MASTER OF SALT & BONES

KERI LAKE

MASTER OF SALT & BONES
Published by KERI LAKE
www.KeriLake.com

Copyright © 2020 Keri Lake

Cover art by Hang Le
Photography by Morten Munthe
Editing: Julie Belfield
Warning: This book contains explicit sexual content, and violent scenes that some readers may find disturbing.

Media vita in morte sumus

(In the midst of life, we are in death)

For Diane
Because even those who write fairy tales with happy endings need a fairy godmother of their own.

Keep up with Keri Lake's new releases, exclusive extras and more by signing up to her VIP Email List:
VIP EMAIL SIGN UP

Join her reading group for giveaways, fun chats, and a chance to win advance copies of her books: VIGILANTE VIXENS

PLAYLIST

This book would not have been possible without the talented musicians who provided inspiration along the way.

"Unspoken" -Myuu
"Come Back For Me" -Jaymes Young
"Love Is A Bitch" -Two Feet
"Soda" -Nothing But Thieves
"I Walk The Line" -Halsey
"Why Don't You Save Me?" -Kan Wakan
"Oceans" -Seafret
"Fear Of The Water" -SYML
"Bottom of the Deep Blue Sea" -MISSIO
"Curse" -Koda
"Million Dollar Man" -Lana Del Rey
"Chopin: Nocturne in C-Sharp Minor" -Frédéric Chopin, Alexandre Tharaud
"Madness" -Ruelle
"Drown" -Seafret
"Liebestraume No. 3: Nocturne in A-Flat Major" -Franz Liszt
"Twisted" -Two Feet

DEAR READER,

In an effort to preserve the setting and characters in my head, this story is set in a fictional town, on a fictional island off the coast of Massachusetts. It's very loosely based on Martha's Vineyard, with Bonesalt Bluff inspired by the Aquinnah Cliffs. A quaint little fishing community with a modern-day castle.

This book contains a number of potentially triggering situations. You can find the full list of trigger warnings-with spoilers-on my website: https://www.kerilake.com/master-of-salt-bones-trigger-list

Thank you for reading, and I hope you enjoy Lucian and Isa's story 🤍 ~Keri

PROLOGUE

LUCIAN

Fifteen years ago ...

"Mother, I want to go home."

Straps across my face limit the movement of my jaw, where I lie bound to a stiff bed in the middle of a mostly empty, dark cell. An incessant chill burrows deep within my bones, over the thrum of anxiety that's only mildly subdued by the drugs they've forced down my throat. Restraints at my wrists and ankles ensure that I won't leap from this bed and follow her when she leaves.

"This place is hell."

A hospital, from the looks of it, but far from any place designed to heal. Their method is torment. Aversion therapy. Experimental medicine that hasn't been approved by any governing body. I doubt any *practicing* doctor has ever set foot inside.

Considering where it's nestled, deep in the northern woods of Vermont, it's a wonder my parents managed to stumble upon it.

"You're ill, Lucian. The doctors here ... they'll help you." Tears gather in Mother's eyes that're red and swollen, from days of crying, no doubt. "They'll make you better."

"There's ... nothing wrong with me." I manage to grit the words past the tight clench of my teeth that's reinforced by unyielding leather stretched across my chin. The pressure against my jaw sends a throbbing ache to my skull that pulses behind my eyeballs, and the shape of her blurs behind a watery shield, while little snippets of memory, things they've done to me here, flash through my head.

Injections. Drugs. Clamps. Cuffs. Electric shock. Hissing. The screams.

"Take me home!"

"She's lucky she's already dead, or I'd insist she get the worst of it." Fingers curling around the strap of her designer purse, she stares off, lips clamped tight with her disgust, but then her eye twitches, and her expression changes into what I surmise as satisfaction. "My God, do you have any idea what they do to *female* child predators here?"

CHAPTER 1

ISADORA

Present day ...

"**Y**ou seem nervous."

Cigarette smoke mingles with the warm, salty sea air that's breezing through the cracked window, as my aunt taps her thumb like a metronome against the steering wheel. "Yeah, you would be, too, if you paid any attention to the *rumors*, as you call them." Cheeks caving with a drag of her smoke, she doesn't bother to look away from the road ahead, toward me.

Wind whips my too-long hair, which I don't fuss to brush away, while the old junker she affectionately named Hal in an ode to her ex rattles along the seaside road. The early morning sky, with its heavy gray clouds, is the foreboding threat of a storm later, and the barometric pressure seems to be adding a nice dose of anxiety to her already cantankerous mood.

"What bliss it must be to ignore everything around you, like it's all one big lie."

I have heard some of the rumors of Blackthorne Manor. A

modern-day castle that sits on the edge of a seaside bluff, otherwise known to the locals as Bonesalt, for the white clay and sand that covers its steep walls. The place is now owned by the only heir, Lucian Blackthorne, affectionately called the *Devil of Bonesalt*. And I'll be tasked to serve as a companion to his ailing mother over the next few months. "Oh, right. What's that again? He runs naked through the woods to eat animals alive? Or is it the one where he bathes in human blood?" In mocking, I shake my head and point at nothing in the air. "No, wait, you're talking about the one where he sneaks into town to snatch children from their beds at night."

"Go ahead. Poke your fun. Won't take long for you to find out for yourself."

"That people in this town have too much time on their hands? Already knew that."

"That the man is madder than a hatter. Why else would they call him *The Mad Son*."

Oh, Lucian Blackthorne is also said to have spent some time in a psychiatric ward, earning him the second nickname, but just like every other ridiculous rumor that surrounds the guy, I'm not sure I believe that one either. "You're just pissed that you don't really know anything about him. Facts, anyway."

"It's unnerving that a man keeps to himself that way. Just isn't right." Tongue resting on her lip, she shakes her head. "Only ones who stay away from people are the ones who have something to hide."

"Maybe he just likes his privacy."

"Most *murderers* do."

Snorting, I shake my head and look away, knowing it'll piss her off. From what I've *read*, his wife committed suicide and his son went missing. Somehow, the locals equated that to a double homicide. "If you honestly thought he murdered her, you wouldn't be driving me to his house." I glance back at her. "So, why *are you* driving me to his house?"

"Because I know ya well enough to know you'd find a way, with or without me. That, and I figured the drive would give me enough time to change your mind." After a quick once-over, she huffs. "Should've known you'd be stubborn. You don't have to do this, you know. There are plenty of jobs--"

"Bartending?" It's a knock at my aunt, but I'll resort to a whole list of unsavory jobs before I'll consider doing what she's done day in and day out for the last twenty years. I refuse to be yet another Quinn sopping up the leftovers in this town.

"Hey, The Shoal's been good to me. Good people. Good work."

Shitty pay. "Look, I'm not doing this to rattle your cage. We need the money. You need it."

"I don't need it this bad, Isa."

This bad.

Tempest Cove is a town ruled by its superstitions. Etched in the northern cliffs on a small island off the coast of Massachusetts, it's a place where most of the redheads are single, and no one, no matter how ambitious, leaves port on a Thursday or Friday, because *Sunday sails never fails.* Women are said to be bad luck aboard a ship, and there's no whistling for fear of a gale. Also, the dudes walking around with shaggy hair and unkempt nails aren't bums, but die-hard fishermen who believe good hygiene spoils a catch. Hell, half the regulars who close down The Shoal every night look like they stumbled in from the streets, because of their crazy superstitions.

Here? It's just the way of life.

They also believe that *if you cross paths with a Blackthorne, you're doomed to an unfortunate and indeterminate fate.*

Which probably explains why I got the job of looking after Mrs. Blackthorne based on nothing more than a phone interview. No one else in Tempest Cove is crazy enough to tempt their luck by working for them.

I just happen to be desperate enough.

As I understand, the family owns the most successful shipping company in the whole United States, so I'm not the only crazy person in need of a paycheck. To be fair, though, the business is said to operate out of Gloucester, where their employees aren't likely to know much about the family history, like folks here.

Or what folks here think they know about them, anyway.

The only thing I *really* know about the Blackthornes is that they are the richest family in Tempest Cove, true royalty, and they own the only castle I'm aware of, which can be seen from any point downtown.

Oh, and they're cursed, too. Supposedly by a siren, although some accounts reference a sea witch. Depends on who's telling the story.

Ask anyone in Tempest Cove, and they won't so much as bat an eye at the mention of a sea witch, or siren. They believe in such things nearly as much as the God they insist will deliver them from the evils of the world.

Including the Blackthornes.

"What about an education?" Eyes on the road, she doesn't bother to look at me, while she sucks in another drag of her cigarette. Good thing, because we've already gone over this, and I'd hate for her to see the exasperated look on my face. "You have a gift. One that shouldn't go to waste."

Since childhood, I've had an uncanny ability to play music by ear. Note for note, even though I can't actually read a lick of music. My high school music teacher referred to me as lost potential before I graduated six months ago. *A prodigious waste of talent*, I believe were his exact words. Not that he ever believed I'd amount to anything if I did pursue my music. After all, kids in this town are cursed to follow in their parents' footsteps.

Sons become fishermen. Daughters become their lonely wives. It's been that way for generations.

It so happens, though, my mother has been, and still is, the reigning whore on this island who's kept their husbands from becoming lonely, too. A somewhat colorful deviation from the town's norm, I suppose. While my real father died when I was born, my mother insists it could've been any of the men who got her pregnant. She's always made a point to tell me how lucky I am to have a whole damn town as a father. My own personal kingdom, she once called it.

As if that makes it easier to fit in here.

What I wouldn't give to be ignorant to this town's disapproving stares and whispers. The way the women shield their husbands and sons, as if I walk around with snakes wriggling about my head, ready to turn them to stone.

Unfortunately, I grew up as the daughter of a sinner, and as far as they're concerned, that's all I'll ever be.

"Need money for an education," I answer, drawing a dollar symbol in the nicotine stained film on the window beside me. "That's the problem. I'm cursed with impractical potential. Just like you're cursed to meddle where you shouldn't."

"And if I didn't meddle, you'd be living under a viaduct right now."

She's not lying, although I haven't visited my mom in weeks to know if she's still camped out off the highway. Last I checked, she'd gone on another bender with one of her many junkie boyfriends.

"Your mother wasn't always bad, for the record."

Sometimes I forget that, if anyone is capable of understanding what it's like to be the daughter of the town's blacksheep, it's the sister of said sheep. Maybe that's why Aunt Midge is so hardened and jaded by life.

Could be that my mother made her that way, too. Or maybe it was having to raise me all these years.

Either way, we're both cursed, just like the Blackthornes, so it doesn't make sense that she'd side with the rumors.

A thick fog hovers over the road where the oceanside gives way to trees. An object ahead, off to the right, draws my attention, and I squint my eyes to focus through the white haze, only noticing the shape of a cross once we pass it. Another stands a few feet ahead of that.

I twist around in my seat and catch a third on the opposite side of the road, through the back window. "What's with the crosses?"

"Churchy types like to come up here sometimes and remind us all how useless they are." In spite of the crucifix around her neck, my aunt has always had a certain disdain for religion. All those years of catechism seem to have burned her out on it.

That, or the people who tried to cram it down her throat after finding out my uncle cheated on her.

"Have the Blackthornes always been hated this much?" I ask.

Flicking her cigarette out the window, she blows out the last of the smoke. "Thought you didn't like the rumors?"

I don't. I hate this town and its gossip, but something about this particular family intrigues me. "I'm just curious to know if it's a generational thing, or if Lucian's the only accused *murderer*." Rolling my eyes, I turn in time to catch yet another cross at the side of the road.

"Roll your eyes, but you didn't know Amelia. She was the princess of Tempest Cove. Everyone loved her. And when she started hanging around that man? Well, we just knew trouble would follow. Always does with a Blackthorne."

"Amelia. That's his wife?"

"*Was*. She ain't around anymore, remember?" Staring through the windshield, she sighs and shakes her head. "Such a shame. But to answer your question, I suppose there's always been something off about that family. Whether the older ones murdered their wives is unknown—to me, anyway. But who knows, with as much as they keep to themselves."

The fact that they almost never venture into town has given rise to the mythological rumors about Lucian being some hungry creature that hunts the surrounding woods.

8

"Well, there's a difference between suicide and homicide, and last I checked, he was never charged for murder."

A squawk of laughter jerks her head back, before she flashes me a dubious look. "You think a man with as much money as he has, as much power, would ever be convicted?"

I think this town likes to make up stories when facts don't quite line up the way they'd like. Take my mother, for example. They nicknamed her the Siren of Tempest Cove, simply because the women couldn't deal with the fact that their husbands were just as guilty of adultery as she was.

"I think, no matter what, science is science. And evidence doesn't favor the rich."

Face washed in mirthless amusement, she shakes her head. "Beauty. Brains. But as naive as a seal pup in a pool of sharks." When she glances toward me, I swear her eyes are rimmed in darker circles than before. "Evidence don't always tell the whole story. Sometimes, we have to rely on instinct, Isa. Remember that?"

There's a subtlety to my aunt's words. Where she can be downright crass and rude, laying her personality on the table like tarnished silver that hasn't been polished in decades, there are times I find her to be more shrewd than I am. Her comment is meant to give me pause, to remind me that, only a few months ago, I'd made the tragic mistake of ignoring my instincts.

A thought I cast aside. I don't need those memories pulling me under and clouding a new start.

"You're curious, too. That's why you're driving me." I say, searching through the dark silhouettes of passing trees for distraction. Even with the sun cresting the horizon, the canopy of the forest still gives the impression of night here.

"I'm curious to know what would change your mind, yes."

Inwardly groaning, I shake my head. "It'd take an act of God to make me turn down this cash."

A black object swoops into my periphery, and Aunt Midge

slams on the breaks, sending me crashing forward into the dashboard. Hard vinyl thumps against my palms, and needles of electricity shoot up my unbent arms, as the car squeals to a stop.

"Son of a bitch!" Aunt Midge sits with her arms outstretched, both hands white-knuckling the steering wheel.

I lift my head to find an eerie swirl of fog dancing in the beam of the lights, before it parts around a black bird in the middle of the road that hops alongside the bloody remains of a dead animal. "Jesus. What the hell is it?" Unbuckling my seatbelt, I slide forward for a better view.

"Crow? I've no idea."

"Not the bird." The animal beside the bird is hardly recognizable, sprawled out in a pool of entrails that the wretched creature pecks at as though unfettered by the headlights.

"Who gives a shit? Damn thing almost ran us off the road!" She rails on the horn, but fails to move the bird.

In fact, it doesn't even spare us a glance, still feasting on the carrion strewn across our path. A bulbous object is wedged in its beak--an eyeball, which it gulps back, and I grimace, imagining myself lying there in the road while it feeds on me.

"What in the Sam Hill?" As Aunt Midge idles past the bird, I stare down at it from the passenger window, and when it cranes its neck toward me, I frown, noticing one of its own eyes missing. "Never seen such a thing in all my life," my aunt says beside me. "Wasn't even bothered by us."

Twisting in my seat, I breathe deep to settle my nerves and peer through the back window, where the bird still hasn't moved. "Must've been starving, or something."

With a dry chuckle, she shakes her head. "Act of God, you say. How 'bout the devil himself? This bluff is cursed, I tell ya. Cursed. Every creature here bears the burden of it. I hope it won't be you when all is said and done. You're nineteen now, so I can't very well be telling you what you can and can't do anymore. But I'm strongly urging you to consider something else."

There is nothing else, unless I want to work alongside my best friend, Kelsey, at Barnaby's Baubles on the boardwalk, selling overpriced trinkets to the few tourists we get. Or better yet, slopping out bowls of chowder and beers at The Shoal with Aunt Midge.

"I'm taking this job." The money is enough to clear some of her debts, get caught up on the mortgage, *and* save up for a car to get the hell out of this place, eventually. "I'll be fine. Look, I get it, okay? You're just watching out for me." As she's done since the night my mom left me on her doorstep and bailed on parenthood. "But this is it. All those times we talked about me getting out of here? It's not happening with my music. Or working at some tourist trap in town."

"It could, if you gave it a chan--"

"It won't. It takes money to make money, remember? You told me that."

"You don't have to listen to everything I say, kid. You know that, right?" The glance she shoots back at me holds a smile that actually touches her eyes this time. "Sometimes, I'm fulla shit."

"More than sometimes, I'd say."

With a slap on my shoulder, she snorts. "Smartass."

A few more miles up the road, the fog breaks, and the forest opens to a clearing. A black wrought iron gate, with Blackthorne Manor etched into the metal at either side of an unwelcoming skull with white stones for sockets, greets us at the entrance. Standing off to the side of the driveway is a silver box with a black button, and Aunt Midge reaches through the window to press it. Seconds later, the gate opens onto a long narrow driveway flanked by more trees, and the path widens to an expansive neglected lawn ahead.

The occasional shrubs and bushes that dot the unkempt landscape must've once been trimmed into shapes, given their odd contortions that now simply make them look old and tired. In the center of a circular drive stands a dried-up cement fountain, and the figure of a woman whose single arm reaches up toward the sky, her other arm broken at the elbow.

"Place looks downright abandoned," Aunt Midge says, slowing the car to a stop.

Gaze shifting to the front entrance, I stare up the stone staircase, which is guarded by menacing gargoyles at either side, toward an enormous turret situated beside the most elaborate wooden doors I've ever seen in my life. Carved in thick cherry timber, they match the topiary boxes that house small, wilting shrubs.

I've never actually laid eyes on a castle in person. Only in books and on the internet. Blackthorne seems far too elaborate for this town, as if I've slipped into some medieval time bubble.

The doors open up, and a man in a crisp suit, with gray hair and spectacles, fills the gap. Given the stories I have heard, it doesn't seem likely that he's the master of the house, particularly as he doesn't wear the scars said to mar Lucian Blackthorne's face. The very scars that earned him the devil moniker.

The Devil of Bonesalt. My new boss.

What fodder that'll make when Aunt Midge begins her shift this evening at The Shoal.

We exit the vehicle, and I follow Aunt Midge up the staircase, my eyes drinking in the forlorn beauty of this place. I don't know why it speaks to some part of me, but where Aunt Midge looks like a cat who just got the shit scared out of it, with her shoulders bunched and her jaw clenched, I find the place oddly intriguing. Peaceful, really. Almost like a graveyard.

Movement draws my eyes to a window three stories up the turret, where I can just make out the shadowy figure of someone standing there. The surrounding darkness conceals much of the face, but the discernible parts are big and imposing. Definitely masculine. If I had to guess, I'm staring up at Lucian Blackthorne.

Or one of his rumored bodyguards.

It's amazing how many stories surround a single man.

"Isadora Quinn?" The older gentleman standing in the doorway tips his chin up in a regal sort of way that'd make half the men back in town laugh if they were standing here.

"That's her." Aunt Midge hikes a thumb in my direction. "I'm her aunt. Just makin' sure everything is kosher before I drop her off."

His face crinkles into a frown as his eyes appraise me, prompting me to look down at the outfit I've chosen to wear for my first day. Ripped up jeans tucked into rubber fishing mucks, and the only T-shirt I own that doesn't have a coffee or ketchup stain. Imagining the way I look through his eyes, with my long ink black hair, the tattoo visible on my right forearm that reads *Invulnerable* in bold, cursive print, and the dark eyeliner that Aunt Midge likens to Alice Cooper's just to tease me, has me thinking casual dress holds a vastly different meaning here. The guy probably thinks I'm another local punk. Oddly enough, dressing this way keeps me *out* of trouble. Keeps others away. In high school, I was called Goth Girl and considered most likely to shoot up the place.

Couldn't be farther from the truth. While my classmates partied on the weekends and wreaked havoc, I stayed home reading books and listening to Chopin.

I'm polite to a degree, when others are polite to me, and defiant when I have to be.

"You said it was casual dress, right?"

"I suppose we all have a subjective interpretation of the word. Very well. Come on, Isadora."

"Isa, or Izzy, is fine."

He steps aside, ushering us through the doors that stand at least twice my height. A large brass knocker in the shape of a lion makes me wonder if it's ever actually been used, and I stare up at the intricate carvings that decorate an otherwise benign door-frame while passing through the threshold.

"I'm Mr. Rand, Master Blackthorne's assistant," the man says from behind. "We spoke on the phone."

We come to a stop in an elegant foyer, with a beautiful, dark gray, marble floor, the center of which holds a crest that I'm guessing is Blackthorne. An obscenely large and gaudy crystal chandelier hangs over a winding staircase that converges into an upper level, the dark, wooden bannisters and matching dark walls like something out of a gothic horror movie. Rich tapestries hang from gilded rods, along with paintings that I would bet cost more money than my aunt makes in a year. Maybe even two years. The extravagance of this place is overwhelming, and yet, the dark and neglected tones that linger beneath all of it tug at some invisible string inside my chest.

Like an undercurrent of sadness hangs on the air.

"You did say you play piano, correct?" Rand asks, while I continue to scope the place out.

"Yes. I can play. I'm not like Mozart, or anything, but I can play some songs."

"Mrs. Blackthorne enjoys classics. Are you versed in those?"

"Chopin, Liszt, Bach ... sure."

"Excellent. The office is to the left. Please follow me."

Rand takes the lead toward an arched door that I have to believe was custom fitted, and pushes through to an open space filled with elegant cherrywood furniture and leather. The rich scent of expensive cigars and wealth assaults my senses as I step inside. Books line the shelves alongside a credenza, and I take note of a few that appear to be business references.

On the shiny surface of the mostly-clean desk is a stack of white papers that reflects the dim light they're below.

"Please, take a seat." The older man gestures toward two small, leather chairs set before the desk, before rounding the other side to a much bigger chair.

The unyielding surface catches my fall as I plop into the seat. As a side gig, I've cleaned enough homes outside of Tempest

Cove to know expensive furniture is neither comfortable, nor practical, and this chair is no exception.

Though, with as many business transactions as I imagine take place in this room, perhaps that's the point.

"I've drafted the contract we discussed over the phone." Rand pushes half the stack of papers toward me.

I slide the documents in front of me. They're written in the overwhelming language of the serious businessman I imagine Blackthorne to be, although I frown down at the confidentiality agreement laid out on the first page. "What's this?"

"The last companion we hired took it upon herself to snap *selfies*, which she proceeded to post to social media. Master Blackthorne is very particular about his privacy. During your time here, you will be entrusted to roam the castle freely, which invariably places the master in a compromised position."

"If you think she's gonna take pictures of the guy's underwear, I can assure you it ain't gonna happen." Aunt Midge gives an unappealing snort and chuckles. "His tidy whities are safe with Isa." No sooner do the words tumble from her mouth than the smirk on Aunt Midge's face fades to a frown. "Professionally speaking, of course."

Face screwed up in what must be a grimace reserved for the most uncouth locals, Rand rolls his shoulders. "Yes, well, just the same, we'd like to cover all bases." His dark eyes fall on me like a stormcloud, and I'm guessing the guy's assuming I'm like most other teenagers of my generation who have social media. In truth, I probably don't exist in today's modern world, considering I don't even have a phone with internet. Mine is a simple design, meant only to field the occasional frantic call, or text, from Aunt Midge when I've stayed too long at the library.

Without hesitation, I sign the document.

"I hope it doesn't state in the contract that she has to call him Master, because we Quinns don't answer to anyone that way." If I didn't know this job was already in the bag, Aunt Midge would surely be reason for this guy to reconsider. "Always been captain of our own ships."

"*Mister* Blackthorne is fine. Though I don't suspect you'll have much contact with him during your time here. As I said, he's a man who values his privacy above all else. And he's quite busy."

With the kind of urban legends that surround this place, I wonder what makes a man like Rand remain faithful to his much-loathed employer. Money?

It takes a couple minutes to fill out all of the paperwork and sign the documents, and when I've finished, I let out an exasperated breath. "Hope I didn't just sign my soul over."

"Of course you did." Rand's voice carries no trace of humor.

Frozen in my seat, I dare a glance toward Aunt Midge.

The chasing sound that fills the room might be mistaken for a chuckle, but one that hasn't gotten much practice in the last couple of years. Rand sits with a hand covering his mouth, his eyes bunched in mirth.

For a moment, I feel like I'm caught in an episode of *The Twilight Zone*, the room blanching to white and black in some alternate version of reality.

Thankfully, the laughter doesn't last long, dying down to a sigh.

Removing a handkerchief that he sets to his eyes, Rand clears his throat. "Well, then. Allow me to show you around Blackthorne."

"Shouldn't I meet Mrs. Blackthorne first?" *Make sure the woman even likes me?*

"We'll do that last. Mrs. Blackthorne tends to be very … *disagreeable* first thing in the morning."

CHAPTER 2

LUCIAN

Sixteen years ago ...

Drawing back the rock I've tucked into the pouch, I line my slingshot up with an acorn hangs from a limp branch, one mostly hidden in the early morning darkness and thick foliage. Snapping the rubberband, I let the shrapnel fly through the air, until it hits its mark, and something black, far bigger than an acorn, falls to the ground with a thud.

"Oh, shit, you hit a bird!" My best friend Jude scrambles to his feet over the crackling brush, and I follow after him as he slides to the ground beside what looks like a large raven. "Shot his eye out! Look!" he adds in his native British accent.

Where there should be an eyeball sits the fleshy remains inside a bloody socket. The mutilated organ lies a couple feet away from the animal.

"It was an accident."

"Fucking hell, that's disgusting! Pretty sure you killed him." Jude's lips stretch into a smile as he looks up at me. The delight in his eyes reminds me of a child, instead of the sixteen-year-old I've grown up with most of my life. "Couldn't do that again if you tried. Nailed the bastard."

I kneel down alongside the fallen creature, studying the lack of movement in its chest. Some believe it's a bad omen to kill a bird. Seagulls are said to carry the souls of fishermen. Killing an albatross means getting lost at sea. I've no idea what it means to kill a raven. "It's bad luck."

"Nah. That's crows. Ravens are just evil shit-eaters." Nabbing a stick beside him, Jude lifts the bird's tiny, dark eyeball and flings it at me.

I leap back, but not before it lands square on the crotch of my pants. "Asshole!" The eyeball tumbles to the ground, and I grab a nearby stone to chuck at him.

He chuckles. "Your face! Priceless."

A flash of black knocks him in the head, and Jude lets out a screech. Black wings flap over him, the bird pecking and clawing as it squawks.

"Get it off of me! Get it the fuck off of me!" He flails his hands, and when I grab a stick to fend it off, the bird abandons Jude for me.

The sharp sting of its beak blazes across my skin, as I raise my arms to shield my face. It caws, its nails digging at my flesh while it needles past my limbs to my hair, ripping strands from my head. "Grab a fucking stick!" I manage to belt out, and as the first swing knocks into my elbow, I cry out, lowering my arms to cradle the vibrating ache in my bones. Opening my clenched eyes shows Jude standing alongside me, crouched and ready to swing again. "Not me, stupid bastard, the bird!"

Except, there is no bird.

"Didn't see it fly off. Did you?" The harrowing tone of Jude's voice sends a tickle down my spine.

"No. Must've … just vanished." I glance up at the canopy of

trees above us, toward the small bits of sky peeking through the leaves, but find no sign of the bird.

"Vanished. Yeah, right."

When I lower my gaze toward my friend, I notice where a long slice of skin at his hairline hangs by a thread of torn-away flesh.

Like he just realises the pain, he reaches up to touch the wound. "The cocksucker tore into my skin!"

At a lingering burn on my arms, and I lift both limbs to find pocks, and deep grooves filled with a dark red blood, where the bird nipped at my flesh. I look like I've survived a war, with all the marks marring my skin. "My mom will have my ass for this. Family portraits are tomorrow afternoon."

With a snort, he swipes up my sling from where I threw it on the ground. "Fitting, then, for your macabre family."

Much as I know my mother will be upset, I can't help but chuckle at the visual of standing alongside her, coated in blood, while my father looks on behind me, pissed off and stern, as always. "The locals would surely have a field day with that one."

"Speaking of which, I thought, *surely*, you'd be a more gracious host and gift an old friend some pussy while I'm stuck here."

Jude and I met at the boarding school my father shipped me off to, up until I managed to get myself expelled for setting the headmaster's couch on fire. Now I'm forced to slog through boring lessons with a tutor every day, with only the occasional visit from my friend when school is out of session.

"One of the local girls?" I say. "You'd end up with crabs."

A bellow of Jude's laughter echoes through the forest, while we trek back to the castle grounds. "Still, a little T and A would've been a nice touch."

"Touch to what?"

Shoving his hands into his shirt pocket, he pulls out two perfectly rolled joints.

"How'd you manage that here at the *Chateau de Prison*."

"You really should pay more attention to your help. The gardener hooked me up for a modest fee."

Swiping one of them up from his palm, I drag it across my nose, inhaling the scent of crisp herb and wood. "We'll meet down in the cave tonight, after my mother takes her Valium."

"And the girls?" he asks, tucking both joints back into his pocket.

"Forget the girls, man. There's nothing in this town that would interest you."

They're a strange breed in Tempest Cove. The kind who smile and flirt, while spreading their gossip behind your back. I once made out with a local girl, nothing more than kissing and some fumbling of hands, and by the end of the week, half the town was talking about my dick.

I hadn't even bothered to whip it out.

That's how they operate here, though. For whatever dirt they can spill, they'll dig as deep as they have to.

The forest breaks up for the open lawn of Blackthorne, and we stride past Easton, the gardener, who flashes a smirk that makes a whole lot more sense than it would've ten minutes ago.

"I think you're wrong, my friend." Slowing his steps, Jude grabs hold of my shoulder. "I think there's definitely something interesting."

I follow the path of his gaze, toward where a woman gathers up her suitcase in the circular drive in front of the manor.

Jude strides ahead of me. "Please, allow me to help you."

As the woman turns around, my heart screeches to a halt inside my chest.

Her eyes are a deep gray beneath long black lashes, in a narrow face framed by long, lazy curls that tumble over slender shoulders, which widen with the edges of large breasts stretching her tight sweater. When she smiles back at Jude, one of her teeth in front is twisted just enough to lift her plump lip into a crooked sort of smile. A painfully beautiful woman who must be at least ten years older than me, judging by the maturity in her features.

"*Merci*," she says, her lips pursing when she slides her gaze to mine. "My name is Solange. I'm here to clean." A thick French accent only adds to the sultry nature of the woman.

"Jude." My forward friend prods a hand in front of her, but her eyes remain locked on mine as she rests her palm in his. Jude leans forward to kiss the back of her hand. "It's a pleasure to meet you, Solange."

"The pleasure is mine," she says, smiling as she slips her hand out of his. "You must be Lucian."

My name rolling off her tongue sends a shiver down my spine. "You know my name?"

Her gray eyes dip from mine and back. "You're hurt," she says, rather than answer the question.

"I'm sorry?"

"You're bleeding."

A quick glance at my arms reminds me of the ass-kicking I suffered at the beak of a bird. "I'm fine."

"Lucian! I've been calling you for the last hour."

At the unwelcomed clamor of my mother's voice, I cringe, trying to ignore her, where she stands at the front of the castle, hands crossed in front of her conservative beige pantsuit.

"And what happened to you?" As the fussy woman makes her way down the stone staircase toward me, I groan, waiting for the onslaught of motherly concern. "You're a bloody mess!"

"Ah, you're picking up my dialect, Mrs. B." Jude says, his snicker dying beneath the clearing of his throat.

Expression more stern than before, my mother snatches up my arm, and my cheeks instantly heat as I catch the amused look Solange shoots Jude. "Mother, I'm fine."

"You've got literal gouges in your arm, Lucian. What did this?"

"He tangoed with the wrong bird." The humor in Jude's tone

grates on me, while my arm is twisted and tugged in examination.

"As I said, I'm fine."

"Those could be infected. You'll need to get them cleaned up. Come on, we'll have the nurse check you--"

"Would you back the hell off? I said I'm fine!" I wrench my arm from her grip, the anger finally exploding to the surface.

With her mouth agape, a shocked expression widens her eyes. "Lucian Darius Blackthorne, you will not speak to your mother that way. As I see it, you're already in deep shit with your father." What started out as a small food fight between Jude and me turned into a full on war, when we broke into the fire extinguishers and sprayed dry powder all over the kitchen and parlor, causing what she estimated to be *thousands of dollars in damage* to the furniture and carpets.

In spite of the annoying grin I know is plastered to Jude's face, I grind my teeth, keeping my mouth shut.

"Go clean yourself. We'll talk later."

Lurching a step toward her, Solange holds out her hand. "It's nice to meet you, Mrs. Blackthorne."

Shoulders stiff with her usual haughty posture, my mother keeps her steely gaze on me, not bothering to acknowledge the woman beside her.

Solange lowers her hand and clears her throat.

Jesus Christ, the woman can't even spare a glance at the girl who'll be washing the piss out of her bedsheets after my mother has another one of her Valium-induced nightmares.

"If you could … show me to my room, I'll get settled and begin my work." The meek tone of Solange's voice is inconsistent with the woman who greeted me just before my mother showed up.

"One more thing, Lucian. You're not to go near that cave tonight." Still ignoring the new girl, my mother spins around and makes her way back up the stone staircase, where she pauses to look back. "Are you coming?"

With a sheepish smile, Solange slides her suitcases from Jude's grasp and raises a brow that my mother can't see. "She's delightful," she whispers, before following after the woman.

"Not gonna lie. Your mum?" Jude says. "She's worse than my own."

"She'll drive me to drink before I'm even of age." In spite of the irritating encounter with my mother, I'm somehow fixated on the woman who follows her inside.

"Goddamn, that is one fine piece of ass, though."

Frowning, I twist to look at my friend, whose eyes are glued as he licks his lips. "Solange, not your mum. If you don't fuck that at some point, I'm afraid we can't remain friends. I say we invite her to our little soiree tonight."

"And what the hell would she want with a couple of sixteen-year-olds, huh?"

"We're not like most sixteen-year-olds." He wraps one arm around my neck, pulling me in. "We're obscenely wealthy, and equally good looking. Not to mention, I refuse to fuck your dad's sloppy seconds. Better to get our digs in first."

"'The hell's that supposed to mean?"

"You honestly think your father, a man with more bad habits than a convent of dirty nuns, won't be tapping that ass at some point?"

I slam my fist into his shoulder. "In case you've forgotten, he's married to my mother, asshole."

"As my old man is married to my mum. Doesn't keep him from fucking anything in a tight skirt."

"Your father has no concept of family. If he did, he wouldn't send you off to school, then send you off to stay with me every time you come home for break."

"True. But I admire his passion for the extracurricular." Jude turns to face me, his lip kicking up to a half smile. "I'll gift you the entire contents of my left ball-sack if you invite Solange to the cave tonight."

Lips curled in disgust, I shake my head and walk ahead of him. "I wouldn't touch your curdled spunk if you gifted me your entire trust fund on top of it. Piss off."

"I meant my future firstborn." Falling into step behind me, he leaps ahead and turns to face me, walking backward. "I'm kidding. But seriously, whatever you want, it's yours."

"How the hell am I supposed to make that happen? She's new. They spend the first week kissing my parents' asses. No doubt, she'll do the same."

"Exactly. She's new. She wants to please." He reaches out to grip my shoulders, bringing me to a halt. "I saved you from a goddamn bird today. The least you can do is return the favor."

"You're comparing apples to oranges."

"No, I'm comparing one dangerous bird to another. Did you see her tits?" His grip squeezes my arms as if he's imagining his hands on them. "Couldn't wrap my palm around them if I wanted to. I need to fuck this woman before my balls explode."

"Then, you ask her."

"It's not the same." Finally releasing me, he crosses his arms over his chest. "You're the master of the house when your father is away. Make her go."

"How?"

"Your infamous Blackthorne charm. What else?"

CHAPTER 3

LUCIAN

Present day ...

I stare through the window of my father's old office. Even two years after his death, the room still reeks of cigar smoke and the cheap perfume of his last whore.

In the aftermath of my mother's declining mental health, he let the place fall into disrepair. Took to drinking gin all hours of the day, and keeping with prostitutes he forced Rand to recruit from the mainland on his behalf.

A dull ache in my skull radiates over the right side of my head, and I set a hand to where small patches of hair are missing. In light circles, I try to abate the needling sensation that settles deep inside my bones. A quiet ringing in my ears intensifies just enough to add a zap of sharp pain.

Eyes flinched, I breathe through my nose until it subsides, and loosen the tight clench of my teeth.

"She's arrived, sir," Makaio says from behind.

I let out a shaky exhale, not bothering to turn to where the giant Hawaiian stands behind me.

At six-five, he's only about an inch taller, but his mass makes up the difference between us. That, and Makaio happens to be far more deadly with his MMA background. I loathe the idea of having a bodyguard shadow me everywhere, but I've had enough attempts on my life to warrant the man's services. I've known him for nearly half my life, he and Rand being longtime associates of my father. The only two people left in the world that I trust.

"You want Rand to bring her up so you can meet her?"

"Rand assisted my father in making multi-million dollar decisions every day. I'm sure he can handle hiring a companion for my mother."

"This one looks young. Hot, but can't dress worth a damn."

I couldn't care less about the new help. They rarely last here, so I find it pointless to learn more than I need. Whether from having to put up with my mother, or from staying in this rotting corpse of a house, they have a tendency to quit the job before they've begun. "Please have Giulia bring me some coffee."

"Breakfast, too?"

"No. I'm not hungry."

"How is that even possible? I don't get it."

I smirk, in spite of my mood. "I weigh about a hundred pounds less than you do. I certainly don't have the same love affair you seem to have with food."

"Doesn't cheat. Doesn't piss and moan every time I want a piece. And I don't have to worry about some other asshole coming along to swipe it up."

"Depends on what you're eating."

Snorting, Makaio shakes his head. "I'll have Giulia bring the coffee."

With a nod, I turn my attention back toward the window. From here, I can see over the surrounding forest that lines the

26

property's perimeter, and beyond to where the ocean dances in the distance, past the edge of a steep cliff.

Blackthorne Manor is the pillar of excess, a fortress designed to divide the rich from the poor. My great-grandfather had the castle built on the highest cliff, where it could be seen from anywhere in Tempest Cove. A grim reminder to generations that followed why one should never cross paths with a Blackthorne. It's said the foundations, upon which this place was built, are the crushed remains of his enemies' bones. Dramatic really. Even my own family isn't immune to making up fables.

The ocean view morphs and sharpens into my reflection in the glass, where a cluster of grisly scars stretch across the lower part of my cheek. Twisting my head slightly to the side shows the unaffected half, the part that wasn't torn away that night. Touching it with my hand offers palpable evidence to the visuals of the grotesque, uneven landscape of my skin. Gashes so deep that not even scar revision could hide them.

As the familiar revulsion bubbles to the surface, my hands instinctively ball into fists. I've punched enough mirrors to know that breaking things doesn't make it go away. Doesn't change what happened. But the pain feels good.

"Master?" At the sound of Giulia's voice, I tamp down my frustration and turn only slightly to face her. "Will you be needing my services this evening?" she asks, setting down the cup of coffee on a coaster atop the desk.

Sometimes we fuck. It's part of the contract I have with her, which keeps her employed, and her daughter at a prestigious boarding school instead of public schools on the mainland that're riddled with drug dealers.

"That won't be necessary."

As much as I enjoy the pleasures of a woman, it's not enough. It never is. Giulia is accommodating, indulging in whatever I ask, but what I *need* is something that would turn her stomach.

27

And I just don't have the energy to slog through the mundane tonight.

If I didn't know her as well as I do, I'd almost mistake the chasing expression on her face for disappointment. I know better, though.

"Very well."

Wasn't that long ago, she would've scoffed at the idea of bowing her head in acquiescence. Nowadays, she's far more agreeable, without much commentary, or objection. Not that she'd object to my dismissal. In spite of the moans, the kisses, seemingly kind caresses, I'm certain the sight of me repulses her enough to feign enjoyment during sex. Even her climax is achieved through shuttered eyes, as if one glance would ruin it.

"This pleases you?" I ask her.

"Your satisfaction pleases me, sir."

"But you're relieved that you don't have to fuck me tonight. The abhorrent, hideous Mad Son."

"I don't think of you as such."

"*Everyone* thinks of me as such. Including you."

If she lowered her head any more, she'd be kissing the floor. "Do you need anything else from me?"

Twisting away from her, I catch her fidgeting in the window's reflection. Aside from Makaio, everyone fidgets around me. If my face isn't enough to frighten them, the rumors about me surely keep them on edge. "No. Nothing."

I watch her retreat, the light of the hallway adding a soft glow to the glass as she exits my office.

The ache strikes again, stronger than before, the ringing between my ears like a sewing needle spearing my eardrum. Spasms of pain shoot through my jaw, as I grind my teeth while clutching either side of my head.

Fuck. They've gotten worse in the last year. Almost unbearable. The ache reaches my eye sockets, and for a moment the view outside the window blurs into an impressionist painting of green and blue.

Through heavy lids, I try to focus on the water, something that might draw my thoughts away from the agony. *An object of focus*, the doc once told me. There's nothing but jagged flashes of light and the vertigo that always follows.

Voices outside the door could be real, or imagined, it's hard to tell, but as they grow louder, I concentrate on the sound for distraction. A female voice, whose intonation is soft, but enough to break through the ringing.

I stumble toward the door and press my ear to the wood. The cool panels and solid surface I lean against offer some relief, and I close my eyes, listening to her speak. Rand's voice follows, as he prattles off the history of Blackthorne Manor. Another woman's voice chimes in, deep and raspy, like a smoker's, but then it's the first voice again. The sound is so soothing, and at a melodic vibrato of laughter, I can no longer hear the painful ringing.

I open the door a crack, only catching their backs as they continue down the hallway.

Raven black hair dances around her slim shoulders, as she scans the walls of my home. An older woman moves beside her, perhaps her mother, judging by the hardened lines in her face. The raven-haired girl turns just enough to reveal her profile, and God help me, she's beautiful, with her golden skin, high cheekbones, and the perfect slope of her nose. A kind of radiant beauty that'll soon be snuffed by the vapid gloom of this place.

But young. Far too young.

My mother will eat her alive before week's end.

What a shame that will be.

CHAPTER 4

ISADORA

I t takes over an hour to give us a *brief* tour, which only covered the west wing of the castle. The single theme in every room we passed was opulence. The Blackthornes evidently have more money than any of the locals can probably fathom. Even Aunt Midge, who tends to consider elegance a frivolous waste, stood wide-eyed a few times.

One would never guess, given the abandoned appearance outside the walls, that such wealth and luxury still pulses through its veins.

In spite of my subtle protest, Rand insisted that she come along, because it didn't take a psychoanalyst to see my aunt's panties hadn't unbunched with the small meeting we had an hour ago. I admire her commitment to look after me, particularly after the hell I went through months ago, but her overbearing nature has become one of the many reasons I can't wait to leave this town. It reminds me of the time I watched two baby squirrels trapped in a cage, when one of the boys down the street swiped them up after they'd crawled up his pant leg. The boys laughed cruelly as the tiny animals ran in circles over the thin bars. Over and over again. Never eating. Never resting.

They climbed their barriers as if they didn't realize something held them inside that cramped space, and eventually, they both died.

That won't be me. Not in this town.

"Should you get hungry, the kitchen staff is at your disposal while you're here. We have a gourmet chef on staff, who is happy to prepare whatever you like." Rand breaks my thoughts with even more of the amenities of this place.

Gourmet chef? What the hell would I ask of a gourmet chef? I don't even know what gourmet chefs cook.

"Fancy," Aunt Midge whispers as we follow Rand down a dark corridor. "Still don't like this place. Makes the hairs on my neck stand up."

I trail my gaze over the high ceilings and dark walls, the elaborate portraits either side of us. Relatives, I'd bet. A richness in the history of a family like nothing I've ever seen before. "I like it. And I'll be home on weekends."

"What happens on the weekends here? 'Sat when they hold their séances?" Aunt Midge chuckles at herself, and I silently groan, taking in another sweep of the walls.

"It's when the Master enjoys a bit of privacy," Rand says, coming to a stop at the top of the staircase overlooking the foyer where we first came in. "He finds himself surrounded by others far more than he cares to be, and weekends give him a break from social interactions. However, you may be called on to attend a party, or the occasional dinner as added help."

"What? Like serving the other richies?" The derision in Aunt Midge's voice makes me regret letting her accompany me. How childish it must seem to have my aunt along for a job interview.

"I'm happy to assist. However I'm needed." Even with my gaze cast away from her, I can feel Aunt Midge's eyes burning into me as I seal my decision to take this job.

"Very good." Continuing on down the staircase, Rand takes the lead once again, toward the front entrance, where we gather over the Blackthorne crest. "I trust you're satisfied with the arrangement?"

The question is directed toward Aunt Midge, and a flare of irritation blazes beneath my skin when she tips her chin, as if she's got any place being haughty and demanding. As if this man owes her an explanation for all the nosy gossip she's been instrumental in perpetrating about this family. At the same time, the gesture makes me nervous. I know my aunt well enough that this is the point when she makes a bold and wildly inappropriate inquiry, like *Is it true Lucian Blackthorne murdered his wife and son?*

Say something, my head goads, but the words fail to breach my frozen lips.

"I guess, yeah. She have to hand out any medications, or anything?" Her response leaves me dumbfounded for a moment. So much so, I almost don't appreciate the importance of her question--one I hadn't bothered to ask myself. Jesus.

"Mrs. Blackthorne has a nurse who attends to her medical needs, as well as an occasional visiting physician. The role of the companion is strictly to spend time with her, in whatever capacity Mrs. Blackthorne finds comfortable, whether it be walks in the garden, or reading a book. She's quite the bibliophile."

"Sounds like the two of you will get along *swimmingly.*" Rolling her eyes, she crosses her arms in her usual defensive stance. "So do I … come pick her up on the weekends? How does that work?"

"Master Blackthorne has a personal driver who will be at the disposal of Miss Quinn, should she need to venture into town for anything."

"His personal driver? Doesn't he need him?" I'm clueless when it comes to the affairs of rich people and whether, or not, they commute to work like everyone else.

"Much of his business dealings are handled remotely, over the computer. Those that are held in person take place here, in his personal office. The Master rarely leaves his home for anything.

He has occasional business trips on the mainland, or out of state, but those are fairly limited."

The visual of the squirrels climbing the cage comes to mind again, and I catch myself frowning. "I don't expect I'll need to venture into town much, either, then."

"Except to visit your aunt." Aunt Midge adds.

"Of course."

"If you're satisfied with the amenities for your niece, I'd like to get Miss Quinn acquainted with her routine, so that she can begin her day with Mrs. Blackthorne."

"Yeah. Sure." Hiking a thumb over her shoulder, Aunt Midge tips her head. "I'll just grab her bags and bring them inside."

"Makaio is waiting at your car to gather Miss Quinn's personal effects. There's no need to come back inside. You're free to go from there."

"Oh. Uh. I guess this is ... goodbye, then?" The uncertainty hasn't faded from my aunt's eyes when she steps toward me and wraps her arms around me in a hug. "You got your cell. Call me if you need anything. Or if anything seems shady," she whispers.

With a nod, I grasp her elbows, breaking the embrace, and smile like I'm not nervous as all hell to meet the lady of the house. "I'll be fine. Call you tonight, okay?"

"You better." She turns her attention toward Rand and offers him a handshake, which turns into an awkward exchange between them when Rand only rests his palm in her hand for a moment, before nabbing a handkerchief to wipe away what I'm guessing he deems is germs on his skin.

"Yeah, so. I'll go, then." She slides her hands into her pockets, as if she doesn't know what else to do with them. "See you .... See you this weekend."

"Drive careful." I don't bother to follow her toward the door, for fear she'll make a last ditch effort to sway me.

Nothing can sway me now that I've actually set foot inside the castle. There is a haunting ambience, but it's not the emptiness and desolation I was expecting. Probably not quite what Aunt Midge was expecting, either, otherwise I doubt she'd concede so quickly. There's a heartbeat inside this place, however faint, hidden beneath its bones.

Rand opens the door for her, and I watch from the foyer as she stands in the doorway, looking small and almost cartoonish within the enormous threshold, grasping the hem of her shirt. One more glance back, and she makes her way down the stone staircase, where a large man, perhaps six-foot-five, with darker skin, and black hair pulled back in a bun, waits for her. I'd guess him to be Polynesian, based on his looks.

The moment Rand closes the door behind her is the moment I realize, for the first time, I'm truly on my own.

"Do you like tea?"

The question breaks my thoughts, and I clear my throat. "No, not really. More of a coffee drinker."

"Shame. Mrs. Blackthorne loves her tea. It's perhaps when she's most cordial."

The woman sounds like her patience for people is thinner than my savings account. Can't be any worse than Aunt Midge when she attempted to quit smoking a year ago, though. Moody as a bat sunbathing on the beach.

"Come, let's go meet her, shall we?"

"Sure." The uncertainty creeps back down my spine again.

When I was fifteen years old, I was asked to stay one night with my great-aunt and -uncle, my grandfather's only brother, who had advance stage muscular sclerosis. Great-Aunt Sophie had wanted a night out with some old friends, and needed a break from the daily care she administered to her husband. My job? To make sure he didn't drown in his own saliva. So, every so often, when I heard uncle Conlan gagging, I was tasked with shoving a tube down into his throat and clearing the fluids. The mere thought of it was enough to give me hives, but it wasn't until I had to perform the act, panicking when I couldn't get the tube properly placed down his throat, and shaking when he looked at me like I was some kind of imbecile, that I vowed never to place myself in such a position again.

Yet, here I am, jumping at the opportunity to entertain an elderly recluse.

In the interview, though, Rand assured me Mrs. Blackthorne was mostly mobile and capable, requiring only the slightest assistance getting around.

Instead of taking the staircase, as before, we venture down a hallway on the first level, past a room on the right that has me slowing my steps. Every inch of the walls is covered in mirrors. Big elaborate mirrors. Small mirrors. Oddly shaped mirrors. An entire room devoted to reflection. So strange. I can't imagine having so much space for something so useless. Aunt Midge and I are always running into one another at home, it seems.

A chime breaks my stare, and Rand comes to a stop in the middle of the hallway. "Excuse me a moment." Setting the phone to his ear, he walks three paces ahead. "Yes?" In his profile, I catch the lowering of his brows. "You can't be serious. The girl left abruptly with no communication, never once said a word to our in-house doctor, or nurse. She left the door to the balcony unlocked, placing Mrs. Blackthorne at grave risk." The intensity in his voice fades as he continues down the hallway. "Whatever hallucinations she claims she's suffered since leaving, it's likely her own conscience biting her in the ass."

Hallucinations? Pretending not to listen to the conversation, I look back at the room with the mirrors, but feel the light tap on my shoulder. On instinct, I flinch, and turn to find Rand holding up a finger, phone still pressed to his ear, before he walks off.

"She's lucky the Master isn't privy to all of this, or we'd have a far less equitable day in court." His voice echoes down the hallway, and I keep on in the opposite direction, past the elevator toward more rooms ahead.

My wandering brings me to a doorway halfway down the

corridor, and I halt mid-step, my heart leaping into my throat when I peer through the French doors.

Completely encased in windows and iron that converge into an arched, translucent ceiling, it reminds me of a cross between a greenhouse and a birdcage. An atrium with hardwood flooring and enough early morning light to illuminate the gossamer cobwebs clinging to the room. Dying plants lie about in what must've been a room brimming with life at one time, given the number of pots scattered throughout. In the center of it, sits the most beautiful black piano I've ever seen. Like the one from my dreams, where I sit and play my own compositions for a room of people who listen. Before I even realize it, my feet carry me across the room, until I'm standing in front of the beastly thing. Giving one furtive glance toward the doorway, I glide my fingertips over the ivory and ebony keys. Off to the side, on a pedestal table, is a snifter glass with an amber fluid and mostly melted ice cubes.

Swinging around, I search for another presence, but find nothing aside from scattered bits of furniture, stacked books, and what look like outdoor streetlights, the kind of Victorian era decor unfound in a town like Tempest Cove. The vines crawling over the windows outside remind me of an old London alleyway.

Mesmerizing.

I can only imagine what this room must look like in winter.

I settle my attention back on the keys and press a note, one I couldn't recognize if someone paid me, but a common sound, found in many of the pieces I've played. Unlike on the old piano at school, broken down from age and overuse, these keys are even and smooth, yet slightly stiffer than what I'm used to. Heavier and crisp, as I play a simple scale. Sometimes, my music teacher would have me play at concerts when his usual pianist wasn't available. I only have to listen to a piece once before I know the entire song, note for note. I've always appreciated consistent rhythms and the *tick tick tick* of the metronome.

A strange sensation winds down my spine, and I pause my playing, turning my attention toward the door in time to catch a flickering shadow of movement outside the room. "Rand?"

A cold sensation sweeps over my skin, springing goosebumps. I step around the piano to get a better look at what I'm certain is someone beyond the doorway. "Rand, is that you?"

Fine tendrils tickle the back of my neck, and I rub a hand across my nape over the creeping prickle.

It's broad daylight, Isa. Relax.

The feeling of being watched has my eyes scanning the room. "Hello?"

"Miss Quinn!"

A scream flies out of my throat, and I stumble backward, setting a hand to my chest.

Rand peers in from the doorway. "I didn't mean to startle you. And my apologies for the delay. Shall we?"

Eyes fluttering shut, I exhale a breath, and nodding, I follow him out of the room and down the hallway toward a set of silver doors, which appear to be an elevator. Of course, the place has an elevator. Why wouldn't it?

"Only two rooms can be accessed from this elevator. Mrs. Blackthorne's chambers, and the Master's personal office. I'd caution you against snooping around the third level, as Master Blackthorne is very particular."

"About his privacy," I finish for him. "I understand."

"Good." He presses the button on the wall, and the panel overhead shows the third floor lit up, then the second. "You're free to roam all other rooms, aside from the Master's bedroom and the catacombs, of course." At a ding, the silver doors slide open, and with a wave of his hand, Rand ushers me inside.

"Catacombs?" I ask.

"The bottommost level in the castle. It's where the Blackthorne mausoleum, or *ossuary*, rather, is located."

That cold sensation sweeps over me again. "Mausoleum? As in … human remains? In this house?"

"Yes. The Blackthornes have obtained special documentation that has permitted them to bury their ancestors right here on the property. However, the catacombs are off limits to you."

"Of course." Why the hell would I care to go snooping around for dead bodies, anyway?

"You'd be surprised what lengths some will go to, to see what's off limits. I'd advise you don't. One other small thing I want to mention. Should, by chance, you run into Master Blackthorne, I'd advise you not to make eye contact for long. Makes him a little … edgy."

Guy must be sensitive about his scars. I get it. "Sure. He doesn't wander about much, I take it."

"Aside from his office and the gym, not much, no."

"There's a gym here?"

"And a pool, as well as an indoor track. The Master was quite an athlete in his youth. You're welcome to use them, if you wish."

Jesus, it must take a crew just to keep up the daily cleaning here. I'd've hated getting assigned this place back when I worked for the cleaning company.

The elevator comes to a stop on floor number two and opens directly into what appears to be a parlor, with an antique-looking settee upholstered in a black satiny material that has my palms itching to touch. The entire wall to the left is one giant glass curio cabinet filled with what I'm guessing are porcelain dolls. Hundreds of them. In the light through the window ahead, I can see their beady eyes staring forward through the glass, where each appears to be propped on some kind of stand.

Creepy.

As I step into the room, another cold rush of air dances over my skin, and the abandonment of this place becomes palpable.

"Mrs. Blackthorne has one of the most expensive and coveted porcelain and bisque doll collections in the world."

"She's been collecting them for a while, then?"

"Since she was a little girl. Please have a seat on the couch. I'll fetch her." With his parting words, he wanders off through a doorway, and I don't yet bother to sit. I'll do nothing but fidget, which will only bring my wracked-out nerves to my attention.

Eyes scanning over the lifeless faces, I take in the variety of dolls in her collection--some I bet came from different countries. Some with cracked faces, others smooth and flawless. I never grew up with dolls to appreciate them much. My mother always called them pointless, and by the time I went to live with my aunt, I was too old for them.

"She'll be out in a moment." Rand starts toward the elevator doors, and I spin around.

"Wait. You're leaving?"

Pausing, he turns to face me, a smile widening his lips. "The fewer triggers, the better. Besides, she tends to do much better in a one-on-one situation. Her nurse is flitting about somewhere, so you're not entirely alone. If you need anything, there's an intercom on the wall. One of the staff can fetch me."

After all he's told me about the woman, I feel like he's leaving me with Norman Bates's mother. "Okay."

"You'll be fine. She seems to be in an unusually good mood."

That's a relief. "Thank you, Rand."

With a sharp nod, he resumes his exit, smiling again when the elevator doors close, but just before they seal, I catch the dramatic change in his expression that morphs from pleasant to distressed.

The phone call, maybe?

Shrugging it off, I lean into the cabinet, staring down at one particular doll that looks so lifelike, given the detail in her dark green irises, the waves of red hair cascading over her shoulder. It's uncanny how much she looks like my mother. So much so, I chuckle at the resemblance, thinking it amusing to find her in such an extravagant-looking dress amongst all the other expensive dolls. Like staring at an alternate version of the woman.

"Shauna. Princess of Blarney Castle." The voice from behind draws my attention toward an older, but no less elegant, woman than the doll in the case. Graying hair betrays the silky texture of her skin, and though she must be near the age of sixty, her lithe form and regal stance don't give the impression she's in much need of assistance. Only the cane she leans slightly against gives any indication of physical deficiencies. "Certainly not the most expensive one I've purchased, but I appreciate the fire in her eyes."

Fire is definitely how I'd describe my mother, though her flame has dimmed over the last decade to a dullness just short of death.

"She's beautiful."

"She is." The woman's eyes dip to my outfit and back to me, the disapproval hidden behind a slight smile. "You must be my new babysitter."

"Just … a companion."

"Companion is just an adult word for babysitter." Again her eyes appraise me. "You're a local girl."

"It's obvious, I guess."

"No proper teenage girl would choose to wear *fishing* mucks."

Cheeks burning with embarrassment, I swallow back the catty sarcasm I've always reserved for the pretentious bitches I grew up with, the ones who had a problem with my clothes. The fact is, they're Aunt Midge's old shoes. The only pair I own that don't have as many holes as my jeans. "I'll be sure to get a better pair."

"I'll have Rand get in touch with Amy to have you outfitted for the job."

I have no idea who Amy is, or how much of this is going to be taken out of my pay, but it sounds well beyond what I can afford. "I … um. I didn't realize there was a specific wardrobe requirement." My comment isn't meant to sound snarky, but somehow that's how it comes out. To me, anyway.

"You'll be attending some important engagements with me. I'll not have you looking like you crawled onto port."

This woman doesn't seem in need of medical assistance, or companionship, though she could benefit from some manners. I'm the last person to care about etiquette, but within a relatively short span of time, she's already made me feel inferior, which I'm certain is her MO. My purpose here has officially eluded me. I guess I had the impression she was less alert and aware. Maybe not quite a vegetable, but not full-on capable of slinging insults so proficiently, either.

"Are you going to sit there, admiring dolls all day, or make yourself useful?"

Blinking out of my thoughts, I stare back at her. "I'm sorry, I think I may have misunderstood my purpose here."

"Well, that makes two of us."

"I just mean, I was under the impression you needed more … assistance. You seem perfectly capable to me."

Her eyes narrow, before softening to amusement, as she hobbles across the room toward where a teapot and cups are set out on a small table. "Tea?"

Rand's words from before come to mind, and though I hate tea as much as I do an overcooked plate of crab legs, I nod. I'm damn well determined to find some common ground with this woman, even if it leaves a bitter flavor on my tongue.

After pouring the tea into a porcelain cup that looks like an adult version of the set Aunt Midge bought me for my tenth birthday, Mrs. Blackthorne hands it off to me. It's an amber colored tea with a slight sweet scent, and I let the warmth of the cup leach into my ice cold hands.

"What do I call you?"

Nice, I forgot to mention my name. "I'm sorry, I should've told you earlier. I'm Isa. Izzy, if you prefer."

"I never bothered to ask. Isa. As in Isabelle?" She lowers herself to the seat across from me, setting the cane off to the side, and lifts the teacup to her lips.

"Isadora."

There's only a slight tremble in her hand, as she sips the drink and sets the teacup tittering against the saucer on the table in front of her. "Shame. I love the name Isabelle."

Shame. The only kind thing my mother ever did for me was naming me after my grandmother.

"Have you met Lucian yet?" Her question interrupts my thoughts.

"No. Rand says I probably won't have much contact with him."

"It's probably just as well. He's not much for socializing these days."

"He likes his privacy. I respect that."

"Do you?" For the third time, her gaze slips to my outfit, which I'm guessing, in this alternate existence, would be like a fisherman rolling up to port in a three-piece suit back home.

"I've no intentions of imposing. I'm merely here to assist you in whatever capacity you require."

"I'll give you this, you don't talk like a typical adolescent. The last one we had could barely speak in full sentences. I felt like I was verbally texting with her."

I can't help the chuckle that escapes me, and I clear my throat, straightening in my seat just enough not to spill the cup of tea I haven't yet sipped. "I have very little in common with most girls my age," I say, lifting the teacup to my lips. *Dear God, please don't let me gag.* I tip the drink back, taking tiny sips of the sweet flavor that warms my tongue.

"How many boys have fucked you, Isa?"

Fluids expel past my lips on a gasp, and a good portion of the tea splashes onto the saucer below the cup, sloshing around the dish as I set it onto the table in front of me.

"Da Hong Pao is the most expensive tea in the world. More than thirty times its weight in gold. In China, it's reserved for honored guests."

"I'm sorry. I was caught off guard."

"My question offended you? See, it's important for me to gauge your interests. A number of women we've hired have gone on to behave rather inappropriately toward my son. The rumors of his *cock* seem to be legendary. A source of amusement amongst you local girls."

"As I said, I've nothing in common with my peers. And I can assure you, I'm not here for your son's cock. Legendary, or not."

"Good. You should be safe to introduce to Roark, then."

"Roark?"

"My grandson."

"Oh, I was … under the impression you only had one grandson."

"I do only have one grandson. That's all Lucian and Amelia gifted me, but I count my blessings for him every day."

A cold chill winds down my spine as I stare back at her, and I school my face over my confusion. Unless rumors have it all wrong, she's talking about her *missing* grandson. Did they find him? I don't even know how to ask her this question.

"Roark! Roark! Come here please, I've someone to introduce to you!" She doesn't take her eyes off me as she calls out for him, smiling in such a way that makes me roll my shoulders back to ward off the sudden discomfort. "Roark! Nonna is calling for you!"

"Perhaps he's asleep?"

"It's the dolls. They've always frightened him, ever since he was a baby." Shooting up out of her chair, she knocks over the pot, spilling her expensive tea all over the carpet. "Roark Lucian Blackthorne, you come here now, or I'll have Anna spank your behind!"

I kneel down to the carpet, grabbing one of the napkins from the tray to daub the tea, while I tease out the possibility that she might not be mentally sound. "It's okay, if he doesn't want to meet me. I don't want to make him uncomfortable."

"He's a child. He doesn't know what discomfort is. No child understands the burdens we adults carry." She swings around toward the door wall behind her. "I'll bet he's playing on the balcony again. Amelia must be sleeping."

Amelia. From what I've heard, Amelia *is* dead. Is it possible that rumor was wrong, as well?

As she tromps toward the door, I recall Rand mentioning something on the phone earlier, about someone leaving the door unlocked and placing Mrs. Blackthorne at grave risk. I jump to my feet and step in front of her, immediately regretting my decision when she frowns back at me. The last thing I need, though, is to have this lady leap from the balcony to her death on my first day here.

"Wait, let me look for him. I love surprises."

After a dubious side-eye glance, she rolls her shoulders back. "Roark enjoys them, as well. All right, I'll let you surprise him."

With a nod, I twist toward the door wall, and the moment I step out onto the balcony, I exhale a breath, closing the door behind me. Mentally unstable isn't something new for me. Hell, my mom was a meth addict, for Christ's sake. Crazy was a way of life growing up, and I learned early on not to trust everything that flies out of an adult's mouth. I once found her sitting outside completely topless, telling passersby that the sky was being sucked into the sun.

I know crazy when I see it.

But I have to admit, hearing Mrs. Blackthorne call out for her dead daughter-in-law and missing grandson was about as confusing as getting knocked in the head by an acorn in the middle of the desert.

Resting my head against the wall, I mentally tell myself this isn't a mistake. In spite of the fact that I wasn't aware the woman had some mental issues, this isn't a mistake.

"Hey."

A gasp flies past my lips, and I leap to the side, away from the direction of the voice.

A woman, only slightly older than me, I think, sits bent forward smoking a cigarette that dangles from her long, slender fingers. Decked out in navy blue scrubs, she must be the nurse. "Sorry. I didn't mean to make you jump. When you didn't look over at me, I figured one way, or another, you were going to be startled."

"It's okay. I'm just a little edgy right now, is all. First day."

"Yeah. My first day sucked. Heard her yelling, but she always yells, so ..." Her cheeks cave as she sucks in a drag of her smoke.

"She was calling for her grandson. Roark?"

Snorting, the woman shakes her head. "Roark's been gone for five years. Amelia, too, in case she tries to get you to fetch her next." Reaching around her cigarette, she extends a hand toward me. "I'm Nell. Anella, but just call me Nell."

"Isadora, but just call me Isa. Hey, is she always ..."

"Out of it? Yeah. Dementia with Lewy Bodies to be specific. Similar to what folks with Parkinsons suffer from. Doc's trying to get her meds right."

"She seemed fine up until she started talking about Roark."

"Unnerving, isn't it? One minute, she's prattling on about current world events, the next she's playing hide and seek with her dead grandson."

"He's ... dead? For sure?"

"Depends on who you ask. After five years? Yeah, it's a safe bet he's dead." Taking in another drag, she leans back on the chair and blows the smoke away from me. "The nightmares are always a good time, too. Sometimes have to strap her down." With a sigh, she stamps her cigarette out into an ashtray filled with used butts. "I should probably get her settled back into bed. She have her tea yet?"

"Yeah. Not much, after spilling it onto the floor. Broke the teapot."

The girl flinches as she pushes to her feet. "That teapot, along with the tea, is worth more than I make in a month."

"No kidding. I just got an education in tea."

Her eyes dip to my outfit and back. "You're young."

"Nineteen. Just graduated last year."

"Two weeks. That's if you keep to yourself."

Frowning, I mentally tease the meaning of her words. "What's two weeks?"

"How long you'll last. That's giving you some credit, too. Girl before you lasted a week. One before her? Three whole days. You met Lucian yet?"

Why does everyone ask me that after scoping my outfit?

"No. Why do you ask?"

"You think his mom's a whackjob? Wait 'til you meet the Devil of Bonesalt, himself." She steps past me, knocking me in the shoulder on her way to the door. "Whole damn place is one big asylum."

"I didn't say his mom was a whack--" The door slams shut before I can finish. "Job."

Staring out over the yard, I can make out the edge of the bluff and the endless sea beyond it. Miles of isolation.

On one hand, I appreciate the peace and quiet.

On the other, I hope I didn't make a mistake in taking this job.

CHAPTER 5

LUCIAN

Sixteen years ago ...

With a thin twig, I draw my initials in the sandy bed of the cave while I wait for Jude to arrive. Heat from the small fire I've lit keeps the evening chill away, but my mind twists with what will happen when my father returns from his business trip. The fire extinguishers weren't the smartest idea, but fuck, being trapped in this hellhole for months is prison. I'm losing my mind in this place, day in and day out. The only reprieves are the few times like these, when I steal away without anyone knowing.

Rushing of water at the mouth of the cave is the first taunt of the rising tide. In just a few hours, this place will be half full of sea water, and the pull of the tide will sweep whatever's in here beneath the surface and out to sea. For that reason, locals call it Pirates Cove.

A young kid, fourteen, ventured in here a few years back and was believed to have drowned and gotten pulled out to sea.

According to reports, he might've hit his head, knocking him out long enough for the tide to take him away. Since then, it's been made off limits to beach goers, and children, in particular. The cave sits on the edge of our property and the state-owned land beside us, so the family attempted to sue my father, but no one files a lawsuit against a Blackthorne and wins.

Jude and I typically hang out until the water reaches our calves, but leave before it becomes impossible to wade through. We once played chicken, the water rising as high as our chests before we were forced to climb out. With its rough and choppy waves that hammer against the rocks, if the sea doesn't take you alive, it'll surely take what's left of you after your body's been tossed around.

Splashing draws my attention toward the entrance, where two figures stand, and I drop my stick on seeing Jude has somehow manipulated the new maid into hanging out with us.

"Brought a friend, hope you don't mind." He guides her toward one of the boulders, the only permanent fixtures in the cave, and plops down on the dry sand at the opposite side of the bonfire. "Solange wanted to see the infamous *Pirates Cove*."

I can't take my eyes off the woman, the way her deep brown eyes and long, curly hair gives her an exotic lure. Her long slender neck and equally slender shoulders dip down to full breasts that, too heavy for such a small frame, strain against the thin fabric of her shirt. From here, I can see her nipples poking through, and my dick lurches at the sight.

"What do you estimate we've got? Two hours?" Reaching into his coat pocket, Jude pulls out one of the joints he scammed from Easton and, without wasting time, lights it up. The end crackles orange, and he puffs it twice, turning it around to suck in the smoke, before puffing it again and passing it to Solange. He runs his finger up and down her arm, shooting me a smirk through the flames. She takes one long drag and leans to the side, reaching around the small fire to pass it to me.

"I say we've got two hours, max." Like Jude, I take a couple tugs of the joint, letting the smoke crackle in my lungs, and I close my eyes, tipping my head back on the exhale. While away at school, Jude and I would sneak down into the basement and get high, or wasted, all night. Sometimes it was weed, other times it was alcohol.

"So, what do you do before the tide comes in?" Her thick French accent carries a breathy quality, like a mid-thrust moan. Nothing like the girls I've messed around with, stealing away to cop a feel, or a quick fuck. Local girls can be fun sometimes, if I've got the time to charm them. Only problem is, they're looking for a way out. A means to keep from becoming their mothers, and I'd rather run a nail through the head of my dick than make that kind of commitment.

"How 'bout you take off that sweater, and we'll show you." Jude has always been ballsy when it comes to women. Kind of a prick, to be honest, but whether it's because he's wealthier than a prostitute in a submarine fleet, or more charming than the devil himself, they never seem bothered by it.

Solange smiles, and her gaze falls on me, for some reason. "Does the young Master wish to see my tits?"

Young Master. Fuck me.

Blowing the smoke off to the side, I give a small nod, catching sight of her nipples again. More prominent than even a minute ago. Without hesitation, she crosses her arms and lifts the sweater over her head, revealing braless tits that're too big for my palms.

Licking his lips beside her, Jude cups one of her breasts and runs a thumb over her nipple.

Still, her eyes are on me.

"Feed it to me," he says, before taking another hit of his joint.

Without hesitation, she leans in, lifting her breast just enough to slide her nipple into his mouth. Smoke curls from his nose as he exhales, tonguing her breast at the same time.

Things seem to progress quickly between them from there. Or maybe I'm just fucked up on weed, it's hard to tell. It isn't long before I'm watching her tits bounce as she rides him across from me.

A hard smack echoes through the cave as Jude slaps her ass. "I knew you were a whore. Dick gobbling slut."

She seems to like this, her lips stretching with a smile. "Come, Young Master. Fuck me."

The thought of my dick in close contact with Jude's leaves me shaking my head, but it isn't long before they finish, and Jude's bellows of pleasure echoes through the cave. With his come likely dripping down her thighs, she crawls around the firepit toward me, like it's my turn. As she buries her face in my neck, the scent of her perfume mingles with sex, and I set my hand on her shoulder, giving a small nudge to push her away. Her brows lower with telling disappointment, and she paws at me a second time.

Again, I push her away from me. "I don't fuck seconds."

Jude snorts, and Solange sits back on her heels, her naked body perfect, glowing in the dimming flame of the bonfire.

"I should've let you have me first, then," she says, shoving two fingers up inside her. "I'll just have to pretend." Biting her lip, she tips her head back, fingers plunging in and out, and I watch as they shimmer on each withdrawal. Falling back onto her outstretched arm, she holds herself up, thrusting her pussy in my face, while she fingers herself.

I'd be lying if I said I don't want to take her right now, but I meant what I said.

I don't do sloppy seconds, no matter how hot she is, or how high I get.

Within minutes, she's moaning, thrusting faster. Behind her, Jude lights up the second joint and smiles as he passes it to me. My dick is harder than the rock I'm leaning against just to keep myself upright, as I watch this chick go to town on her cunt, the wet sounds audible over the waves in the distance.

As I hit the joint, everything feels good, and when she cries out, I almost don't recognize my name bouncing against the walls of the cave. "Lucian!"

Her fingers are soaking wet when she withdraws them again, and she leans forward, cramming them into my mouth. "This was for you. Next time, I'll have you first."

CHAPTER 6

ISADORA

Present day ...

I tap my fork against the plate, staring down at the fancy dinner I had the chef repeat the name of twice when he served it. Roasted chicken with fennel panza-something.

The long dining table could probably seat about two-dozen guests. It seems to go on forever, but here I sit by myself. Apparently, everyone, except Rand, Nell and Makaio, has already cleared out of here for the night. Even the chef who graciously served me had one foot out the door. The Blackthornes seem to like their privacy in the evening, too, but for whatever reason, they insist that I remain on castle grounds all five days of the week.

Not that I mind. It's not every day a girl from Tempest Cove gets to sleep in a castle. I just thought it'd be a bit more bustling than this. That's what I get for watching *Annie* too many times.

After Nell put Mrs. Blackthorne to bed earlier, there really wasn't much for me to do, aside from sitting in that unsettling room full of dolls, until Nell suggested I go grab something to eat. Kinda depressing, really. Nell sat on her phone, smoking cigarettes out on the balcony most of the time, while Mrs. Black-thorne lay passed out all afternoon. Can't say I'd have the energy to do much of anything, if that was my life.

I shove another forkful into my mouth, focusing on the taste of the oniony green stuff mingled with the succulent chicken flavor. For a girl who grew up on seafood and cans of spam most of her life, I actually have a fairly picky palate. Gourmet food is something new to me. Something I'll have to get used to while living here.

Movement in my periphery draws my attention, and I slowly turn my head to where an enormous figure sits off to the side, watching me. A black, beastly animal that looks like a dog and a horse had a baby sits on its haunches, staring at me. Its head is level with mine. Meaning it could lean in and chew my face off, if it felt so inclined.

A monster.

My muscles turn rigid. My jaw stiff.

Slowly, so as not to set it off into attack mode, I look around for a master, anyone who might claim ownership of this thing, but it's just me and the beast.

Staring at one another.

"Um. Hi."

Its ear twitches as it slides its gaze toward my plate. A long string of drool falls from its chops, and only when I lift my fork does the animal break its stare to look up at me, though only for a second, or two, before returning its attention to my food.

At least there's enough chicken on my plate to maybe afford me a few minutes to reach the door, before it can tear after me and make me its next meal.

"Do you … um. Like chicken?" So as not to draw too much attention, I slide my hand into my lap to grab the napkin there, and more drool oozes from the dog's mouth. A downward glance shows a tiny pool of it on the floor in front of its enormous paw. Jesus. Like a lion's paw.

With as much subtlety as I can muster, given the tremble running through me, I set the napkin onto the table, not bothering to look where, and pat around until my fingertips hit the wet meat on my plate.

"Let's just … see if this will buy me some time. Okay?"

My muscles spring on instinct, and I toss the chicken to the dog, who makes a snorting sound as he catches it midair. Not a second later, he straightens again, tongue sweeping over his jowls, eyes locked on my plate.

"Did you even taste that?" I could set the plate down and run, or leave it on the table and hope the scramble to get to it affords me extra time. Doesn't look like it'll buy me much, considering this beast just scarfed down a chunk like it was air.

The fork clinks against the china as I lower the plate to the floor, noting the unwavering attention of the dog staring down at the food once it's set before him. He doesn't make a move, though. Only a quick glance up at me breaks his concentration before he goes back to staring down at the food.

Like he's waiting for something.

I take the opportunity to slide out of my chair, pushing to my feet. Still, the dog doesn't go after the plate of gourmet chicken I've just offered him. Hoping that'll buy me a few extra seconds, I back slow and easy toward the other end of the dining table.

An endless strand of drool hangs like a shimmering cable from the dog's mouth, but for some reason, it won't. Touch. The food.

"What the hell are you waiting for? Eat!"

As soon as the words pass my lips, the dog lunges for the plate like it's in a hurry, its body poised to run as soon as every bite of chicken is gone. Taking the cue, I spin on my heel, and race out of the room and down the hallway.

The surrounding darkness conceals the path ahead, and for a

moment, I've lost my bearings in this house. Momentary brainless with fear thrumming through my veins--not a good combination.

Any second now, that beast is going to come plowing through the dining area, looking for me. Why the hell would they let it roam unattended?

I search the obscure walls for something familiar to help lead me back to my room, and when I dare a backward glance, I see the dog barreling straight for me.

"Oh, my God!" The air withers in my chest as I force speed from my legs, and when I look back again, the damn beast has already gained on me, hoofing it on all fours.

It's going to maul me right here in this hallway.

The staff are going to come back tomorrow morning to find my body half eaten by a monster.

Aunt Midge was right. This was stupid. So fucking stupid it hurts.

An unyielding force hits me from the side and something grips my shoulders. A scream rips from my chest as the ache of the blow settles into my bones, and I look up to see a massive chest with a light covering of dark hair behind the few unbuttoned clasps of a black shirt. Broad shoulders stretch the fabric that clings tight to massive biceps that're bunched at either side of me, while fingers dig into my arms. A chiseled jawline, dusted in a five o'clock shadow, bears grisly scars and slices, the fine lines of contractured skin fanning out from each wound.

He releases me and I take a step back, my whole body quaking as I stare into liquid amber eyes, which are narrowed in a royally pissed-off expression that screws up the mangled half of his face. Ghastly to look at, but nowhere near the monstrous appearance I'd heard others describe. Personally, I think he's kind of handsome, in a rough, edgy sort of way, but I'll keep that to myself. In a matter of seconds, my eyes suck in as many details as they can grasp.

The flawless half of his face lends insight into how he might have once looked --olive-toned skin, deep chestnut colored hair that has a slightly ruffled appeal, the perfect symmetry just begging to be captured by a sharp charcoal pencil, while the other half is ruined by the scars for which he's known.

Shadows hide much of what I imagine is hard to look at in bright light, but those eyes practically glow with malice as he stares back at me.

Don't stare. Shit!

"I … I'm sorry. I didn't mean to … I was just …" *The dog. Christ, the dog!* I turn away from the man to find the dog sitting at attention behind me, its tongue lolled out to the side, tail wagging.

As if the bastard was *playing* with me?

Turning my attention back toward the man, undoubtedly Lucian Blackthorne, whose stature and size leaves me feeling small and insignificant, I lower my gaze to his hands, the right mutilated by fewer scars than his face. Strong with long fingers and a map of veins that extends up into his forearms, they seem well designed for throttling, if he gets the notion. "He chased me."

"You run. He chases. That's what dogs do." His voice is a deep, rich sound that practically vibrates on the air. Smooth and immaculate, it doesn't match his scars. It's a sound that hums in my chest, the kind of hypnotic timbre that lingers in the ear after he's spoken.

"I didn't realize it was in play."

"You're the new girl." It isn't a question, because it's apparently obvious, and he says it as if he's just tasted something sour and bitter and is looking to spit it out. In spite of the fact that I'm on his payroll, making more money here than any of the odd jobs I'd find downtown, he doesn't even know my name. Imagine that. A place in this town where someone is disgusted with me as a person and not simply because I'm Jenny Quinn's daughter.

"Yes. I'm Isa. Or Izzy. Whichever you'd prefer."

"I'd *prefer* that you watch where you're going."

"Takes two to collide." It's a bad habit, talking back. One that's gotten me in trouble more times than I care to admit, but it's also completely reflexive. I can't help the things that fly out of my mouth sometimes, and it sucks, because he's obviously been through some stuff. I know from my own experience how things like rejection and ridicule can turn someone into a stony wall of *Back the hell off.* "I just mean, you could've easily stepped aside when you saw me coming."

"Smartass?" Leaning forward just enough that I can feel the heat of his frustration rolling off his skin, can practically taste the delicious cologne he's wearing, he drills those fiery eyes into me as if they're laser beams shooting out his sockets. "You'll find the best way to stay employed in this house is by staying on my good side."

I literally have to bite my lips together to keep from asking which half he considers his good side. Again, reflexive, brought on by years of torment at the hands of my asshole classmates, when I was forced to stand my ground, or swallow their crap.

This job means too much to me. My freedom. My independence. And I am singlehandedly blowing this first meeting, so to respond with, "My apologies," requires a kind of tongue-biting self-control I've not yet mastered.

"Your boots are loud and clumsy. I can hear them all the way in the east wing. Find a different pair, if you insist on running through the halls."

"These are the only shoes I brought with me." Eyes on his, I lift my leg, bending my knee as I stand on one foot, hopping to keep balanced while I slide the boot off and set it to the floor beside me. Same with the other. "Anything else about my outfit you don't like?"

Chin tipped at a condescending angle, he dips his gaze, and a sneer tugs at his ruined lips. "Perhaps a pair of pants that don't make you look like you were in a brawl with a wolverine."

This guy is something else.

"Would you have me remove those, too?" Biting my tongue once again, I set my fingers to the buttons of my jeans in mocking, as if to take them off, and catch a flicker of something in his eyes. Amusement, maybe? A dare?

Ignoring my question, he steps past me, as if already bored with our exchange, and snaps his fingers. "Sampson."

The dog follows after him, down the hallway.

There's a regal arrogance to the way he walks, the easy stroll of a powerful man who doesn't give a shit about some local Townie clown who wears fishing mucks for shoes.

I turn away toward my path again and exhale a shaky breath. I've never met a human being so intense in my life. As if the very air crackled around him, threatening to strike out at me. Which probably would've felt better than the fly-in-the-soup attitude I got instead. Like I was nothing in this guy's day, aside from the nuisance who didn't watch where she was going.

All this time, I've given him some measure of credit, benefit of the doubt, and all that.

Turns out, the Devil of Bonesalt really is an asshole.

L ight physical, mostly emotional support, I text to Aunt Midge, when she asked what was wrong with Lady Blackthorne that she needs a companion. *She's probably lonely after her husband's death.*

If I tell her the truth, that the entire family is bat-shit crazy, or moody as hell, she'll not only tell me she was right, but it'll be passed around The Shoal for the next week like a donation basket at church, everyone adding their version of the story. I refuse to give this town more gossip to devour.

Well, I'm sure she'll find you a good source of entertainment. How's your room? They lock you in a tower?

I lift my gaze to the room I've been assigned, and just like the first time, my eyes can hardly imbibe the magic of it all. Tall windows curtained by thick, black drapes allow in the shimmer of moon's light. The bed and vanity are a heavy, but ornate dark wood that I'm guessing would take a half dozen men to move. The linens are velvet grays and black, with only a splash of white for the sheets. A black crystal chandelier hangs from the center of the room, giving it a gothic Victorian appeal. In spite of the incessant chill that hangs on the air, the bedroom is cozy, and the fireplace across from me crackles as it burns.

Perhaps the only thing I'd change is removing the creepy doll that's propped on the nightstand beside my bed. One of Laura's, I'll bet. Long, blonde hair and blue eyes hardly detract from the stern angle of its brow and the devious smile stretching its lips, as if it might come to life while I sleep. Other than that, the room is somehow fitting for me.

Like a fairy tale, I text back.

Yeah, well. Fairy tales are just that. Tales. Don't get too caught up in it.

Like I would. Try not to have too much fun while I'm gone.

In the time it takes Aunt Midge to text back, which is three times as long as it takes me, there's a knock at the door, and I nearly drop my phone on the floor.

Climbing off the bed, I type back, *Talk later. Love you.*

The floors creak as I make my way across the room, and I throw back the door to find a woman with dark bronze skin, about the same age as Nell, though slightly less gloomy and fairly attractive. Silky black hair is pulled into a tight bun that sits at the back of her head, and bright red lipstick adds a pop of color.

"Hi, I'm Giulia. You must be Isa." The first person besides Rand who actually knows my name. "I'm a couple rooms down. Just thought I'd stop in and say hello." The gray double-breasted dress with white collar and cuffs, and a white apron tied to the front, is a dead giveaway that she's housekeeping.

"Thought all the employees in this place left for the day."

"Blackthornes keep me overnight. Just in case. But I'm the only one, besides the nurse. And you, it seems." She peeks past me, as if trying to see into the room. "Can I come in?"

"Sure." She's probably been in here to clean it at some point, anyway. Who am I to tell her she can't come in?

Ambling to a stop in the middle of the room, she tips her head back, as if she's absorbing something in the air, and when she turns to face me, there's a slight smile on her lips. "Beautiful, isn't it? Never in a million years did I think someone with my background would end up living in a castle by the ocean."

"Your background?"

"Poor. I lived on the streets. My daughter and I did."

"She lives here with you?"

"No. Didn't think this was a place for children. She stays in a boarding school now." Nodding toward the fireplace and back, she asks, "Are you comfortable in here?"

"Yeah. It's a little drafty, but other than that, I'm fine."

"This was Amelia's old room."

My enthusiasm for this place deflates like a balloon. The long, drawn out squeal of a balloon.

Of the many rooms throughout this castle, why the hell would they place me in the dead wife's?

"I wasn't aware."

She glances over her shoulder toward that creepy-looking, porcelain doll. "Here, I'll put that in the closet for you."

"Thanks. Was kind of giving me the creeps."

"Used to give Roark the creeps, too. He refused to come in here."

"You knew the two of them? Personally?"

"Oh, yes, but not long. Amelia died only a few weeks after I started. So, so sad, what happened to them."

"Wait ... so they know what happened to Roark, then? I mean, I thought he disappeared? If you don't mind me asking?"

The smile on her face is empty, as if she's holding it simply to be polite, while her eyes study me. Perhaps she's gauging whether, or not, to say anything. Wondering if I'll take the information and spread it around Tempest Cove, like Aunt Midge would do.

"You don't have to tell me. It's okay."

"Isn't really my place. But you care for Mrs. Blackthorne, right? Maybe she'll tell you."

The woman who thinks her possibly dead grandson is alive? Sure. "It's not important for me to know."

"You've met Lucian?"

I'm beginning to think everyone keeps asking me about him to see what I think of him, like he's some kind of deal breaker for me. Devil, or not, he's not scaring me out of this job. "I have. He's … pretty intense."

"Yes. Very. But not so bad, once you get to know him."

"I don't think he likes me very much."

"He's not a people person. Assuming you stay, he'll warm up eventually."

Warm up? I can't imagine that. I found the guy's personality frigid enough to replenish the polar icecaps. "It seems I'm not expected to stay long."

With a sigh, she glances around my room again. "This place isn't for everyone. Some find it depressing. Morose. Maybe even a little frightening, at times. It's a matter of perspective, I suppose. It can be a peaceful place for some. And drive others absolutely mad."

"You find it peaceful, then?"

"Sure. It's sort of like … sitting in a cemetery. Being surrounded by death can either make you feel incredibly vulnerable and alone, or it can make you grateful to be alive."

Giulia's is a personality that I can't quite place in our first meeting. A part of me appreciates her perspective, as I've always had a sort of fondness for the macabre. A cracked dead rose. A spider web in morning light. Even a cemetery. Yet, I find her demeanor almost oddly un-genuine, unlike Nell's. It's as if she's hiding something.

"I met Sampson, as well," I tell her.

"Oh, he's a big sweetie. Scary looking, but a sweetie."

"Scary, for sure. He looks like he could devour a person in under a minute."

"Minute and thirty, actually."

"Excuse me?"

Her head kicks back on a quiet chuckle, and even that strikes me as somewhat fake. "I'm joking. I've only seen him go after the occasional trespasser. We get them more often than not. Folks who like to dig up dirt on the Blackthornes. It's troublesome, the way people behave, sometimes."

"I agree. My asking about Roark was merely curiosity. Nothing else." My gaze falls to the shiny cross clasped around her neck.

"I didn't think anything bad of it. I've just grown accustomed to not talking with anyone about it."

"I'm sure you've had a lot of people pry. I promise I'm not one of them."

"Good. Also, I should let you know that this place can get pretty unsettling at night, sometimes." She reaches for her cross in what is perhaps a mindless gesture, drawing it back and forth along its delicate chain. "Think it's the wind coming off the cliff, but it can sound like someone crying. Freaked me out, the first few nights."

"Good to know."

"Well, I'll let you get settled. If you need anything, just holler."

"Or I can just knock on the door."

"I won't answer if you do. Just holler. I'll hear you through the vents."

"O. Kay. I'll do that."

"Oh, and you may want to lock your door at night."

CHAPTER 7

LUCIAN

Sixteen years ago ...

My father comes home today. With Jude having left, on his way back to school, there's nothing to keep me distracted from that thought. Blowing out an exasperated breath, I fix my gaze toward the tall ceiling in my bedroom. Adorned with gods of war, there isn't an inch of it that isn't painted with men in armor, clashing in blood and battle. Somehow, my parents thought staring up at it night after night would turn me into a complacent and obedient teenager.

Disaster with the fire extinguisher aside, homecomings with my father are never something I look forward to, but this one promises to be exceptionally bad, as I understand negotiations didn't go as he'd hoped. Which means his shitty mood will permeate every corner of this castle before the night is over. I'll get the brunt of it, as usual, but so will everyone else.

Perhaps even Solange.

At the flash of her tits, I screw my eyes shut and run a hand down my face. After spending the entire night battling the most horrific case of blue balls I've ever felt, I'll now be forced to tamp down the raging hard-on she's incited once again.

A knock at the door stiffens my muscles. Surely, my father hasn't arrived home already.

I lift my head, waiting to see if he'll slam through the door cursing my name, like the last time I got in trouble.

Another knock arrives, instead.

Likely not either of my parents, since my mom would've pushed her way in by now.

"Yeah?"

Instead of an answer, I get another knock at the door.

Groaning in frustration, I clamber out of bed, and with quick strides across the room, I throw the door open.

Solange stands outside my room. "Forgive my intrusion." Her voice is like an intoxicating poison made for a slow death. "May I come in?"

After a quick glance around, I step aside, allowing her entry.

"I have to admit, of all the rooms I've seen, so far, this one is my favorite." She points to the ceiling and smiles. "Nothing sexier than gods in battle."

"What do you want?"

"You disappointed me the other night. I was a little … how you say … *humiliated.*"

"What'd you expect, after screwing my friend in front of me?"

"Did you like the taste of my pussy?"

Setting one hand on my hip, I rub my jaw with the other to keep from grabbing my straining dick in front of her. "Nothing I haven't tasted before."

Amusement flickers in her eyes as she licks her lips, and her gaze nosedives toward where my groin must look like I'm smuggling tennis balls. "I've got a secret, young master." She, somehow, manages a slow and easy saunter back toward my bed, and runs her fingertips over the duvet as she comes to a stop alongside it.

Eyes on mine, she kneels and reaches beneath the bed, a smile lifting the corner of her lips as she pulls something from beneath and rises to a stand. "What would your mother think of this?"

Frowning, I focus on what she holds up in front of me. Porn, based on the cover of the magazine that shows a couple fucking, but not just any porn. These two are clad in leather, and the woman is tied up. The expression on her face, twisted up in fear, makes it look like rape.

"That isn't mine."

"Sure, sure."

"I'm serious. I've never seen that before." Jesus Christ, if this is Jude's little prank, he's a dead man the next time I see him. My mom would have a heart attack if she got her hands on this.

On a slow saunter back toward me, Solange doesn't lower the magazine from my sight. "The question is, do you like what you see?"

I don't answer that. Of course I like what I see. Any guy who says he doesn't fantasize about forced sex on occasion is a fucking liar.

Would I act on it, though? No, I'm no rapist.

"Would you like to do that, say ... to *me*?"

"I already told you. I don't do sloppy--"

She slaps a hand over my mouth, and she's lucky I'm already in the shithouse with my father, or she'd regret laying a hand on me. No one touches without asking.

I pry her fingers from my lips and throw her hand off to prove that point.

"I want you to meet me down in the cave tonight. I want to show you something."

This chick is relentless. She's got to be ten years older than me, at least. What the hell does she want with me?

"I'm sure I'll be grounded."

"Oh, poor baby." Testing my limits again, she sets her palm against my chest. "Do they lock your crib at night, so you can't crawl out?" Not even giving me the chance to make a smartass comment, she leans into me. "I wanted to show you a trick."

"What kind of trick?"

Something brushes the head of my dick through the slacks, and my stomach knots up. My mom could come through the door at any second, and this woman doesn't seem to care. "You'll have to *come*, if you want to find out."

Pressing the magazine into my chest, she guides my hand to take it from her.

"A gift from me," she whispers, and steps past me. "Enjoy."

Athrobbing ache swells behind my eye socket, and I set an ice pack there to numb the pain as I sit on a boulder inside the cave. A fist to the eye is nothing to me. Besides growing up with a violent bastard for a father, I got into more fights than I can count in school. This one's just another chip against my dwindling self-control. The truth is, even if Solange didn't invite me down here, I'd have ended up here eventually. It's where I go when I need to escape the prick. My mother had conveniently already swallowed back her valium before he arrived home. Not that she'd have stopped him. Sure, she'd have protested, like any mom, but she isn't stupid. Griffin Blackthorne would've happily doled out the same punishment to her, so it's better she didn't get in the middle of it. Asshole didn't even seem all that pissed about the fire extinguisher, so I'm guessing I merely served as a punching bag to his frustrations over a botched business deal.

Second one in the last couple of months, which means the old man is losing his touch.

Shadows at the mouth of the cave draw my attention to where a lithe form stands at the entrance. I daresay she's a welcomed sight right now, as I solemnly nurse the wounds that'll ultimately leave me with a black eye. I lower the pack of ice, confirming that

I still can't see out of my left eye, and she rushes toward me, falling to her knees before the boulder.

"*Mon bébé*! My sweet boy, what happened to you?" Her fingertips brush over the bruise, and even the slightest pressure intensifies the ache.

Sweet boy? She hardly knows me.

"I'm fine." Pushing her hand aside, I catch the pout of her lips, telling of her disappointment.

"I didn't think you'd come."

"I didn't come for you."

"Are you not attracted to me?"

"What does it matter? You're too old for me."

Her eyes flinch at that, as if I've slapped her. "Old," she echoes, and pushes to her feet. "May I show you the trick now, young master?"

"Whatever floats your boat." The dismissal in my tone is the result of the increasingly aching throb behind my eyeball. What I wouldn't give for some weed to help dull the misery.

Like she senses as much, she hooks her finger beneath my chin, tipping my head back. "You're in pain?"

"I said I'm fine."

Reaching down into her shirt, she pulls a silver flask out from between her breasts. "I've brought you something that might help."

Accepting the proffered drink, I open the cap and take a sniff of what's undoubtedly liquor, but sweet, like sugar. "What is it?"

"Rum. Have some. It'll help take the pain away."

With a sniff, I throw back the flask on a long swill. A burn slides down my throat, warming my chest as it makes its way to my stomach. I tip it back again.

Solange chuckles and sinks to her knees before me, wedging herself between my thighs. Running her hands up and down my legs, she smiles and licks her lips. "Such powerful legs. You play sports?"

For a second, her face blurs, and I double blink to bring her back into focus. "Lacrosse and swim." The slur in my words is unexpected, and with a frown, I lift the flask again. "D'you spike this w'something?" Two sips of liquor would've hardly left me feeling this woozy so fast. At school, Jude and I did tequila shots when we played cards, and I still won eighty percent of the time.

With a devious smile, she leans forward and licks the shell of my ear. "Yes," she whispers.

My muscles turn weak, lax, with that fireplace coziness that makes me want to lie down somewhere. I don't even realize I've slid down the rock onto the sand until Solange straddles my thighs, lifting my arms above my head as she removes my shirt.

Should I be doing this? What's happening?

Without protest, I let her undress me, as I stare up at the ceiling of the cave. There are brief moments of blackness, like a long blink. A cold sensation. Then warmth. I lift my hand to rub my eyes, surprised to find it's already raised, and I follow the path of my limb to a pair of handcuffs that bind my wrists together, and a rope tied to an old, rusted post that used to be a *'Danger Stay Out'* sign. It's somehow weathered years of high tide, though the actual sign popped off a while back.

Long blink.

My muscles jerk, and I'm staring up at the rope tied to the post. I tug, but it doesn't give.

Long blink.

A spasm rocks me awake. Something cold tickles my feet. I lift my head to find the water splashing around my legs.

Rising with the tide.

Panic freezes my veins. I tug at the rope again, to no avail.

Long blink.

Ice cold liquid crashes against my face, and I gasp, kicking myself back. The water has risen up to my chest, my legs fully submerged. Perched on a boulder off to the side is a black object that doesn't immediately come into focus until I squint. It's a bird. A black bird. I zero in on the missing eyeball. The bird I shot with Jude.

Its caw echoes through the cave, and a fist of salt and fury smashes against my face with an incoming wave, kicking my head to the side. The sea is rough tonight.

"Help me!" I manage to call out, the sound of my voice bouncing inside the empty cave. "Somebody help!"

The bird flies off.

Long blink.

"Tell me more about swim." Solange kneels beside me, looking down on me, and warmth engulfs my exposed cock as she curls her hand around it. To my surprise, it feels good. So fucking good. When did she pull down my pants? I tug at the rope, but only for leverage, as I arch into her strokes.

"The water ... it gets deep." Before I can finish the thought, a wave crashes against my face again, and I shake my head, snorting the salt that shoots up into my sinuses.

"Your mother told me you had an accident as a child. You almost drowned."

It's true. When I was three years old, I fell into the pool. Fortunately, we had a number of staff, and someone managed to pull me out before I *officially* kicked the bucket. It was traumatic enough to keep me from the water for years, though, until my father demanded that I join the swim team.

Therapy, he called it.

Might've helped my fear of water, but it didn't help my fear of drowning.

"The tide's strong. We have to get out of here." My voice is weak, and I feel my consciousness waning again, the darkness on the fringes closing in.

"We will." She runs her hand up and down my tenacious hard-on. "After you come."

"I can't. N'when we're about to drown."

"You're already halfway there, from the feel of it."

The water rushes over my head, and I hardly have the opportunity to suck in a breath as it washes over me, pulling me when it retreats.

She strokes faster. "Come for me, Lucian."

I want to tell her to fuck off, to push her away, but I can't. I'm too caught up in the feeling of her palm, the precise pressure of it as she pumps her fist.

"If you refuse, you'll drown. Here, in this cave."

"So will you." I groan, the sound vibrating in my chest, punctuated by sheer bliss as the water provides a wet slide. Cold, but not frigid.

"I'll go before it gets too deep. I'll leave you here to die."

She's fucking crazy!

Another wave crashes over me, this one lifting my body up off the sand and pulling at the binds when it recedes.

Coughing up the fluids from my sinuses, I brace for another wave.

Her strokes hasten.

My body hardens.

The salt burns as it floods my nostrils again, the waves coming faster than before. Higher than the last.

Another wave.

My muffled shouts beneath the water pound through my ears, over the muted crash against the rocks. Bubbles expel the last breath, but the sensation between my thighs diverts my attention from everything else. Once again the water is yanked away, and I suck in as much air as I can.

The next wave doesn't retreat this time.

I kick against her hand pressing into my thigh, while the other works me to orgasm. The breath I managed before the wave punches at my chest for release. The desperate pull for air leaves me arched underwater. Panic reaches its height. My body eases into the next phase. Drowning. I'm going to be the next kid to drown in this fucking cave.

70

But somehow, *somehow* I don't care, because even as the ocean rubs its palms for another sacrifice, I'm still in tune to every incredible rub of my dick.

Dizziness settles over me while she plays with my balls, and the sensations clash together, the fear, the panic, the excitement, tightening my muscles, until I have no choice but to let go.

More bubbles expel from my mouth, light crashes behind my eyes, and for a split second, I wonder if I'm dead.

The next thing I know, I'm sitting upright, the water reaching my neck, my body cold and shaky, the way it feels just before a person passes out. Coughing and gasping for air, I turn to the side, while the next wave pummels my face. Tucking her arms beneath mine, Solange stumbles forward, knocking into me, but I kick back and push to my feet. Still coughing, muscles loose with weakness, I hobble toward the entrance, the water up to my thighs, as we round the mouth of the cave and climb the slope.

Once elevated enough, I fall back against the rocky outer surface, and heave, trying to catch my breath. It's then I realize I'm still completely naked. Solange stands bent forward, hands on her knees, and chuckles as she lifts her gaze to mine.

I want to fucking strangle her, but whatever she gave me earlier, along with having almost died a second ago, has rendered me weak. So weak, I can't even fight her when she steps toward me, caging me against the rock.

"Tell me that wasn't the best fucking orgasm you've ever had."

I wish I could tell her it wasn't.

I wish I could say I'd been more consumed with the panic of dying than the possibility of climax.

I wish I could tell her what a crazy bitch she is, and that when my parents hear of what just happened, she'll never work again on this island.

I wish I could tell her it was, hands down, the worst fucking experience I've ever had in my life.

I wish I could tell her all these things, but I can't. Because I'd be lying through my teeth.

Something has awakened inside of me. At the intersection of fear and ecstasy, I've found something dangerous. Thrilling.

Inexplicable.

Licking her lips, she hikes up her skirt and pushes her panties down. Taking hold of my partially flaccid cock, she drags my tip over her slit. In the next breath, I'm hard and inside of her, and I spin us around, so she's against the rock and I'm fucking her.

Hard.

Her screams and moans echo around me, winding down my spine, and the climax pulses through my body again.

I slow my thrusts on a shuddered breath and rest my forehead in the crook of her neck. "What happened to me? Why?"

"In French, the word for orgasm is *la petite mort*. The little death. Not like real death, from which you never return. This gives new life. Over. And over. And over." She strokes her hand over my hair and rakes her nails across my back, the sensation intensifying the shiver that ruffles over me. "From this point on, nothing else will compare. No one else."

CHAPTER 8

ISADORA

Present day ...

Through sounds of screaming breach the void, and on a gasp of breath, I jolt upright.

Darkness swallows me, confusion clouding my head as I search the unfamiliar surroundings. For a split second, I forget where I am, but with the slow trickle of memory, I settle back onto the plush pillows and exhale a shaky breath.

Running a trembling hand across my brow, I try to recall the last few minutes of my dream.

The dark shadow of a man with intense golden eyes, standing over me, staring down at me.

Lucian?

I lift my head and find the door of my bedroom cracked open, the dim light from the hallway slicing across the floor. I closed it the night before, but didn't lock it, as Giulia suggested.

A cold sliver of panic ripples over my skin again, and I reach under the pillow, my fingertips prodding the cold metal of a pocketknife I stuffed there before bed. For a while, storing it under the pillow was an attempt to keep my cutting hidden from Aunt Midge. These days, it's mostly for my own comfort.

Eyes locked on the cracked door, I mentally rewind to sometime in the night when, in dreams, I felt something tickle my arm. The memory of it spurs a phantom sensation that has me scratching at the spot, while a shiver spirals up my spine.

Was someone in my room?

Throwing my legs over the edge of the bed, I sit upright. With light steps, I pad across the room and push the door closed. A twist of the lock clicks it, and for a brief moment, I wonder if I've locked myself in with someone. The thought lingers on my mind as I dash across the hardwood floor in the direction of the bed.

When something jams against my toe, I halt, stumbling forward. "Ow! Shit!" In blinding darkness, I lift my foot, setting my hand over the throbbing, and pat around for the bedside lamp.

Finding the chain, I flick it on noting only a small bit of redness at the tip. I wriggle it around to be sure it's not broken and sigh, as the pulsing swell begins to calm.

An object beneath the nightstand draws my attention there, a welcomed diversion from my throbbing toe.

I bend forward and slip my fingers below the elaborate carved wood, and slide out a picture. Turning it to the side, I study the family, who're standing in a colorful garden with a stone fountain in the background. A woman with short blonde hair. A small boy with sandy blond tufts, who stands alongside Sampson, the beast I met earlier. But my eyes linger on the man. He's strikingly handsome. Golden eyes and dark chestnut hair. Broad shoulders stretching the casual polo shirt that shows off toned biceps. His lips pressed to a hard line.

Lucian.

Without the scars.

It's strange to see him this way, as if I'm looking at a forbidden memory. A forgotten moment in time.

In spite of the slight smile of the woman, the beaming smile on the boy on the verge of laughter, Lucian's solemn eyes don't match the sunny disposition of everyone else. The way he stares back at me from the image, it's as if he's trying to say something. Plead with his unknowing observer.

For the next couple minutes, I study the image a bit more, running my finger over his flawless face, its perfect symmetry, and focus on the darkness behind those bright eyes. They could be any color, and just as intense, but gold is fitting for him. Exotic, almost. Yes, that's it. In the image, he looks like an exotic animal that's been captured as a pet. Caged.

I open the drawer of the nightstand and set the image inside the empty space where one might typically find a Bible.

Clicking off the lamp, I cover up and turn to face the tall windows, beyond which the moon sits high. Winds howl, just as Giulia warned earlier, like angry whispers of night against the glass. The phantom tickle at my arm returns, as I lie scratching at it again. But the image lingers inside my head, distracting me from the eerie undercurrent in this room, this haunted place where Amelia once slept. The sight of Lucian's painfully handsome face now ruined by whatever happened to him, and I wonder:

What *did* happen to him?

CHAPTER 9

LUCIAN

Sixteen years ago ...

Ripples chase my hand as I stir the bathwater and test its temperature. Only a couple years ago, I couldn't so much as look at water so deep without my chest turning cold and my palms sweating. That was before my father demanded I join swim team, and somehow, my competitive nature overrode my fears enough that I won meets and earned medals.

But then, Griffin Blackthorne's main objective was never really about helping me overcome my fears, as much as I'd like to believe that.

My teammate's father owned one of the largest chains of grocery stores in the country, with whom my father eventually partnered, and he used the occasional meet as a means of talking business, while he pretended to watch me swim.

I close my eyes, recalling the moments in the cave with Solange, when my chest burned for air, my muscles stiff with fear and excitement. I focus on the memory of her hand gliding up and down my cock, and the way my body tingled with a rush of what I suppose must've been adrenaline. I've thought about those moments a number of times since then.

Fully unclothed, I step into the tub, much warmer than the cold and salty ocean water, and my body hardens with a thrill of what's to come. Jacking off in water is nothing new for me. I've done it a number of times in the shower, but never like this.

Like giving my fear a big *fuck you*, and coming while I do it.

I draw the curtains that surround the enormous, circular sunken tub, leaving only a crack of light.

Warmth engulfs me as I settle into the water until it sits at my shoulders, and I run-through some diaphragmatic breathing, in and out, like we did before practice. I've grown accustomed to holding my breath for long periods of time, and this time, I intend to put that skill to good use.

I slip below the water's surface, where the world is muted and I'm alone, and stare up at the distorted constellations painted across the circular ceiling that mirrors the diameter of the tub. My own dark world.

The strokes begin light and teasing. This time, I intend to draw it out. Maximize the climax. It doesn't take long for my balls to tighten, though, while the first rush of adrenaline pulses through me.

Fuck, yes.

I imagine Solange straddling me, holding me underwater as she rides my cock. Every muscle turns rigid, the burn inside my chest intensifying. I can practically feel the tiny electric shocks inside my brain, the warning signals demanding I take a sip of air.

I don't.

Blood rushes to my dick as I stroke hard, the water furious and agitated, echoing the chaos inside my body right now. Tunnel vision sets in. I'm preparing to pass out.

I need air. Every cell in my body is desperate for the oxygen that I intentionally withhold.

Muscles wind tighter. Tighter. So fucking tight. I arch with the impending climax, the cool air on where my groin sticks up out of the water while I continue to pump my slick erection.

A flash of light behind my eyes hits at the same time as a blast of heat rushes through my body, and jets of hot fluid pulse from the head of my cock.

I jolt upright on a gasp of breath. I can't get enough air, and I lean over the edge of the tub, digging my nails into the cold tiles. Through rapid shallow breaths, my body does its best to fill my lungs, until each inhale is no longer labored, but long and easy.

Not an ounce of strength left in me. I'm so fucking relaxed right now, I can't even fathom moving from this spot. A chuckle escapes while I lie with my head pressed against the tiles.

Solange was right.

Nothing will ever compare now.

CHAPTER 10

ISADORA

Present day ...

Heat falls on my face, the intense light piercing through the void. I frown and shield my eyes, turning away from the open window through which sunlight streams. The clock beside me reads ten minutes to seven, and I groan at the small bit of missed sleep, yet I don't feel exhausted, the way I typically do when I wake up at home. My neck isn't stiff, nor is my back the way it sometimes feels after sleeping on the cardboard-like mattress at Aunt Midge's.

I feel like I've slept on clouds all night.

Yawning and stretching, I turn over in the bed and flip off the alarm, which hasn't yet gone off. I can't remember the last time I felt so relaxed waking up. Probably the time I slipped on the wharf and landed on my shoulder. The doc gave Aunt Midge some heavy Tylenols that knocked me out for a few hours, and when I woke up, I felt like I'd slept for days.

I climb out of bed and gather up clean clothes, then make my way to the bathroom. After shutting myself inside, I flip on the water for the shower, letting it heat up while I brush my teeth and floss. Standing before the mirror, I cross my arms to lift my shirt over my head, tossing it to the floor beside me. Perhaps it's the light of the bathroom, but the scars on my forearms seem to stick out even more than before. Thin, tiny lines, unevenly spaced, where I spent months cutting myself. Of course, that was after what happened. I wouldn't have resorted to this level of self-mutilation before then. Maybe the occasional cut every so often, just to take the pressure off when things got stressful at school, but nothing like this.

We're just having a little fun.

You're so beautiful.

I close my eyes on the unbidden lies reverberating through my head. *Don't, don't, don't. Not now.*

No one will know.

Images flash through my brain as my mind scrambles for some distraction.

Teeth clenched, I shake my head, and the voice of my memories fades into the constant hum of water spilling from the shower. Steam rolls over the glass door, and I step inside, letting the warmth of the water sweep me away into the visual of the picture I saw the night before.

Lucian.

I couldn't stop thinking about it. *Him.* What I imagined him to be then, not the asshole I met in the hallway. Though maybe he's always been that way. He certainly didn't look happy in the picture. In fact, he looked very *un*happy.

Almost haunting. Like he was begging to be set free.

I wash and dry quickly, and don't bother to style, or primp, my hair. Aside from eyeliner on occasion, I don't apply much makeup, either. My bronze skin supposedly comes from my dad, though I wouldn't begin to know what he looked like. Mom never had pictures of him, never talked about him, at all, and neither did Aunt Midge. Any time I asked about him, I got a short and sweet answer, and an even faster change of topic.

It never made sense to me that my mom could hate him so much, that even after his death, after he was no longer around to disgust her, she still couldn't say one good thing about the man, but that's Jenny Quinn. The most spiteful, shallow and selfish woman I've ever met.

I rush to dress, then head down for a cup of coffee and something light. Breakfast has never really been my thing, so the gluttonous spread of food I find waiting for me when I arrive at the dining room is unexpected.

Jose, a different chef from the night before, pulls out my chair with a foxy sort of smile stretching his lips. He never actually told me his name, it's just what's etched on his uniform, and when I sit down, he offers a wink before brushing his finger across my cheek.

Oh, no.

I do my best to school my face, so I don't look entirely put off by the gesture, but the guy reminds me of a cartel boss, with his slicked-back hair and chevron mustache. "Thank you," I say just above a whisper, as he walks off with his stare on me the whole time. Aunt Midge always said my face was a trouble magnet, drawing the kind of bad boys whose imaginations were confined to the brain between their thighs.

Her words, not mine.

Guys have always been this way around me, like wolves whose intent always seems transparent behind wide smiles. Or maybe I've just become keen on recognizing it as of late. Unfortunately for Jose, or whatever his name is, I'm not as naive as Red Riding Hood, so even the perfectly brewed French press coffee set before me won't earn the kind of attention he's apparently looking for.

Waiting until he's out of sight, I grab a Danish from the smorgasbord of food, and push the large plate of eggs, bacon and toast, with a stack of pancakes off to the side.

Who the hell could eat this much in one sitting? If I were Aunt Midge, I'd be stuffing it in one of the many plastic Ziploc bags she often stores in her purse, for the few occasions we go to a restaurant. A habit she's known for in Tempest Cove. So much so, the waitresses at one restaurant often leave a bag for her at the table.

As I finish up the last of my coffee, Giulia enters the dining room, rolling her eyes as she approaches.

"Looks like Jose found a new love interest. You done eating?"

"Yes. I don't think I'll have eaten this much after a week."

Shaking her head, she nabs a piece of bacon, munching on it while she gathers up the many dishes. "His mother apparently told him the quickest way to a woman's heart is through an excessive breakfast that one person can't possibly finish."

With a chuckle, I help her gather the plates, watching her scrape the fruit and yogurt onto the same dish as the eggs and pancakes. "It's a shame to waste all this food."

"Dinner parties are the worst. You could probably feed a village with the leftover food. Where I come from? There'd be fights over who gets to finish it."

"Must've been hard living on the streets."

"Winters were the worst. Had to stay in shelters most of the time, just to keep warm. But Jackie was good about it." A slight smile lights up her face, and I'm guessing she's talking about her daughter. "She always woke up each morning and asked, *Momma, what adventures are we going on today?*"

"You must miss her while she's at school."

"I do. But … she gets the life I never had. She's going to be important someday. Respected. Blackthorne is a respected name in those kinds of places."

Those kinds of places meaning, anywhere but Tempest Cove.

Basically, anywhere people have as much money as the Blackthornes and aren't blinded by their gossip.

"Hey, I woke up last night, and my door was cracked. I forgot to lock it."

"I didn't mean to worry you. Just that, sometimes Lucian sleepwalks. In this place, it can be unnerving to see him pass by your bedroom. He looks like a zombie, or something. Really spaced out."

"He's completely out of it, then?"

"I once called out to him, not realizing he was asleep." She sets dishes on the tray Jose must've used to serve the breakfast. "He turned very slowly and looked at me, like he was trying to decide what to do, then kept on down the hallway. But the *way* he looked at me had the hairs on the back of my neck standing up."

"That sounds like something out of *The Exorcist*."

"Makaio thinks he has nightmares, from the time he spent in that mental institute." She shakes her head, waving her hand in dismissal. "Not that I want to gossip about it. Forget what I said. I'm sorry."

"Makaio the big guy?"

"Lucian's bodyguard." The dimples in her cheek as she tries to hide a smile tells me he's something more to her, but I don't bother to pry. "Anyway, it's just better if you don't answer the door."

"And lock it." I nod toward the plates she's stacked on the tray, the food mixed together in one big massive slop. "Do you need help with those?"

"No. Probably best you don't run into Jose in the kitchen. He tends to be touchy-feely."

"Ah. Yeah, I'll pass."

"Catch up with you later, then."

It's almost eight-thirty by the time I reach the elevator, and I'm hoping that Mrs. Blackthorne got enough sleep that she won't be needing another nap today, because the thought of sitting in the doll room, staring off at the walls, is enough to want to scratch my eyeballs out.

The elevator door opens on Rand, who offers only a half-smile as he exits the car. "I trust you slept well?"

"Yes, thank you. Best sleep I've gotten in a while."

"Very good. And your first day with Mrs. Blackthorne?"

"Uneventful."

What an understatement.

"I was thinking perhaps you could take her down to the piano room today. She'd love to hear you play."

"Sure, I can do that."

"Excellent." Arms behind his back, he turns to face me, as I step inside the elevator. "The Master has important meetings today, so it's best if Laura isn't within earshot. She's never been fond of business talk."

"I'll keep her entertained."

With a sharp nod, he walks off, and I hit the button for the second floor. The doors open on the familiar doll room, one I've come to dread after yesterday, but the deep and hearty laughter I hear is a good sign.

I follow the sound to the most luxurious bedroom I've ever laid eyes on. Dark, rich wood furniture with gold trimming, paintings of cherubs and goddesses on the walls and ceilings, with lush greenery dotted about the wide open space. Perhaps the only room brimming with life in this place.

A man stands alongside Laura, where she sits in a wheelchair, allowing him to listen to her heart through the stethoscope.

"Steady as a metronome." He tugs the ear-tips out and drapes the instrument over his neck. "Except for that slight flutter when I touched your hand."

With a demure smile, she pretends to push him away. "Oh, stop, you old flirt." Her gaze lands on me in the doorway, and she waves me over. "Michael, this is my babysitter, Isabelle."

"Isadora, actually." I stretch my hand out to him, and when he bends to kiss it, I clear my throat. The desire to pull my hand away twitches my muscles. "I'm her companion."

"Lucky girl. I've wanted to be her companion for many years. Stubborn woman still turns me down."

A gust of laughter flies out of Laura, and she sets her hand to her chest. "You are shameless, Michael."

"You must be the doctor?"

Frowning, he tips his head. "What gave you that impression?"

Another burst of laughter, this time from the two of them in unison, leaves me feeling small and stupid.

"I'm only playing with you darling, yes. I'm her longtime physician and friend of the family. Dr. Powell." He glances down at his watch and huffs. "And I'm afraid if I don't cut this right now, I'm going to be late for my next appointment."

"You're cheating on me?" The flirtatious trill to Laura's voice is painful to listen to, or maybe I'm just not accustomed to this kind of play. No one flirted with Aunt Midge--not even the fishermen who're out at sea for months. Not that she's an unattractive woman. I'm guessing, in her heyday, she was probably quite a catch, but she never tolerated that kind of behavior from the men.

"You know I'm solely devoted to you, Lady Blackthorne." As he did with me, he bends forward and kisses the back of her hand. "Until we meet again."

"I'll be sure to wear something ... decent next time." The raspberry shade of lipstick is smudged in the corner of her lips, and a rose color blush is scattered too low on her pale cheeks, as if she rushed to apply it. "No more unexpected visits."

"I promise. And I've given the new formulation to Nell. I sent her out to pick up the script for you this morning."

"Excellent."

I give a tight-lipped smile as he passes, and once he's out of the room, I notice the sparkle in her eyes has immediately dulled.

"I'd like to take you down to the piano room. To play for a bit. Would you like that?"

"I don't know." She crosses her hands in her lap and looks away from me. "I may as well go back to bed."

"No Chopin, then?"

"You know Chopin?" From the corner of her eye, she gives me a onceover. "I find that hard to believe."

"Well, I guess you'll have to come with me to find out, won't you?"

A harsh breath escapes through her nose, and she rolls her eyes. "If you insist. And then after, I'd like you to put me to bed."

Taking the handles of her wheelchair, I inwardly groan at the thought of another long and boring afternoon spent counting her dolls.

CHAPTER 11

LUCIAN

In the mirror's reflection, I straighten my tie, while Rand runs a wooden suit brush over my shoulders and down my back.

"Are they refusing to reschedule this?" I ask, tugging the cuffs of my sleeves.

"I'm afraid we've put it off too long, Master. They've grown impatient."

In the tray of jewelry that's on the table beside the full-length mirror, I fish through the few rings, including my discarded wedding band, for a silver oxidized, moth signet ring. The skull on its thorax signifies the Death's Head species.

I slide it onto my pinky finger and curl my hand to a fist. "It seems they always grow impatient where money is concerned."

"You know as well as I do, it isn't money that draws them. They want assurance that you're prepared to take over your father's position in this organization."

"And what do I have to do to prove that? What haven't I already done to prove that over and over to them?"

"Your absence makes them nervous."

"Does grieving count for nothing these days?"

"After two years?" He drops his gaze at the question. "Forgive me, Master."

It's no secret that I harbored little love for my father while he was alive, or that I've done my best to avoid as many of his business affairs as possible. Rand is also well aware that I don't care for someone challenging my authority on the matter, either.

"I've provided the funding. The connections." All the promises my father insisted I deliver, up until the bastard took his last breath.

"It's your presence. Or, and I mean no disrespect, lack thereof."

Groaning, I step away from the mirror and clip on a set of cufflinks. "Is it my face they wish to stare at? Then, perhaps we should do away with the masks. That'll be my first order of business."

"Lucian ..." Rand's voice carries the weary exhaustion of a man who's had to wrangle two generations of Blackthorns. "They meet once every quarter. It's always been about strengthening your alliances."

"Is that what it is? So, we've moved away from the carnival fuck-show to something more respectable, is that it?"

With a huff, Rand shifts his gaze. "While I don't agree with your father's decisions to invite female subjects to mingle at these gatherings, I do think there is some validity in them."

"You're saying you support the purpose behind this group?"

One thing about Rand is he's never one to respond impulsively, so when he stares off for a moment, I know he's chewing on the question. "If it's mutually beneficial to both parties, I see no harm in it. It's no different than these BDSM sex clubs, and bear in mind, these subjects seek out the group, not the other way around."

"Do you think I sought out the group, when I was thrown into that hellhole institute for weeks?"

"Of course not. But respectfully, Sir, you were a bit reckless in your ... pursuits. Your father felt an intervention was in order."

"An intervention? Is that what he called it?" There's no point arguing with Rand over what happened to me. He doesn't know the details of my time there, the punishments I personally suffered at their hands, and never will. "I saw a man beaten to within an inch of his life because the amount of money he requested *warranted* it, according to the group. The difference between BDSM sex clubs and Schadenfreude comes down to desire. If given the money without the punishment, none of them would choose the torture."

"Likely not. But nothing in this world is free, I'm afraid. If you'd prefer, we can arrange for a dinner party in lieu of the *carnival fuck show*, as you so eloquently put it."

The thought of a dinner party would be my idea of torment. "You know how much I love social engagements."

"A masquerade, then. We'll hire a crew to brighten up the atrium a bit."

"If it'll get them off my back ..."

"May I speak candidly?" Rand has never meant any disrespect, even on the occasions he has challenged my authority.

"Have at it."

"They're afraid your commitment has never been as staunch as your father's and grandfather's."

"Well, they're not wrong. But what's the worry? I never had a choice growing up, why would I suddenly have one now? Because the dictatorship has ended? All my father's death afforded me was the same damn shackles he and every generation since my great grandfather have worn without fail."

"You know I understand, perhaps more than anyone. But this is your legacy, Lucian. If you won't stay committed for your father, then do it for the son you were never given the opportunity to raise."

"I wouldn't have subjected him to my curse. I would've set him free, given him choices."

"And forgive my being frank, but you know better than I do that the organization would never have allowed such a thing."

They want me because I know things. Secrets they'd kill to keep buried. I only know such things because my own father made me privy to them. The day he introduced me to their little society was the day he slung the albatross around my neck.

"You would've undoubtedly been a better father than your own. But that is no longer your choice. Just as this is no longer your father's."

Odd to hear him liken my situation to death. Rand has always seemed to favor the organization above all other things. I've not yet determined if that's of his own will, or what my father pounded into his skull all these years.

"What an absolute tragedy."

On the way to my office, the unmistakable sound of Chopin fills the dark and dreary hallway, drawing me toward the atrium. Peeking around the doorway, I find my mother in her wheelchair beside the piano, on which the new girl plays with the finesse of a seasoned pianist. Chin lifted in the air, she doesn't seem to follow any music, and I frown watching her. Not once has she dipped her gaze to the page, or bothered to flip to the next. As if she's memorized the entire piece, note for note.

"I was told she can't read music." Rand's voice from behind interrupts my staring, and I glance back to find him craning his neck for a peek. "Remarkable ability, wouldn't you say?"

Turning my attention back to her, I don't bother to answer, too focused on the dampness of her hair, as if she didn't bother with it after a shower. The way those long black tresses fall about her slim shoulders and frame the warm glow of her face that's obviously been touched by sunlight.

Vibrant with youth, she's beautiful without even trying. Mesmerizing.

Beside her, my mother sits with her head tipped, eyes closed, drinking in every note, the way she often would when I played for her. Unlike my father, who ridiculed my love for piano, she encouraged it, would often have me play while she trimmed her flowers, or sat drinking her tea. The only true connection I ever really had with my mother.

"We shouldn't keep them waiting, Master."

"No. We shouldn't. Let's get this shit show over with."

I steal one more glance at the girl, the way she sways when she plays, as if the notes move through her onto the keys like a conduit. She opens her eyes and directs her gaze toward me. For one brief moment, a zap of embarrassment heats my face, and I turn away, like a school boy caught peeking through the windows.

The meeting with who I call The Blacksuits, or Chairmen of the Schadenfreude Collective, is always a dog and pony act. Established generations ago, the purpose of the organization is essentially to glean power, money, entertainment and stature from the misfortune of others, though they would undoubtedly have a far more eloquent and scientific way of describing it.

"Gentlemen." I stride toward the two older men who're waiting for me in the chairs in front of my desk. Both decked in black suits, they remind me of old Italian mafia dons, though their role in the great scheme of things is far less important. These are merely just the messengers.

"Lucian, good to see you." Dominic must be in his seventies now, and practically grew up with my father. I've always liked him, but never trusted him. "Thanks for taking the time to meet with us. How's your mother doing?"

"Just fine."

He shifts his attention slightly to my left, where Rand stands behind me. "And Rand? How are you?"

"I'm well, Dominic, thank you."

The other guy, Louis, is mostly just here for moral support, as he rarely ever says much of anything in these meetings. Together, the two are a harmless irritation, but one that represents some of the most powerful individuals in the country, so while the idea of meeting with them is about as exciting as taking inventory of the hair on my balls, it's worth the effort of being polite.

I shake both their hands, each bearing the same signet ring as mine, and round the desk to my chair. Rand stands off to the side, as usual. As many times as I've asked him to take a seat in these meetings, he always politely declines. So I stopped asking.

"What can I do for you?" Cold leather presses into my back as I lean into the chair.

"We've had an inquiry into the group. Someone has expressed interest in becoming a *member*."

Schadenfreude isn't the kind of group someone stumbles across on Facebook, or something. For generations, it's remained hidden in the shadows, below the radar, a secret society whose members are some of the most affluent in the world. An inquiry is a big deal. "Oh? What is the nature of his interest?"

"Well, that's why we're here. Happens to be your former father-in-law."

"Patrick Boyd?" *Of all the unholy fucks.*

"That's him. He's been asking around. And quite frankly, he's making too much noise doing so."

"How did he hear--?"

"He apparently heard about us through your father, who introduced him to Thomas, and he's been showing up at his work place inquiring about Schadenfreude."

Jesus Christ. Thomas is a highly respected surgeon, an active member of the group with some of the most impressive connections, including a Middle Eastern king who once made a special visit to the hospital where he works.

"We think his motivations might be entirely political." The disapproving tone of Dominic's voice is what I'd expect. The group tends to frown on inquiries from those whose intentions aren't aligned with their philosophies.

"They definitely are. He has no business seeking membership." I toss a quick glance back to Rand, whose face remains stoic, as if he's not even listening.

"Maybe. But as you know, we like to keep an open mind to those with strong alliances."

Strong alliances. The man has lost favor with his public after a scandal involving a young teenage girl, whom he apparently paid to have sex with. He claimed to be in a severe depression after Amelia's death, which prompted him to go a little crazy. His wife subsequently left him afterward. My guess is, he's trying to build his alliances back up.

"Trust me when I say we don't need his alliances."

"Well, to be frank, Lucian, we're a little concerned about the direction of things since your father passed. God rest his soul."

Unfortunately, I doubt my father's soul is with God. "You've nothing to be concerned about, Domini--"

"You just don't have the same presence as your father, and that just isn't good for rapport." He throws up his hands, having cut me off. The guy wears a hearing aid the size of California, so I can't get too pissed off. "People start to forget who is in charge. They start doing their own thing. I know things are different in this age, but in my generation, face to face was the way of business. Handshakes sealed the deal. Eye contact meant assurance. Confidence."

Or a strong desire to murder someone. "I understand. Rand and I were just discussing a dinner--"

"We were thinking maybe you should host a party, or something. A gathering. Invite some of the big players. Let them mingle. We haven't had one of those in … well, in quite a long time, to be frank."

That's his thing. *To be frank.* By the end of this meeting, I'll be about ready to kill frank.

"A masquerade? What do you think?"

"Bingo. Something fancy. Maybe invite some women." In other words, prostitutes, to keep the married men entertained while their wives are left at home, because not even they know this group exists. "I want you to invite Boyd. We'll see how he interacts. Make our own determinations based on observation. Like we've always done."

"Of course." I can't muster more than a crooked smile in response, but it doesn't matter. The scars on my face make me look like I'm frowning even when I'm not.

"Going forward, I'd ask that you meet with us on a more regular basis. Let us know how things are going. How's business, by the way?"

At this point, I only serve as the Chair for the family shipping business, and my meetings are few and far between. It's the other engagements, like these, that take up most of my day. The minutiae my father dumped on me when he kicked the bucket.

"Well. Up from last quarter." It's the same phrase I use at every meeting, to avoid an hour-long inquiry into the finances of Blackthorne Enterprises. Short and sweet.

"Fantastic. That's what we like to hear."

"Well, gentlemen, I don't mean to rush things along, but I have other meetings--"

"I'm sure you've got other meetings today, so we won't take up any more of your time."

A feigned smile works the muscles of my face as I nod. "Thank you."

Both men push to their feet and offer another handshake. "You have Rand give us the details of the dinner party."

"Will do. Thank you for taking the time to meet with me."

He gives a sharp nod, and both men exit my office. The moment the elevator doors close, I push back in my chair and kick my feet up on the desk.

"I want a meeting with Boyd. As soon as possible." It's strange that he didn't come to me about this in the first place, but I sense the man has always harbored both contempt and fear towards me.

"I'll arrange it immediately." Rand straightens the departed chairs in front of my desk.

"As for this masquerade dinner." I run a hand down my face, pausing over my eyes to rub them. "What a production that'll be."

"I'll handle the details and get the crew working on the atrium. In the meantime, we'll get you a tux and a mask." He clears his throat, his hands clasped behind his back. "Should I procure a date for the evening?"

"No." I pinch the bridge of my nose. "Absolutely not."

"Pardon my meddling, Master, but it may put them at ease to see you with a ... lady friend. The Widow Lancaster has been asking about you."

"Lancaster?" I lower my hand from my face, frowning. "And what is their concern? That I be married? A possible heir to the Blackthorne throne of shit that they can watch and observe over the course of his life? Let them think what they want. I'm not out to marry some desperate woman who's ten years older than me and looking to secure her future country club membership. I've done an arranged marriage once."

"I understand. Merely a suggestion. I'll get started on these plans."

"Rand? How old did you say my mother's companion was?"

He raises his brows as if the question has caught him off guard. "Isadora? She's nineteen, according to her file."

Young. "What made you choose her?"

"During the phone interview, I found her to be pleasant, conversant, and well … pardon my saying so, pretty much everything your mother isn't."

With an ungracious snort, I nod. "Isn't that the truth."

"In spite of her appearance, she's actually quite intelligent, and well-versed in much of the music and literature your mother seems to enjoy."

Rolling my eyes, I shake my head. "A repertoire of useless romance novels and outdated composers."

"Indeed. Have you had the opportunity to meet her yet?"

"Briefly. We ran into each other last night. Seems *snarky.*" I don't bother to say that I found her bold attitude somewhat amusing, the way one might prod a cat to lash its claws. Exotically attractive, too, which I also keep to myself.

"That's odd. I didn't get that impression, at all."

"Well, it wouldn't be the first time I've brought out the best in someone."

"And I'm sure her snark was met with your unwavering charm." To his credit, he lowers his gaze and smiles.

I sneer at the remark, tugging a case of hand-rolled cigarettes from the inside pocket of my suit. "I'm afraid not." Before I can snag the Zippo from my desk, Rand is at my side, the flame already waiting for me.

"I'd like to give her a chance. Lord knows your mother hasn't been receptive to, well … any of the companions we've brought in. Ones well-bred and educated. Isadora is young, but she's different. And so far, she's proven to keep your mother out of her bed longer than the others ever could."

It's been weeks since I last saw my mother outside of her room. While it's made it easy to avoid her, it's also gnawed at my conscience to think of her wasting away in there.

Forgiveness has never been my best suit, but she's still my mother, regardless of our history.

"Well, let's hope the new girl works out. In the meantime, I guess we've got a party to plan."

"I know dinner parties have always made you anxious, but I think this is the right step."

"I'm sure. I'll give you a raise, if you can find me a costume that makes me invisible."

"I believe they call that mundane, sir, and unfortunately, you don't wear that well."

With a slight chuckle, I lean forward and flick the ash off my cigarette. "I see you're trying for the raise anyway."

"One must always aspire."

CHAPTER 12

LUCIAN

Sixteen years ago ...

I hate dinner parties.

Wedged between my mother and the recently married Darla Lancaster, I'd rather sit between two dentists performing root canals on either side of my face without Novocain. Darla leans in, showing my mother the five carat diamond weighing down her ring finger, over which my mother acts like it's the most impressive thing she's ever seen.

I have to give it to my mother, she knows how to play this game better than any woman in this room. If she didn't, I'm certain my father wouldn't have bothered with her.

Not that Darla's new beau is anything to write home about. The guy is twice her age and, in spite of the money he likes to flaunt, hasn't bothered to get the enormous wart removed from his nose that's earned him the nickname The Troll of Lancaster.

As something grabs hold of my thigh, I stiffen, and catch the wily grin on Darla's face, while she continues to converse with my mother. As she prattles on about her nuptials, running her hand higher up my thigh, my mother sits oblivious on the other side of me.

"I cannot wait for the day Lucian takes an interest in girls."

"Oh ..." Darla's hand slides back down. "Is he ... gay?"

I open my mouth to respond, but my mother answers for me.

"Oh, God, no. He just hasn't found the right girl, yet."

For fucks sake, I hate that they talk about me like I'm not sitting between them, while one feels me up.

I twist in my chair, catching sight of Solange, who stands off to the side, ready to clear plates, fill drinks, whatever is needed of her. She slides her gaze to me, only briefly, and the tightening of my stomach comes as a surprise.

I shouldn't feel this way toward her. The *help*, as my mother calls them.

We arranged to meet down in the cave later this evening, and the sooner this party ends, the faster we can sneak away together.

Darla's hand slides over my thigh again, squeezing too close to the growing erection that I'm certain she'll happily take credit for. Clearing my throat, I straighten in my chair, drawing her hand down to my knee.

"Mayor Boyd! So good to see you!" Pushing up from her seat, my mother stands to greet yet another dinner guest, and when she nudges my arm, my shoulders sag, and I follow suit. For once, I don't mind playing polite, if it gets this woman's hands off me.

Beside Mayor Boyd, whom I've only met once before, stands a blonde, maybe around my age, with a bright smile and blue eyes. The smooth shine of her hair, coupled with a poufy dress, reminds me of one of the dolls my mom keeps imprisoned in her sitting room.

No doubt my mother is thinking the same, as she takes the girl's hands, holding them out to get a good look at her dress.

"My, aren't you a vision! Look at this dress, Lucian, isn't it gorgeous?"

The girl's doe eyes fall on me, her smile turning demure with the blush of her cheeks.

"This is my daughter, Amelia." Mayor Boyd sets his hand on the girl's shoulder, and I spot the slight twitch of her arm. "Her mother fell ill this evening, so she's graciously decided to be my date for the night."

"Amelia, this is my son. Lucian." Another nudge is a cue from my mother to play the role I've been bred to play since I was old enough to shake hands and kiss knuckles.

"Nice to meet you, Amelia."

"Not so much enthusiasm, Lucian." My mother chuckles, but I know better. It's a warning that I'm not playing nicely enough. "After dinner, perhaps you can show Amelia the grounds. Take her for a walk in the gardens."

"I'd like that." Once again, the girl's eyes sparkle like those of a well-bred politician's daughter.

"Sure." I can't bring myself to fabricate the enthusiasm my mother is expecting from me, but at the same time, it was only two weeks ago that I nursed a black eye for my insolence.

"Excellent. Now, which school do you attend, Amelia?" It's a trick my mother has developed over the years. She can gauge how much money and pull someone has by which school their son, or daughter, attends, and no doubt, she's reading Mayor Boyd like one of the many bodice rippers she tears through a week in her sitting room.

"We, uh … opted for public schools. I thought it would establish rapport with the locals to know their mayor's daughter attends the same schools as their children."

"Of course." Not even her best smile can hide the disgust riding on her voice.

I have to hold back the snort trapped in my throat. Suddenly, Amelia Boyd isn't so fascinating to my mother, which means she's just stepped up a notch in my book. "I'll look for you after dinner."

The smile on her face reveals perfect teeth that have undoubtedly seen their share of orthodontic work.

We settle down to eat, and between Darla's hand on my thigh, the shy glances from Amelia, and the sultry, jealous stares from Solange, I'm ready to blow this fucking popstand by the time dessert is served.

"Lucian is quite the athlete!" Darla says with enthusiasm beside me, having worked her way up my leg, where her knuckles have brushed my balls twice. "Does he get that from you, or his father?"

"Oh, God, Griffin never played a sport in school. I, however, twirled baton in gymnastics up until my senior year."

"You were a gymnast?" Mayor Boyd says from across the table, raising a glass of wine to his lips. "Fascinating."

"Yes, I did competitive gymnastics for a number of years."

Beside my mother, my father grinds his jaw, staring back at Mayor Boyd, but seems to cap whatever thoughts are spinning through his head with a long swill of his drink. He holds up the empty glass, and Solange lurches forward, filling it with more wine.

"I still have my baton hanging up in my sitting room. Sometimes, I take it down to see if I still have it." With a chuckle, my mother sips her wine, staring over the glass in the flirtatious way that I know gnaws at my father's pride. "I may be forty-two, but I can do a backbend like it's nobody's business."

"Seriously?" Boyd clears his throat. "You are full of surprises, Lady Blackthorne."

"Please. Call me Laura."

"The talent in your family is … incredible." Darla cups me, and I jolt upright, setting my hand on hers and swallowing hard as the erection meant for Solange has made itself known.

My mother couldn't be more oblivious if she were deaf and blindfolded. "Have you heard Lucian play piano?"

God. No. The moment I stand up from this table, the better half of New England is going to know I'm hard.

Clearly tipsy, my mother hooks her arm in mine and tugs. "Come on, let's go to the atrium to listen to him play."

"We're not going to the atrium." My father's voice carries all the annoyance of the evening, and for once, I'm relieved to hear him speak up. "My son toys around with piano, but he's no Mozart. Certainly not worth uprooting an entire dinner party for."

"He's quite good, Griffin, you've just never taken the time to notice, is all."

"I notice more than you think, Laura." He's undoubtedly caught on to Mayor Boyd's interest most of the night. Kind of hard to miss his puppy dog fascination with my mother.

"I suppose you do. Certainly didn't take you long to learn the *help's* name."

My gaze flits to Solange, whose tight jaw betrays the fake smile plastered to her face.

"Somebody has to treat them as if they're more than pets."

My mother releases me and reaches for her glass, shaking her head on a mirthless chuckle. "I'm sure you do."

"What do you play?" Amelia asks from across the table.

Everyone's eyes land back on me, and for a split second, I hate Amelia Boyd for putting me in this position.

"Lots of things."

"Lots of things." My father echoes in mocking. "You see? No Mozart."

"You're right. I prefer Beethoven, Father. It has the structural perfection of Mozart, but more emotion."

I catch the twitch of my father's eye, and I'm certain, if we weren't sitting in a room filled with elite members of society, my father would've already backhanded me.

"I'd love to hear you play." Amelia lowers her head, but lifts her eyes toward me. "Will you show me to the atrium?"

A quick glance toward my mother, who is undoubtedly absorbing the insults of my father, making a case for what will be an explosive argument between them tomorrow, and my father, whose red face is the culmination of embarrassment, anger, and too many drinks, and I nod, pushing back away from Darla's wandering hand.

~

I take the lead down the hallway toward the atrium, not bothering to look back at Amelia. I didn't agree to this for her benefit, but to get the fuck out of that suffocating room.

"You're so lucky to live in a castle. Like a prince."

There's no point in answering her. Whatever this is, it's only show on her part, as well as mine. I'm certain she was coached by her father prior to arriving, just as my mother continues to coach me before every social gathering.

"You, um ... you go to private school?"

With a huff, I spare her a quick glance. Christ, I thought she'd take the cue that being away from our parents meant she didn't have to do this shit. "Private tutor. I was kicked out of school."

"Really? For what?"

"Burning the headmaster's couch."

Hearing her chuckle behind me, I do my best to hide the smile, recalling Jude and I sitting in his office the following day. I took the fall, of course. My father may be a bastard, but Jude's is a bastard with a fucking cherry on top.

"That's great."

"Great? I was expelled. Now I'm stuck here until I graduate."

"Well ... was it worth it?"

Trying to hide my smile is pointless, as I recall the pissed-off expression on the headmaster's face. The prick who warned me when the year began that, just because I was a Blackthorne, it didn't mean I was immune to the flames of hell he'd raise if I gave him shit that year. I later found out the couch in his office was something of a souvenir from his old college days, gifted to him by his frat brothers. So I stuffed some dog shit into a paper bag and lit it on fire, tossing it onto the couch.

Yeah. It was worth it.

"I guess so." I come to a stop in front of the atrium and lean against the doorframe. "You don't have to do this, you know? *We* don't have to do this. We can just sit in here until the party's over."

"I want to hear you play. Unless you were lying."

"Fine." I have to admit, this girl is a little more interesting than I gave her credit for.

I take a seat at the piano, while she sits across from me on one of the few chairs in the room. The second my fingers hit the keys, everything around me falls away. My father. My mother. This stupid fucking dinner party. I'm floating underwater, the notes all around me, pulsing through me, as I pound *Les Adieux* out on the keys, taking my frustrations from the night out on the music. I'm so wrapped up in the piece that I don't immediately notice Amelia is sitting beside me, until her hand rests against my knee.

I stop playing, and it's then I realize, this hasn't been a political game for her. She's in it for something else.

"Your mother was right. You are quite good." Before I can stop her, she leans in and presses her lips to mine.

It's a kiss I neither want, nor asked for, and yet, I can't stop myself from kissing her back. I blame it on the anger running through me. The rush of adrenaline brought on by my parents and the anxiety of the evening.

I break the kiss, turning my face away from her. "I'm sorry, I shouldn't have done that."

"I'm not sorry, Lucian Blackthorne. In fact, I intend to kiss you again someday."

The house is quiet, the last guest having left about a half hour ago. As usual, my father will be in the library, sipping his scotch, until he finally passes out and falls asleep on the couch. After tonight's events, I suspect he's already unconscious, but to ensure that he doesn't catch me sneaking about and decide to take his frustrations out on me, I make my way toward the library. Sounds echo down the hall. My father mumbling something quietly over a distinctly feminine voice.

As I approach, the female voice drawls out into soft moans. For a moment, I pause, thinking it's my mother, but then I hear her speak, the accent thick.

She cries out, and I peek through the crack in the door to find Solange naked, bent over the arm of the couch. Her wrists have been tied with rope that's stretched across the furniture out until of my view. My father stands behind her, holding my mother's baton in one hand, his drink in the other.

"*I'm forty-two and I can do a backbend like nobody's business,*" he mocks before taking a sip of his drink.

Solange giggles, craning her neck to look back at him. "Is she more flexible than me?"

"Let's find out." He pushes the baton up into her, and at her first cry of lust, a ripple of disgust churns in my stomach.

Hands balled into fists, I will myself to walk away, as my father proceeds to fuck Solange with my mother's old baton.

"The next time she decides to see if she's still got it, it will smell like your cunt."

Solange moans again and bites her lip. "I want you to fuck me. Fuck me like you've never fucked her."

With rage pounding through my veins, I walk away.

CHAPTER 13

ISADORA

Present day ...

"What should I play next?" Hands folded in my lap, I sit at the piano, waiting for Mrs. Blackthorne to rattle off the next piece.

"How did you come to memorize the music?" Whether it's by nature or intentional, there always seems to be a suspicious edge to her tone.

"My aunt played it for me once, and I listened."

"Your Aunt plays piano?"

"No. She had it playing in the background, while I was doing my homework. She read somewhere that playing classical music makes you smarter, or something."

Her eyes narrow on me while she taps her finger on a book sitting on her lap. "You heard it once. And you memorized it."

"Yes. I um ..." I gesture toward my head, trying to think of the word my counselor used to describe it. "Have a gift, of sorts. More of a curse. I can't listen to a song without my fingers moving." The thought of how that must look to someone else makes me chuckle, but she clearly isn't amused, judging by the stern expression still claiming her face.

This woman is going to be impossible to crack.

"So, why are you working here, if you have such an amazing *gift*." She says this as if it's not a gift, at all.

"You don't believe me, even after I *just* played it for you?"

"That piece could've taken you months, years to learn. You claim you heard it once. I taught piano for many years. I know what's possible and impossible."

"Would you like me to play another?"

"I insist."

"Okay, then." Twisting back around to the piano, I set my fingers to the first note of Vivaldi's *Summer*. I wish I knew the difference between easy and difficult pieces, but for me, they're all the same. It's only the music my fingers tend to stumble through that distinguishes them from one another. The first time I heard this one, I closed my eyes, imagining my every stroke at a spasmic speed, and I could picture every sound from every key I pressed. I've no idea what standard note I was playing, or whether sharp, or flat. I only knew sound, and when my ears heard it, my fingers longed to find it.

My music teacher would toy with me at times, speeding the song up to see if it affected my ability to copy. Not to be jealous, or angry of my talent, but to test my capabilities. No matter what speed, or tempo, I caught onto the keystrokes every time.

On the last note, I keep my fingers to the keys and smile. Not for Mrs. Blackthorne, but for how quickly I recalled a piece I hadn't heard in years. One my music teacher played in broken segments, to see if I could assemble it as one fluid song in my head.

"Vivaldi. One of the more difficult compositions."

For a woman whose mind isn't always reliable, she certainly

has some surprising intuitive moments when it comes to music and dolls.

"My Lucian liked to play for me. He was very good." As she stares off, the corner of her lips lift with a smile. "He knew the notes, of course." Pausing, she tips her head, her expression hardening with a frown. "His father hated it. Thought it as a weakness in our son." With a scoff, she shakes her head. "Can you imagine? The level of concentration and focus of the mind that goes into playing these complex pieces, and he thought it weak."

"That's a shame. I've always wanted to learn notes."

"Did you not have someone in school to show you?"

"My music teacher, but the idea of staying alone with him after school gave me the creeps."

A slight smile curves her lips. "Isn't it funny, the way we deny ourselves based on our fears?"

Absorbing her words, I sit quietly for a moment. "You taught piano. Could you teach me?"

"God, no. My piano teaching days are long gone. I've no interest anymore." Frail fingers lift, and she scratches her chin. "Lucian still remembers, I'm sure. He could teach you."

Seems she's lost her mind again, if she thinks I'd ask her son for piano lessons.

"Never mind. It's not important."

"You're afraid of Lucian, as well?"

"No, I just ... I know he's a busy man. I'm sure he doesn't have time for piano lessons."

"He has time to fuck the help. I'm sure he can squeeze an hour, or two, to show you some notes on the piano."

A flare of discomfort snakes beneath my skin with her comment, until I'm left wondering which of *the help* he's fucking. Giulia? Or one of the other maids I've seen bustling about over the last two days?

"Even with half his face ruined, he still manages to charm the ladies."

Maybe the ones he's attracted to.

The image I found the night before comes to mind, and as much as I want to ask her what happened to him, I believe I have to be careful around Laura, and treat every question as a possible trigger. "He's always had a way with the ladies, then?"

"My God." Rolling her eyes, she shifts on the chair. "In school, they literally wouldn't leave him alone. He attended an all-boys school but there was a sister campus, as well, and those girls …" She shakes her head. "No shame, at all. Sending him notes of what they fantasized doing with him. I found one in his schoolbag at the start of his sophomore year. A girl who claimed she'd adored him since elementary. Respectable daughter of a bank CEO. Yet, she described an addiction she'd developed to … *doing things*, while thinking of him. Disgusting."

A part of me wants to chuckle, while another part of me feels as if her words are directed at me, somehow, though I have nothing to do with her son. "Sometimes … a person just wants to be noticed."

"For the wrong reasons."

"Of course."

"Some, he did ignore. Others, I'm sure he indulged. Boys will be boys, and all that. He was handsome, athletic, and it didn't matter what age they were, women just gravitated to him."

"Did he ever love?" I don't know why I'm asking these questions. I shouldn't be asking, but I slept with the image of his face, his sad, morose face, and I can't stop thinking about it.

"Lucian loves, in as much as he's capable. Whether it's for an hour, a day, or a week. But I don't think any *woman* will ever have his heart completely. The closest was his only son."

Studying her for a moment, to be sure she doesn't slip into another hallucination at the mention of Roark, I nod and rise up from the piano bench. "Would you like to go for a walk, or something?"

Following a light knock, Giulia stands in the doorway, straightening her posture when Laura twists to face her.

"Pardon the interruption, ladies. Miss Amy is here for wardrobe."

"Ah, fantastic!" Laura turns around, her eyes as lit with just as earlier, when the doctor stood flirting at her side. "Time to find you some proper clothing."

Oh, Christ.

～

"I don't know …" With her finger pressed against her cheek, Laura tips her head in the reflection of all three mirrors that are set before a fitting platform, where I stand on display in her bedroom. "Looks too garish, if you ask me."

I'm guessing Amy is in her thirties, considering the youthful, wrinkle-free glow of her face. Her style reminds me of something more bohemian, in patterned pants and an airy, off-the-shoulder top. Strings of necklaces dangle from her neck, different sized beads that match the colors of her pants.

I stare down at the outfit she's chosen for me: a white, flowy peasant top and jeans, with a thin braided leather necklace. A little too hippy for my taste, but better than the tweed suits I imagined she'd show up with.

"You asked me to choose a wardrobe appropriate for a nineteen-year-old. Not you, Laura."

I'm guessing this chick is one of few who gets away with talking to her like that. In some ways, I envy her. Her hair is flipped to the side, highlighted from the strands of darks and lights weaved together, and when she smiles, it's the straightest, whitest set of teeth I've ever seen. "Don't worry, I'm not going to steer you wrong," she whispers, leaning in as she tucks only the front of my shirt into the jeans.

"What else do you have? Any dresses?"

"Oh, I … I don't do dresses." In truth, I stopped wearing dresses when I was about twelve and Abigail Watson told everyone in the class that I had too much hair on my legs. I began shaving soon after, of course, but never bothered with dresses, or shorts, for that matter. Not even when I worked a summer at a marina.

"I did bring one. But I'm guessing you'd think it too garish." Amy rolls her eyes, clearly offended by Laura's earlier comment.

"I want to see it on her," Laura insists, and I'd give anything right now for the platform below me to open up and swallow me whole.

When she turns around, Amy's eyebrows lift in silent apology.

With a huff, I step down from the platform and make my way to the bathroom for the dress, which I find hanging on the rack beside the wardrobe of clothes Amy brought with her.

White and linen, with thin straps and a hook and eye closure bodice, it's everything I loathe. Reminds me of what the rich tourist women wear on the beach, when they're trying to update their social media. I reluctantly change into it, horrified to find it fits me perfectly. My only hope at this point is that Laura will hate it as much as I do. The lines on my forearms practically scream for attention, and there's no hiding them, or my tattoo. Crossing my arms in front of my body, at least, shields the worst of the damage. The few on the outer part of my forearm could be mistaken for injury.

The moment I step through the bathroom's threshold, the first gasp tells me I'm doomed.

"Oh, my, Amy. That is … perfection. Absolute perfection!"

Shaking my head, I don't bother to climb the stage of shame so they can ogle me from every angle. "Truly, I can't do dresses."

"You have no choice, my dear. You're representing me. Do you think Giulia *likes* the uniform she wears for cleaning?"

"No."

"On weekends and after hours, you're welcome to wear what

you like. While you're serving as my companion? You'll wear what *I like*. Are we clear?"

Ugh. I can't even look in the mirror. I feel like a fraud. Like a child trying on high heels for the first time and stumbling about in them. It's unnaturally feminine. "Yes, of course."

"What is that on your arm there? A *tattoo*?" The disapproval in Laura's tone sounds like she said it around a mouthful of worms.

"Yes." She's not the first, oddly enough. Hard to believe anyone still scoffs at tattoos, as common as they are these days, but that's Tempest Cove.

"What does that even mean, *invulnerable*?"

I glance at Amy, whose curious expression tells me she's just as interested in my explanation as Laura. "Nothing, really," I lie.

"In my day, we called those tramp stamps." Laura chuckles, running her finger over her top lip. "I always wanted one, though." Her unexpected remark at the end caps the snarky response cocked at the back of my throat. Not bothering to elaborate, she waves her hand in dismissal. "What shoes do you have to go with this dress, Amy?"

For the next hour, I stand before the mirror, like one of the many dolls encased in the other room, until I have an entire wardrobe of clothes I'd have never chosen myself. Not that I'm complaining, since the entire cost of it was courtesy of the Blackthornes.

By the time Amy leaves, I find myself stuck in the white dress again--at Laura's request.

"It really is flattering on you. I'm not one to admit such things so freely, as you know."

"Thank you."

"Do me a favor, will you?"

"Sure." Anything to get the hell out of this room.

"Go to the library and fetch me some books. A good selection of them. I've already read these at least twice in the last two months." She points to a stack of books beside the bed that ranges from thrillers to bodice rippers. "Take those ones back."

"You like historical and thrillers?" I gather the dozen, or so books, into my arms, my muscles twitching to keep from dropping them.

"Griffin used to call my romance novels ridiculous. I find it interesting, the one thing our marriage lacked was the one thing he found ridiculous." Her comment brings a smile to my face.

"If it makes you feel better, my aunt thought they were ridiculous, too. *Frivolous reading*, she called it."

"Was your aunt ever married?"

"Once. He cheated on her."

Scoffing, she turns her head toward the window. "It's the nature of men to cheat. What else would we hate them for, if they didn't?"

"I'll grab the books." Taking the elevator to the first floor, I hurry toward the library that I remembered from the tour with Rand. My hope is that no one will see me in this absurd dress and the strappy sandals she insisted I wear with it. At least they don't have a heel and cover my unpainted toes.

Once in the library, a familiar curtain of relief passes over me, as if I stepped into another world. It's always been that way for me, a source of escape when things became too stressful. As a child, I'd get lost in worlds and fairy tales that were far from where I lived. Magical stories of princesses and princes, knights and maidens. It wasn't until I got older that I realized life didn't imitate fiction, at all. In fact, if I wanted a more accurate account, I should've been looking through the memoirs of broken children and homes, because not even *Cinderella*, who had a pretty shitty home life, had to wake up with a junkie for a mom.

I stare up at the levels upon levels of books that stretch all the way to the ceiling and smile at the possibilities. An endless selection of stories that line shelves upon shelves. Anxious to begin, I spin around, and as I crash into a wall, the handful of books in my arms tumble to the floor. "Oh, shit!"

Turns out, the wall is actually a body. The same body I ran into the night before, with the solid arms and a smattering of chest hair peeking through his unbuttoned shirt.

Without bothering to look at his undoubtedly pissed-off face this time, I kneel to the floor and gather the fallen books. "I'm so sorry."

"Can't seem to avoid you," he says, with an edge of annoyance.

I frown at that, slightly offended.

Shiny patent leather shoes become knees, as he drops down beside me and picks up a few of the novels that have landed on their pages, splayed in such a way that makes me cringe. "My mother's choice of literature hasn't changed, I see. Unless this belongs to you."

My cheeks heat with embarrassment, as he hands me a book, its cover a shirtless man groping the exposed thigh of a woman whose dress is hiked up, his face buried in breasts that bulge out of a demi-cup bodice. Recalling Laura's earlier comments about her husband's disapproval of her reading, I frown harder, my forehead practically cramping with the effort. I swipe the book out of his hands. "Nothing wrong with it, if it did."

"I never said there was."

I finally lift my gaze to his, just catching the diversion of his eyes. A downward glance shows my own cleavage sticking up from this stupid dress, and I quickly straighten, rolling my shoulders back.

A gentle grip of my arm stiffens my muscles, and when he turns my forearm over to the scars, his brows lowering with what I'd interpret as disgust, panic blooms inside my chest. I want to pull away, but my body is frozen in shock, while I wait for him to ask why I did this to myself. How could I mutilate my own skin, and worse, for what purpose?

It's a question I can't answer myself, except that it felt good at the time. It felt good to release that pain and rage that left me feeling like I could explode. As if I was releasing all of the toxins in my life and decontaminating my blood of all the demons, like an exorcism.

His thumb passes over a cluster of skinny scars, the worst of my pain permanently written in my skin, and my face feels like a sealed-up volcano, with all the pressure and mortification kettled inside my head.

Without a single question about them, he releases me and passes me the last book. Stack clutched tight to my breasts, I do my best to hide the flush of my chest. The evidence of my humiliation.

Fingertips grip my elbow, the soft strokes from before still lingering on my forearm, casting a chill across my skin as he guides me to my feet. Once upright, he releases me, stuffing his hands into his pockets.

"I don't suppose a set of side mirrors would do you any good."

The tension from seconds ago is tamped down by my offense. "No more than a horn for you."

His jaw shifts as if this amuses him. A gesture that I don't find amusing. "Yet, you're the one who can't seem to avoid running into things."

"Maybe if those *things* didn't blend into the wall, I'd take notice of them." Oh, my God. I didn't even mean to spew that one. The fact is, this man is *unblendable*, if such a word exists. He's the kind of mysterious, imposing presence that could shrink any room he walks into. Intriguing and majestic, in spite of his scars.

The humor in his eyes hardens with malice. "Nice dress. I'm sure my mother loved picking it out for you. I've no doubt it gets boring dressing up dolls all day."

"I am not her ... dress-up thing."

What?

Again, his lips twitch as if he's holding back a laugh, which only stirs my frustration. "I suspect you'll have a closetful of dresses by the time she's done playing with you."

My jaw comes unhinged, while my mind scrambles for a proper insult to throw back at him. Gaze dipping to his outfit, which, if I'm being honest, really does look good on him, a fact that only pisses me off further, I tip my head with a smirk. "I see she chooses your wardrobe, as well."

What is it about this man? Twice now, he's brought out this nasty side of me, like he *wants* to fire me for my insolence.

He steps toward me, to which I step backward, until the wall behind me is pressing against my spine. Planting a hand against the wall, he leans forward. It's not his face that scares the shit out of me right now, but the proximity of his body, and I'm suddenly very much aware of his size compared to mine. How small and delicate I must look beside him. Small. Delicate. Totally breakable.

"Careful, girl," he whispers in my ear, casting a shiver of goosebumps across my skin with the dark promise in his tone. The air of authority that radiates from every cell of his body like the crack of a whip. He pushes away from me and gathers up the books from the table behind him--references for music composition, I notice--and taps his knuckles on the wood. "At least I get to wear pants."

As he steps past me, leaving a delicious trail of whatever cologne he's wearing, I exhale a breath and shake my head.

Stupid dress.

Arms brimming with a selection of books, I exit the elevator, and at the sounds of screaming, I rush toward Laura's bedroom, shoulder slamming into the door. "Laura?"

From beside the bed, Nell pins down her arms, while Laura squirms, trying to break free.

"Amelia! Why aren't you answering me? Answer me!"

I drop the books onto a nearby chair and dart across the room to the opposite side of the bed. "What happened?"

"You can't leave without telling me." The anger in Nell's voice strikes like a slap across the face.

"She sent me down for some books. I was only …. I was only gone a few minutes."

"I found her out on the balcony, calling for Amelia."

Oh, my God. This woman's mental status is about as predictable as a category five hurricane. "I'm sorry. It won't happen again. I'll inform you each time I leave. Is there anything I can do?"

"No. I gave her something to sleep. Just waiting for her to calm down. You might as well go. She'll be out the rest of the day."

Shoulders sagging, I can't help the feeling that I've failed her again. As I leave the room, I glance back to where Laura has finally settled. Only her head rolls back and forth, as she stares up at the ceiling.

CHAPTER 14

LUCIAN

Sixteen years ago ...

With one arm tucked under my head, I lie stretched out on my bed, tossing a tennis ball into the air and catching it one-handedly.

At a knock of my bedroom door, I don't answer, but keep on with my solitary game.

Another knock.

Jaw grinding, I throw the ball harder than the last and catch it again.

The door clicks open, and Solange steps inside, closing it behind her. I can't deny the sight of her hardens my muscles, but at a flash of my father fucking her with the baton, I curl my lips and look away.

Arms behind her back, she rests against the door. "I waited for you. At the cave."

"I'm sure you did."

"You never showed. Why?"

I shrug with disinterest. "I wasn't interested in fucking you after my father's dick was in you."

Lowering her gaze, she purses her lips as if to hold back a laugh, only pissing me off more.

"Get out."

"I saw you kiss her. At the piano." Her huff of disappointment echoes through the room. "I was … out of my mind. Jealous. Angry. Hurt."

Catching the ball one more time, I swing my feet over the edge of the bed and sit upright. "She kissed me. I had nothing to do with it."

"But you didn't push her away."

"No. I guess I didn't. Just like you didn't push my father away."

"I can't stand your mother … constantly making me feel like I'm nothing but shit under her *designer* shoes. The baton? Yeah. It was bad. But I'm tired of feeling like some lowlife." She tips her head, no doubt trying to get my attention, while I do my best to keep from looking at her. "As for your father? I don't have a choice. He threatened to get rid of me if I don't fuck him when he asks."

Frowning, I finally meet her gaze. "Fire you?"

"You're the only one, Lucian." The lower hem of her dress draws my attention to her bare legs as she steps further into the room. "The only one who makes me feel good. Who makes me feel … worth something."

"And you fucked that up. So, like I said, get out." I toss the ball into the air again, but she catches it this time.

"You're angry with me."

"Is it obvious?"

Dropping the ball to the floor, she crawls onto my lap before I can stop her, and pushes me back onto the bed. Straddling my body, she reaches behind her back for something. "I want to show you another trick."

Hands on her thighs, I go to push her off, but her muscles vise around me, holding me captive. "I'm done with your tricks."

"This one you'll find useful." A blade gleams in the corner of my eye as she twists it, smiling. "When you're angry. It's as easy as one long slice to release all that tension inside of you."

Cold metal bleeds through my shirt when she sets the steel tip against my chest and pops one of my buttons. I don't even bother to look where it falls. My eyes are riveted on hers, searching for any sign that she might plunge that blade into my ribs. Another button. Followed by another, until a wide gap shows off my bare chest.

"Just as fear can be an aphrodisiac, so can pain. If you learn to love and embrace it, you become invincible."

The relentless pounding of my heart isn't fear, but excitement, evidenced by the hardening of my body.

A cold burn streaks across my chest where she drags the blade, scoring my flesh, and I clench my teeth to the pain. "Fuck," I grit, muscles flinching with the chasing sting. Never taking her eyes off me, she lifts the blade, showing blood running down the steel, which she licks away.

"You taste like rage and lust."

Everything inside me begs me to throw her off and tell her to get the fuck out of my room. Instead, I grip the back of her neck, the rage exploding to the surface when I push her down onto the bed beside me. I swipe the blade from her hand and twist it in the same taunting manner as she had before.

Her lips part around a smile that I could cut from her face. "What do you wish to do with that knife?"

The blade is a quick diversion, and I stare at my distorted reflection in the metal. Without much prompting from my head, the cold steel is propped at her throat, my eyes locked on hers, as I reach down and tear away her panties beneath the dress. Furious with her.

One-handedly, I spring my dick from my pants.

She squirms beneath me, as if to fight me, but I'm stronger.

I wedge my legs between her thighs, and a cold sting smarts my cheek where she slaps me. The giggle that follows only goads my fury, and I press the blade enough to lift her chin.

"If I ever catch him fucking you again, I'll take this knife and drag it across your throat."

She lets out a moan.

A fucking moan.

Slamming my dick into her, I watch her eyes roll back, her tongue sweep over her lips.

Incoherent words in French dance around my head, while I rock against her.

"Tell me what you're saying," I demand.

Eyes weighted with desire, she gives a heavy blink and moans again. "I said *fuck me harder, young master.*"

So I do.

CHAPTER 15

ISADORA

Present day ...

Whan I was fifteen, Aunt Midge thought it'd be fun if I babysat one of the neighbor kids for extra cash. A little five-year-old girl, whose mom worked late into the afternoons, leaving her daughter with no one to pick her up from the school bus stop. I never had siblings, a pet, or anything that I might be remotely responsible for keeping alive, so I'm not sure where Aunt Midge got the idea this would be good for me.

For eight dollars a day, I met the kid at the stop, walked her home, and hung out watching mind-numbing episodes of *Larva* until her mom got home. Didn't seem like such a bad gig, until, one day, she decided to change it up by asking if she could play in the backyard. It was fenced, so I didn't think anything of it. About ten minutes before her mom was due home, I ventured out to call her in.

She didn't answer.

I searched every corner of the yard.

Didn't find her.

To say I was panicked was an understatement. I literally suffered an anxiety attack while racing through the house in search of her. Wheezing for air, feeling dizzy with the urge to pass out. Full on panic.

With only a couple minutes before her mom showed up, I happened to wander outside to check the front, and found her camped out in the middle of the road, drawing with chalk.

Middle of the goddamn road.

Out of my mind, I swiped her up and carried her, as she kicked and screamed, to the sidewalk, where I could properly ask her what the hell she was thinking.

"Mommy lets me play in the street." She was lying, of course, and not a minute later, her mom pulled up, totally oblivious to the drawn hearts and rainbows she drove over.

I didn't bother to say a word, but later that night, the guilt gnawed at me. So much so, I skipped school the next day, to confess what happened and quit my job, feeling like a total failure. A year later, I learned the little girl was killed. Hit by a car in front of her house while she played. According to the article, she was left home alone after school.

Knees tucked up into my chest, I sit on the bed, staring off at the wall across from me. I don't even know what it means that Laura was on the balcony earlier today. If she's so mentally unstable that she'd try to jump, or chase her dead grandson over the railing. All I know is I can't get the visual of her lying on the pavement with her skull cracked open out of my head. I should be asleep right now, but the scenario just keeps playing on a loop, and experience tells me it won't stop until I check to make sure she's all right.

Cold hardwood floors hit my bare feet, and I pad quietly toward my locked door. Cracking it open, I peek to find the hallway empty and quiet, and continue on down one flight of stairs, and past the foyer, where I skid to a halt. "Shit."

Sampson lifts his head as I approach, but doesn't bother to move from where he's made the Blackthorne crest his bed for the night. Instead, his big blockhead pans slowly after me, as I tiptoe past.

The sight of him rattles my nerves even more, and I gotta believe the dog can sense it, the way he keeps a wary watch, while I scamper toward the elevator. Just a quick check will, hopefully, allow me to close my eyes and get some sleep, though. Start over tomorrow.

The elevator doors open, and I'm hit with the sound of screaming for the second time in one day. I race toward Laura's bedroom, But skid to a halt a second time when I find Lucian camped out on the floor beside her door.

One leg propped up, he rests his elbow atop his knee, a drink dangling from his hand. He only spares me a momentary glance, eyes brimming with exhaustion and apathy.

"I'll ... sorry. I'll leave you alone." I spin around to leave, but pause and turn back toward him. "Is she okay?"

Without bothering to look at me, he gives a subtle nod and tips back his drink.

"Do you need anything?"

Lips pressed to a hard line, he shakes his head.

My heart is pounding in my chest, mostly from the unexpected encounter, but also because the man just makes me nervous as all hell.

Again, I turn away, but stall halfway. "I'm ... sorry about my comment this afternoon. About your outfit? Diarrhea of the mouth sometimes." I catch a flicker of distaste dance across his face, until he lifts his glass again for another sip.

The clink of the ice announces the last of it.

"If you don't mind ... I just want to wait until she settles. Just to make sure she's okay."

He doesn't answer. Doesn't bother to look at me, at all, and I get a sense he's annoyed by my presence. In fact, there're probably very few things, like that glass of liquor, that *doesn't* seem to irritate the man.

Unfortunately for him, I know I won't sleep with the sounds of her screams echoing through my head all night. So I don't really give a damn if he's annoyed.

Taking a seat on the floor at the opposite side of the door, I pull my legs up, wrap my arms around them. From this side, I don't see any of his scars, only the sharp profile of an attractive, but intimidating, man. One who doesn't bother to acknowledge me.

For what feels like an eternity, we sit quietly, the sounds of moaning and sobbing bleeding through the door. Nell's voice is flat and commanding, hardly compassionate toward the woman, as if she's too tired to deal with her.

Lucian sighs and rolls his shoulders back, and I wonder how long he's been sitting here. What's going on with her?

His shirt is unbuttoned some, his tie undone, as though he's had to get comfortable. Still, the awkward silence hangs on the air between us.

"Your mother told me you play piano. Or played. She didn't specify if you still do, or not." I'm not the biggest conversationalist. Lord knows, if there was a book in my hands right now, his breathing would get on my nerves, but this one-way conversation is ridiculous with him. It'd probably be easier if I were staring at his scarred half. At least I'd feel a small amount of pity for him, but from this angle, he just looks like an arrogant, moody prick with a perfect jawline.

At this rate, I'd rather stay awake all night counting cracks on my ceilings.

As I push to my feet, he clears his throat.

"What are you really doing here?"

The familiar pangs of guilt settle in, and for a moment, I feel like fifteen-year-old me preparing to confess to Ms. Phillips that I lost her daughter for a minute. Only, he's not Ms. Phillips. He's the Mad Son. Devil of Bonesalt. And my palms are sweating. "While I was ... down in the library, she apparently went out on the balcony. I had no idea she would ... or that she might try to--"

"That's not what I mean. Why are you here? At the manor?"

"You. I mean, Rand hired me."

"No shit."

"I'm here to work."

His face kicks to the side, his brows lowering. "Yeah? Sure you're not here to gather up dirt about the fucked-up Blackthornes, to take back to your little friends in town? I don't think there's enough crosses out on the road. Maybe you can talk them into adding a few more."

Once again, my face heats with embarrassment. "I'm not here to spread gossip. I'm here to do my job."

"You've already done that well, it seems."

Another shrill scream echoes from the other room, and I drop my gaze as the slap of his words settles beneath my skin. A flare of anger shoots up from my gut. "You only know that because I *told you* I screwed up. Not because you actually give a shit."

Slapping a hand over my mouth is futile after what's already been said, what now exists in the universe. I don't even know the relationship between him and his mother. I only know that, in the two days I've been here, he hasn't shown much interest in her.

The glare he shoots back at me crackles through my bones, and I slide my hands over my face to keep from having to look at him when he fires me right here on the spot. Muscles trembling, I brace myself for the onslaught of insults and the anger I see churning in his eyes.

Seconds tick in an agonizing countdown to my walk of shame, when I'm forced to go back to my room and text Aunt

Midge to come pick me up because my damn mouth spouted off again.

"I'm sorry." It's all I can say, worthless as it is.

"You're not like the last girl."

Daring a peek through my fingers, I find him staring ahead toward the wall of dolls across from us, swirling the ice in his glass.

"They all cower. But you ... you just don't know when to keep your lips zipped."

"It's practically a medical condition. I honestly can't stop myself sometimes."

"*Honest* being the operative word." Still swirling the cubes, he sighs. "I've been surrounded by liars my whole life. It's strange to hear honesty. However brutal."

The screams from before have died down to whimpers and quiet sobbing. "I didn't mean what I said. I don't even know your relationship with your mother."

He thumbs at his nose and sniffs. "When I was younger, she'd have these horrible nightmares. Screaming and kicking, and just ... unsettling to watch her. I couldn't go to her, of course, because the staff were worried she'd end up kicking me in the face, or something. So I'd watch from the door until she calmed. Hours, sometimes. Listening to her cry. It was the most honest thing I've ever heard from her."

His comment sits heavy in my chest, as I recall the nights my own mother would come down from one of her highs, lie on the floor, sobbing, while she apologized to me about how much she fucked things up for us. I hated her every other minute of the day, except for those few when I felt like I'd caught a glimpse of her, naked and vulnerable.

"I was thinking I might take her for a walk tomorrow. Get some fresh air."

The door clicks open, and Nell steps out rubbing her hand

across her forehead, until she sets her sights on me and stops with a gasp.

Eyes wide, she turns toward Lucian and lowers her gaze. "I … didn't realize … you were outside the room."

Pushing to his feet, Lucian straightens, towering over her and me, even after I finally clamber to my feet, as well. "She's settled, then."

"Yes. I've given her something for sleep. She's fine. I would've given you an earlier update … if I'd known." It's strange to see Nell so nervous around him, fidgeting and keeping her gaze from his, when she acts so aloof with everyone else.

"I wasn't looking for an earlier update. Her screams were pretty telling."

"Of course." It doesn't take a genius, or junkie, for that matter, to see that Laura is addicted to whatever they keep giving her for sleep. I've been around addicts enough to know they'll do just about anything to get the drug. These fits of hers could very well be real, but with the way Nell hands out sleep aids like candy, I wonder.

Eyes on me, he steps past both of us without another word, and makes his way onto the elevator. I'm inclined to follow, but I wait.

Once the elevator doors close, Nell sets a hand to her chest and expels a long breath. "He must've been working in his office. Heard her scream. God, he makes me nervous."

She's been here far longer than I have, which means there's no chance of my discomfort around the man going away any time soon.

"Because of the scars?"

"No. Because he's just …" A quick glance back at me, and she frowns. "Never mind. I'm tired. I need some sleep."

"Yeah, of course. I just wanted to check on her. What happened earlier is still bothering me."

"Don't worry about it. We've all done it."

"Really? I can't imagine you doing something stupid." Aside from dispensing pills like a human gumball machine.

"Believe me, everyone in this house does something stupid at one point, or another." She jerks her head toward me. "Go to bed. Tomorrow's another fun day in the funhouse."

With a snort, I make my way back toward the elevator.

"Hey," she calls out to me and, after a glance back at Laura's room, closes the space between us. "Be careful around him. Lucian. I wouldn't get too friendly."

"I wasn't getting friendly. We were just casually chatting about his mom."

"Nothing is ever casual with them. Everyone in this place is a master at hiding who they really are."

"What is he hiding?"

Again, she looks back at Laura's room. "Just watch yourself. I'm going to bed."

CHAPTER 16

LUCIAN

Sixteen years ago ...

Six hours with a tutor is about as thrilling as watching turtles fuck.

I've always been a fast learner, and never required the kind of hammering this tutor employs to teach. Show me once and move on.

Haven't seen Solange today, and I'm anxious to meet up with her, to exhaust some of this pent-up frustration that has my muscles in knots.

Book bag slung over my shoulder, I enter my bedroom, but stop in my tracks on finding my father beside the bed. I let my bag fall to the floor, and he turns toward the sound. The accumulation of different sized knives I've collected over the last couple of weeks from the kitchen lies beside the BDSM magazine Solange gifted me. As I said before, I'm a quick study, and if I happen to find enjoyment in it, I'm even a bit enthusiastic. I've become something of a connoisseur of blades. Dull, sharp, jagged, smooth.

And I've managed to keep all this hidden from my mother, only pulling them out from under the bed on the times when I'm alone and keyed up. Imagining her face, screwed up in a cross between disappointment and repulsion, is enough to make me paranoid and cautious.

Somehow, my father having found it first is worse.

On instinct, I tug at the cuffs of my shirt, the phantom sensation of many slices I've made across my skin itching with my sudden discomfort.

"What is this, Lucian?"

Instead of answering, I lower my gaze and frown. Responding will do me no good. It's obvious he's searching for something that he can use as an excuse to leave another black eye on my face. Humiliate me in front of the staff and my mother. He's never searched my room before, so why now?

He rolls up the magazine, and for a moment, I wonder if that's what he'll use to hit me this time, until he starts gathering up the knives, as well. He jerks his head toward those left on the bed. "Grab those. And follow me."

Fuck.

He wants an audience.

I can see it now, all the maids, including Solange, the butler and cooking staff, all gathered in his office, with my knives and magazine laid out. He'll ask who didn't clean under my bed, who didn't notice the knives going missing, just so there's an excuse to have them there.

Reaching for the hilts, I grab a serrated steak knife and a much smoother paring knife. I've found the steak knife requires a lot of pulling and dragging, more damage and messy, difficult to control. I mostly use it for scraping the skin while I get off-- never cutting. The best knife, I've found, is actually the dagger in my father's hands. Particularly across the thigh. But that's neither here, nor there, now that he's found them.

I follow my father out of the bedroom, keeping my head low to avoid eye contact with anyone we might pass. We reach the elevator, and whereas there was a time I would plead for his forgiveness, to spare me whatever wrath is brewing inside of him, I don't bother. I've grown to realize it's useless where he's concerned.

The silver doors open, and my father steps inside first. I follow after, and the doors close. Only, instead of pushing the button to the third floor, for his office, he lifts his hand and presses the signet ring to a button I always assumed broken.

I watch with curiosity as the button with the letter 'S' lights up. The strangest thing I've ever seen.

How many times I've toyed with that button, determined to know why it never lit up like the others. Where it took the elevator. Why I never saw anyone else attempt to access it.

Thoughts click into place, as I recall the one time I saw a group of men in black suits, business partners of my father's, enter the elevator. My mother had summoned me to her sitting room, and I waited for the men to clear the elevator first. By accident, I pressed the button to my father's office, which put me in a panic, but when the car arrived, and the doors opened, his office was empty. As if I'd imagined all those men in suits, like a sketchy dream.

My father twists around, facing the back wall. It raises the hairs on my skin, like any moment, he'll turn around and stab me in the back with one of those knives.

The elevator comes to a stop, and a slight tremble snakes over my bones, while I wait for the doors to open. The sound of grinding metal from behind stirs my curiosity, and I turn around to find the back wall has opened on a cavernous room lit by sconces.

The catacombs, I bet, though I haven't been down here to know for certain.

A thin gauze of cold air clings to my skin, when he leads me down hallways that seem to be made of stone. The clang of the metal knives is the only sound between us, over the steady thud of footsteps and the rush of blood pulsing in my ears.

We pass entrances that seem to lead to other tunnels, like a maze of them one could easily get lost in. My father comes to a stop in front of a wooden door brandished with brass moldings, like something out of the medieval era, but recently updated. Once again, he presses his ring to a panel on the door, and it opens to a small, dark room.

"What is this place?" I finally ask.

"Generations ago, your great-great-grandfather had this castle built on an Indian burial ground the locals wanted to bull-doze. He was granted permission to keep it and bury his own relatives here. It's where we keep the bones of our ancestors."

A light flips on, illuminating the room, in which a number of tools hang from the wall. Knives. Whips. Chains. Some I've never seen in my life. An old chair that reminds me of something from a dentist's office sits smack in the middle, only this one comes equipped with straps, and some kind of contraption around the headrest that looks like the dental gear I wore when I was thirteen.

More clanging fills the room as he drops the knives onto a counter opposite the chair.

"They say it starts with animals, but that's not always true. My obsession began with bones." A piece of what looks to be the bottom jaw of something sits out on the counter beneath a cupboard that holds various jars, some filled with solutions and whatever soaks inside of them. "My father brought me here, and I was overwhelmed with the comfort I felt in this place."

"What starts with animals?"

Setting the bone back down, he twists just enough that I see a hint of a smile play on his lips. So odd and rare, I almost wonder if I'm mistaken. "Sadism."

Sadism? Christ, he thinks I'm out cutting up bunnies in the yard with those knives?

"This isn't what it loo--"

"For years, I thought your mother had gotten her claws into you and turned you into some pansy *pianist.* I thought maybe you'd blow my theories out of the water. Turns out, you have the gene, after all."

"Gene?" I thought sadism was learned.

After casually crossing the room, he comes to a stop in front of the wall of weapons and runs his fingers through the braided cords of a whip there. "I'm guessing your fancy education never taught you much about behavior epigenetics. It was something I became fascinated with at an early age. How the trauma that my grandfather suffered could be passed down generations, altering the genes of his offspring. That is the purpose of our group. Evolutionary biology."

"I'm not following."

"I'm talking about your predisposition for inflicting pain on others. It has become part of your genetic makeup."

Brows lowering with a frown, I don't bother to say aloud that I'm still lost in his explanation, because I know my father to be a man of little patience. One who'd belittle me as simple and slow.

"Our group seeks to explain--"

"Group? What group?"

"We call ourselves Schadenfreude. We are a collective. Generations of those dedicated to studying the epigenetics of sadism. The evolution of dominance and survival." From his pocket, he tugs out a cigar and lights the end of it, while my mind reels in a poor attempt to keep up. "It began with your Great-Grandfather Dane. There was a time, before all of this." He gestures to our surroundings. "After the Great Depression. When he was so poor, he couldn't afford to feed himself, or his family. At the time, he

was working for the New England Fishing Company in Gloucester. Profitability was low, and fleets were reduced during the war,
to be used as naval trawlers for mine sweeps. Men were out of
work." In the pause that follows, he puffs on his cigar, staring
back at me. "Starvation makes a man do desperate things. Irrational things. There were whispers through the neighborhood of
two Germans. At the time, they claimed to have worked in a
factory during the war. It would later be determined that these
men were actually Nazi physicians, war criminals who fled
Germany to avoid persecution. But I digress. Their study was the
effects of sadism on future generations. The concept of DNA had
recently been discovered and eugenics was huge. Heredity was
fascinating to the Nazis, in particular."

I slide my gaze toward the dentist chair, my chest cold with
the thoughts of what he intends to do. If the point of this story is
to prepare me for tortures that he intends to carry out on me.

"These men offered a large sum of money to essentially
torture your great-grandfather for a period of time. Their theory
was that the trauma suffered would alter his behaviors and
produce future offspring with sadistic tendencies."

"How? If he was the one who was tortured?"

"That's the nature of Schadenfreude. Part of his torture was
witnessing the torture of others. In time, his empathy began to
shift. Of course, the Germans rewarded this behavior. It's not to
say their experiments weren't founded in some personal motivations, you know. And at the end of it, he had enough money to
purchase his own fishing boat, start his own company. Build the
foundations of what we are today. But the psychological effects
of what he suffered never left him, and so he maintained a sort of
friendship with the Germans. And it wasn't long before he began
to partake in the study himself."

"He tortured innocent people?"

"Those who were poor, or required some sort of favor he
could fulfill. It was mutually beneficial, as many went on to

become successful themselves. That's the nature of this study. Sadism is a genetically superior trait. And the idea of our collective is to feed what starves us. My grandfather would soon find, over time, the mind's hunger is far more powerful than that of the stomach."

Lowering my gaze from his fails to shield me from the scrutiny burning in his eyes. I've no doubt he's watching for my reaction, waiting for me to tell him those knives were hidden under my bed for the same reason. That I'm some fucked-up result of my great-grandfather.

"Why are you telling me this?"

"Because the experiment continues, Lucian."

"I'm not like that. I don't …. I'm not out to hurt people."

"Not yet. As I said, it began with something simple for me. Bones. It wasn't long before I was collecting my own."

My gaze snaps to his, the cold tickle in my chest exploding with panic. "You've killed?"

"The purpose of Schadenfreude isn't to kill, but a man doesn't amass this much power without making enemies. If you knew how many times someone plotted to kill me, your mother, you, I suspect you'd never leave this home. Fortunately for me, I am genetically equipped to eliminate what threatens my survival."

His words snake beneath my skin, absorbing deep inside my own bones, as the curtain of my life yanks back to expose the harrowing reality I've failed to see.

"You would kill, if someone threatened what you love, wouldn't you?"

I've never thought of it. Do I, or have I, loved anything so much in my life? So much I would kill for it?

"Why did you bring me down here?"

"Because it's time you know your place in this family. In Schadenfreude. There will be expectations in this role. Things you can't elect to ignore."

"Like what? Torturing innocent people?"

"Those people will come to you someday. You will not seek them out. They'll hear whispers of us, and they will come in desperation. They will give themselves over to you for a chance to have the life you live."

"And if I don't want to help them?"

"I'm afraid you don't have a choice."

I frown back at him, studying his eyes for any sign of amusement, or humor, but my gaze is met with the same austerity I've come to know from him.

"The men who make up Schadenfreude are some of the most powerful people in the world. You will come to know secrets that would destroy them. And therefore, they would destroy you. You will do the same. Protect our collective. Preserve generations of study. To observe the effects of environment on genetics. Your genetic makeup is changed, based on what happened to your great-grandfather. And it'll be interesting to see how it manifests in future generations."

"You said those men were Nazis. Why would I protect, or preserve, anything to do with them? Why would *you*?"

"This isn't about them. They were eventually found out by the group, and let's just say, it was a quiet matter of two individuals being consumed by their work. Poetic justice, I suppose."

In not so many words, the Germans were tortured and murdered for their lies.

"It still doesn't make it right. So you ... you create generations of people who enjoy hurting others? How does that make the world a better place?"

Chuckling, he flicks the ash of his cigar and puffs on it again. "The world is filled with sadists and masochists. You either find pleasure in doling pain, or receiving it."

"I'm not a psychopath. I don't get off on callously hurting others."

He lifts the magazine beside him, silencing my argument. "Your books would say otherwise. And it isn't about callousness.

You get off because you know how it feels. Because you've felt the blade slide across your own skin. You've felt the punch beneath your ribs as you fight for a breath of air."

My muscles turn stiff.

The air withers inside my chest.

He knows about Solange. He's seen the two of us together. There is no other explanation.

"It began that way for me, as well. Experimenting. Testing my limits. And soon, my boy, you'll find joy in watching others discover what you now know to be true. That there is pleasure in pain."

CHAPTER 17

LUCIAN

Present day ...

"Lucian! So good to see you!" Patrick Boyd reminds me of a cross between an evangelist and a car salesman. Bright goody-two-shoes smile in place, he wears his hair slicked back like a wanna-be gangster who can spout Bible verses while soliciting your vote. The thin-rimmed glasses are supposed to give him an educated air, but really, he just comes off as confused.

Thin, cold skin greets mine when I shake his hand. "It's been a long time, Patrick."

"How's your mother?"

"Well." I never cared much for my father-in-law, who never hid the fact that he favored my mother. Given his predilection toward younger women, though, it didn't make sense that he'd find her all that attractive, which leads me to believe his feelings were also politically motivated. "Let's not beat around the bush with formalities. I understand you've been inquiring about Schadenfreude."

Brows winging up in surprise, he shifts in his chair and smiles. "Word travels quickly."

"When you make enough noise, sure."

"It was actually your father who told me about the secret group. Before he died. Just never really had the chance to fully connect me."

Perhaps I gave my father too much credit for being shrewd. Of course, that's the nature of my meeting with Boyd now. To see what the hell Griffin Blackthorne was thinking, when he made the guy privy to so many powerful individuals. Like allowing a child to play with the controls of a missile. "And what is your interest?"

"I want to be a part of it. One of the elite."

Eyes locked on his, I study the fine, subtle movements of his body that betray the calm he's trying to convince me of. The incessant twitch of his eye. The bobbing of his throat. The occasional flutter of his lashes and tip of his head. As if every nerve ending is firing at once and he can't get a handle on it. Politicians are strange people, in that they have an ability to wear a mask for most of their public. But set them down in front of someone they might actually fear a little, and they tend to be a bit more transparent. "Are you aware of the nature of this group?"

"People come to you for favors. In exchange for ... a particular recreation."

"Sadism. And why would a man of your stature want to be affiliated with something like that? Considering your past transgressions?" *Say it, Boyd. It's political.*

"As I understand, this group has existed for generations without anyone's awareness, or interference."

"You don't strike me as the type of man who could stand by and watch the suffering of others."

Lips curving to a grin, he crosses his legs and eases back into his seat. "I'm a politician, Lucian. I've done it my whole career."

Rising up from my chair, I bite back the frustration of this meeting and come to a stand in front of the window. Below me, Isa pushes my mother in a wheelchair, stopping to point at something out of my view. The greenhouse, if the angle of her finger is anything to go by.

From here, the pale pink top she's wearing cuts low enough that I can see her cleavage, just like I spotted it the day in the library, when she wore that *godforsaken* white dress. In fact, it's God I blame in general for throwing this peculiar girl into my path.

Dark tresses fall over her shoulders, and my hands crumple into fists with the thoughts of how many times I could wrap her hair around them. Pulling her neck taught, mouth gaping while I hold a blade …

"Lucian?" The annoying tone of Boyd's voice hits me like a wet towel to the face, and my previous thoughts dissipate with my returning irritation.

It's just as well, really. I have no business looking at her that way.

So young.

These lecherous thoughts she's stirred inside of me are wrong, yet the temptation pulls at me every time I'm near her. The cloying, sweet scent of her skin, and oozing sensuality in her voice that serves as an aggravating distraction every time she talks. The way she challenges me, in spite of the sliver of fear behind her eyes. It messes with my head and if there's one thing I hate more than anything, it's when shit messes with my head.

Nineteen. Not a huge gap, but she's young enough to make me feel like my father ogling the help, a thought that crimps my lips.

"You don't understand," Boyd prattles on behind me, while I continue to watch my mother and her disarming companion. "I didn't mean to screw things up with that Krishner girl. It was just

… she was so young and pretty. So … different. I missed my Amelia terribly. I was distraught. Particularly when Greta left me. I was alone."

The comment leaves me frowning, and I break from the window to face him. "So, you fucked a teenager to soothe your broken heart? That's disturbing, Patrick."

"It was stupid. Irresponsible. And for the record, she was of consenting age."

She was barely eighteen, and him fifty-six. Consenting, or not, it's fucking gross.

"I'm making amends. Building my castle back up, so to speak."

"You're looking for connections." To hell with beating around the bush. This guy is literally a professional at the game, and I'll get nowhere unless I come right out and say it.

"That's only partly true. I am very curious in the study."

"You'd have to be sick in the head to hold any curiosity about this study."

"Then, why are you involved?"

Because I *am* the study. Of course, I'll never tell him that. "Why didn't you come to me first?"

"I didn't think you'd want anything to do with me after … everything."

"And how do I know this isn't your attempt to spy?"

"Considering who the members are--you, in particular--I'd consider that a pretty costly endeavor." He isn't kidding. If any one of the members, some of whom are former military and FBI, politicians and even royalty, ever got wind of malicious intent on his part, he'd find himself strung up like every other poor sap who comes begging for a handout.

Spinning my chair around, I plop back down and tug my cigarette case from my pocket. "It isn't up to me," I say, tapping one against the case. "They've asked me to invite you to a masquerade in two weeks. I'm asking you to decline."

Snorting a laugh, Boyd shakes his head. "You ... you owe me this. Your whole family owes me."

"Consider this a favor. A friendly warning."

"I'm not declining, Lucian. I want Senate, and this is my opportunity. If I have to pretend to enjoy busting kneecaps and smacking around a few unfortunate souls. So be it."

The collective will see right through his request. They already have, which means I don't have to say anything else on the matter.

"Then, we have nothing more to discuss. Rand will see you out."

Lips pressed tight, he pushes up from his chair. "I really hoped to have a better relationship with you. For Amelia and Roark's sake."

"My wife and son are dead. I see no point."

Clearing his throat, he rolls his shoulders back, clearly offended. "Have a nice day."

Without another word, he slithers toward the door like the snake he is, and I huff in exasperation.

In-laws.

CHAPTER 18

ISADORA

It occurs to me how long it's been since I've ventured outside for leisure. Used to be I'd spend long hours at the beach with Aunt Midge, reading books and soaking up the sun on days when she didn't have to be at The Shoal until later. Working on my tan was about the only thing I accomplished those days, back when everything was so carefree.

Before the incident, anyway.

Afterward, life got complicated. Darker. The sun didn't seem to shine as bright, and nothing in my world was carefree.

"It's a damn shame, the way this place has gone to shambles." With her hands set in her lap, atop a blanket that seems way too thick for the summer sun beating against my neck right now, Laura huffs, the sound of her voice breaking my thoughts. "I hired the best gardeners in the state. Blackthorne Manor was featured in a *magazine*. Did you know that?"

"I didn't." Glancing around at the withered husks of what must've once been vibrant and colorful flowers, I can't even imagine such a thing. "It must've been beautiful at one time."

"Oh … Easton was an artist. Absolutely incredible. If only the man wasn't so damn stupid, getting himself caught up in drugs and hustling."

"Easton?"

"The gardener. We found out he was pushing his drugs on Lucian, and promptly put a stop to that."

At the mention of his name, I look up to the office window and catch the devil himself staring down at me. I can't imagine a serious man like him high on drugs. With a slight smile, I wave.

He merely continues to stare down at me, and all that moves is the upward curl of smoke from his cigarette.

"Asshole," I mutter under my breath.

"Oh, my word, look who decided to grace us with his presence! Patrick Boyd." Laura's voice snaps me out of my trance, and I turn to see an older man, perhaps in his sixties, with graying hair and a matching gray suit, stroll toward us. Slightly handsome for his age, I can almost hear Aunt Midge referring to him as a *silver fox*, as she sometimes says. He adjusts his glasses and extends a hand toward the woman beside me.

"Laura Blackthorne, you are, and always have been, a sight for sore eyes." Taking her hand, he bends just enough to kiss her knuckles. "I wondered why the sun was shining so brightly today."

"Oh, you charmer. Enough with that."

His gaze falls on me, and for some reason, my stomach curls. Deep-set blue eyes carry a dull weariness, while his lips stretch in a too-bright smile. "And who might this be?"

"My companion, Isadora. This is the former Mayor Boyd."

"Soon, I'll have a fresh new title that sounds more impressive." He holds out his hand, and I hesitate to offer him mine.

With reluctance, I allow him to kiss my knuckles, just as he did Laura's a moment ago. "Nice to meet you."

"My, my. You must be … eighteen?"

"Nineteen."

"You remind me so much …" Lips slamming together, he

shakes his head, his grip tightening around my fingertips. "Of my Amelia."

Jesus. It's then I remember he's Amelia's father. I was so focused on his appearance, I forgot who the hell he was.

"I'm sorry. For your loss." I've always been terrible with these things. Words of sympathy and gratitude. While Aunt Midge always seems to know the right thing to say, probably from working so many years as a bartender, I've always stumbled in awkward silence.

"She was a ..."

"Vision of grace and beauty," Laura finishes. "Is she resting now? I swear that child sleeps all hours of the day."

Mayor Boyd's hand slips from mine, his brows crinkling. "Is that supposed to be funny?"

"She's, um ..." A quick glance to the side shows Laura staring up at me, and I offer a subtle shake of my head, hoping to implore him with my eyes. "Might be time for another ... dose."

His gaze flicks to mine, then hers, and back to mine. "I see. It was good to see you again, Laura." He takes her hand in his, wearing a smile that even I can see is fake. "I've got lots of work to do."

"Well, let me fetch Roark so you can say goodbye. Roark! Roark!"

Wrenching his hand away, he pushes his glasses up onto his nose and strides off in the other direction.

"Well ... how rude. Do you have any idea how much Roark misses his grandfather? Well, he hardly gets to see the man, and this is how he acts? Griffin would've been furious. After all we've done for that man."

Would've?

"Where is Griffin now?"

"You can't be serious. He's been dead for a few years now."

Interesting. She recognizes that her husband is dead, but not her daughter-in-law and grandson.

"I have to admit, I was never a child person. Yes, Lucian was my sweet baby boy, but I didn't flock to children, the way some women do. They made me uncomfortable most times. Lambs of Satan, I called them. But Roark. Roark is my little angel. My delicious little ball of sunshine." There's a fondness in her chuckle, and her eyes seem to sparkle as she speaks of him. "I wonder if he's awake from his nap."

With a sigh, I lower my gaze. "No. Not yet." I don't know if it's wise to play into her confusion, or not. My understanding of psychology is about as extensive as my understanding of microsurgery. It's only having lived with an addict that I know to change the subject when things start getting squirrely with them. "Hey, what if I plant some flowers. Clean out these flowerbeds for you."

"What's the point? They'll die. Everything dies here."

"Maybe just a few pots, then? We can work on it together."

Head tipped, she eyes me up and down. "What do you know of gardening?"

"I worked for a landscaping company for about two months. What's so complicated? Dig a hole, and throw in some seeds and water. Voila. Flowers."

"You're hopeless, child. If nothing else, I suppose a lesson might do you some good. Have one of the servants fetch my gardening supplies. In the meantime, I want to lie down."

"It's only midday. There's still so much we can do."

"I'm tired. And cold."

Jesus, it's gotta be eighty degrees outside right now. "You're sure? I'm happy to do all of the grunt work. Filling pots, digging the holes."

"Tomorrow. Take me to my room."

CHAPTER 19

LUCIAN

Sixteen years ago ...

Darkness swallows me, while I follow the path through the trees toward the clearing up ahead. The moon is still high enough that the tides haven't yet swept through the cave, just below the grassy knoll that marks its spot. Beyond the edge, the sea almost looks calm, where fishing boats sit off in the distance.

The conversation with my father weighs like an anchor around my neck. For the last sixteen years, I've struggled to find a commonality with him, to the extent that I pretty much gave up trying. We're different. We always have been.

And yet, a part of me yearns to understand this fascination I've developed. The tipping point between pain and pleasure, life and death. What if the only person who understands it is the very person I can't relate to on any level. The one I can't stand in this world?

The concept of Schadenfreude is beyond my comprehension.

Like a group of sadistic children who chose not to evolve in favor of their amusements. I don't find pleasure in suffering, only the perception and fantasy of it.

But what if he's right? What if it continues to evolve? What if my future children suffer from the same uncontrollable urges he's inflicted on me? Could I seek out excuses to punish and abuse my son, the way he's done to me all my life? Would I be just as cruel someday?

The answer is no. Not because I don't believe his theories, but because I've no intentions of bringing children into this world. Whatever it is he thinks he's discovered will die with me.

The path narrows along the edge of the cave, and my thoughts are tamped down by the crash of waves as I approach the beach. A thrill winds in my stomach, hardening my muscles at the thought of what's to come. The excitement of testing my limits again, and the exquisite reward of climax that always follows. As I enter the cave, I find the lithe form of Solange, her long dark curls spread out over the sand, hands already trussed over her head by rope attached to the signpost set deep in the sand, her gown in disarray and exposing her thighs.

"Well, you didn't waste any time, did you?"

She doesn't answer, and it's only as I approach that I notice the irregular pallor of her skin.

I slow my steps.

Purple blossoms of bruises dot her legs and her bound arms. The abnormal contortion of her bent elbow, as if it's twisted the wrong way, stirs nausea in my stomach, and I slap my hand to my mouth.

It's not until I'm standing over her that I finally see the vacancy in her stare, assuring there is no life left in her, and terror explodes inside my chest, my head urging my muscles to move and get the hell out of here, but I can't. I can't move. I can't stop looking at her lifeless face. The image now permanently seared inside my head.

My throat flexes with the need to scream, but a tight fist clamps around my lungs and keeps it from escaping.

She's dead.

What did you do?

A black insect emerges from the corner of her gaping mouth, and I curl my lip as it scampers across her face and burrows in her hair that's matted down by sand.

My leg twitches, and I stumble backward, falling onto the boulder behind me. Spinning on my heel, I race out of the cave, up the path along the edge of it, and across the field. My chest burns, the muscles in my legs ready to collapse with fatigue, but I don't stop. I keep running until I reach the stone staircase, where Rand greets me.

"Help!" A hearty cough slices through the rasp of my voice. "She's …. Help!"

My knees finally buckle, and the gravel of the driveway chews at my skin when I hit the ground. I throw my palms out to keep from smacking my teeth. "She's … dead. I …. Dead!"

"Calm down, Lucian." His hands settle across my back, and he tugs me to my feet. "What is it? What are you saying?"

"Solange! She's dead! In the cave! I saw her!"

Brows furrowed, he tips his head and lifts his gaze toward the direction from where I came running. "Are you certain that's what you saw?"

"Yes!" The shock releases its hold, and my muscles give out on me again. I collapse in his arms as a sob rips from my chest. "She's … dead."

CHAPTER 20

ISADORA

Present day ...

I wheel the chair into Laura's doll room, where Nell meets us.

"Short excursion today." Handing over Laura's cane, she stands off to the side, allowing the woman to push to her feet. As she reaches for one of Laura's hands to steady her, the older woman bats her away.

"One moment." Laura hobbles toward the glass case of dolls, her reflection showing a content smile. "Look how beautiful. My beautiful little children."

I exchange a glance with Nell, who rolls her eyes with impatience, and approach Laura from behind. "Which is your favorite?"

"A mother doesn't have favorites."

"Fair enough, which is the most priceless?"

"Ironically, it's the one I paid the most for." She points to one of the smaller dolls, one that seems old fashioned in rag clothes and a bonnet, with puffy cheeks and heart-shaped lips. Completely unnoticeable in a sea of dolls with far more color and detail. "I'd almost forgotten about her. I purchased her from Theriault's for three hundred thousand dollars."

My heart damn near cuts out, and I cough at the absurdity of paying so much for a doll.

Laura lifts her hand to the bracelet at her wrist and the small key that dangles from the linked chains. She unlocks the door and reaches in for the doll, her thumb gently brushing over its cheek while she smiles admirably. "She was created by the French sculptor Albert Marque, for the Parisian couturier, Jeanne Margaix-LaCroix, back in the early nineteen-hundreds."

"It must be very special to you."

"Griffin thought it was the most ridiculous thing I'd ever purchased." Leaning into her cane, she sets the doll back in the case and locks the glass. "A man who spared no expense for his little dinner parties. Do you know, he once paid a half-dozen women to pose naked as live sculptures?" She scoffs, hobbling back toward her bedroom. "A hundred-thousand dollars for a few hours of lewd entertainment. And how many men stood fondling those young girls."

The more time I spend here, the more I realize what little discretion the Blackthornes have when it comes to money.

Nell and I follow after her, and I hold back the covers of her bed, while Nell scurries ahead of Laura to help settle her in.

"I need to use the ladies room. A little privacy, if you will." Cane clicking across the floor, Laura shuffles toward the bathroom with little trouble.

Nell jerks her head toward me. "I'm going out on the balcony. Wanna join?"

"Sure." I lock the wheelchair in place, glancing back to see Laura closing the door behind her, and follow Nell out the door.

With a huff, Nell takes the chair farthest away, presumably to keep her smoke sequestered from me, but the light breeze on the air ensures it'll blow in my face.

"Can you imagine? Three-hundred grand for a fucking doll?" she asks, plopping into the seat. "I can't even afford a decent used car, and she's dropping cash on a goddamn doll that she keeps locked up in a box with all her other toys."

"It's definitely not something I'm accustomed to. I can think of a lot of things I'd spend that kind of money on."

"You and me both." As she lifts the cigarette to her lips, I notice her shirt pulled up to her elbows, revealing a couple tattoos.

I nod toward the anchor inked on the back of her wrist. "Nice ink."

Taking a long drag, she twists her arm, then blows the smoke to the side. "Thanks. It's my little reminder."

"Of what?"

"To hold on. Stay grounded." She pauses for a moment, before taking another drag and staring off. "I got a son. Lives with my sister. Been busting my ass to get him back."

"Does he live far?"

"California. That's where I'm from. Why I decided to come out to this shit island, I'll never know, but here I am."

"Was it school that made you move so far away?"

She runs her tongue across the bottom of her teeth, seemingly lost in quiet contemplation. "I was an addict for five years. Alcohol, pills, coke. Whatever I could get my hands on, I did it."

A part of me isn't surprised. Call it radar I've picked up from having a junkie mom, but this woman had former addict written all over her face. Just strange that she chose to be a nurse, administering drugs.

She scratches her chin with her thumb. "Keep that to yourself. I've passed all the drug tests, and I don't have any criminal history. I'm just an LPN right now. Still going to school."

"I think that's great. Takes a lot to turn things around like that."

"Yeah. It's been rough sometimes." Her eyes fall to my wrist, and she juts her chin toward it. "What's yours?"

I run my thumb over the word inked on my arm. The tattoo I got a few months after things started to settle down a bit, and I was finally able to get out of bed. "I've been through some stuff, too. Not drugs, but ... personal stuff."

"I didn't tell you my shit to get all personal. You asked. I answered."

"I'm sorry. It's not an easy topic for me."

"It's okay. I get it." Stuffing her cigarette butt into the cup beside her, she blows off the last of her smoke. "Look, I wanted to ask you, I have something going on this evening. I don't want to make a big fuss and have them call in another nurse. Any chance you can keep an eye on her tonight? Just until about ten, or so?"

"What if she has a nightmare? I mean, I don't even know what to give for medications."

"Half her medications are sugar pills."

"Seriously?"

"She had a bad addiction to Valium for a while. Sometimes, there's just no reasoning with her. When she has those nightmares? It's mostly me settling her down. Haven't had to give her anything in months."

"Here I thought you guys were over-medicating her, or something."

"If we don't give her anything, she freaks the fuck out. One sugar pill?" She smacks her hands together. "She's down like it's the real deal."

"That's crazy."

"So is she. Anyway, is it cool if I sneak out a couple hours?"

"Yeah, sure."

"*If* she has a nightmare, you mostly just have to hold her

154

down, so she doesn't hurt herself. But watch yourself, too." Her lips twist with a smile. "Woman's got a nasty left hook."

"Okay."

"I'm gonna go now." Pushing up from the chair, she grabs the cup full of cigarette butts from the railing of the balcony. A day's worth, I'd bet. "If she asks where I went, tell her I had to run out to renew a script, or something. That'll make her giddy. And thanks for this," she says, before slipping back inside.

"No problem."

Shit. There are a number of things I suck at, but lying certainly takes the cake. As Nell makes her great escape, the door to what I presume is Laura's bathroom clicks, and I head back in.

"Nell, please help me to bed!"

Awkward smile plastered to my face, I enter her room and stride toward her. "Nell went to grab a script. She asked me to help you."

"She's supposed to tell me when she leaves. Suppose I had a heart attack just now. Or a stroke. Are you equipped to deal with that? Certainly not."

Definitely not, but I don't bother to tell her that would be the case whether Nell informed her, or not. Instead, I pull back the covers and steady her arm, while she scoots herself up onto the bed.

"Will you read to me, Isa?" Laura tucks the blanket around her and lies back on the pile of plush pillows behind her.

"Of course. Any requests?"

"That one." She points toward a murder mystery in the stack beside her.

I open the book, and something flutters out from the pages of it. Bending forward to grab what looks to be a photograph, I reach out and turn it over. On the other side is an image of two young boys, no more than ten, I'm guessing, standing side by side. By the color of his hair and eyes, it's clear the one on the left is Lucian. Arm wrapped around the back of Lucian's neck, the other boy wears a wily smirk on his face that makes me smile. Wet hair and sand scattered over their shirtless chests suggest they're at the beach.

"What is it you have there?" Laura asks.

I hand off the picture to her, and her eyes crinkle with the smile she gives. "Oh, look at this. My Lucian and his best friend, Jude. Ten years old in this picture, if I recall." The smile on her face withers to a frown. "Such a shame, what happened to that boy."

"What happened?"

"Ah, it was all over the news, his father being so well known. The two were playing down in a cave. Must've been about four years after this photo was taken."

"How old is Lucian now?"

"Oh, let's see." Tapping her cheek, she looks away, seems contemplative for a moment, and I wonder if she'll remember, at all. "He's going to be thirty-three in December."

Thirty-three. Strange to think that I wasn't even born when that picture was taken. "I'm sorry, go on."

"So, anyway, they liked to explore. Boys, you know. One of their favorite games was chicken. Seeing how long they could wait out the tide. Well, the tide came in fast, and they tried to swim out. It was believed Jude lost his footing on one of the rocks." The groove in her forehead deepens, and she shakes her head. "Wasn't until Lucian was safely out that he watched his friend get swept out to sea. It took a number of years to get over the death of Jude. Even as he got older, he had vivid hallucinations of him. Rand would catch him down in the cave, sometimes, talking to himself."

"Lucian had bad hallucinations?"

"The doctors called it trauma. But then I had him admitted, and they just ... stopped." Gaze cast to the side, it's like she's trying to avoid looking at me. "I don't know what they did. But it worked." The more she talks, the more troubled her expression turns. "Until it stopped working."

She shifts on the bed and tugs the blankets up higher. "On second thought, I'd rather you didn't read. I'm just going to sleep."

CHAPTER 21

LUCIAN

Fifteen years ago ...

"Lucian." At the sound of my mother's voice, I turn to find her standing alongside me. "This is Dr. Voigt. He's going to help you."

"Help?" Whatever was given to me has rendered me weak and listless, where I lie flat on my back with bright fluorescent lights blinding me. "Wh ... where am I?"

"We're in a hospital." The unfamiliar voice belonging to a man answers this time. "We treat young men and women with your afflictions."

"Affliction?"

"Sexual deviances." At the side of the bed, a tall, slim man with dark hair and spectacles stands with his hands crossed over a clipboard in front of him, and on his finger, I notice the ring. The same one my father wears.

Ice curls through my veins, and eyes wide, I shake my head.

"I don't ... belong here." Tugging at the straps on my arms is futile, as they don't seem to give, the leather biting into my skin.

"For God's sake, Lucian, you drowned." My mother opens her purse, rifling around until she pulls out a Kleenex that she lifts to her nose, and it's then I notice tears in her eyes. "You had to be revived. Don't pretend like it didn't happen. Do you have any idea what we've been through, the last couple of weeks? How this looks?"

"I wasn't trying to kill myself."

"I wish you were! Do you honestly think the alternative *sounds* better?"

Through the haze of drugs, I vaguely remember the bath. Holding my breath. Getting off. Consumed by my loss of Solange. "Mother, I was just playing around. I don't need to be admitted for this."

"Your father insisted that you be admitted here, and I pray to God they can help you. I'll not have my only son engaging in sick and disgusting acts. You're sick, Lucian. You need therapy."

"I'm not sick! Did it ever occur to you that it might've fucked me up a little seeing a dead woman?"

"That was years ago. You were just a little boy. You wouldn't have remembered."

"What are you talking about? It was a week ago! I saw her in that cave!"

"Lucian, there was no woman in that cave. Rand investigated himself. There was no woman tied to the post."

"There was! It was Solange! I know what I saw!"

"Who's Solange?" Dr. Voigt asks, tipping his head with the same curiosity I imagine he'd have for a lab rat curled over the tip of a syringe needle.

"I honestly haven't a clue what he's talking about." Lifting her chin, my mother diverts her eyes away, as if she can't stand to look at me through the lies.

"No. No, no, no. You know who she is. You know who she is!"

"Tell me, Lucian. Who is she?" Dr. Voigt's tone suggests he's humoring me. That he doesn't believe me any more than I believe my mother's bullshit right now.

"The maid!" Lifting my head from the bed, I stare at the side of her face, forcing her to look at me, to give in to whatever facade she's creating, trying to make me look crazy. "You hated her. You wouldn't spare her the slightest bit of your attention."

"We've never had a maid named Solange."

"We did." The rage inside of me festers, in spite of the drugs. My whole body trembles, my head on the verge of exploding from the tension. "And you hated her. So much, you had her killed."

When she finally sets her gaze on mine, a tear slips down her cheek. "She was a hallucination, Lucian. Just like Jude."

"No. No, no, no. She's lying. Her name was Solange, and they killed her!"

Lowering her head, my mother jerks with a sob and daubs her face with the Kleenex still clutched in her palm. "You're not well, my sweet boy. You haven't been for quite some time."

Through a shield of tears, I stare back at her, realizing there is nothing I can do to convince her. Nothing I can say to convince the doctor, who has already decided that I belong in this place. "Mother, please."

"Don't worry, Lucian." Dr. Voigt pats my leg and gives a squeeze where my ankle is also bound by restraints. "There is still time for you. Your mother did the right thing, having you admitted here. We have a one hundred percent success rate with our aversion therapy."

She still hasn't bothered to look at me, her eyes cast toward the floor. "He'll be okay, then, doctor?"

"He's in good hands, Laura. Don't worry."

"His father doesn't want anyone to know he's here."

"You can put your confidence in us. We'll keep all communications strictly through you."

"I appreciate that, Doctor. Thank you."

"And, Lucian." She stares down at me, the sadness in her eyes turning more resolute. "Don't fight them, darling. This is for your own good."

I open my eyes to see masked faces standing over me. A too-bright light bends from the ceiling, like an insect clawing its way inside the room. Nausea gurgles in my stomach. The throbbing ache at my temples is a hammer pounding into my skull.

I try to lift my arm to shield the piercing brightness, and it won't move, still bound by the leather straps of the bed. My heart beats in time to the blood rushing through my ears. "What is this?"

No one answers.

A white towel is placed over my face, and I snap my head back and forth to remove it, but something is strapped around my neck, holding it in place. Writhing and kicking is futile against the straps holding me down.

Ice cold fluids are poured over the towel, and when I gasp in shock, the saturated fabric sucks into my gaping mouth.

The air diminishes.

A sharp pain strikes my groin, and I arch on the bed, crying out. A burning snap, like a spark on my most sensitive flesh.

More fluids trickle around my face, and I shake my head back and forth on another gasp. A second zap lashes at my balls, like an electric current running over me. "Fuck!" Teeth clenched against the pain, I arch as much as the binds will allow.

The pressure at my throat loosens, and the towel is pulled away. Blurred figures stand over me, while I blink away the water dripping from my eyelashes and draw in long, agonizing breaths, my chest pounding with the need for air. Dr. Voigt stands beside a woman I've never seen before. Dark hair and almond-shaped brown eyes. Maybe Asian.

"I understand you have a fascination with water. Do you remember drowning, Lucian?"

Still trying to catch my breath, I don't bother to answer them.

Another jolt of electricity strikes my groin, and my eyes screw shut as my stomach clenches over a cramping ache. "No. I ... I remember taking a bath. And I fell asleep."

Another snap, like the strike of a whip across my nuts.

"Ah, fuck!"

"I don't think you fell asleep. There was evidence that you had ejaculated. Semen found on the tiles."

"Since when is ... jerking off ... considered a fucking crime?" The pain vibrates in my thighs and lower stomach, stirring cold nausea in my chest.

"It's not the jerking off that concerns me, Lucian." He removes his gloves, revealing the signet ring. The moth etched into steel. "It's finding out just how far you're willing to go."

"No." I shake my head, but the room disappears, blurred to a stark white behind the wet towel they place back over my face.

"No!"

CHAPTER 22

LUCIAN

Present day ...

It's not often that I venture out of the manor, but one thing I've learned from doing business with a crook: never let him see where you live. The ferry ride, plus hour and a half drive to Boston, is worth not having a scumbag like Franco Scarpinato step foot in the place where I sleep.

I sit on a bench at the end of McCorkle fishing pier, elbow kicked over the back, as I watch a young kid eyeing me. Beside him, an older guy, I'm guessing his father, hooks a worm on a fishing pole, holding it up in as if instruction, but the kid seems too focused on me to care.

The scars on my face tend to scare the younger ones, but the unwavering stare of this kid has me wondering what he's seen, so much worse that he can look a monster square in the eyes without flinching.

I tug my cigarettes from my pocket, and that's when his father grabs him by the jaw, giving a hard jerk toward the hook. The kid keeps his head cocked where his dad put it, only sliding his eyes toward me when the asshole goes back to baiting the line.

I light my smoke, thinking back to the one time my father took me on a chartered fishing trip, miles out from shore. The idea of floating out on the open sea with him was unsettling enough, but when I saw the liquor he packed away for the excursion, I wondered if it was worth the risk of him calling me a pansy for backing out. At no point was any part of the trip what I'd consider to be a happy memory, but there was a single moment, before he got too drunk, when he set his hand on my shoulder. He was introducing me to the captain of the boat, and for a fleeting second, I felt like any other son accompanying his father.

An hour later, the same hand that'd rested on my shoulder pushed me with enough force to knock me over the edge, into the water. He'd gotten trashed and belligerent, and it took three crew members to pull me aboard, while my father sobbed in the galley of the boat.

As I bobbed in the ice-cold waters with whatever the hell swam below the surface, my lifejacket tight around my throat, all I could think about was how good it felt to scare the shit out of him for once.

"You had to pick the last fucking bench on this pier, didn't you?" Franco's voice reminds me of something out of *Goodfellas*, a wanna-be mafioso who just didn't make the cut. Our family lines go way back to the days when my great-grandfather bootlegged liquor for his great-grandfather. Not that we grew up together. My father never trusted the Scarpinatos enough for family barbecues and other recreations. He kept everything business. Smart, considering they were affiliated with the Boston faction of the New England Mafia.

At five-foot-five, Franco doesn't seem like much of a threat, but considering his connections, he isn't someone to piss off, either.

Unfortunately for him, I never really had what I'd call a healthy appreciation for the line that separates life from death, so I anticipate this meeting to go over like a porno mag at a Catholic school. Makaio waits within shooting distance, and Rand sits alongside him, probably ready to respectfully chide my ass when he finds out what actually went down. I'm not stupid enough to come alone, despite sitting here by myself.

"Thought it'd be quiet out here," I say.

Franco plops down at the other end of the bench, lights up his own cigarette, and looks around the pier, no doubt gauging the proximity of ears that might be listening. "Sorry I'm late. Got some shit going down with one of my distributors who skipped town with about fifty grand worth of product."

"Sounds like a management issue."

"I had a bad feeling about this kid, but he was buddies with my best guy. Who'd have fuckin' thought? Just goes to show, you can't put in a good word for anyone these days." Leaning forward and resting his elbows on his knees, he flicks his ash onto the deck. "So, we got a shipment coming in. Big. Over a mil, direct from Columbia. Your guy told me they loaded it on a container two days ago."

For the last few years, his family has relied on my father's shipping company to bring in pallets of cocaine straight out of South America, by offloading a few miles offshore and having local fishing fleets deliver and, in some cases, distribute the drugs, while offering a modest cut for our troubles. It's a system that has existed below the radar, fortunately, but I believe a man's luck only lasts so long.

I turn my attention toward the kid again, who stands holding the fishing line at the railing of the pier. Arms crossed, his father stands beside him, shaking his head like the kid's doing something wrong. "This is the last job I'm running for you, Franco. I want you to let your uncle know."

"What?"

On a sigh, I turn to face him and take another drag of my smoke. "You'll have to find another company to run your shipments."

With the usual Scarpinato theatrics, he throws himself back against the seat, then leans forward again, tossing his cigarette to the ground. "Are you fucking kidding me? Do you even realize what you're saying right now?" Holding up a finger, he shakes his head when I open my mouth to answer. "I'll give you a minute, because I think this fucking fresh air is messing with your brain."

"I know exactly what I'm doing. You're to find another company."

"That's not the way it works, Lucian. We've been partners a long time. You can't just back out."

I stretch my arms across the top of the bench and look out at the water. "It's a big ocean, Franco. I'd hate for a million-dollars-worth of cocaine to get lost at the bottom of the sea somewhere."

He shoots up off the bench. "Are you fucking nuts?"

As I turn to look up at him, the sun hits my face, and I'm forced to squint. "Depends on who you ask."

"My uncle isn't going to let you just walk away. As someone who's known you a long time, I'm urging you to reconsider."

"And I'm urging you to lower your voice."

He looks around, as if he's suddenly aware of the man and his son standing off from us. "This is big, Lucian. Bigger than you realize. You fuck with my family's livelihood, it's not going to end well for you."

"I'm not out to fuck with your family's livelihood. It's no longer worth it to me."

Plopping back down on the bench, he moves in closer. Too close. Asshole is about one hard shove from my personal space.

"We'll talk about a bigger cut. Is that what you want? More money?"

"No. I told you what I want. I'll deliver this shipment, as promised. And we'll part ways. Amicably. Seeing as we've known each other a long time, that's not too much to ask, is it?"

Groaning, he strokes his hands over his head, like he intends to rub the hair right off his skull. "Look. I can't go back to my uncle with this. He's going to go ape-shit, and your face will be on every hitman's shit-list in Boston."

"Is that a threat?"

"It's a fact."

I slide my arms down from the bench and rest them on my thighs as I lean in closer. "Well, since we're sharing facts, let me offer one, as well. I have more money than the entire New England Mafia combined. Certainly more than your scrappy ass. If you even think of retaliating against me, know that I will seek out the most skilled hitmen in the world to hunt down every one of your family members, *and* your henchmen, and have your heads mounted on stakes as a lesson for why you should never fucking cross a Blackthorne again."

Shaking his head, he backs away, eyes wide with what I surmise as disbelief and perhaps a small bit of fear. "You really are the Mad Son, you know that? You're fucking crazy."

"As I said before, Franco. Depends on who you ask."

R and stares out the window, as Makaio drives along I-93, heading back toward the Manor. He hasn't said a word since we left Boston. Not that he would. If anyone knows how crazy I am, it's him.

"You believe it was foolish of me to cut ties."

Clearing his throat, he drags his attention from the window, but doesn't bother to meet my gaze. "Reckless perhaps, but not foolish."

"If I'm to run this company, this mess my father left me, the days of financing criminals are over."

"I understand. I just wish … you would have consulted me. I feel useless in these matters, Lucian." The gulp of his throat betrays his boldness.

I respect his honesty, though.

"You'd have told me not to do it. Just as you advised my father to stay connected with them all these years."

"For his own protection. Not because I agreed with the arrangement."

"Look at my face. Look at me."

He lifts his chin in the same indignant manner of a scorned puppy.

"Do I look like a man who has anything left to fear? I've lost a wife and my only son. There isn't a man who can look me in the eyes without flinching. If they decide to retaliate, I've got nothing to lose."

"With all due respect, Master, your decisions affect more than just yourself. They affect all of us. I don't have access to the kinds of funds it would take to protect myself against a family like the Scarpinatos."

Leaning back against the seat, I stare out the window at the green blur of trees that pass on the highway. "They're not stupid. I expect they'll try to negotiate."

"To which I expect you'll decline."

"Of course. In the meantime, Franco is anticipating a shipment this week, worth over a million. I want it dumped offshore, watertight containers, far enough that their fleets can't sweep for it. We'll hang onto it for a bit, and when they realize how crippling it would be to lose it altogether, I suspect they'll play nice."

"I wasn't aware of this shipment."

"Neither was I. Your second task this week is to find out who dropped the ball and can his ass."

"I'll look into the matter, Master."

"Good. In the meantime, don't worry about Franco Scarpinato. He's my problem. And I don't let problems fester for long."

CHAPTER 23

ISADORA

The sliver of the moon is high, and a slight chill on the air ruffles the thin fabric of my shirt, as I sit out on the balcony, keeping an eye out for Nell. She should've been back an hour ago, and I feel like every second that ticks off in between is one second closer to Laura's next nightmare. The last thing I need is to have Lucian storming down here in search of the nurse who skipped off to do God knows what. There's no way I can lie to a man like that.

A man who'd see right through me.

All my life, I've constructed walls to protect myself from a world that has no regard for boundaries. Some have 'dozed their way past my barriers with little care. But never has a man seen through them, as if they're translucent.

The sound of yelling steels my muscles, and I freeze in my chair, until it occurs to me that the voice belongs to a man, not Mrs. Blackthorne. Reaching me from somewhere above.

Pushing up from my chair, I lean over the railing of the balcony, craning my neck toward the roof of the turret, and Lucian's office above.

My heart skids to a stop, and a gasp flies from my mouth.

With trembling hands, I attempt to reach out, but draw them to my face in shock.

Balanced on the edge of the parapet, Lucian sways with a drink in his hand, shouting obscenities that are so slurred, I can't even entirely make out what the hell he's saying.

To avoid startling him, I don't bother to call to him, and instead scamper inside, making a beeline toward the elevator.

"Fuck!" Halfway there, I stall and turn around, hustling back toward the balcony to close and lock the door so Laura won't escape, before darting around to the elevator again.

Oh, God, please don't jump. If I get to the damn roof and find him lying in a pool of blood on the ground below, I'll probably end up in a psych ward after.

My finger jabs the *up* button, my whole body shaking with adrenaline, while I wait for the goddamn car to slide to a stop and open its doors. Once inside, I press the third button, and when the doors finally open again, I glance around the dark office, hardly taking in much of the surroundings, and find a door at the opposite side of the room. I don't even know if it leads to the roof, but I head toward it anyway.

Another quick sprint through the door and up a flight of stairs brings me to the flat roof of the turret. Ahead of me, Lucian stands with his back to me, his black suit in disarray, the coat falling off one shoulder.

Careful, so as not to startle him, I tiptoe closer.

"N'body fuckin' threatens a Blackthorne. Isn'at what you said t'me? Fuckin' lyin' prick." Bottle of liquor in hand, he attempts to balance himself as he sets the mouth of the bottle to his glass like he's trying to fill it. A small bit trickles over the edge of the glass, and he chucks it off the roof, tipping back the bottle, instead.

My heart is beating so fast I can scarcely draw in a breath, watching him teeter on the edge. Approaching him might make him stumble, though.

"I wanted t'be free of this shit. B'you … y'had one more

punishment t'dole out, didn' you? One more fuckin' hell f'me t'walk through."

I quietly clear my throat and step closer. "Mr. Blackthorne?"

His arm flies out as he spins to face me, and he loses his footing just enough that I reach out on a wheeze of breath, before he catches himself.

Holy shit, that was close!

Balanced again, he stares at me for a moment, his eyes dark and appraising, and I can't even begin to imagine what thoughts are running through his head. "Isa. *Isa Bella.*" Snorting a laugh, he chugs his drink again. "The fuck're you doin' up here?"

"I heard you yelling. Look, whatever is going on right now, you don't have to do this."

Brows crinkled to an incredulous frown, he chuckles, and in spite of the fear thrumming inside my veins, the low-pitched sound is a brief distraction. I hate that I like the sound of his amusement, even if it's meant to mock me. "I'm no coward. I'm Lucian. Fucking. Blackthorne. I make shit happen. People cower t'me."

"I know. I know that."

"Y'know that." His voice is tinged in disbelief, and he licks his lips, his gaze raking over me in disdain. "What things d'you know, Isa *Bella?*"

"Well, for one ... I know that ... alcohol and heights don't mix."

His lips stretch to an incredibly dashing smile, despite his scars, and he rubs his eye on the back of his bottle-toting hand, swaying unsteadily. A long moan, like the end of a laugh, spills from his lips, just before his tongue sweeps over them. "'S'how I get off. Bad decisions like this."

"You're saying that standing at the precipice of death is arousing to you?"

"Oh, yeah." A long blink, and his bottom lip slips between his teeth. "What'd'you know, anyway? You're young. Excessively beau'ful. Men probably pay you t'fuck. Not th'other way 'round."

A flare of embarrassment heats my cheeks, the conversation taking an uncomfortable turn. "No … that's prostitution … and I don't consider that good reason to tempt death."

"Fucking?"

"There's more to life."

"Well …" He lifts the bottle for another sip and pauses halfway to his mouth. "Then, you haven' been fucked properly."

Another blast of humiliation burns beneath my skin. I try to ignore the clench of my thighs, or the truth in his words, coming from an older man who's probably had far more practice with countless women. I've been used, mostly, and nothing more. "Can you …. Can you come down from there now? You're making me nervous."

"Wha're you afraid'f?"

"Oh, I don't know … that you might die in front of me tonight?"

Staring down his nose at me, he seems to chew on the inside of his lip. "That'd bother you?"

"Yes. Very much."

Huffing, he sways again, craning his neck to look back over the edge, toward what I'm certain would be instant death below. "I know why you'really here. Y'came t'haunt me, haven' you?"

"What do you mean?"

He turns his attention back on me. "The bird. When I was jus'a kid. I hurt it. Now you're here. Raven beauty. T'get me back for what I did. My curse."

The words make no sense, nothing but drunken rambling, but his eyes implore me. "I don't know what that means," I whisper. "Please. Just come down."

A long blink, and he chuckles again. "Fine. You win." The second he steps forward, he loses his footing.

His body slips behind the parapet.

My heart seizes in my chest, but I rush forward.

Over the edge of the building, he dangles from the parapet,

held only by his arms. His bottle of liquor lies in a scatter of broken glass on the ground below him. Muscles tremble and stretch as he holds himself from falling.

"Mr. Blackthorne!" I kneel down to put most of my weight on one side, and lean against the wall to reach over the edge. "Take my hand."

The guy probably weighs twice as much as I do, but I don't care. Watching him fall to the cement below is a sight that would stay with me for the rest of my life.

"Take my hand, Lucian."

Still holding onto the edge with one hand, he hoists himself enough to clutch my arm, and I grasp onto him with both hands, straining and flexing to keep him from slipping.

"If this ain't some shit karma." He chuckles again, slipping enough to yank me forward until my breasts are pressed into the stone wall.

"Somebody, help! Help us! Makaio!"

"Makaio can't hear you. He's on th'other side of th'castle."

"Rand!"

"Rand, too."

"Jesus Christ, somebody help!"

"Stop yellin', girl. Fuck." Jaw hardening with the effort, he pushes himself up, perhaps exerting most of the pressure on the hand clutched to the parapet. Still, I brace myself on the wall of the roof and tug him until my muscles are weak with the effort. My wrists burn where he grips my skin, but once his shoulders breach the edge, I slide my hands beneath his armpits and drag him toward me.

"Don't slip, Lucian. Use your legs!"

Every muscle in my body is both hot and cold with the toil, until his entire upper half is finally on my side of the wall, and he drops down. The gravelly bed crashes into my spine, and his big body topples onto mine, held up by his massive arms planted at either side of me.

In the pause that follows, I pant to catch my breath and look up to see him staring down at me, his eyes dilated, swirling with the excitement of a wily cat, before they shift toward my lips.

"Say my name again," he whispers, eyes riveted on my mouth.

"Lucian."

Stiff and paralyzed beneath him, I watch as his gaze leads his body closer, and he lowers himself, until the first gentle brush of his lips feathers across mine. The scent of him is an intoxicating mix of liquor and cologne, his breath a sweet whiskey that waters my mouth for a taste.

His tongue circles my parted lips, as if he's sampling me, and my stomach clenches with the contact.

My heart is pounding so hard inside my chest right now, it's a wonder he doesn't hear it.

My boss, the Devil himself, the wealthiest, most reclusive man on this island. And he's kissing me. Muscles still trembling, I try to calm my breathing, as the air stutters through my nose on each shaky exhale.

He slants his face over mine, his tongue dipping past my teeth, deepening the kiss. Nothing like the sloppy, gagging tongue-dives of boys my age. Expert and unrushed, his maturity shines through in his focus and attention. I feel so juvenile and inexperienced with this man who's clearly perfected the art of the French kiss.

Air expels from his nose on a groan, and he presses me harder into the gravel, but I don't care. I taste everything pouring out of him, into me--the desperation, the sadness, the loneliness. His kiss speaks to me beyond the slurs of his drunkenness from moments before.

It tastes of whiskey and longing.

A whimper escapes me. I've never been kissed this way before in my life. Boys have taken from me, stolen kisses in teasing and play, but never with so much passion as this. I want to consume it all, commit every second to memory, so I'll never accept anything less again.

The weight of his body presses down on me, trapping me beneath him as his kiss turns aggressive. Forceful. The moan from his throat vibrates in mine, making me dizzy with want. A warm, strong hand slides up the edge of my body, beneath my shirt, and I gasp in his mouth when his fingertips reach the edge of my breast.

He breaks away from me, his hand sliding back down to plant on the ground beside me. Flickers of remorse or shame, I can't tell, are punctuated by the stern pinch of his brows. The mask of his drunken stupor lifting to the sobering reality beneath it all.

"Lucian?" I reach up to cup his face, and he pushes off me, falling backward against the wall behind him. Sitting up from the ground across from him, I watch him silently chide himself through the shocked and disgusted expression on his face.

I don't know what's worse: the way he looks right now, brimming with regret, or the arrogant smirks the boys in school used to wear when they were finished with me.

The thought of them leaves me frowning, as well.

"I'm sorry." Lucian's voice draws my thoughts back to him, where he's slouched with his shirt opened, his tie undone, clutching his skull with one hand. Completely disheveled and tormented.

"You regret kissing me?"

"I regret wanting to. It was wrong."

Wrong. Wrong to kiss me.

No. I won't let him cheapen the moment and turn me into some kind of mistake.

"Maybe for you."

His gaze slices to mine, the darkness in his eyes burning with intensity, but he doesn't reveal whatever is spinning inside his head. There's something sinister there, regardless of his apology. Something devilish. Dangerous. A duality that exists within him, like two personalities trapped in one body, both vying for control. I felt it when he kissed me, the shift from desolation to aggression, ferocity, an animal waking from its slumber.

Starving for something.

Clambering to my feet, I hold his stare and back myself to the door. Perhaps it's not regret that he feels in this moment, but the realization that I got a small peek of the man he hides beneath his business suits and indifference. I just had a taste of the passionate man underneath those scars. One who'd probably never admit that he makes love harder than most.

In fact, I'm pretty sure he just bared his soul in a single kiss.

"Goodnight, Mr. Blackthorne."

～

*C*ool satin sheets slide over my legs as I writhe across the bed, my view trapped behind the pitch blackness of a blindfold. Soft, silky bands tighten at my wrists, when I tug my arms to no avail, while quiet, indiscernible whispers of a man fill my head, as if spoken in another language. A palm slides over top of the sheets, and the sensitive tickle at my thigh, only dulled by the thin barrier, tells me I'm naked beneath.

"Please." Exhaustion weighs heavy on my voice while I plead with my captor. "Let me go."

"Shhh, Isa Bella." The deep timbre of Lucian's voice skims across my skin like a feather, and I shiver, dizzy with the sensation. "I'm afraid that's not possible."

"Why are you doing this?"

"We want to watch."

"We?"

The veil over my eyes is lifted, and I glance to the side, catching sight of my arm tethered to the bed by silk ties. Lucian stands alongside me in my room, wearing a half-buttoned white shirt, and he brushes his knuckles over my cheek.

A hand glides across my belly, and I look to my right. Lying beside me is a second Lucian, this one wearing a black shirt, his hands rough, demanding, as they slip beneath the sheets.

I snap my attention back to the first Lucian, who leans in for a gentle kiss along my jaw.

"You belong to both of us, Isa."

A finger travels down between my thighs, over the sensitive cleft there, and I arch up, pulling my knees together.

"Relax, Isa," the gentle Lucian breathes. "Don't fight him."

My knees are pried apart, and the Lucian beside me settles closer, keeping my leg tucked against him. "He's going to make love to you, Isa. But I'm going to fuck you." His jaw hardens at the same time that he thrusts his fingers hard up inside of me.

I shoot upright on a gasp, fingers curled tight around the bedsheets that I hold to my chest. Quick pants of breath fail to fill my lungs. I search my surroundings for the two of them, finding only the curtain softly fluttering across from me in the otherwise still room.

Sliding my hand beneath the pillow, I prod the pocketknife there, the cold metal a comfort against my fingertips, and exhale a long breath.

I raise a trembling hand to my forehead, mentally noting none of my limbs are tied down, and pat down my chest and legs to find my sweats and T-shirt from earlier in the night are still in place.

"Just a dream," I murmur, resting my forehead against the heel of my palm to catch my breath.

As my heart rate settles, I touch my fingers to my lips, recalling his kiss from earlier. When I returned to Laura's room, and Nell finally arrived, I swore Lucian's scent was embedded in my clothes, that forbidden kiss written all over my face for her to call me out. Even now, I can still feel his skin on mine, the warmth of his breath. The flavor. A small chiding voice inside my head says it was wrong to let him kiss me like that. An older man. My boss, no less.

As if I had a choice!

That same voice tells me to forget the kiss, it was nothing but a drunken mistake. Forget him and go back to sleep. Except, that voice isn't mine. It belongs to my aunt and everyone else who thinks they know what's best for me.

I can't forget the kiss that's now permanently seared within me. And even if I never get the opportunity to kiss Lucian again, I'll never forget how wonderful it felt.

At a cracking sound, like the shifting of walls, I startle out of those musings and scramble for the lamp beside me, switching it on to find nothing there.

But I know there's something there. I can feel it.

Something about this place slips beneath my skin when I'm not looking. It's subtle, but ever present, easily mistaken for a fine stray hair, or a thin web. A tickle of imagination that toys with me every time I close my eyes. The same peculiar feeling I get when I'm around Lucian.

Lucian.

Visuals of those pale amber eyes drilling into mine as he stared down at me earlier, an infernal promise of wicked pleasures, cast a shiver down my spine. I don't know why I find the man so darkly intriguing in a way that draws my curiosity like nothing else. The same curiosity that lures me into dreams that are as delusional as the shadows crawling about the room each time I wake, shaken and unsettled. Questioning my sanity.

Maybe that's the reason they call him the Devil.

Because the madness that breathes within these walls is as real as the man who feeds it.

CHAPTER 24

LUCIAN

Fifteen years ago ...

I find comfort in darkness. The only place they can't see me. In the light, I'm bare, naked, exposed, but here, nothing can touch me. I'm invisible. A silent observer.

Knees bent to my chest, I sit in the corner of my room, staring through the window at the moon. Three weeks ago, I was lying strapped to a bed, with no idea whether it was day, or night. There was only light and darkness, and in the darkness, I found peace.

Where I stayed for all those weeks was no hospital. The place where my mother discarded me like a bag of old, unwanted clothes was a farce. A lie.

It looked like a hospital. Smelled like one. Was cold, and reeked like suffering. But beneath all the sterile veneer and medical equipment was something sinister and wrong. Something designed to slip inside my skull and rearrange the synaptic connections inside my head. To take what I learned to perceive as thrilling and exciting, and turn it into something I fear. Something I associate with pain and loathing. Panic.

Only problem is, none of the so-called doctors who attempted to cure me have ever really walked the line between life and death. If they had, they'd know panic and fear doesn't exist there.

The buzz of an insect tickles my ear, and I bat it away. It flies past again, the vibrating hum louder than before, and I flinch. The hum turns to hissing. The incessant hiss of the moths in their cages. So loud. I slam my palms against my ears, screwing my eyes shut to block it out.

The squealing intensifies turning to screams. They're screaming. High-pitched torment raking through my eardrums.

I open my mouth to call for help, but I can't. If I do, they'll think I'm not well again and send me back.

"Stop," I whisper. "Please stop."

The hisses die down inside my head as I imagine the black moths settling back to the corner of their cages. I open my eyes in search of them, certain they're here with me, while I breathe through my nose to calm the rapid thrumming of my pulse.

There's nothing but darkness—until the door clicks, and the light from the hallway slices into my room.

My father's silhouette fills the space, where he stands half in and out the door. "Feeling better?"

Of course not. I've had things done to me that will never leave my head, all in some grand scheme to reprogram my brain. To make me forget Solange and everything she taught me.

I don't tell my father this, just shrug and nod. "Getting better."

"Good. I want you to come with me."

There was a time those words terrified me, but I've since grown numb to things like that. Words. As many times as he's punished and humiliated me, they can't compare to the pain that has now become a permanent part of me. A layer of flesh on the outside that I won't let penetrate my skin. Instead, I stay anes-thetized to it all, and it's as if it never happened.

I follow my father to the elevator, where he uses his ring as a key to access the catacombs. We arrive at the door of the same room he took me to before, only when we step inside, my guts twist on finding two men waiting for us.

One, I've never seen before. He lies strapped to the dentist-looking chair, his eyes blindfolded, body stripped down to nothing but his boxers and socks. I guess him to be late forties, or fifties, judging by his salt-and-pepper hair.

The sight of the other man sends a tremble through my body, and every muscle tenses up when my father nudges me toward Dr. Voigt.

"I've told you of our study, Lucian. Now you've met the good doctor. He's the leader of Schadenfreude. A highly respected expert on the topic of epigenetics."

The familiar man's lips stretch with a smile, and he opens his arms as if to welcome me. Only weeks ago, he wouldn't spare me so much as a simple explanation for the torment he put me through, treating me like nothing but a lab-rat, but now, it's as if the bastard is happy to see me.

"Ah, Lucian, my boy. You're looking healthier."

Healthier? I've not had the energy, nor inclination, to do anything more than stay in my room all hours of the day.

"The pain you've suffered will carry with you into the next phase of our studies," he adds, clasping his hands together as if this is exciting news for him.

"Next phase?" Gaze flitting toward the man on the table, I notice the quiver of his arms that rattle the metal fasteners of his restraints. It wasn't long ago that I was strapped down like him, uncertain of what I'd be forced to face that day. What torments the 'doctors' and 'nurses' would inflict.

"This is Robert Tackas." Dr. Voigt stands behind the headrest, looking down on the man. "Tell us why you sought out the collective, Robert."

His tongue sweeps over dry, cracked lips, and his Adam's apple bobs with a swallow. "I, um … have debts. I need cash, or I'm going to lose … my home." Mouth quivering, he's obviously trying to hold back tears, but the wobble in his voice betrays him. "My family."

"We've agreed to pay him the sum of money he's requested at the end of his session today. With it, he will be able to pay his mortgage, buy food for his family, get back on track."

"What session?"

Dr. Voigt lifts his chin while staring down at me, and the urge to turn away from him throttles my courage and tells me to cower. But this is my home. In spite of the fear hammering through me, I hold his stare, as he backs himself to the wall behind him. With a quick glance over his shoulder, he grabs one of the objects from the wall: a long stick with leather, knotted braids spilling from the tip of it. I recognize this tool as one of many he used on me in my time at the institute. A flinch of my eye echoes the memory of those braids cracking against my skin, bruising my very bones.

Striding back toward us, he runs his fingers through the braids and smiles.

"Cat o' nine. Nine braids, nine lives. Do you know how it gets its name?" Allowing only a brief pause, he continues, "Egyptians believed that when beaten with cat hide, a victim gained virtue from the whip." He shoves the object into my chest, and with a frown, I shake my head. "Your father thought this might be a good opportunity for you to learn our ways."

"What ways?"

He jerks his head toward Robert. "Fifty lashes. As hard as you can."

"No." Looking back at my father only weakens my resolve, as the man stares down at me, his lips peeled back with disgust.

"I'd hate to think you've grown soft since our therapy sessions, Lucian. You know firsthand what this whip feels like against your flesh. You survived."

"With not even half the lashes." My gaze flits to Robert, who seems to tremble even more, and back to Dr. Voigt. I remember every strike that came down against my skin. The way it bruised and cut into me. "I won't do this."

"We've watched you over the years. Every fistfight at school. Every expulsion afterward. You bear this inner battle between good and evil, but what if this is your calling, Lucian? What if you are genetically *primed* for this behavior?"

"Every fight was self-defense. I don't go out of my way to hurt others. I won't."

Dr. Voigt's lips flatten, and he sets a hand on Robert's bare shoulders, causing the man to twitch at his touch. "I'm sorry, my friend. We can't help you."

The man shifts as if his body is suddenly possessed by panic. "Please. I'm begging you. Please do this. I need the money. My family needs this money."

A snaking sensation crawls beneath my skin as I listen to the man plead for his punishment. Like I'm the bad guy, all of a sudden, for not wanting to dole it out. I frown down at him, my head swimming in confusion, right and wrong clashing inside my skull.

"It's disgusting, isn't it? How we're willing to suffer for something so common as the paper and the ink that separates the wealthy from the poor. You wouldn't know that feeling, Lucian. From birth, you were born into wealth. You know nothing but comfort and security. You've never known hunger. What it feels like to do whatever it takes to feed your starving family."

"Why not just give him the money, then?"

"Do you have any idea how many of them come to us? Begging for mercy. A handout? What makes him any more deserving than the others?" He rubs his hands over the man's shoulders. "This way, we get something in return, at least."

"By torturing him?"

"This is a study. One rooted in science. Evolution. He's merely a catalyst. A variable to test."

"He's a human being."

"Who came to us. We didn't seek him out. He was well-informed of who we are and what we do."

"Enough of this! You will do as you're told, or by God, I'll throw your ass back into that institute for another week." My father's voice thunders behind me, skating down my spine. "I'll not stand by and--"

Dr. Voigt holds his hand up, silencing my father, and for a moment, I wonder if Griffin Blackthorne will strike out at him, the way he does to anyone who threatens his pride. Instead, he lowers his head.

"The boy chooses for himself," Dr. Voigt says. "Dole out this man's punishment, and we'll pay him what he's asked for. He'll walk away with more money than he earns in a year. Or tell him you refuse."

The man's jaw quivers, as if he wants to cry, but I won't do it. My choice. I won't let them turn me into a monster.

"I refuse."

Two days have passed, and my father has made a point to avoid me. He hasn't punished me for what I'm certain he views as insolence. It's as if I don't exist, at all.

Until today.

I sit in one of the chairs across from his desk, hands in my lap so he won't see my fidgeting.

Across from me, he holds a rolled-up newspaper, tapping it

against the top of his desk, as if in taunting, while he stares back at me.

I wonder if he'll strike me with the thing.

In answer to my thoughts, he tosses the paper in front of me, and it flips open to the front page, where a headline reads: *Boston Man Dies Horrifically After He Throws Himself From Overpass Onto Busy Traffic.*

Nausea gurgles in my stomach when I catch sight of Robert Tackas' name in the body of the article.

"Tell me, what do you think would've resulted in less suffering?" My father's taunting words only twist the blade stabbing at my conscience.

"It's not my fault."

"Not your fault? Imagine if he'd walked out of here with the money he requested?"

"I won't let you blame me for this."

"I don't have to. You blame yourself. It's written all over your face."

Tears spring to my eyes, the anger and guilt pulling and stretching, growing inside of me. "You could've given him the money."

"Nothing is free, Lucian. Nothing. Including you." He pushes up from his desk, and maybe it's just the shadows behind him, but he seems larger than usual. More intimidating. As he rounds the desk, my pulse hastens, my hands balling to fists, waiting for the moment I'll have to defend myself. "This world is made up of strong and weak. It's believed that nature decides who thrives and who perishes, based on certain genetics we're bestowed with at birth. But that isn't true. Your great-grandfather, and his father before him, were starving fishermen. Men who couldn't afford to feed their families. By all accounts, he should've perished with the weak. In suffering, in pain, he found strength, and that strength changed his fate." He reaches for a half-smoked cigar balanced on the edge of an ashtray and lights it up. "One day, this company will be in your hands. And I fear it will perish there. Generations of work and toil--"

"I don't want it."

"Excuse me?"

"I don't want your company, or your secret group. I want out."

His eye twitches as he stares down at me in a brief moment of silence. "And what will you do with your life, Lucian? Play music?" At the derision and mocking in his voice, I grind my teeth, and he chuckles. "There are thousands upon thousands of musicians in the world. There is, however, only one successful shipping company in this entire country. Built by sweat and sacrifice."

"And blood. Blood of innocent people. How many have you killed to stay on top, Father?"

"As many as it takes." He tips his head as if studying me. Always trying to figure out what I'm thinking. "Fucks sake, no son of mine is going to play *piano* for a living. You may as well have studied ballet all these years. It's only by the grace of God that you excelled in sports, the way you did."

Grace of God? I busted my ass. Trained hard. Never missed a practice, and went on to set records for the state. But only *by the grace of God*, it seems.

"You will take over this company. You will take your place in Schadenfreude. Or I will--"

"Kill me? Like you killed *her?*"

"Who?"

"You know exactly who I'm talking about. I *saw* her. In the cave. Dead. I saw you fucking her."

His lips form the malevolent smile of a man who doesn't care that he's been caught. "The pedophile? The one who liked playing with little boys? Yes. I fucked her. And then I got rid of her."

Unbidden flashes of memory flicker through my head like a sketchy dream.

A beautiful woman. Long dark hair. Her hands between my thighs.

Similar to Solange, but perhaps not as exotic, like a watered down version of her.

"You were just a boy when we hired her to be your nanny. Six years old. Your mother was suspicious of anyone who spent excessive amounts of time with you, so we installed cameras throughout the manor." His voice gives narration to the rapid succession of images still slipping through my mind. "It started with fondling. In the bathtub, mostly. She would touch you. Harmless, mostly. Your mother ... she was always so protective, but with Monique, even more so."

Monique. *Miss Monique.* At the sound of her name, more images erupt inside my head.

Giggles. Soft caresses. Tickles and the chasing knots in my stomach.

"Your mother insisted we get rid of her." Eyes on me, he puffs his cigar. "So I did."

Memories spin and tumble in my brain, jumbling into a mish-mash of something that doesn't make sense. "You're lying. The woman you killed was Solange."

"According to Friedrich, this Solange you keep going on about is the result of the trauma you suffered after the death of Jude and the abuse of your nanny. A hallucination."

I didn't imagine her. I couldn't have. She was real. What she did to me was real. I felt everything. I shake my head, but even as I prepare to argue with him, flickering images pass behind my eyes. My mother never acknowledging Solange in the room. The staff giving me strange looks as we'd stroll by together. The way she'd disappear from the castle for days, and show up only when I was upset, or stressed.

No. I couldn't have imagined her. How could I have imagined something that felt so real?

"I won't let you make me out to be crazy. So, you can throw me back into that place. It wasn't a hospital!"

"It's the institute where we meet. A number of studies are

carried out there, but Freidrich thought you might be more comfortable having your first session here."

"They fucking tortured me there!"

"Friedrich wanted to study the nature of your hallucinations. To see how they might affect what we're trying to accomplish. Through these delusions, you put yourself at risk, many times over. Killing yourself accomplishes nothing, Lucian. It proves nothing."

"I wasn't trying to kill myself."

"As we soon learned. You've developed masochistic tendencies." He shrugs and rolls his cigar between his fingers. "Nothing to be ashamed of. I had them myself, though not as dangerous as yours."

"I want out of this study."

"I'm afraid that's not possible." He puffs his cigar again, twisting it around to show the bright orange glow at the other end of it. "The only way out is death."

The percolating anger inside of me explodes, and I push up from my chair. Refusing to listen to another word, I make a mad dash toward the door.

"Lucian!" My father calls from behind, but I run from his office, knocking into Rand on the way.

"Lucian, where are you going?"

I sprint through the foyer, and out the front door. Across the yard and into the woods. Bracken and twigs on the ground gouge the soles of my feet, scratching and scraping at my legs. A light, evening breeze cools the sweat gathered on my exposed skin. It isn't long before the trees give way to a small clearing and the cliff in the distance. I run faster toward it.

The sound of waves crashing below sing like a dirge over the hurricane of thoughts spinning inside my head.

Solange. She wasn't real. She never was. I'm crazy. I imagined her, and only crazy people imagine shit like that. My mother was right. I'm sick. I'm so sick. How does someone imagine a whole person, doing the things she did to me?

Skidding to a halt, I stare down at the dark waters a hundred feet below me. The moon highlights the crest of the waves that crash against the rock. My heart pounds inside my chest. The air thins.

I jump.

A tickle in my stomach explodes with panic.

Nothing flashes before my eyes except the world slipping past at a dizzying speed.

A cold sting smacks my skin, pressure crushing my chest as I plunge into the sea. Ice cold water embraces me, drawing me deeper, toward the bottom. Into the darkness below.

I'm still alive.

I'm still alive.

I kick away from the pull. My muscles burn while I climb the slippery liquid wall all around me. Lungs pulsing with the need for air, I propel myself upward, until I breach the surface.

The cliff stands off in the distance, while the sea carries me further away. With fatigue weighing heavy on me, I push forward and swim toward the shore at the opposite side of the rock.

It must take a good twenty minutes of fighting the water, the lack of air, the muscles that long to give out on me. By the time the shallow bed of sand hits my feet, I can hardly stand.

A shudder of bone-chilling cold shakes my body, my teeth chattering, jaw sore and aching from tension and stiffness. Collapsing to my knees, I crawl against the tug of the waves, until the heel of my hand hits dry sand, and turning over onto my back, I lie staring up at the starry sky and the moon, weak and panting for breath.

I'm alive.

I mentally replay the moment I leapt from that cliff without a single thought of consequence. If I'd died, or lived, didn't matter to me. All that mattered was the exquisite rush of fear and recklessness that burned inside of me. A paradox of racing toward death in order to feel alive.

A burst of laughter tears through my already taxed chest at the thought.

My body hardens, and I slip my hand down inside my sodden pants where my dick stands at full mast.

A few quick pumps, and I come harder than I ever have before.

CHAPTER 25

ISADORA

Present day ...

I t's hard to believe a week has passed already, and as I make my way toward the sleek black vehicle parked in the drive-way, with the tall, beefy guy I've come to learn is Makaio standing beside it, I can't help but feel a little sadness at having to leave for the weekend.

At the same time, I probably need a break from this place.

I glance back at where a figure stands in the window of Lucian's office. They turn away, out of view, disappearing into the room beyond.

Him, no doubt. He's avoided me since the night in his office. Not that I've seen much of him, at all, in the last couple of days. Mostly moments like these, when I catch him staring at me, just before he walks away.

Maybe I should regret that kiss, too, but I can't. Even now, the phantom sensation of his lips against mine still lingers on my skin. The bitter taste of whiskey. The heat of his breath mingling with mine.

Makaio opens the door to the back passenger seat, his lips only halfcocked in a smile.

"Thank you," I say, and pause mid-climb inside. My God, I've never seen the interior of a car so posh as this one. "Holy shit."

"That's a Bentley for ya."

Setting my bag on one of the tan leather seats, I fall into the cushioned one before me, the soft leather like sitting on a cloud. Clean and inviting, the lingering scent of Lucian's cologne makes for a delicious greeting as I settle in.

Makaio reaches over me, and I shrink at his close proximity, but he merely presses a button on the long center console that divides the two passenger seats. A screen slides up from a slit in the seat in front of me. He presses another button, and something pushes against my heels, as he backs himself out of the car.

Startled, I look down to find a footrest, like that of a recliner, lifting my feet up off the floor.

"I have a cooler with some soda and Perrier water in the front. If you push the button beside you, there's a foldout table. And you can close the curtains on the window by pressing the button there." He points to a silvery button on the door panel beside me.

Jesus, I've never been in something so luxurious and high-tech in my life.

"I'm, uh. I'm good." Glancing around, I notice *1 of 25* stitched into the leather seat beside me. "What's one of twenty-five?"

"This car is one of only twenty-five in the United States."

"Seriously?" This thing must have cost a fortune. Thousands of dollars on wheels. "I'm surprised Mr. Blackthorne allows it to be used to transport his employees."

"Not all employees, Miss. Only you. Master Blackthorne insisted that you be comfortable on the ride home."

He insisted? Why? "I'm very comfortable. Thank you."

"Good." He closes the door, shutting me inside, and I glance up at the empty window of Lucian's office. *Devil of Bonesalt.*

The ride home seems almost too short, having killed the time watching *Ever After* on the tablet's Netflix app. Movies aren't usually my thing, but it was that, or dodging glances from Makaio in the rearview mirror and having him ask if I needed something every ten minutes. Besides, the movie was fitting for a visit home, as Aunt Midge and I used to love watching it when I was younger.

Admittedly, I've kind of missed the crotchety old woman.

We roll to a stop at the curb, and I nab the duffle from beside me and reach for the handle of the car door. It swings open before I can, and Makaio stands waiting to help me out. Out of courtesy, I take his hand, otherwise the gesture feels strange to me.

Once I'm free of the vehicle, he bends forward, slipping his hand through the strap of my duffle, while he closes the door behind me.

"It's okay. It's not …"

He swipes up the duffle, leaving me to carry nothing more than my cellphone.

With a huff, I lead the way through the fenced-in lot, toward the broken-down house where I've grown up for the last nine years. Empty pots of dead flowers lay tipped on the front porch as we climb the stairs to the entrance, but whereas the gardens at the Blackthorne's simply look unkempt and neglected, here, they're just a failed attempt to polish another rundown house on the block.

A swing to the left, old with cracked paint, reminds me of the times Aunt Midge and I would sit out talking for hours, on balmy summer nights. As much as it's an added eyesore, I can't imagine it not being there.

The exterior of the house could also use some new paint, but that doesn't even hold a candle to what the interior needs, so I halt at the door and reach for my bag. "I'm good here."

"You sure?"

"Yeah. Thanks for the ride." I refuse to open the door, seeing as the Blackthorne's garden shed is in better shape than this place.

"I'll be back Sunday night to pick you up."

"You sure? I mean, Aunt Midge can probably drive me."

"Master Blackthorne insisted I drop you off and pick you up."

It's hard to imagine a man like him thinking me important enough to make such a demand. "Okay. If that's what he insists."

"It is. Have a nice weekend. Stay out of trouble."

A curtain of familiarity hits me as I step inside the house and lock the door behind me, as usual. Aunt Midge calls me paranoid for checking locks, the stove, and closing curtains, but growing up half my life in abandoned places taught me not to be so quick to trust my fellow man, because sometimes he takes shit without asking.

The tired and broken-down furniture, which I imagine was probably purchased sometime in the eighties, the ugly brown paneling of the living room, and outdated wallpaper stained with nicotine throughout is still a comfort to me, in spite of its hideous appearance.

"Aunt Midge! You home?" I dump my duffle on the couch and make my way into the kitchen. The overwhelming scent of coffee and cigarettes clings to the air. That's one thing I appreciate about the Blackthornes: aside from the occasional rich-cigar scent, there isn't the stale smoky odor that sticks to the back of the throat, the way it does here. "Yo! Aunt Midge!"

The coffee pot is warm, not hot like she used it recently, but not cold like it's been sitting for too long, either.

I peek inside her bedroom to find it empty, her bed unmade, nightclothes flung onto the floor. Maybe ran to the store, or something, seeing as she told me she took the weekend off, and it's only just after noon. Too early for The Shoal.

On the way back into the kitchen, I hear a rattling at the door and freeze. The entrance swings open, and in steps Aunt Midge, shoving a cigarette into her mouth as she wriggles the key from the lock.

Behind her stands the one person in the world who could possibly sour the excitement of coming home.

My mother.

It's been a few months since I saw her hobbling about her little campsite on the freeway. Aunt Midge likes to pop in on her sometimes, to bring her something to eat, or an extra blanket. No idea why she bothers. I stayed inside the car, of course. No sense giving my mother the impression that I give a shit about her after she dumped me on her sister.

The white pallor of her skin only emphasizes the dark circles around her eyes, her sunken cheeks and gaunt figure. Even from here, I can see the scabs and bruises of heroin tracks down her arms.

Anger and disgust roil in my stomach, as I watch her follow Aunt Midge into the house.

"What the hell is she doing here?" Crossing my arms fails to hide the tremble of fury vibrating beneath my skin.

On her way toward the kitchen, Aunt Midge pauses to look me up and down, her left eye squinting as she sucks in a drag of her cigarette. "New clothes?"

"Yeah. Irrelevant. Why is she here?"

"Fancy, schmancy," she says, as she passes me, not answering my question.

My mother stands in the center of the room, rubbing her arm, looking around as though she's searching for a needle to inject. Nervous, from the looks of it.

I follow after Aunt Midge, who throws the coffee pot onto the stove, and lean in to get her attention, lowering my voice. "Why is she here?"

Blowing out an exasperated sigh, she leans closer. "So, I get a call from her from some unknown number. Her boyfriend skipped town. Took a bunch of drugs with him. I guess some bigtime drug dealer is after him now." Her gaze slides from mine. "And her."

"So, you brought her *here*? Are you nuts?"

"What was I gonna do? Tell her to fuck off? She's my sister."

"She's my mother, but that doesn't mean I think you should help her every time she steps in a pile of shit and gets dirty."

Shoving the cigarette back between her lips, she shakes her head and fires up the stove. "You don't get it. That's okay. You're a kid."

"I'm nineteen. I dealt with her shit for ten years. I get it more than you know."

Setting her hand on her hip is the first sign that I'm starting to piss her off, but I don't care. This was not one of her smarter decisions. "And you would've just stood by and let some criminal gun her down?"

"Karma's a bitch. Isn't that what you always say?"

"She's your mother, Isa. Your mother. Yeah, she's done a shit job, but it doesn't change who she is. It's not right to want to see her suffer. Those dealers in Roxbury don't fuck around."

Son of a bitch. "Roxbury? She was in Roxbury?"

"Apparently so."

"Jesus, Aunt Midge." Lodging my fingers in my hair is all I can do to keep from yanking every strand out of my head. "You can't let her stay here. You're going to wake up and find all our shit missing."

"Cash is put away. I stashed all my jewelry, too. Only thing that's worth a damn is the shitty TV, and I doubt she can lift a fucking cup of coffee at the moment."

"I'm not staying here." Crossing my arms, I shake my head. I hate having to make her choose, but she has no idea what kind of shit-storm my mother can create without even trying. "Either she goes, or I go."

"C'mon, Isa. Don't be like that. She's family, for Christ's sake. I'm not choosing between family."

"She's fucked you over more times than I ever would."

"She was also there for me more times. Before the drugs."

"You're a goddamn saint." Tromping back through the living room, I find my mother sitting on the edge of the couch, rubbing her hands together.

"Hey, baby. How you been?"

Ignoring her question, I swipe up my duffle bag and grimace, disgusted by the raspy tone of her voice and the spacy look in her eyes. "I'm staying at Kel's tonight!" I call out to Aunt Midge as I head toward the door.

"Isa, wait!" Aunt Midge calls after me, throwing her hands up in the air. "I had tacos planned for dinner!"

"I'm sure they'll get eaten." Ire coursing through my blood, I push through the door.

The moment fresh air hits my face, tears well in my eyes, and the sidewalk blurs behind the watery shield. It isn't the first time my mother has come looking for a handout. A few months back, she managed to scam fifty bucks from Aunt Midge, leaving us short for the electricity bill, and the time before that, it was the wedding ring Uncle Hal gave her. Granted, it didn't mean much to my aunt, but we certainly could've used the cash my mother undoubtedly hocked for it. Maybe it's because I've never had a sibling that I can't seem to understand my aunt's sympathy toward her. I can't imagine loving something so much after being fucked over that many times. Just seems like, at some point, it's not worth the trouble.

The walk to Kelsey's is about fifteen minutes, and I can already feel the calm returning. In high school, I didn't have many friends, except Kelsey Donovan. Like me, she always had a sincere love for music, which is how we first met. I had earbuds in, with Arctic Monkeys blasting at full volume, when she first strolled up to ask what I was listening to. From then on, a friendship blossomed. Only, unlike me, she was a hell of a lot more popular with the other kids at school. Even after the whole incident with Aeden and Brady. In fact, as odd as it was, when the rest of the school shunned me, Kelsey and I grew closer.

Which probably saved me in the end.

It's something I hate thinking about, but sometimes, when I look in the mirror, it sneaks up on me. Especially when I see the cuts, the evidence of how much that night messed with my head.

Always reminding me that I will never be like them. I'll never belong.

Which is exactly why I took the job at the Blackthornes. The minute I have enough to ditch this island, I'm out of here.

The obnoxious blare of a horn interrupts my thoughts, and I jump back as a car speeds past. I recognize the Jeep as belonging to some of Brady's old football buddies. Likely home on summer break from college.

It's been months since I've had to deal with their torment, and I dreaded the thought of running into them--him--over the summer.

"Fucking psycho!" one of the boys shouts, and something knocks me in the head, spilling liquid down onto my new shirt.

Exhaling a gasp, I stare down at myself, where dark splashes of Coke dot my white shirt, the red can lying on the ground in a dark pool of bubbly soda.

"Touchdown!" they shout over the squeal of tires as they take off down the road.

A sob tugs at my chest, but I swallow it back. I prod the throbbing ache at my temple where the can hit, and more tears sting the rims of my eyes. "Fuck you," I whisper, and keep on to Kelsey's.

~

"That's not coming out."

Mrs. Donovan holds up my stained shirt, as I sit on Kelsey's bed in one of her T-shirts. My best friend lies cuddled up to me, her arm stretched across my stomach. For the last hour, she's tried to comfort me, after I showed up to her house distraught and teary-eyed.

"Such a shame, too," she continues. "This is an Ulla Johnson."

"I don't know what that means." I slide my gaze to Kelsey, who shakes her head, rolling her eyes.

"My mom's planning a trip to New York next weekend," she says, pushing up to sit beside me. "She's trying to up her fashion game by memorizing all the designers."

"One doesn't venture to the fashion capital of the country looking like she came from a fishing town."

Shaking her head, Kelsey sighs. "But you did mom."

"Anyway, how the hell did you afford this, Isa? This shirt probably cost about three-hundred. Easy."

Nausea twists in my stomach, and I cup my face in my palms. "Three hundred? Are you serious?" Bending forward, I clutch my gut, while the threat of puke tickles the back of my throat. "Shit."

"Izzy is working for the Blackthornes." Kelsey strokes my back, while I sit with my head between my knees, trying to calm my breathing. "They bought her an entire wardrobe."

"You're kidding me." Wearing a frown, her mother sets the shirt down on the bed. "Aunt Midge let you do this?"

"I didn't really ask permission."

"Dina!" A familiar voice calls from another room, one I recognize as Tracey's, Mrs. Donovan's best friend who practically lives here.

"In here, Trace!" Mrs. Donovan calls over her shoulder, before directing her attention back on me. "Be careful, okay? You know what they say about crossing a Blackthorne."

"What about the Blackthornes?" Tracey stands in the doorway with a bag of popcorn clutched to her chest. She tosses a couple into her mouth and saunters into the room. At forty-five, she's not bad looking. Sandy brown hair that she pulls back into a messy bun on top of her head. Pale blue eyes, and a decent figure despite having had a few kids. The wrinkles and bad skin from years of sunbathing make her look older, though.

"Isa has taken a job, working for them."

"No shit?" Face alight with fascination, she sits down on the bed beside us and offers some popcorn. "Do you stay at the castle?"

I nod in response to her question and decline the popcorn. With the sickness still twisting my guts, I can't even begin to think of eating anything. Hopefully, Aunt Midge will have something that can remove the stains.

"To stay in a *castle*! Like a princess." Tracey bites her lip, her eyes sparkling all of a sudden. "What's he like these days? Lucian."

"These days? As opposed to what?" Kelsey reaches into the proffered bag, grabbing a handful of popcorn.

"As opposed to ten years ago when I hooked up with him."

What?

I'm guessing she didn't look quite as aged back then, but the woman is still about thirteen years older than him.

"You've got to be kidding me." Mrs. Donovan tips her head to get her friends attention. "Tell me you're kidding. You never told me you hooked up with the Devil of Bonesalt."

"Devil is right." Tracey snorts, shoving more popcorn into her mouth.

"C'mon, there are teenagers present."

Groaning, Kelsey rolls her eyes. "Adults, mother. Tell us what happened, Aunt Trace." She sits back beside me, crossing her legs like we're about to hear a riveting tale. "And don't skip out on the details."

"Kels." I shake my head, the news of her hookup only stoking the gurgling sensation in my gut.

"Well, we're at Tom Garrison's house for a party, right?"

"Tom Garrison? *Tom Garrison?*" Hands at her hips, Mrs. Donovan stares down at Tracey like the name is one we're all supposed to know and loathe, as she apparently does, given the expression of disgust on her face. "Had I known you hung around that crowd, I'd have ended our friendship. The guy was the biggest man-whore I've ever known."

"True. But Lucian and some of his college buddies show up. We're all drinking, getting high at a bonfire on the beach. Lucian is looking fucking *delicious* as all get out." She licks her lips and smiles, sending a sinking feeling through my chest. "Anyway, the guys get this brilliant idea to race bikes. And of course, Lucian wins, despite being drunk as a skunk."

Memories of two nights ago slip behind my eyes, recalling him standing on the edge of the roof, *drunk as a skunk*, and what little care he gave for preserving his life. Sounds about right.

"So, being the bike aficionado that I am ..."

"Oh, like hell you are," Mrs. Donovan interrupts, shoving her hand into the popcorn bag. "You probably asked him all these questions about his bike, and you couldn't give two shits about riding."

Tracey's grin stretches wider. "You're absolutely right, but I couldn't pass up the opportunity. I mean, this guy looked like a goddamn rock star. And the way women flirted with him? I just couldn't stand the idea of not approaching him. So we talk for a few minutes. He decides to give me a ride on his bike after, and before I know it, we're going about a hundred-thirty on the highway."

"Tracey! Are you nuts?" Mrs. Donovan slaps her, shaking her head. "You girls better not do something so stupid."

"It was ... fucking awesome." Tracey giggles and leans forward to dodge another swat from her friend. "He's apparently a total adrenaline junkie. Gets off on that shit. So, he pulls the bike off to the side of the road, and he is all over me. I mean, an absolute beast. Pulling my hair. Yanking my clothes off. Kissing me like he means it." The smile on her face withers to a frown. "I'm lying there, damn near buck-ass naked, *panting* for this guy. Like, just take me already, right? And … nothing happens. He's hard as stone, but he won't let me get him off. So he takes me back to the party, we part ways, and …" Lips pursed, she shrugs. "I never hear from him again."

"What's up with that?" Kelsey's lip curls, but a part of me is relieved. I don't know why, really, but I'm glad that nothing happened between them.

"No idea. Worst part is? I know he would've been good. You can just tell, that devious look in their eyes, like they're about to fuck up your world, you know?"

"Okay. Story time is officially over." Mrs. Donovan swipes the bag out of Tracey's hand and ushers her friend up off the bed. "C'mon. These girls don't want a bunch of old ladies hanging around all night."

Tracey's eyes zero in on mine. "Be careful around him, Izzy. I have a feeling he hasn't changed all that much. Something sweet and innocent like yourself? Well, the bad ones just seem to flock to that. Like a moth to flame." With a sigh, she pushes off the bed and pats my leg. "'Course, everybody knows you can take care of yourself."

CHAPTER 26

LUCIAN

I swirl the liquor in my glass, staring at the empty bed on camera, where Isa has slept all week.

The kiss on the roof was an act of a drunken fool, but the lingering effects of it are something I can't seem to ignore, as much as I've tried. Even in my stupor, I could taste the temptation on her lips, the black magic behind her kiss. Like the sound of her voice, it calls to some dark and primitive side of me that longs to place her on a shelf, so no one else can touch her.

What is it about this girl? Watching her leave this afternoon left me with a strange sensation I've not felt in a long time. I hate that I wonder what she's doing right now. Who she's with. Experience tells me these feelings will begin to fester and evolve into my least favorite thing of all: obsession.

A knock at the door interrupts my thoughts, and I lift my gaze to find Rand standing in the doorway.

"A minute of your time, Sir?"

"Of course." I lean forward and click the remote that shuts off the camera I've been staring at for the last half hour.

"It seems the shipment was an oversight. A new employee. I've taken the liberty of firing him."

"Good. And how is our friend behaving?" Leaving Franco Scarpinato in a state of shock and anger probably wasn't the best idea.

"It seems you were right about holding the shipment offshore. All has been quiet, and they've offered to discuss negotiations at your leisure."

"We'll let them wait a bit longer. Wouldn't want to seem too hasty."

"Of course, Sir. A very wise move on your part." Arms crossed in front of him, Rand gives a nod. "I just wanted to provide a quick update. I'll let you get back to your work."

"Before you go, I'd like you to look into something for me."

"Absolutely. What can I do?"

"I want you to find whatever you can on Isadora."

Clearing his throat, he rolls his shoulders back, as if the request is a discomfort he doesn't want to confess. Understandable, as I've never inquired about any of the workers before. Never really gave a shit. But then, none of them ever pulled me from the edge of a three-story building, either. "I have her interview file, Master. I'll fetch it immediately."

"No. Dig deeper. Use whatever resources you need. I want everything on her. Everything."

"Yes, of course. I'll get in touch with our contacts and see what I can find."

"Keep this between you and me. Whatever you find on her."

"You have my word." He nods and shifts his arms behind his back. "Is there anything else? Would you like me to fetch Giulia for you?"

Giulia. There was a time she was a source of relief. A means of relieving tension, but lately, I can't even bring myself to entertain so much as a blowjob from her. "No. I wouldn't."

"If I may speak freely, Master."

"I'd rather you didn't."

"Very well." Turning away from me, he heads toward the door, and I sigh.

"What?"

When he spins around to face me, his brows are crinkled, hands fidgeting. "It's just that … the times you've opted not to use her services, you've been rather …"

I stay quiet, waiting to see if he has the balls to tell me.

"Irritable. I've noticed that hasn't been the case, particularly in the last week."

My thoughts flicker back to three nights ago, when I had Isa beneath me, and the sweet flavor of whatever strawberry shit she had on her lips puckering my tongue. "Threatening the mafia seems to agree with me, I guess."

Rand snorts a laugh and lowers his gaze. "Perhaps. I'll find what I can on the girl. I should also mention that renovations for the atrium begin tomorrow. Any particular theme you'd like the designer to focus on?"

"Surprise me."

"Very well. Goodnight, Master."

"'Night." The moment he exits the office, I grab my drink, lean back in my chair, and flick the monitor back on.

CHAPTER 27

LUCIAN

Eight years ago ...

"You make me proud, my boy." My father stretches across his desk to fill the glass set before me with the same amber liquor that fills his own. "Top of your class, and a Masters from Harvard. The world is your oyster, Lucian." He lifts his glass in a toast, and tips it back.

I don't consider my degree much of a feat, having been bred for ruthless business from the time I swiped my first toy from another child, but after a moment of hesitation, I pitch back my own.

"A week from now, you'll embark on a new journey at Blackthorne Enterprises, but tonight, we celebrate."

As I understand, he's invited half of New England to my graduation party. While I should be thrilled to see my father beaming with so much pride, all I can think about is how much I want to tell him to shove his pride up his ass and smoke it.

Waving his finger in the air, he pushes up from his chair. "I've got a gift for you."

"Father, it's not nec--"

"I'll not have you telling me what is, or isn't, necessary." He hobbles over to a closet, where he rifles around, before returning with something enclosed in his palm. Flicking his hand for mine, he waits until I offer a stretched palm, and drops an object into the center of it.

I stare down at the ring, the same one he wears on his own finger, where a wedding band should be. "Father, I--"

"Not a word. It was Friedrich's idea. With this ring, you now have access to the secret chambers at the institute, where all our meetings are held, as well as the catacombs here at the Manor."

I don't want this. I never asked for it. By accepting this gift, I'm allowing myself to become indoctrinated into their ways. For the last few years, I've played along, in an effort to avoid my father's wrath, but I have neither the desire, nor inclination, to become an active participant in their little club. "I don't know what to say."

"Say nothing. You are now an official member of Schadenfreude. Whatever you want is at your fingertips, my boy. As I said before, the world is yours."

Only an hour into the party, and I'm bored, sipping my third glass of wine, while I watch all of my father's friends and acquaintances mingle in honor of me.

Sebastian strides toward me, one of only a handful of my friends that my father bothered to invite, and only because of his father. "I say we ditch this lame party, and head to the cliff for a late-night dive."

Snorting a chuckle, I lift my drink. "You lead, I shall follow," I say, before tipping back the last of my drink. "At this rate, I'll be wasted before the bastard even bothers to toast."

"And I'll be in the corner, flogging my cock until then."

As both of us laugh, I signal the hired wait staff for another drink.

"Lucian Blackthorne. Well, you haven't changed a bit." The sweet feminine voice has me twisting in my chair.

Amelia Boyd stands off to the side behind me. In a pastel pink dress, her hair coifed in a perfect twist of curls that spill over her ears, she's the vision of a political princess. Same girl I kissed all those years ago, just with bigger tits and a wiser edge to her stare.

"Amelia Boyd."

"Sebastian Thoms." My friend reaches out a hand that she doesn't bother to acknowledge while keeping her gaze locked on mine. "I'll just … head for the corner."

With a smile, I break my ogling to watch him retreat. "His father owns the largest pharmaceutical company on the east coast. You might be the reason he OD's on antidepressants tonight."

"Serves him right for the way he was looking at my breasts."

My gaze dips to the deep-set cleavage peeking out the top of her demi-cut dress. A far cry from the innocent little doll I first met. "Perhaps he couldn't help himself."

"And what's your excuse?"

"I don't bother with excuses. I find your tits to be very appealing."

The corner of her lips twitch. "Would you like to find a quiet place to talk?"

"Very much."

"Show me the way, then."

Pushing up from my chair, I take her hand, leading her toward the doorway that exits to the main hallway.

"Lucian! Lucian, my boy, where are you?" my father calls for me over the cacophony of wealthy men boasting and bragging.

Amelia comes to a stop, tugging at my arm. "Is it time for the toast?"

Shaking my head, I yank her forward. "C'mon. Let's get out of here before he sees me."

"Lucian! Lucian, where are you?" my father calls again from the center of the room, where he's drowning in black tuxedos.

With a giggle, she scampers behind me, as we battle our way through the crowd and out the door.

"Lucian!" Halfway down the hallway, I hear a familiar voice calling out to me. "Wait! Your father is looking for you!"

Rand.

Chuckling over our escape, I drag Amelia down the endless corridor and around the corner. Her giggles echo from behind, as we hustle to get away.

"Lucian!" Rand calls, still chasing after us.

"In here." I bang a left and plow through the first door, tugging her inside with me, and the door clicks as I close it shut. In the darkness of the closet, I feel her fingers curl into mine, while we wait.

"Lucian!" Rand's voice is closer than before. "Lucian Blackthorne!"

Pitch blackness blankets the room, and her hand slides across my abdomen, clenching my stomach muscles on contact. Soft fingertips linger there, toying along the top of my belt. With her other hand still captured in mine, I loosen my buckle one-handedly, unzip my pants, and guide her hand down inside, curling her fingers around my shaft.

"Oh, my," she whispers, stroking my cock without much direction.

"Lucian!" Rand seems to be right outside the door, and I bite my bottom lip, stomach muscles tight, as she runs her small and delicate hands up and down my dick. "Dear God, I don't get paid enough for this shit," he says, his voice growing weary and distant.

At the sound of his retreating footsteps, I twist around, slamming Amelia into a shelf that rattles whatever is stored there. Blindly hiking up her skirt, my fingertips are greeted by smooth skin up to her damp cotton panties.

She lets out a quiet moan.

Our movements are quick and frantic, punctuated by harsh breaths and clawing fingers. I slide her panties down her thighs, and feel a tight grip of my arm.

"Wait. Do you have a condom?"

Of course I do. If there's one thing six years at an Ivy League college taught me, it's never attend a party without one. I slide the condom from my back pocket, tear it open, and roll it down my shaft in the dark. Once in place, I gather up her dress and run my finger over her clit for a quick check.

Soaking wet.

I line my dick at her entrance and push forward, feeling her fingers dig into my nape on a whimper.

"Oh, God, Lucian. It's ... you're going to split me half."

"Relax," I whisper, and reach through the darkness for her jaw.

Holding tight, I press my lips to hers, silencing her, and thrust again. This time harder than before, and the vibration of her outcry rumbles against my lips. Her warm, wet walls greet me each time I drive my hips forward, and it isn't long before she's panting for breath.

"Oh, God, oh, God, oh, God. Don't stop. Please." The soft, breathy voice tickles my ear.

I hammer into her, and something crashes to the floor beside us. My whole body is hard, begging for release. Her pussy contracts around me as she cries out, but I can't pull the trigger. Twenty minutes pass.

I can't come.

"Lucian? What's wrong?" Her fingertips slide down my hairline, and I snap my head away, irritated by the distraction.

Frustrated, I pull out of her and slide the condom off, tossing it to the floor, and furiously pump my dick with my own hand.

Still nothing.

I dip my fingers up inside of her, where the remnants of her climax leaves a warm sticky coating on my skin, and hold it to my nose, breathing in the smell of her pussy.

Nothing.

"Fuck!" Humiliation gets the best of me, the anger swelling inside of me as my cock turns flaccid.

"Do you want me to suck on it?"

"No." I rest my head in the crook of her neck, and half-heartedly stroke myself in a futile attempt to come. Disappointed, I still against her, giving one last squeeze to the limp flesh in my hands. Through the agony of missed climax, I tuck myself back into my pants and flick the chain beside me, flipping on the light in the closet.

Stray hairs stick out from Amelia's up-do, the chiffon of her dress crinkled and disheveled. On the floor beside us lies a broken glass jar of some kind of cleaning fluid, the potent scent of which now fills the small closet space. The discarded condom and its wrapper sit in the pool of clear fluid, and I reach down to grab it, tossing both the condom and bits of broken glass into a nearby trash can that sits against the wall.

Once decent again, the two of us exit the closet and return to the party, neither one of us saying a word. As we enter the room, my mother spins away from a group of hens she's been chatting with since the night began, and her eyes light up.

"Lucian! Your father's been looking for you!" Her attention falls on Amelia. "And, Amelia, how nice to see you again, my dear. You look lovely in pink. Where have the two of you--" Eyes narrowed, her gaze turns appraising like she's suddenly noticed the mess of Amelia's hair. A subtle smile plays on her lips, and she clears her throat, the way she does when something makes her uncomfortable. "Amelia, darling, your father and I were discussing having you stay here at the manor for a few days. Would you like that?"

My blood freezes inside my veins, and I snap my gaze to Amelia, and back to my mother.

"Well, that's very kind, but ..." Amelia stammers, like she's shy all of a sudden.

"Please. We'd be delighted to have you." Tipping her head, my mother shoots me the same fake smile she reserves for the wives of my father's friends. "Wouldn't we, Lucian?"

CHAPTER 28

ISADORA

Present day ...

D uffle bag slung over my shoulder, I slam the passenger door of Kelsey's old Corolla, and wave as I make my way toward the front door of my house, mentally praying my mother isn't here.

The slightly cracked door is the first cue that something isn't right. Although Aunt Midge isn't one to lock all the doors and windows, like me, she also isn't so trusting as to leave the front door open for anyone to stroll in.

I step inside, eyeing the blankets strewn in disarray on the couch, where my mother must've slept the night before. An ashtray on the coffee table, overflowing with cigarettes, tells me it was a long night. One of a half-dozen beer bottles lies tipped on its side, dripping into a small pool collected below its mouth. A sulfur-like, burnt smell lingers on the air as if they tried to cook while drunk.

Must've had a party last night.

The sound of sniveling draws my attention toward the kitchen, and I tip my head just enough to see bare feet sticking out from the end of the counter. "Aunt Midge?"

Dropping my duffle, I hustle toward the feet, and round the counter to find her lying on her side, in the fetal position, her hands tucked into her chest while she sobs.

"Aunt Midge!" Hard tiles hit my knees, when I fall to the floor beside her and help turn her over.

Her eye is swollen like a plum, her lip split and caked in dried blood. When she looks up at me, deep red swirls fill the whites of her bruised eye, like one long, irregular pupil. Body trembling, she tucks her hand closer, but I reach for it, gently pulling it away from her.

Unraveling her fingers sends a shot of nausea to my stomach. Bruised and swollen, almost black, two of them appear to be bent the wrong way, undeniably broken.

"Who did this?" I release her hand and brush away the strands of hair that're matted to her face by tears and blood. "Was this my mother?" Though she isn't known to be violent, my mother is desperate for drugs, and stupid, at times.

She shakes her head, eyes shuttering with another sob. "No, it wasn't your ma."

At the raspy sound of her voice, I scramble to the cupboard, snatch a glass that I fill with water, and return to her side. Setting my hand to her nape, I help her into a sitting position, cringing when she cries out, and set the glass to her lips. Water trickles from the corner of her mouth as she guzzles the fluids, and at her first cough, I lower the glass.

"We were ... sitting. Talking. It was nice, you know? Catching up with her. It got late." Lip quivering, she stares into her glass. "I was sleeping when they dragged me out of bed. He said he was looking for Tony, your mom's boyfriend."

"The drug dealer. Jesus, Aunt Midge." Threading my fingers through my hair, I cap the irritation and the *told you so* that's cocked at the back of my throat. Instead, I busy myself with gathering ice from the freezer, wrapping it up in a cloth, which I set to her broken fingers.

"They kept … punching me. Asking me what I knew. I heard Jenny in the other room. One of 'em must've been burning her 'cause I could smell it." Another sob leaves her bent forward, shaking, and I lean in, letting her rest her forehead on my shoulder.

"Where is she now?"

"They took her." She lifts her head from my shoulder, her nose and cheeks shining with snot and the tracks of tears. So helpless looking and terrified. The sight of her brings tears to my own eyes. "They said … they're going to kill her."

I should feel something after hearing this. An urgency, like the one that has my aunt's eyes widening, in spite of the swelling. I can't even muster surprise at this point. "If what?"

"If we don't pay him fifty grand. The fifty grand worth of drugs that asshole took off with."

My chest turns cold, disgust sinking to the pit of my stomach.

"He's coming back … in three days to collect it." The worry in her voice isn't right for Aunt Midge. No matter what we got into financially, she always had a plan, or faith that it'd all work out. Whoever this guy is, he scared the crap out of her. "He says, if I don't have it, he'll kill both Jenny and me."

"Who? Who's coming back?"

"His name was Franco. Franco Scar-*something*. Oh, God, he's coming back."

Anger rattles my grinding teeth. "This is … this is why I said. You can't help her, Aunt Midge. She's a fucking walking disaster!"

"I didn't want to see her get hurt, Isa. She's my sister."

Cold waves of shock leave my body feeling numb. The logic I'm desperate for, in order to get us out of this mess, is tamped down by the tension squeezing my brain. I tip my head to get her attention. "We have to go to the police. Hear me? We have to report this."

"No!" The fingers of her good hand claw at my arm, digging into my skin. "No police! He said he'll give her a slow and painful death, if we go to the police."

"Aunt Midge, this is a criminal. From Roxbury. This isn't some local neighborhood kid threatening you. We have to do something! If he comes back …" My words falter, falling off my tongue as the thought of someone coming back for her clamps my chest and hardens it to a ball of bitter hate. Hatred for my mother. "She did this. This is her problem, not ours."

"I won't let them murder my sister."

I'll never understand my aunt's sense of loyalty to her. Why, in spite of all she's done, Aunt Midge continues to do anything for her. No matter the risk.

It doesn't matter, though. As a kid from the streets, I never put that much faith in police, anyway. Particularly local police. They just don't get this kind of thing around here, and with my drugged-out mom involved, I doubt they'd take it seriously. I'd venture to say, the worst case Tempest Cove cops have seen is probably when someone stole Old Man Murphy's metal detector from his shed.

A drug dealer from Roxbury would have their heads spinning.

Besides that, it's hard to know who might be on this Franco's payroll. Maybe he's expecting that we'd go to the cops. Maybe he's buddies with them. It's not so much my mom I'm worried about, as Aunt Midge. She doesn't deserve this.

"We'll figure this out. Don't worry."

"We don't have that kind of money, Isa." Her lip quivers again. "I can't get that kind of money in a year, let alone three days."

In the thick of all the confusion swirling inside my head, a thought pops there. The conversation I had with Laura a week ago. The doll.

The one she said was worth over three-hundred grand. Small

enough that I could tuck it inside my shirt without anyone noticing, including Laura. Hell, she'd forgotten that she even had the thing.

I can't see myself asking a stern man like Lucian for a glass of water, let alone fifty grand. And what would I tell him? It's to pay off a drug dealer for my mother's junkie boyfriend who skipped town? He'd probably flick me off like an annoying fly and tell me to go to hell. "Like I said. We'll figure something out. Don't worry."

After helping her into the car, I drive Aunt Midge to the emergency room, listening to her complain about the hundred-dollar deductible she'll have to pay over and above the fifty grand we now have to cough up.

After three hours, her fingers are set and splinted. When asked by the doctor, Aunt Midge said she smashed her fingers while trying to move her dresser by herself. A crappy lie, but I didn't dispute her story.

By the time we arrive back home, it's midafternoon. Makaio will be here soon to drive me back to the Blackthornes, and as much as I don't want to leave Aunt Midge alone tonight, I need time to swipe the doll and find somewhere to hock it. I don't even know where to start with that, but at the moment, it's the only plan I have. The only one that might ensure Franco Scar-*something* doesn't return with a hard-on for blood.

With only minutes left before Lucian's car arrives, I head to my bedroom and pull one of my extra pocket knives from underneath the mattress of my bed, which I hand off to Aunt Midge. It isn't much, and if the guy returns, I doubt he'll be unarmed. A pocket knife is no match for a gun, but it gives me a small peace of mind to know she has some means of defense.

"I'm begging you. Lock the doors. And if anyone comes knocking, call the police. Don't screw around with this, Aunt Midge. I might know how to get that cash."

The thought of leaving her alone sits like bricks in my stomach, but the whole reason behind my return to the Blackthornes is to help her. I'll plan to swipe the key from Laura during one of her many naps and grab the doll from the case. Then text Aunt Midge to come pick me up. I'll say there's a family emergency at home. We'll find a place to hock the doll and get the cash.

Yeah, it's shitty.

Yeah, I feel like an absolute scumball for taking advantage of the Blackthornes this way.

But I would do anything for my aunt.

Even this.

"I'm so scared, Isa." The constant shudder of her body proves the point. "What if he comes back tonight?"

"Can you stay with Shelly?" As much as her coworker from The Shoal annoys the hell out of me, she's the closest Aunt Midge has to a best friend.

"Yeah, probably."

"Do you need me to drive you there?"

"Nah." Reaching for her pack of smokes, she shakes her head. "I'll have Shel come get me. She ain't got nothing better to do, anyway."

"Good. Stay with her tonight."

The sound of a horn outside is probably Makaio, but to be sure, I pad toward the window, and peer through the curtains. The sleek black car sits at the curb, and Makaio stands alongside the passenger door. What I wouldn't have given for him to be around the night before. I bet Franco would've run scared shitless, if Makaio had been here.

Nabbing my duffle, I head back toward Aunt Midge for a quick peck on the forehead. "Text me when you get to Shelly's, okay?"

"I will." Fingers fidgeting with the cigarette she hasn't yet lit, she lowers her gaze. "Isa, I'm sorry for this. I'm sorry I roped you into this."

"It's okay. We're going to be okay, I promise."

~

G uilt weighs heavy on me, while I sit in the backseat of the luxury car, knowing that some time tomorrow, I'll be scamming three-hundred grand. I wipe my sweaty palms across my jeans for the dozenth time and try not to look at Makaio, but I feel him staring at me through the rearview mirror.

"You okay, Miss Quinn? You look kinda pale."

"Just ... something I ate. Not sitting right with me."

"You need me to pull over, let me know. Don't want you blowing chunks in the backseat."

The visual of that tickles the back of my throat, and lips clamped over the real possibility of throwing up, I nod.

We finally reach the manor, and I'm pretty sure my heartrate has doubled since we left Aunt Midge's. Taking Makaio's hand, I climb out of the Bentley and glance up toward the empty window of Lucian's office.

Good. I can't bear to see him tonight.

Shuffling up the staircase, I pass Rand, who holds the front door open for me.

"Good evening, Miss Quinn. I trust you had an enjoyable weekend."

Enjoyable? Not even close. "Yes, it was ... nice."

"Excellent." He closes the door behind me, and in spite of the spacious surroundings, I suddenly feel claustrophobic. "I'll have the chef prepare dinner for you, while you get settled into your room."

I can't even think of food right now. I can't even think of how *he* can think of food right now. "That won't be necessary, Rand. I ate before I left," I lie. "It's not sitting well with me."

"Ah, yes. Happens after a week of meals prepared by a chef. Do you need anything for indigestion?"

"No. Thank you. I'm just going to lie down."

"Very well. It's good to have you back at the Manor."

Anxious to hide away in my room, I hustle up the staircase, counting the stairs while my head swirls in a number of thoughts, until something hard smashes into me. Knocked off balance, I flail my arms, and a hand reaches out to grab my wrist before I fall.

Hand to my chest, I catch my breath and look up to find Lucian frowning down at me.

Of all the times in the world to run into him, literally, why now?

Why, when my guilt is at its height?

"I'm really thinking a horn might be more appropriate for you."

In spite of the anxiety tearing up my insides, I force a smile at that. In a parallel universe, I'd steal the opportunity to flirt. At the moment, I'm just being nice. "I almost think you enjoy watching me stumble into you."

"I'd be lying if I said I didn't find it somewhat amusing."

As much as I'd love to engage our usual banter, a much heavier weight presses down on me. Slipping my wrist from his grasp, I clear my throat and hike my duffle higher onto my shoulder. "Excuse me. I'll try to watch where I'm going."

He doesn't say a word, while I continue on up the staircase, the desperate impulse reminding me I'm not the pretty delicate thing who flirts and minds her manners. I'm a crude thief, a former street kid, one who does what she has to in order to survive.

Even if that means fucking over those who are willing to catch my fall.

CHAPTER 29

ISADORA

Wringing the fabric of my dress, I stand in the elevator, waiting to reach Laura's room on the second floor. The long maxi certainly wouldn't have been my first choice, but the oversized, lightweight military jacket that Amy paired with it is perfect for tucking the doll inside. The trembling of my fingers, coupled with the cold, hollow feeling in my chest, is hard to ignore. It's my body's way of telling me I'm not the slick and heartless swindler I've spent all night convincing myself that I am. The physical manifestations of a girl with a conscience, who isn't out to hurt anyone. In fact, this whole fiasco is about *ensuring* that no one gets hurt.

The elevator doors open on the empty sitting room, and from here, I can see the doll beneath the glow of light that shines down on her inside the glass case. I try to imagine her missing. Would anyone even notice, with all the dolls crammed together?

Nell wanders into the room, tipping her head. "You're early this morning. She's still under."

"Think I got too much sleep over the weekend, myself. Feeling kind of antsy."

"Well, hey, I'm going to grab some coffee from the kitchen. Can you listen for her?"

"Of course."

It's almost too easy. Or maybe I've just grown accustomed to how predictable and efficient things work in this place. I knew she'd still be asleep. The woman never wakes before her morning alarm that's set for nine. I knew Nell would run down for her usual cup of coffee before things begin, taking her time, which would leave me completely alone.

The doors to the elevator close, and I glance at my watch. Twenty-to nine. I have just under that to grab the key, snatch the doll, store it away in my room, and return to Laura's room before Nell gets back. When she does return, I'll check my texts, where Aunt Midge will already have sent the message we discussed the night before, telling me she's coming to pick me up.

It's stupid. Perhaps the most under-thought plan I've come up with, and I'm certain there are a number of consequences that I haven't even begun to explore.

But I don't have the luxury of time, and even if I did, would it stop me?

Not when Aunt Midge's life is on the line.

I shuffle across the room, into Laura's bedroom, where the shades are still drawn. Her snores trail my steps through the dim light, as I tiptoe across the floor toward the tray on her vanity dresser, where she stores all of her jewelry. Halfway there, the floorboard beneath me creaks, and I halt, eyes screwed shut, as she sniffles and shifts in her bed. Daring a peek through the darkness of the room, I find her lying with her head turned away from me, and the sound of snores fills the room again.

The bracelet lies on top of her discarded jewelry, and I carefully lift it from the tray, the jitter in my hands threatening to drop the damn thing.

With the bracelet secured, I hurry out of the room. Seconds

later, I'm lifting the doll from its stand, and rearranging the surrounding dolls to fill the gap left there.

Slightly bigger than I originally remember, I tuck it beneath my arm inside the jacket, feeling stiff and awkward as it rests against my ribs.

And just like that, I have officially stolen the most valuable thing I'll ever touch in my life.

I close and lock up the case, before returning the bracelet to Laura's jewelry tray, and hustle back out of the room.

Ten-to nine.

The elevator seems to take forever, and when it opens on Rand, the urge to throw up sends bile shooting up my throat.

"Miss Quinn! Are you on your way down?"

"I'm, um ... I forgot to grab a coffee."

"Ah, excellent. I'm off to grab some breakfast. I'll accompany you to the kitchen."

"I ... okay."

Shit. Shit, shit, shit.

The elevator reaches the bottom floor, where a number of people are bustling around. Construction workers, or something, judging by the tool belts strapped at their waists and one of the men carrying a ladder.

"What's going on?" I ask, trying to distract myself from the guilt.

"Renovations for the atrium. The master is planning a masquerade ball, three weeks from today. There's quite a bit of work that needs done before then."

"Masquerade?"

"Yes. Some very important guests will be here."

We wait for one of the workers to pass, a younger guy, maybe in his twenties, who winks and smiles as he passes.

Gaze trailing after him, Rand frowns. "I trust you'll keep your distance from these men. I haven't a clue what their background is." He leans in, raising the hair on my skin with his proximity. "We've installed extra cameras, just in case."

My blood turns cold. "Cameras?"

I didn't even think of cameras. Why would I? It's not like they have security here to monitor them.

"Yes. Master Griffin had them installed quite a few years ago. We've expanded the coverage to most of the common rooms."

Common room? What the hell constitutes common? A sitting room? I swallow hard, my throat suddenly parched, lips dry. "Hey, I, um …. I need to stop at my room. I'm still not feeling the greatest."

"Ah, yes, of course. Might I suggest some Pepto-Bismol? You'll find some in the cupboard of your bathroom."

"Thanks. I'll catch up with you later, Rand." On the verge of hyperventilating, I race down the hallway, practically sliding to a stop in front of my room.

"Isa?"

At the sound of my name, I jump back, and the doll falls to the floor. On impact, one of the hands cracks off.

Oh, no. Oh, my God.

My gaze snaps to Giulia, who frowns down at it before lifting eyes cold with suspicion back to me. "It's … it's not what you think." Every muscle in my body is in a frenzy as I kneel down and gather up the doll with its broken hand.

"What is this, Isa?"

Glancing around, I open the door and usher her inside.

She shakes her head, shrugging my hand away. "I don't want any part of this."

"Please, let me explain."

With hesitation, she steps inside the room, looking over her shoulder as she comes to a stop a few paces in.

I scan the hallway once more, before clicking the door shut.

"Are you crazy? Stealing one of her dolls?"

"Believe me, Giulia. I wouldn't do this if I didn't need the money."

"We all need the money. You don't see me stealing it! Do you have any idea what they'll do, if they catch you?"

String me up? Hide my body? I have no idea.

If there's one person who might have any inkling what I'm going through right now, it's a woman who lived on the streets. "I went home this weekend. My mom ... she's a junkie. It's a long story, but she's seeing some asshole who skipped off with about fifty grand worth of drugs. The drug dealer beat up my mom, and aunt, broke two of her fingers, and threatened to kill them, if we don't pay him the money." Tiny fissures in my composure bleed out the urgency ready to burst inside of me. "I'm freaking out here, Giulia."

Dubious brown eyes stare back at me, the way I often looked at my mom when she told me similar ridiculous stories of desperation.

"I know this sounds nuts. It is nuts. But I can't let him hurt my aunt. Or my mom." It's not my mom that concerns me, but I don't tell her that.

Sighing, she steps past me, deeper into the room, and I wonder if she's contemplating ratting me out. Not that she'd have to. I'm sure the camera caught everything. And now, even if I want to return the damn thing, its hand is broken.

"There's no other way for you?" Back turned to me, she can't see the hilarity of such a possibility written all over my face.

"Do you honestly think I'd be stealing this thing, *a doll,* if there was? I've wracked my brain trying to figure out how to fix this."

"There might be another way. The question is, how much would you be willing to sacrifice to save your mother's life?"

"What?"

She turns around, and the resolution etched in her expression is almost more terrifying than the look of shock from before.

"What would you sacrifice to save your mother and aunt? Pain? Your dignity?"

"I just stole a freakin' doll. I'd say dignity is out the window at this point. What are you getting at?"

A sharp exhale, and she presses her lips together, casting her gaze to the side. "There is a group. It's how I got out of my situation. They help people. Lucian is a member of it."

"What group?"

"I don't know what they call themselves, but--"

A hard knock at the door startles my muscles, and I almost drop the doll again. "Oh, no."

Looking around the room, I zero in on the dresser and shove the doll inside, beneath my underwear. At the other end of the drawer, I slide out my pocket knife from where I stored it to keep the maids from finding it under my pillow. Tucking it tight to my body so Giulia can't see, I drop it into the pocket of my military jacket. I don't know how this place handles thieves.

On my way to the door, Giulia grabs my arm. "Ask him about it," she whispers. "Lucian. He'll know what you mean."

"I don't think that's going to help me now." I twist my arm out of hers. "I've no doubt they've seen what I've done."

With heavy steps, I clutch my stomach and stride toward the door, throwing it back on where Rand stands in the hallway. Chin lifted in the air, he stares down his nose at me, his brows stern with disappointment.

"Miss Quinn, Master Blackthorne has requested you report to his office immediately."

CHAPTER 30

LUCIAN

Leaning back in my chair, I rewind the footage of Isa swiping the doll out of the glass case. I couldn't give a damn about the overpriced toy, it's the betrayal that gnaws at me. The idea that this girl has the balls to steal from right under my nose.

At the ding of the elevator door, I pause the footage, and when Rand escorts her into the office, I want to throttle my dick for lurching against my zipper. Head bowed, she comes to a stop in the middle of the room, not bothering to look me in the eye, and when I give Rand a nod, he exits the room.

Once the elevator doors close, I push forward in my chair, resting my hands against the desk. "Anything you want to tell me?"

She gives a subtle shake of her head that only stokes my anger. "Nothing I'm guessing you haven't already seen." Hands clasped in front of her, she looks ridiculous in that dress. A walking lie. Yet, at the same time, I can picture the flowy fabric draped across the back of my neck, with my head between her thighs.

A thought that pisses me off even more.

"Where is it?"

"In my drawer."

"*Your* drawer. The dresser belongs to you, now, as well?"

Flinching, she shakes her head. "No, of course not."

"It takes an enormous amount of trust to put someone in charge of caring for my mother."

She bows her head further, probably so weighed down by guilt, it feels like a bowling ball propped on her neck.

"Why did you betray my trust in you, Isa?"

Eyes hiding behind long, black lashes, she sighs. "I didn't mean to."

"I don't give a fuck what you didn't mean to do. I want to know *why* you *did* do it?"

"I'll return the doll and leave. If it's all the same to you."

I push up from my chair, adjusting the lapels of my coat as I round the desk and lean against the front of it. "As I understand, it's broken now. Practically worthless."

Flinching, she turns away from me and shakes her head. "I'm …. I don't know what to say, Mr. Blackthorne."

"I'm sure you don't. There's nothing you can say. Hundreds of thousands of dollars are gone to waste."

"I find that excessive for something so fragile," she says under her breath.

Shooting up from the desk, my frustration gets the best of me, and in three quick strides, I'm standing in front of her. "It's not your place to say what's excessive, or not. The fact is, you've destroyed something worth far more than yourself."

Her eyes snap to mine, the thin sheen of tears gathered there bringing her bright gray eyes to life. Lips quivering, it's like something snarky and smartass waits to tear free from her mouth. That's how this girl is--quick with the quips--but instead, her gaze falls from mine once more. "I didn't mean to break it."

"The least you can do is tell me what was so important that you felt compelled to steal from me."

Slim shoulders roll back, her eyes brimming with enough challenge to trip my switch.

My temper is on the cusp of exploding as I stare down at her, practically blazing with the heat of irritation that simmers inside of me.

Seconds pass, and she doesn't say a word, the insolence of her silence slowly chipping away at my patience.

"Answer me!"

She flinches and lifts her chin in defiance. "What does it matter now?"

As I lurch toward her, she backs herself up, stumbling into the chair behind her, and when I set my hands at either side of her and lean in, the bite of cold steel hits the bottom of my chin.

The unyielding expression on her face, along with the blade at my throat, strums a fine and precarious thread inside of me. It awakens a sensation I haven't felt in a very long time. One that has my dick ready to tear through my trousers. Chills race beneath my skin, my muscles burning with the urge to keep from kissing her right now. What I feel is beyond anger. Beyond the rush of adrenaline. It's lust. Pure, black, poisonous lust.

"My family is in trouble. Someone told me of a group that can help me. Said you'd know about it. A secret group."

Fuck. "No idea what you're talking about."

"I think you do." She looks away for only a second, perhaps a moment of uncertainty, before holding my stare again. "I think you're a member of this group."

My eye twitches at that, this bold and sassy little shit who thinks she knows what she's doing right now. There's no way in hell an innocent thing like her knows about Schadenfreude. If she had a clue what it was, she surely wouldn't be throwing herself at it. "A bit late for that now, don't you think? Seeing as you not only stole from me, but have the balls to hold a blade to my throat."

"I'm desperate."

"Not desperate enough for the consequences, I can assure you."

"This man threatened to kill my mother. He beat the hell out of my aunt and broke two of her fingers over the weekend. If I don't come up with fifty grand, he's going to kill both of them. I doubt he'll leave any loose ends, which means he'll come for me next."

"Who is this man?"

"Franco Scar-something."

Franco Scarpinato. Fucking hell. How the hell did she get tangled up with scumbag like him?

"What does he want with you?"

Still holding the blade to my neck, she licks her lips that look dry as a bone. "My mother's boyfriend skipped town with his drugs. We don't know where he is, so he's trying to get the money out of us."

Must be the guy Franco was bitching about when we met up. Somehow, my gaze lands on her lips again, and I could kick my own ass for wondering how they'd feel between my teeth. "How did you hear about this secret group?"

Again, she lowers her gaze, as if she has no intentions of telling me. Stubborn. I don't know what it is about this girl, the way she makes me want to spank her bare ass while kissing her at the same time.

"How?"

"Giulia." She deadpanned the name as if I might dispute her. "She said you might help me. The way you helped her."

"Do you even know what it is you're asking me for?"

"No. But I'd be willing to work for you for free. To pay off what I owe. As long as you'll have me."

I want to laugh at that, the naiveté beneath her brassiness, like a bad joke. I lean further into her, pressing against the blade at my throat. "I fuck Giulia. That's how she repays me. Whenever I want. Wherever I want. Is that what you had in mind, Isa? To let me use you, however I see fit?"

Throat bobbing with a swallow, she can't possibly imagine the ways I'd ruin an innocent thing like her. "If that's what it takes to save my family. Yes."

The twitch of my eye fails to conceal the chaos exploding inside of me. This girl. This fucking beautiful, painfully fascinating girl. Snatching up her wrist, I grind my jaw as I twist the knife from her grasp, the glare on her face almost comical. The quick rise and fall of her chest betrays the defiance burning in her eyes, the courage she's wearing like a shitty makeover.

Lifting her wrist between us, I run my thumb over her hammering pulse. "Do you feel that, Isa? The rapid pulse in your veins? The hard pounding in your chest? That's your body's natural defenses, warning you to stay the fuck away. Listen to it." I push off her, all I can do to keep from acting on the sudden appetite I've developed for a sassy nineteen-year-old. The phantom sensation of the blade still lingers across my throat.

Get her out of here before you do something stupid.

"Please. You're the only chance I have."

I fold up the blade and toss it onto her lap. "I can't help you. Return the doll, and we'll have it repaired. Consider this a warning that, if you ever steal from me again, I'll take pleasure in watching the police cuff you before locking you away."

"What about my family?"

"I said I can't help you. You're far too young for what you're offering."

"I'm of age. I'm not a child. I've had boyfriends, you know. And sex!" The desperation in her voice only strums the depraved visuals tickling my thoughts.

"If ever I was desperate and stupid enough to have you, Isa, make no mistake, that'd be the day you're properly fucked by a *man*, not a boy. It's not an amusing diversion, but something I put a very concentrated effort into. Pleasure is business for me, and you're not equipped to handle my ruthless nature. Now, if you'll excuse me, I have work to do."

"Please. I'm begging you, Lucian."

"Get out of my office before I change my mind and press charges for stealing." I lean toward her again, sliding my hand over the delicate curve of her neck. "And if you ever hold a knife to my throat again, you'll find out how adept I am at disarming a threat." My head blares a warning, as my eyes dip to her lips once more, and I release her, instantly regretting the missed contact.

As hard-pressed as she was to hide her tears, the sniffling as she dashes for the door is unmistakable. The moment she's gone, Rand reenters my office.

"My apologies, Sir. I did my best to ensure she was the right candidate for--"

"I want you to set up a meeting with Franco. Let him know I'm ready to discuss negotiations, and I'd like to invite him here for it."

"Here, Master? Your father always felt it was too dangerous to invite the Scarpinatos to the Manor."

"In case you've forgotten, my father isn't here running the show. I am." I fall into my chair, while my body scrambles to undo whatever the hell it is that happens when I'm around that girl. The way I can't seem to control myself, like a prepubescent schoolboy who hasn't yet learned how to deal with a hard-on.

"I've not forgotten, Master. I meant no disrespect. I'll arrange this meeting, as you requested."

"Good. And send Makaio in. He'll be thrilled to know I have a real task for him."

"Of course. I'll fetch him immediately. And what of the girl?"

The girl. The girl. The aggravating, beautiful girl. "Keep an eye on her. I have a feeling she may try to leave. I want her to remain here, at least until I've decided what I want to do with her."

"I'll see it done. My contact should have the information you requested soon. I'll forward it on to you, once he's gathered it."

"Fantastic." As if my curiosity wasn't already piqued, the incident with the knife only solidifies my interest in her. I can't even look at the screen where the video remains paused.

And now I have the perfect excuse to do something completely reckless and impulsive. Only took the tears of a desperate girl to give me the opportunity I've been waiting for.

CHAPTER 31

ISADORA

I set the doll, with its broken hand, into Rand's awaiting palms, unable to look him in the eye.

"To say that I'm disappointed is an understatement. I thought very highly of you, Isa. I thought you were the perfect fit for our family."

As much as I want to feel bad for what I've done, the truth is, I still have a shit-storm to take care of at home, and at the moment, that takes precedence over guilt. "I'm sorry."

"I'll see if I can salvage Mrs. Blackthorne's doll. We'll keep this under wraps, as I'm sure she'll be less forgiving than her son."

With a solemn nod, I dare to look up at him. "I appreciate that."

"It's of no concern to me what you appreciate. I'm doing this for Mrs. Blackthorne's sake. She, too, thinks very highly of you."

This man deserves a Master's Degree in guilt-tripping. If I wasn't so preoccupied over a dangerous criminal showing up at my aunt's house in the next couple of days, I'd probably find myself teetering on the edge of the roof, like Lucian the other night, weighted down by shame.

Without another word, Rand walks off, and I close the door

to my bedroom. From beneath the bed, I grab my suitcase to begin packing up my stuff.

A text chimes on my phone, and I open it to see the message my aunt has been waiting to send me.

You need to come home. Family emergency.

Tension winds inside my muscles, the disappointment of having failed her pressing down on my conscience.

Abort mission. Something came up. I have to figure out another plan.

Are you in trouble, Isa?

No, it's okay. Just let me figure this out.

A knock at the door leaves me huffing with exhaustion. Maybe Rand decided to smear my nose in it some more?

"Come in!" I don't even have the energy to face him at this point. My whole world is crumbling around me, and I can't muster the will to care about some stupid fucking doll that's worth more than my aunt's life.

The door clicks, and I twist to find Giulia standing in the doorway. Her gaze dips toward my suitcase and back as she steps into the room and closes the door behind her. "I take it he declined."

"Is it obvious?" Perhaps it's the presence of another woman, one who was also desperate at one time, that finally punches through my defenses. I turn away from her to hide the tears welling in my eyes again. If there's one thing I hate, it's crying in front of someone. "I feel … lost right now."

The gentle touch on my shoulder twitches my muscles. "What will you do?"

"All I *can* do. Go home and be there for my aunt. I can't leave her alone in all this."

"Do you think that's a good idea? Do you think she'd want you to place yourself in danger that way?"

"Versus what? Staying here and pretending my life is as perfect as everyone else's? I'm not going to play house with a nut job, while some drug dealer decides to use my aunt as target practice."

Sighing, she lowers her head. "You asked him for help?"

"He said … that I was too young for whatever help I didn't realize I was requesting."

Gaze still cast from mine, she picks at her thumb, fidgeting. "Then, he told you of our arrangement."

"In so many words."

"I'm surprised he denied you."

"Why's that?"

"Because he hasn't touched me since the day you arrived here."

An agitated laugh escapes me, as I unzip the bag I intend to have packed within the next ten minutes. "I don't think that has anything to do with me."

"Maybe not. But as recent as the night before you arrived, he called for me every night. Now, he wants nothing to do with me."

Called for her? For some reason, all that comes to mind is the scene in *Dracula*, when Lucy fucks the wolf. "Lucian thinks I'm a child. He treats me like a little girl. An irritating little girl."

"Well, I've seen the way he's dealt with thieves. The fact that he didn't fire you tells me he thinks more of you than you probably realize." Backing away from me, she heads toward the door. "Anyway, I just wanted to check on you. I'll pray that everything works out in the end."

"Thanks. But I don't think God gives a shit about a girl who doesn't have much faith in prayer."

"He might surprise you, Isa. They say he works in mysterious ways."

Mysterious indeed. I couldn't have guessed when I woke up this morning that I'd be sacrificing myself to the Devil.

Once she's out of the room, I go back to packing up my clothes. I leave the new wardrobe hanging in the armoire, cringing at the soda-stained shirt. It's then I realize I forgot to send Aunt Midge a text to come pick me up, with all the Giulia distraction.

"Shit." When I lift my phone, there's a text message from her.

Holy shit on a shingle, that was fast!!!!

I frown down at her message and the barrage of exclamations she uses and text her back.

What was fast?

I have to bite my nails to keep from losing my mind, as she takes a turtle's lifetime to answer, so I shake my head and dial her number instead.

The moment she picks up, I can hear laughter in her voice. "You're a saint. I'm convinced of it!"

"What are you talking about?"

"He returned your mother, Isa. And apologized on top of it all."

"Who?"

"Franco."

Franco? The guy who broke fingers, burned my mother, and threatened to kill both of them Franco? Somehow, I can't picture an apology in all of that violence. It's unfitting, only adding to my disbelief.

"He showed up here with that Hawaiian guy, driving a fancy black car. I nearly had a heart attack when he walked up into the yard, but he had your mother with him. She's a little worse for the wear, looks like they roughed her up most of the night, but she's going to be okay. She's resting now."

Makaio? I pull the phone away to see it's only been an hour since I left Lucian's office. "What happened? What did he say?"

"He just said it was a misunderstanding. He apologized and said he won't bother us again. That was it. He left with the Hawaiian."

"You're sure it was Makaio."

"Same guy who carried in your luggage that first night? Yeah. There's no mistaking that one."

This has Lucian written all over it. He has to be the one behind this. Who else would send Makaio to return my mother?

"I don't know what you did, but thank you. I know you're not a fan of Jenny, but you saved your mom's life today. You saved mine. I love ya, Isa." Her voice is shaky again, like she might cry, which is my cue to cut the call short.

"Sure, sure. Love you, too. Look, um, send me a text later, to make sure all is still okay." I still can't wrap my head around this. Everything feels numb and spacey, but cold and tingly at the same time. Shock, maybe?

"I will. In the meantime, your mom's gonna need some time to heal. I'm letting her stay a few days."

"Yeah. Okay. I'm glad it worked out."

"Okay, I'll see you this weekend, hun."

I click out of the call and close my eyes over tears of relief. My knees buckle beneath me, and I collapse to the floor, finally breaking down.

Humble pie was never my favorite flavor.

Swallowing back the relief and humiliation, I stand in the elevator, waiting for the doors to open on the third floor. Arriving unannounced is as frightening as having to ask the guy for help, but seeing as I held a blade to his throat a mere hour ago, this is probably the easiest thing I've had to do today.

The door opens at Lucian's office, and just like when I arrived this morning, I'm greeted by the delicious scent of cologne and leather. A masculine aroma that naturally waters the mouth.

With his feet kicked up on the desk, Lucian is leaning back in his chair, watching me approach, a glass half full of what is probably liquor beside an actively burning cigarette he holds over the ashtray.

With the top of his shirt unbuttoned and his tie loosened, the sight of him sends butterflies to my stomach, the way he watches me like a predator eyeing prey.

"I see your balls haven't shrunk in the last hour." He flicks his cigarette before taking a drag, never taking his eyes off me.

The comment brings a smile to my face, and I bite the inside of my cheek to hide my amusement. "It seems I owe you an apology."

"You owe me more than that, as I recall."

"The doll."

"Rand is having a fuck of a time gluing its small hand back in place. Keeps falling off."

A snort of laughter escapes me, and I slap a palm to my face and clear my throat. "I'm sorry. You're welcome to take the cost of repair out of my wages." Exhaling a shaky breath, I cross my arms over my chest so he can't see the shallow breaths of my anxiety. I'm convinced the guy feeds off fear. "My aunt contacted me to let me know that Franco returned my mother."

Reaching forward, he grabs the drink from the desk and takes a sip. "And?"

"And he apologized. She said Makaio was with him, so I'm assuming you had a hand in that."

"It's possible. A lot of weird shit's gone down today."

Again, I find myself biting the inside of my cheek to stifle the urge to smile. "I just wanted to thank you. I don't know what you told him, or what you did, but I appreciate it."

"Franco is a long-time associate of mine."

A drug dealer? Why the hell would he be associated with a drug dealer?

"His family, I should say." Something about his voice always carries an air of boredom. "He's dabbled in some less than admirable hobbies, as of late. At any rate, he'll no longer be an issue for you, or your family."

Gaze glued to the floor, I breathe in the relief once again and nod. "I feel that I owe you something for all of this ... mess."

He reaches for the decanter of liquor, filling his glass while he shoves the cigarette between his lips. "Consider it payment for saving my life," he says around it.

"What?"

"The other night. On the roof. Had you not been there, well, I'd probably be a spatter of bones and blood."

Grimacing, I swallow back the visual of that. "It was nothing special."

"Saving my life, or what followed?"

"The, um ... the kiss was ... very good. I enjoyed it very much."

Leaning forward again to flick his smoke, he tips his head, as if to study me. "You found enjoyment in a drunken kiss?" His cheeks cave with a long draw of his cigarette, before he stamps it out in the ashtray. "You'd have to be quite inexperienced to fancy something so meaningless."

Ouch.

"I guess I didn't consider it all that meaningless."

"I guess you haven't been kissed enough to know the difference."

What the hell is wrong with this guy? "Is it your intent to constantly insult me? Here, I'm trying to thank you for helping me out, and suddenly I'm feeling under attack."

"Attack?" He chuffs a laugh, and his tongue sweeps across his lips before they curve into a mocking smirk. "No, I don't intend to *constantly insult* you. Your gratitude is noted."

"Good."

"I trust you'll be back to assist my mother tomorrow. She's asked for you, as I understand."

"I promise. No more shenanigans."

"Fantastic. If that's all, I have some pressing matters to attend to."

"That's all."

I never know how to take Lucian Blackthorne. He's an enigma to me. Even as I make my way back toward the elevator, having accomplished what I came up here to do, I feel unraveled. As if I've spent the last twenty minutes spinning in place, watching layers of my skin peel away. I hate that he has this effect on me, as though he sees right through me, with one of my weaknesses down to a science: my pride. If only I knew his. The one soft spot that I could punch through to find out if there's anything on the other side of it. There has to be a heart inside this man. Why else would he help someone who means so little to him?

The elevator door opens, and I step inside, keeping my attention glued to the red paisley carpeting. It's only when they begin to close that I look up and catch him staring back at me. The eyes of the devil, burning right through me, and if not for the thick silver doors shutting him out, I'd probably crumble into a pile of ash.

On the first floor, I exit past Makaio and Rand escorting a man I've never seen at the Manor before. Dark hair, and equally dark eyes beneath bushy eyebrows that lower with a scowl, he doesn't divert his gaze as polite people do when passed.

Like he recognizes me, or something.

I don't recognize him, at all. Should I?

Confused, I turn around as Makaio leads him onto the elevator, and when he turns to face me again, his eyes pop wide.

"Wait!" He lurches forward, held back by the massive Hawaiian beside him, and the doors close shut.

In that moment, I wonder if I've just come face to face with Franco.

CHAPTER 32

LUCIAN

Stepping from the elevator on the floor to the catacombs, I casually sip my drink, as the sound of screaming echoes down the shadowy corridor. I open the door to the room on the right, where Makaio blocks most of my view. All I can see from the doorway is a pair of trembling feet sticking out from the right of the massive bodyguard, as Makaio goes to work on removing Franco's tongue, per my earlier request.

Because the best meetings are the ones where I talk, and assholes listen.

I stroll to the other side of the chair, getting a front row view of the carnage, where Franco lies in a bloody mess on the old dentist chair, his tongue on a silver tray beside him.

I tip back another sip of my drink and tuck my hand into my pocket, listening to him sob like a child. "I apologize for the haste of this meeting, but I'm afraid the matter was urgent. I've come to the decision that I'm neither going to return your shipment, nor entertain any bullshit from your uncle. No one will find your body. You'll be nothing more than another pile of bones to add to my collection."

As he moans and writhes in the chair, Makaio grabs one of

the tools from beside him and prods a sharp-looking object into the man's side.

Franco arches, his voice cracking on a scream before it dies down to another sob.

The sight of his tears tugs a smile that I bury in the last of my drink. "Turns out, you were right, Franco. I am fucking crazy."

CHAPTER 33

LUCIAN

Eight years ago ...

Annoying giggles echo down the hall as I pass the atrium on the way to answer my father's summons. The sound is as much a nuisance as the girl's presence, and when I catch sight of Amelia, sitting on one of the chairs beside my mother, while the two of them appear to trim flowers, I can't help but wonder how much longer this will go on. What started as an invitation to spend the week with us has turned into nearly a month of her and my mother running around this place like two obnoxious teenagers.

Amelia flashes yet another flirtatious smile, one of many in the last month, and I turn my head to dodge it and keep on down the hall, toward my father's office.

It seems she's always there, wherever I am. Whether it's in the pool, the gym, the garden, the hallways. I can't stand that she's everywhere. Always flirting and offering things I'm pretty sure my mother wouldn't approve of, if she heard them.

Of course, I always refuse.

I don't know what it is about her. She's undeniably one of the most beautiful girls in Tempest Cove, and yet, I'm not attracted to her in the least. Not since I've been forced to spend every day avoiding her, anyway. I'm waiting for my mother to bring up marriage, and that'll be when I put my foot down.

There's no way in hell I'll marry Amelia Boyd.

The elevator opens, and I slow my steps on entering my father's office, where he sits across from Mayor Boyd. Frowning, I keep my eyes on Boyd, while I take my seat beside him and look back to my father, whose flat expression offers no indication as to what this meeting is about.

"Hello, Lucian," Boyd says, his voice tense as he stares down at his entwined hands.

"Hello."

"Lucian, you know I'm not one to beat around the bush, so I'm just going to get right to the point of this meeting." My father has a way of setting my nerves on edge with his honesty, and today will be no exception. "Did you fuck Amelia?"

A bolt of shock pierces my chest, squeezing my lungs, and I sit forward to cough. "I'm sorry, what?" I try not to look at Boyd, whose glare is practically burning a hole in the side of my head right now. The last time I touched the girl was the night of my party, holed up in the cleaning closet, and I haven't had the inclination to go near her since. "I mean, we fooled around. A little."

"Did the two of you have sex?"

"It's … not what …" I swallow a harsh gulp and glance to the side, catching sight of Boyd's stern brows and unamused expression. "I wouldn't call it sex, really."

"'Fucks sakes, boy. Did you stick your dick inside her?" My father's questions have my hands sweating.

"For a couple minutes, I guess. Yeah."

Rolling his eyes, my father groans.

"Why are you asking me this?" Shifting my attention between

Boyd, whose flat lips and balled hands are a pretty good sign he wants to kill me, and my father who slouches in his chair, rubbing a hand down his face, I don't know whether to duck or run. "It was completely consensual between us. She wanted it as much--"

"She's pregnant, Lucian." My father's words punch my gut, and I clutch my stomach as bile shoots up my throat.

"Pregnant?" The back of my hand muffles the question, as I try to hold back the torrent of vomit itching to break free. "I didn't even … I wore a condom. And I never …"

"Condoms break. Surely your prestigious education has taught you something on sex ed." The ire in Boyd's voice confirms what I already suspected--the man would probably try to kill me, if my father weren't sitting across from him right now.

"Are you sure it's …" I know the answer to this, though. Amelia hasn't left the Manor since the night of the party, a month ago. As terrifying as it may be, I am the most probable suspect.

"Come on now, boy." My father swipes up the glass of liquor on the desk in front of him and guzzles what's left of it. "If that girl pined any harder for you, her feet would be stuck in the dirt, with roots coming out of her ass."

Boyd clears his throat, rolling his shoulders back. "Kindly bear in mind this is my *only* daughter."

"The Boyds are Catholic, as you know. It's not their way to terminate a pregnancy, or get knocked up out of wedlock, for that matter." Tapping his finger on the desktop, my father stares off for a moment, seeming to chew on his lips. "You're going to marry her."

Another punch to the gut. This one harder, the pain of it shooting up into my ribcage. "What? No. I can't."

"You have no choice, Lucian. You got yourself into this mess."

"I'll be there for her. I'll raise the child. Ensure that it never wants for anything, but I cannot marry her."

"You can desecrate her, though? Put your filth inside her?"

Boyd speaks through gritted teeth, his anger burgeoning before my eyes.

"It doesn't work that way, Son. Mayor Boyd has a reputation to uphold. How do you think it looks if his only daughter is pregnant, without a husband?"

I don't care how the fuck it looks. It's my life he's looking to muddle, and it's not like she didn't have a say in what we did that night. "This isn't the seventeenth century. Women get pregnant and have children, without marriage, all the time."

Cheeks puffed, my father lets out a long, dramatic exhale. "The decision has been made. You'll marry Amelia Boyd, and that's final."

CHAPTER 34

ISADORA

Nearly two weeks have passed since the incident with my mother and the drug dealer. I've texted Aunt Midge every day, twice sometimes, to see how she's doing. If she's heard anything. Seen anything. Gotten a sense that he might come back.

Everything has been quiet.

Lucian hasn't said a word to me since I braved barging into his office to thank him. We pass each other in the hallway sometimes, but it's like two ships passing on a placid sea. Not a word spoken between us. I've caught him watching me a few times, when I've been out in the garden, or playing piano, but never longer than a fleeting moment before he looks away.

Maybe I've thought too much of it, because I've had more dreams of him lately. Dark dreams I wouldn't dare tell a soul about, not even Kelsey. Ones where he keeps me imprisoned in this place, and I find myself questioning whether he's good, or evil. The other night, I woke up sweating and panting, calling out for him.

Humiliating to think that Giulia may have heard me.

I suppose I've always been drawn to older men, having

developed well before most girls my age. The boys I grew up with were immature and plain stupid, always touching. Fondling.

Taking without asking.

Grown men tend to be different toward me. Careful, if not curious.

The dark hallway of the first floor greets me, as I step out of the elevator and make my way to the dining room. En route, I pause at the atrium, and look inside where the last few weeks of contractors and construction workers have turned what was once unkempt and neglected into a vision of wonder and fascination. Healthy vines spill down the gilded iron bars, braided in small white lights. Newly painted walls and lush greenery give a splash of spectacular color. Lanterns hang from the ceiling like stars in the night sky, while the floors, polished and shining, reflect the glow above.

Breathtaking.

I step inside the room, empty of workers who must be on their lunchbreak, and take a seat at the piano. A device sits propped against the music rack. Small and clunky, it reminds me of a walkie-talkie.

A large, round button in the center of it carries the symbol for play, and out of sheer nosiness, I press it. Music drifts from its speakers like black ribbons flitting around me. Haunting and darkly beautiful.

It's a piece I've not heard before, I close my eyes, taking in every stroke of the keys, letting it wind around my senses.

The sadness. The longing.

The notes take shape inside my head like a living, breathing entity. A vision of Lucian's hands dancing over white keys, and up over my arms, his fingertips dragging across my skin. I breathe in through my nose, and exhale through parted lips, while the music takes me back to my most recent dream of him. I reach up to touch my lips, recalling the night he kissed me on the rooftop, my eyes still shuttered to everything but the scene playing behind my lids.

"What are you doing?"

At the sharp, menacing tone, I jolt from my musings and scramble to turn off the device, pressing the first button that stops the music. Muscles vibrating, I turn to find Lucian standing across from me, with a notepad clutched at his hip.

"Tell me you didn't mess anything up."

"I ... I didn't."

Scowl plastered to his face, he strides toward me and swipes up the device.

"I saw the recorder sitting there, and ..."

"It's a Tascam," he says, examining the equipment.

"A what?"

"A Tascam. Used to record tracks."

"It's your music, then?" I can't help the wonder in my voice, imagining such a beautiful piece originating inside his head. "I swear I only listened to it."

Shoulders sagging, he tips his head back, eyes screwed shut, as he presses the play button.

"Tell me you didn't mess anything up."

"I ... I didn't. I saw the recorder sitting there, and ..."

"It's a Tascam."

The playback is our conversation. I must've accidentally recorded over the music.

I slap a hand to my face, the needling pangs of shock stabbing my gut. "Oh, no."

"Hours, I tried to get that piece right. Now, it's gone." He waves his notebook in the air. "Ran to get something to jot down the notes." Jaw hard, he chucks the book across the piano strings beneath the lid.

"Lucian, I'm so sorry." Remorse hammers through me, crushing my chest like a heavy fist. "I didn't mean to touch it."

"You just can't keep your hands off anything, can you?" The

growl in his tone likely only represents a fraction of his anger. He tosses the Tascam onto the music stand, and when it falls to the keys, slamming out a hard note, I flinch. "I'll never remember it."

Lowering my gaze, I stare down at the keys, and while echoes of the song linger in my head, my eyes scan over every placement of my fingers. I see them. I *know* them. "I can."

Still turned away from me, he doesn't bother to acknowledge my response.

Exhaling a shaky breath, I set my fingers to the keys and close my eyes. At the first note, I feel the black ribbons dance around me as I play the song from memory. The soft caress of his hands on my skin. The warmth of his breath at my neck. Every moment of the song permanently seared by his imagined seduction that winds around each keystroke. The dream plays exactly as before, every look, every touch. Up until the point when it ends, and I open my eyes to Lucian's incredulous stare.

"How did you do that?" Disbelief blazes in his eyes while riding the tone of his voice.

"I played it from memory."

"I literally wrote that minutes before. How could you possibly know the notes?"

"I didn't know the notes. I can't read music."

Frown deepening, he crosses his arms. "How? I've heard you play Chopin. Liszt. Bach."

"All from memory. But I've never learned notes." The awe in his stare is too much, and I shift on the bench. "So ... are you going to stand there? Or are we going to figure out these notes?"

He reaches beneath the piano lid for his notebook, and I set my hands to the keys once more. For the next hour, he has me play small segments of the song, while he furiously jots down the notes, capturing every single one. Each time I play, the same images come to mind, making it almost impossible to look at him, for fear he'll see the desire burning in my eyes. By the time we're finished, I've mentally made love to Lucian over and over again.

He sits beside me on the bench, a partial smile playing on his lips as he stares down at the last page of music. For a man so serious, so focused on business and his work, there is a vulnerability to him in the pride he exudes right now. This is it. His soft spot, where the steel bends around the notes, and the shadows that always seem to follow him dance across the walls. Beneath the leathery skin and hardened bones, this is where his happiness hides.

I finally found it.

"Thank you for this."

Tucking my hands into my lap, I nod. "It's a beautiful piece. Would've been a shame to lose it."

"It would've."

"What will you do with it?" I try not to stare at his magnificent hands, the long fingers and perfectly trimmed nails, his skin slightly weathered with age.

"Nothing."

"Nothing?" This must be what my high school teacher felt like when I told him I had no plans to follow through with music. I can't fathom that Lucian would let such a beautiful piece collect dust.

"I didn't write it to do anything with it. I wrote it to get it out of my head."

What a wondrous place it must be inside his mind. A dark and wicked place, brimming with the bizarre and peculiar, just like the song.

His eyes finally fall on me, the soft amber glow of his irises eclipsed by shadows. "It reminds me of you."

The dryness of my throat becomes apparent when I attempt to swallow. "How so?"

"The way it's haunting. Delicate. Perilous, yet somehow alluring." Precisely the words I'd use to describe the song. "Annoying as fuck."

At a burst of laughter through my nose, I cover my face. "I annoy you?"

"Incessantly."

My laughter wilts to a sigh as his lips snare my attention, lulling me into the memory of being on the rooftop, lying beneath him. The many times I've thought about his kiss since that night, tasted the whiskey on my tongue, and have longed to feel the butterflies in my stomach again. The right and wrong waging war inside my head. The lure of it all, so intoxicating, I don't even realize I'm leaning into him until my lips brush his.

What are you doing! The warning blares inside my head.

His thigh twitches beneath my palm where I've unwittingly placed my hand.

Oh, my God.

Mortification washes over me in excruciating colors of red, as I back away enough to see the disapproval darkening his eyes.

He snatches up my wrist from his lap, startling me, and I wonder if he'll slap me across the face with my own hand. "You misunderstand my intent."

"I'm sorry." Cheeks burning with humiliation, I can't bring myself to look at him. "I thought you …. I mean we …. I thought you wanted …"

"You're a teenager. Practically a child. I'm a grown man." The derision in his voice is thick and condescending.

"I'm not a child," I snap, the distraction of his insult smoldering my embarrassment. "You had no problem kissing me before, as I recall."

Eye twitching, jaw shifting, he stares back at me. "A drunken mistake, as I said."

A mistake. I was a mistake.

I try not to let the harsh blow of his mockery slip beneath my skin, but I can't help it. "You really are something." I hate that my voice cracks on the last word, and I have to look away momentarily when the stinging rims of my eyes threaten tears. "You and I aren't so different, you know." Twisting my arm still caught in his grasp, I break loose and peel back the sleeve of my shirt to show the scars across my arm. "I know what it's like to push people away, too."

He doesn't spare them so much as a glance. "You think your small inconspicuous scars make us alike? You are *nothing* like me, Isa. You have no idea what I am, or what I've done to earn my scars."

"You're not a monster. Nor the devil everyone says you are. Devils don't help people." Beneath the cold shadows in his eyes lies a flicker of warmth, so subtle, I almost wonder if I'm imagining it. "You're just alone. Like me."

He snorts a mirthless laugh. "I've never been alone. That's the problem with having money. There's always someone who wants it."

"Is money always your excuse? Because mine was always that they weren't smart enough. Mature enough."

A muscle in his jaw tics, as I imagine him grinding my words in his teeth.

"What do you want, Isa?" He lifts my wrist to his face, holding it there as he kisses the skinny white lines across my skin. "You want me to fuck you? So you can add more to your collection?"

"Fuck *you*." I wrench my arm back, but he tightens his grip. "You don't have to be cruel."

"I do. It's the nature of my being. You're right, though. I've done a number of sadistic things to myself over the years." He runs his thumb over my scars, as if reading them, and that flickering warmth returns again. "But depriving myself has always been the worst."

The sadness, the loneliness in his voice tugs at my heart, and for a brief moment, I wonder if this is his honesty bleeding through the steel. Arm still propped in the air, I uncurl my fist to touch his face.

He recoils, throwing my hand off of him, his expression guarded and hard all over again.

The humiliation flares to life a second time, and I jolt up from the piano bench. "Never mind. I'm just …. It was stupid."

A hard tug of my arm jerks me into him until my butt slams back against the bench. Palm to my chin, he holds my face, and devours my breath in a white hot kiss.

Butterflies explode in my stomach, my heart fluttering out of control, a menagerie of wings and victory trapped inside of me. My head is dizzy and my muscles are weak, and it's a damn good thing I'm sitting down, or I'd have probably passed out. I reach out to hold onto something, and my fingertips are greeted by the hard bunched muscles of his biceps.

A feral growl rattles in his chest, and his fingers curl tighter, his tongue dipping past my teeth. With heightened fervor, he kisses me harder, and his hand slides to my nape, the tight grip there thwarting any chance to steal a breath. "I'm tired of these fucking games with you," he says through his teeth.

A warm palm skates up my thigh, and when he reaches beyond the hem of my skirt, I gasp into his mouth.

His touch falls away, and he breaks the kiss, leaving a cold and bitter emptiness between us. Tongue sweeping across his lips, he stares back at me, with rapid breaths and flared nostrils.

The enthralled look on his face reminds me of an animal that's just gotten a taste of blood and hasn't decided whether to spare, or finish off, the rest.

Gaze locked on his, I escort his hand up my thigh and beneath my skirt, my own hands trembling with fear and excitement. "It's okay," I whisper.

His breaths hasten, and the amber of his eyes is swallowed up by the blackness of his dilated pupils. At the first skim of his fingertips over the damp cotton of my panties, I watch his expression sharpen to a knowing smirk. I suck in a breath and close my eyes, concentrating on the tickle at the barrier to my flesh beneath.

I've been with boys, I've been touched by boys, but never a man so forbidden and off-limits as Lucian Blackthorne. The exotic animal trapped in a cage. It's like falling into a tank, not knowing if the circling shark will ultimately devour me.

Warm breath hits my neck, just as in my dreams, as he runs his finger up and down the indentation he's made, the slit of sensitivity. A shaky blast of air escapes my parted lips.

I brace one palm on the bench, squirming against his intrusive fingers, and spread my knees open to allow him access. "Oh, yes," I breathe, and suck my bottom lip between my teeth, until the coppery flavor puckers my tongue.

"You're my curse. Staying away from you, is like trying to hold my breath when the tide is rising." His words dance around my head, the deep timbre of his voice titillating my senses. "I want to drown in you."

I tip my head back, and the coarse scratch of his facial hair against my throat adds a delicious tickle, as he pushes my panties aside, rougher than expected, for the bare skin beneath.

He doesn't fumble in his movements, like boys my age. Every touch is deliberate and brimming with assurance that I'll be a hot, wet mess afterward.

"I hate that I could fuck you for hours and never tire of it." He kisses along the edge of my jaw, and on instinct I turn to face him. Tongue dancing over my lips, he licks the blood I've drawn, before sealing my mouth in a possessive kiss. His fingertips gather the sticky fluids he's worked up between my thighs, and he spreads it up over my swollen clit, gently rubbing my sensitive nub like a tiny pet he's trying to rouse from slumber. "Everything about you pisses me off," he grits against my mouth, the radiating tension hot and dangerous, while his fingertips work me beneath my skirt.

I let out a moan and lift my hips off the bench toward his unforgiving strokes. My belly curls, muscles tight, and my shirt is suddenly too tight, the scratchy fabric tickling my nipples through the lacy bra. Releasing my neck, he seems to take notice of the hard peaks and scrapes the tip of his thumb over the sensitive buds.

A tortured whimper leaks from my mouth, my whole body stiff, as if wires run beneath my skin.

"The way your body responds to my touch. Like the strings of a piano when the hammer strikes it. Every note of a song that I write. A song you keep begging me to play."

There's a hypnotic darkness in his eyes, malicious and desiring, and I wonder if this is how it feels just before the devil claims a soul. I pant with his movements, his fingers tunneling deeper, circling against my soaked slit, creating chords of music that escape my lips. He hasn't even penetrated me. "I dream of you sometimes." The ragged texture of my voice mirrors my slowly dissolving composure.

"What do you dream, Isa?"

"Of this. Of … of your hands on me."

"How far do we take this in your dreams? Am I fucking you?"

The mere thought of that sends tingles of excitement shooting through my core, and I can't answer him, for fear of sounding like a pervert who's fantasized about him. The ache between my thighs swells, as if attached by some invisible string that he pulls for his own amusement, and I cry out instead.

"Of course I'm fucking you. How do I feel inside of you?"

The heat of his breath on my skin, the touch of his fingers, the sound of his voice. It's all too much. *Too much.* My senses are on overload right now, spinning me out of control.

"So good. I don't want it to stop."

"You want my finger inside of you, Isa? To fill this tender little hole with something thick and warm." The tip of his relentless little weapon circles my entrance for emphasis, stirring the wet sticky juices over my skin, and I curl my hand around the bench, desperate to squeeze something.

I mindlessly nod, my body lost to the sensations he's stoked. Lust blazes through me, an inferno of need building at my core. I can't sit still. I can't move. My body is in chaos, waiting for the moment he puts it out of its misery and penetrates me.

His dark chuckle rakes over me. "Too bad," he says, and the moment he withdraws his fingers, the heat inside of me fizzles to a cold and bitter yearning.

"What?"

He captures my jaw in his hand, the same hand that stroked my overly sensitive clit moments before, and I can smell the arousal on his fingers. He presses his lips to mine, taking another piece of me. "I get off on pain. And there is nothing more exquisite than the pain of denying myself." Shoving his fingers into his mouth, he closes his eyes, as if savoring the taste of me on his tongue. "You're too young for me."

Too young. Too poor. Too unpopular. I've heard these things my whole life. Reasons for rejection. Yet from him, it somehow bites harder. The mercurial nature of the man, this hot and cold, is enough to make me scream with all the tension burning me up like a fever.

Bitterness explodes inside of me. "Why did you touch me, at all, if you had no intentions of following through?"

A smirk takes hold of his lips, one I want to smack right off his face. "Why do we bother to breathe, when we know we're going to die?" Standing up from the bench, he twists to look back at me. "I'd fuck you up in ways you've never been fucked before, Isa. Consider this a kindness."

The sensation fluttering in my gut is one I'm intimately familiar with when it comes to this man. Humiliation. Wet and disheveled, I'm pretty sure this is exactly why he bothered to touch me, at all, to show me he doesn't have to finish me off to leave me hot and panting for him like a stupid schoolgirl who's hot for teacher.

"There's a masquerade ball coming up this weekend. I'd like you to play for me."

My mind longs to cling to the conversation of what happened between us, but the curiosity of his request draws me out of those thoughts. "Piano?"

"Yes. Can you do that? For me?"

I want to deny him, just as he did me, but I can't. I'm ashamed to admit that I like this side of him. This teasing game of cat and mouse between us. I don't know why. Maybe I'm sick, but there's something thrilling about taunting the devil. "Of course. Whatever you like."

He slides his hands into his pants pockets, moving further away from the topic of us. "You'll need something to wear. I'll make arrangements for you to get what you like. There's a boutique in town. They have my credit card on file."

A dress. Another goddamn dress. Even if the guy is paying for it, like something out of *Pretty Woman*, I still dread the thought of having to wear something fancy. And no doubt, any *boutique* that has his credit card on file is going to be fancy. "Okay."

"Something elegant. There will be a number of very powerful and important people at this ball. Dress accordingly." He walks from the room.

CHAPTER 35

LUCIAN

Notebook still tucked beneath my arm, I descend the stone staircase to the awaiting vehicle, where Makaio opens the passenger door for me.

Rand is already inside, fingers entwined with telling impatience, as I fall into the seat beside him. For the opportunity to have my fingers down Isa's panties, I rush for no one. Not even the Scarpinato men, who'll be anxious to know where Franco disappeared to, I'll bet. They requested a meeting with me a few days ago, one I was reluctant to oblige at first, until a crazy idea popped into my head.

"I don't know how you act so calmly, facing these men." Rand keeps his attention toward the passenger window, as the car idles down the long drive.

"I don't look at them as anything more than flesh and bone."

"An army of flesh and bone, with the kind of weaponry that'd make the military jealous."

"Words are the most powerful weapon in the world. Alongside money. And if you combine the two, you're practically a God."

Sighing, he shakes his head. "Well, I must admit, I'm dying to know what words you plan to exchange during this meeting."

"I'm sure you are. And I can assure you, you have nothing to worry about with this meeting."

"The more you talk about it, the more I worry."

"Then, let's not talk about it." I smooth my hand over the notebook. If only I could've captured the notes of her moans, I'd claim the song as mine and no one else's. The sound was everything I dreamed it would be, and coupled to that pleading look in her eyes, it's enough to make a man lose control.

As if I needed another reason to be excruciatingly intrigued by this girl. She's like a bad hangover after a long night of drinking, but hell if that's going to keep me from grabbing the bottle again. One sip is enough for now, while my conscience pummels away at my head for trying to corrupt an innocent teenager.

It takes over two hours to drive and ferry to the restaurant in Boston, where the Scarpinatos requested to meet. I've no doubt it'll be teeming with their men, waiting for the moment they can open fire on me. But all that bullshit about family being the most important thing in the mafia is just that: bullshit. The truth is, they haven't been relevant in a number of years, and their numbers are dwindling. They'd have to fuck their own sisters to keep a pure bloodline nowadays. If not me, some other asshole would've come along and silenced Franco, because you don't walk around with a mouth that big without someone wanting to shove the barrel of a gun into it.

Straightening my jacket, I enter the dimly-lit restaurant that looks like a two-dimensional wanna-be of Tuscany, with painted arched doorways and awnings on brick walls. Out the rear door on the patio, I find Vincent and Stefano, Franco's uncle and cousin, seated at a table toward the back. Stefano, the younger one, reminds me of a dark-eyed Ray Liotta, with his black hair and dimples, who waves me over.

"Here we go," Rand says beside me, the nervous wobble in his voice bringing a smile to my face.

Standing off to the side, behind the Scarpinatos, are two stocky men, bodyguards judging by their stiff and guarded posture, who eye-fuck Makaio as we approach.

"Gentlemen," I say, taking a seat across from them, alongside Rand, while Makaio stands off to the side behind me, eye-fucking the men right back.

Ordinarily, they'd offer a hug and a handshake, but I didn't give them the opportunity, which is why I'm guessing Vincent is looking at me like I tried to cop a feel under the table, or something.

"Been a long time, Lucian. How you been?" Stefano asks, nowhere near concerned with etiquette. That's the problem with the new generation--they just don't care anymore.

"Excellent."

"Sorry to hear about your father. He was a good guy."

"Yeah, well, when the big man says it's time ..."

I watch the two of them give the sign of the cross, before kissing the crucifixes dangling from the chains at their neck. It's incredible. The obligations of religion that force them to show respect to a man they've plotted to kill on at least one occasion. As much as my father tried to keep the peace with them throughout his life, nobody's perfect. I almost want to say it again, to see if they'll repeat the ritual.

Stefano leans in and rests his elbows on the table. "We called you to this meeting to discuss the status of our arrangement."

"Which one are we talking about? The shipment I've with-held? Or the future shipments I refuse to deliver?"

Rand clears his throat beside me, probably holding back a torrent of piss right now.

An un-genuine smile stretches Stefano's lips, and he sits back in his chair, hiking his elbow up on the seat. "See, that's not gonna work. We have a longstanding history with your company. A contract."

"If you'll kindly produce the contract, I'm happy to discuss the terms of it."

"It's a verbal contract, asshole. Between our grandfathers."

"Both of whom are now decaying in the ground, *asshole*." This meeting's off to a great start. I can practically hear the fragile threads of Stefano's patience snapping inside his head.

Nostrils flaring, he shifts his jaw in annoyance. "We have suppliers looking to move a shit-ton of product."

"Fantastic. I trust you won't be at a loss finding a replacement to ship it for you."

Jerking forward, he slams his fist against the table, like an angry toddler, and at Makaio's lurch beside me, the two body-guards behind Stefano reach behind their backs for what I presume are guns.

"I ought to knock that smug fucking smile off your face!"

Still wearing that smug fucking smile, I quirk a brow. "Careful now. I wouldn't want over a million-dollars-worth of product to end up as fish food."

Rolling his shoulders back, he exhales a long breath and raises his hand, signaling for his men to stand down. "You've been doing this a long time. Why the sudden change of heart?"

As I pull my cigarette case from inside my coat pocket, his men lurch again, but I hold the case up for them to see, and pop it open, sliding one of my smokes out. Makaio already has the Zippo lit beside me, and I lean in to light the end of it.

"I fucking hate my job. Hate. My job. If I didn't have to deal with all my father's shitty loose ends, I'd buy a boat and sail around the world, fucking every woman at every port, until I die of some raging STD. You're the first of many loose ends."

"What are you saying? You're gonna ... sell the fucking company?"

"That's exactly what I'm saying. Do I look like I'm over here trying to produce an heir?" With a shrug, I take another drag of my smoke. "It's going to happen eventually, unless the key to everlasting life suddenly comes in the form of daily suppositories and denture glue."

"You can't do that. We've been partners a long time. You don't just ditch a business partnership."

"I believe a man's odds eventually catch up to him, Stefano. We have been doing this a long time. And at some point, someone is going to get wise to the fact that I have been moving large shipments for the mafia. It's going to be very bad. And my dreams of sailing and fucking? Gone like a prostitute when the meth runs out."

Beside Stefano, Vincent sits rubbing his fingers together, the harsh breaths coming out of his nose reminding me of a bull seeing red. "What do you propose?"

"I'm glad you asked." I lean forward to flick the ash of my cigarette in Stefano's drink. "I'll hand off your shipment and, as a courtesy, waive the usual cut. To honor my grandfather's *verbal* contract with your grandfather, which, let's face it, with the rising inflation, probably didn't amount to much back then, I'll buy out your arrangement for three-million up front, and another three-million when the business sells." I catch the quick exchange of glances between Stefano and Vincent, as I ease back into my seat.

"How soon?" Vincent also reaches for a pack of cigarettes out on the table in front of him and lights one up.

"I'll have Rand draft the paperwork immediately." I lean forward to toss the remains of my cigarette in Stefano's drink, catching the glare he shoots back. "Provide an account number to wire funds to. Your shipment will be at port as early as tomorrow morning."

"And what about our suppliers?"

Rubbing my hand across my jaw, I breathe in the heady scent of Isa still clinging to my fingers. "I'll provide the name of a smaller operation. I'm afraid that's the best I can do."

"You honor this ... and we'll once again be in good standing."

Vincent's eye squints as he takes another drag of his cigarette and points his finger at me. "A man's word is gold."

"And I'm a man of my word. Now, if you gentlemen will excuse me, I have boats to shop for." I push up from my seat, and Stefano leans forward.

"One more thing. We haven't heard from Franco in a few weeks. As I understand, he was in contact with you just before he went missing. You wouldn't happen to know anything about that, would you?"

Lips tight, I lower myself back into my seat and set my hands on the table. "As a matter of fact, I would. It so happens, I killed him."

The slow descent of Stefano's brows must mirror the slow realization that my reputation is everything they say with an extra helping of bat-shit.

"'The fuck? Are you fucking nuts? Tell me you're fucking playing right now, because no way a man comes into another man's territory, sits down at his table, and confesses to killing his family. You've lost your goddamn mind."

"I'm probably a little unstable. But that's not really my excuse. The truth is, it was bound to happen eventually. And might I add, Franco threatened me on your behalf. I'm certain I'm not the first."

As Stefano lurches forward, Vincent sets his hand on his son's arm to settle him. "What did you do?"

"Cut his tongue out first."

"I oughta have my men gun you down where you sit, you crazy piece of shit."

Wouldn't surprise me if Stefano opened his mouth to expel a cloud of dust, as much as he's grinding his teeth.

"I suppose you'll have to ask yourself, was Franco worth almost seven-million dollars alive?"

Stefano slams his mouth shut, rolling his head against his shoulders in a piss poor attempt to calm his anger.

"You're right. He was bound to get himself in trouble. If not you, then someone else." Vincent takes another drag of his cigarette and blows it off to the side. "Little prick had a mouth the size of Massachusetts."

Stefano snaps his gaze toward Vincent. "Pop. He was family."

Vincent waves his hand in dismissal. "My brother's son. Half Irish."

As I said, so much for family. I could've probably offered half the amount, and they'd have come up with a reason Franco wasn't worth the retaliation.

"All I gotta say is, if that shipment ain't at port tomorrow morning, all hell is gonna break loose." Stefano has a funny way of going about negotiations, reminds me of a pitbull with a set of false teeth. If it wasn't for his father's leash, he'd have been put down already.

Hell isn't going to break loose. Not when I'm already running the ship and the crew.

I push up from the table again and step aside to let Rand out. I'm sure the guy is about one breath away from a stroke, after this meeting. "I said I was crazy. I didn't say I was stupid. We have a deal, gentlemen?" Stretching my hand toward him, I wait for Stefano to shake it. It's Vincent who shakes my hand first, and Stefano reluctantly follows suit.

"Honesty is a rare, if not foolish, quality in a man, Lucian," Vincent says.

"Isn't that the fucking truth."

"Master Blackthorne, I don't know if you're a genius, or if you've absolutely lost your mind." Rand sits beside me, rubbing his forehead. "I've never felt the urge to throw up in a meeting in my whole life, until today."

I snort a laugh, but as I stare out the window, my thoughts

aren't dwelling on the Scarpinatos. They're wrapped around a nineteen-year-old, whose toned thighs have somehow squeezed every other thought out of my mind.

"I don't even think your father, as bold as he could be, had the gumption to confess to killing a Scarpinato. He wouldn't even think of it."

My father allowed himself to amass what I call enemy debt. Too many favors that amount to too many potential enemies. "He was never much of a risk-taker."

"You certainly have a more reckless approach to negotiations, but I admire your audacity."

"Had I not confessed to killing Franco, they'd have come sniffing around eventually. You saw the accusation written all over their faces, when we first sat down. I could practically smell it on Stefano."

"Pretty sure that was spaghetti sauce, boss." Makaio chuckles from the front seat, and I can't help but share his amusement. After all, it's not every day a man gets to press the mafia's buttons.

"Anyway, they now know I'm a man with nothing to hide."

"Well, it's certainly nice to know that I won't have to sleep with a gun beneath my pillow."

"Wait. You don't usually sleep with a gun beneath your pillow?" Makaio frowns back at us from the rearview mirror. "Who doesn't sleep with a gun beneath their pillow? I do. Do you, boss?"

"Always."

Rand sneers and turns his gaze back toward the passenger window. "Well, I doubt either of you sleep wearing an undergarment for incontinence, so there's that."

CHAPTER 36

LUCIAN

Eight years ago ...

I gulp back the entire glass of champagne and signal the waiter for another, while my buddy, Sebastian, does his best to piece together a shit best man speech. The only time he's ever met the bride was at my graduation party, when she snubbed him, so I've gotta give him some credit for not making her out to look like a total bitch.

"And I wish you a long and happy life together. Cheers."

With his official toast, I polish off my fourth glass. At this rate, I'll be too trashed for the first dance. Maybe someone else will fill my place for it.

I catch sight of my father, standing off with Mayor Boyd, both of them laughing. It makes sense why Boyd would be delighted, marrying into power and wealth, but I haven't quite figured out the payoff for my father, aside from strapping me down with domesticated life. Perhaps that's the only payoff, but I've known my father long enough to recognize he doesn't do anything that isn't wholly for his own gain.

"It's beautiful, isn't it?" Amelia sits beside me, not having said much for most of the night, aside from the templated vows the two of us memorized this morning. "Your mother did such a nice job planning *everything.*"

There's a dash of animosity in her tone, though subtle, as she's cunning enough to disguise her contempt beneath layers of polished etiquette.

"I'm sure she paid someone to take care of the details." It's a chip at her pride, but I'm too drunk to care.

"Have you given any thought to the honeymoon?" She sips a glass of water, and I reckon everyone at this dog and pony show knows she's knocked up because of it.

"What's the point? You're already carrying my child, aren't you?"

The flinch of her eyes betrays the indifference she's struggling to hold in place like a mask that's too small for her face. "I understand this whole thing isn't what either one of us would have chosen. But the least you can do is pretend to enjoy the evening."

I lift yet another glass of champagne. "I'm working on that."

As the night rolls on, I stumble my way through the first dance and the sloppy cake cutting, walking off before she has the opportunity to smash the twenty-thousand dollar cake my mother ordered in my face. By the time it's over, I feel like I've been strung up by my briefs most of the night, my ass hanging out.

With the music blasting through the atrium, I stumble my way out into the hallway, my brain swimming in at least three bottles worth of champagne.

"Lucian." The sound of Amelia's voice is fine china scraping against ground glass.

I want to claw it out of my skull.

"Lucian, wait."

On unsteady feet, I pause halfway down the hall, while she scurries to catch up to me. It's only because she's the pregnant bride of the evening that I give her the time.

"I'll help you to our bed."

"*Our* bed? No. There is no *our* bed. You sleep in *your* bed. I sleep in *my* bed."

Tears well in her eyes as she turns away from me. "It was a surprise to me, as well. I didn't do this to trap you."

"Then how th'fuck did my father know about it b'fore me? Huh? How th'fuck did your father know b'fore me?"

"It was wrong of me not to tell you right away. I should have. I'm sorry."

"You're sorry? Th'only thing I'm sorry about is sticking my dick in you." It's then I notice the music has cut out, and I turn to see a crowd of guests standing outside the atrium.

The potent fog of alcohol tamps down the flare of irritation burning inside of me.

Amelia breaks into tears, and runs off down the hall.

And once again, I stand here looking like the villain.

CHAPTER 37

ISADORA

Present day ...

I stare in the mirror, as Giulia pins the last curl in place with a clip adorned in crystals. My hair hangs in long, lazy curls over my shoulders, gleaming with whatever products she used to make it shine. Since I never bothered with prom, or any of the dances in school, I've really never had the opportunity to dress up this way, aside from for the few weddings Aunt Midge has dragged me to, but she was often the one to do my hair, and all I can say about her efforts is *she tried.*

The dress is not one I would've chosen myself. Long, black and vampy, it clings to my curves, and flares out past my knees. The obscene slit up the side feels almost too racy, but the woman at the boutique insisted I was the epitome of grace and elegance, in spite of my trepidations. Lace and jewels make up the bodice that emphasizes my breasts, while long sleeves cover my scars. The black, Swarovski rhinestone, Venetian mask punctuates what I've always been told are cat-like eyes, and the red lipstick plumps my already too-fat lips.

"My God, Isa. You look like a maleficent goddess." The solemn expression on Giulia's face belies the awe in her words. I'd believe it jealousy, for not having been invited to the masquerade, but she wouldn't have gone through so much trouble, fussing over me, if that were the case. And that's not what I've gathered of her personality so far.

"Is everything okay?"

In the mirror's reflection, she frowns, before her gaze falls away, prompting me to turn around.

"Giulia?"

"You need to be careful around these men tonight. They're not what they seem." Before I can ask her more, she crosses the room and grabs the shoes set out for me, and when she returns, she lowers herself to the floor at my feet. "I don't know why he would ask you to do this."

"What is it about them that concerns you?"

Raising the hem of my dress, she slips the black stiletto heel over my foot, which fits snugly, followed by the other, then pushes upright again. "These are not just random guests he's invited. They're very powerful."

I recall Lucian's comment a while ago, about the men being important. I imagine a lot of *important men* come and go in this place, so what makes these so exceptionally unnerving to her?

"I'll be on my best behavior." Smiling, I take one step toward the bathroom to blot some of this obnoxious lipstick, but feel a tight grip of my arm.

"It's not like that, Isa. These men are ... dangerous." A flicker of remorse dances across her face, and it's then, I realize she's trying not to divulge too much.

"How are they dangerous?"

"I can't say much. I won't, so don't ask. But stay by Lucian's side. And if one of these men try to proposition you, tell him your debt is with Lucian."

"What?"

"Trust me." Her fingers squeeze my arm, emphasizing the urgency in her eyes.

"Is this the *secret group* thing you told me about a while ago?"

"Yes. And no more questions."

"Just one more. Please. Why did you go through so much trouble, making me look like this, if I'm to avoid drawing attention to myself?"

"Because Lucian demanded that I help you look elegant for the evening. But I'm afraid, even he couldn't anticipate that you'd look like this."

"Like what?"

"Food for the sharks."

I have to remind myself not to wring my dress, as I stand outside the door of the atrium, palms sweating and trembling, while the clamor of voices on the other side tells me it's a full house.

A couple walks toward me, arms linked, wearing masks, and evening attire that I imagine cost as much as this dress the woman at the boutique insisted I charge to Lucian's credit card. The man's stare through the holes in his mask lingers long after they pass, forcing me to turn away as I recall Giulia's warning.

Damn this dress. The *consultant*, as she called herself, wouldn't take no for an answer, when I insisted on something less flashy and ... sexy. I'm certain it was the most expensive in the shop, as Lucian had apparently told her, before I arrived, to spare no expense. Even Makaio shifted uncomfortably, when I emerged from the dressing room wearing the thing.

"Breathe, Isa." *They're just people.* Human beings who sat on toilets sometime today looking as undignified as everyone else. It was a saying Aunt Midge used to have about the haughty tourists she encountered at the The Shoal on occasion: *They shit in toilets like the rest of us.* Crude, but it's always put things into perspective for me. Aunt Midge was good for that, never letting others make her feel inferior.

"Isa? Is that you?" At the sound of Rand's voice, I glance up to see him approaching in a black tuxedo, and catch the widening of his eyes through the mask. "Oh, my. You look … stunning. Why are you standing out here? Master Blackthorne requested you play piano this evening, did he not?"

"He did. I'm just … trying to settle my nerves."

"Well, come on, then. I'm sure he'll be very anxious to know you haven't backed out on your promise." He bends his arm toward me and jerks his head. "Shall we?"

"Of course." Linking my arm in his, I take another long inhale and stand in the entrance of the atrium behind the couple who passed me moments ago.

Breath hitches in my throat as I take in the beauty of the room within. Lights have been dimmed enough that the hundreds of lit candles give the room a soft flicker and glow. The various-sized lanterns overhead are falling stars against the night sky, and the glow of lights winding through the vines only adds to the ambience. From the curved steel beams overhead, what look like bird-cages hang over the crowd below, though it's hard to make out what's inside of them. Around the room stand a few more cages on pedestals, and though I can detect something moving within, I can't identify what they are.

A small line forms where Makaio runs a metal detector over each guest, before checking what must be an invitation and allowing them to pass.

The man in front of us cranes his neck, looking back at me, and I catch the corner of his lips lift with a smile--the sight of which has me turning away to avoid eye contact. Thankfully, the masks do a fairly good job of concealing everyone's identity. If not for his voice, I'd have never recognized Rand in the hallway.

It isn't long before we reach Makaio, who waves us inside.

"Master Blackthorne would like you to start playing in about twenty minutes, or so. That's when the orchestra is due for a break." As soon as Rand says it, I notice the music beneath the din of laughter and conversation. A stage has been set up toward the back of the room, where a small orchestra sits, and beside them, the piano that I'll be playing.

"Got it." The scenery continues to lure my gaze, drawing my eyes toward the ceiling that I can see, now I'm inside the room, has been made to look like the glow of a flame overhead. Still, I can't make out what's in the cages, but the spectacle of it enthralls me so much, I don't notice Rand is no longer beside me.

Curious, I cross the room, ignoring the unwanted stares of those I pass, both men and women, as I make my way toward one of the beautiful, gilded cages. It's only when I'm up close that I can finally make out the dark creatures fluttering around inside. Large moths from the looks of it, and on their backs is a strange marking that resembles a skull.

"*Acherontia atropos.*"

The deep, rich sound in my ear sends a flutter through my chest, mirroring that of the moths' wings against the cage. My blood sizzles, and the air seems to grow thinner. I turn to find a tall, handsome figure rounding the cage from the other side.

Wearing a demi-mask, and a perfectly-tailored black brocade coat over a gray vest and white shirt beneath, Lucian looks both handsome and diabolically wicked, like something out of a gothic novel. "It's named after Archeron, the river of pain and sorrows, and atropos, eldest of three fates who cut the thread of life. More commonly known as the death's-head hawkmoth," he continues, and my cheeks flush at the sight of him. The mask completely covers the scarred half of his face, leaving only the too-handsome side of him exposed. "People once believed they were an evil omen." He runs his fingers along the outside of the cage. "Two moths were discovered in the bedchamber of Mad King George the Third during a bout of psychosis. It's said the incessant squealing sounds they made plagued on his weakened mind."

"And you keep them in beautiful cages as pets."

"I appreciate things that others tend to fear and cast off as evil."

Stepping to the side, he lifts one of the candles from a cluster on a nearby table and holds it up to the cage. The moths flutter and climb the spindles of the cage toward the flickering light.

"Fascinating, isn't it?" he asks, keeping the candle just far enough away so as not to harm the insects inside. "The way they flock to torment. Death. A fatal attraction."

"Can you blame them? Fire is warm and inviting."

"How tragic, to crave the very thing that can destroy you. If I opened this cage, we'd watch them burn alive."

"That's … macabre when you put it that way."

Twisting around, he sets the candle back down alongside the others and turns his attention back to me. "You chose this dress?" Beneath the shimmer of appreciation in his eyes lies a shadow of annoyance that mirrors the tone of his voice.

"You don't like it?"

"Everyone is looking at you."

Over my shoulder, I glimpse a few gazes in my direction, one of whom comes from the man I followed inside. "This bothers you."

"Yes." He steps around the cage until he's standing beside me, and a shiver skitters down my back when his lips feather my ear. Heat blooms inside of me, the dress suddenly too hot and tight against my skin. "It's as if they want to consume you alive. Or perhaps it's the other way around, like the moths to the candle."

I turn just enough that our lips nearly touch. "You were looking at me, too."

Scintillating amber eyes dip to my dress and back. "If I

suspected any one of these bastards were thinking the same thing I was when I first saw you, I'd kill them all."

"I'm too young for you, remember?"

"You are." The gentle brush of his knuckles along the edge of my neck has my heart hammering inside my chest. "And too tempting."

"What torture that must be."

"You have no idea. Particularly with how ravishing you look tonight."

"Then, why put yourself through it?" I glance around the room at the more scantily clad women, most likely hired as entertainment for anyone who came alone. "There seems to be plenty of women your age here. Why trouble yourself, at all, with me?"

"I ask myself the same question. Somehow, the more I stay away, the more I can't. That's the tragedy in all of this. The cease-less draw of the flame."

"For a ruthless businessman, that's awfully undisciplined of you."

"Ruthless, indeed. And curious as hell."

"What kind of curiosities plague the mind of a devil?"

The richness of his chuckle hits a nerve somewhere inside of me, the mask emphasizing an unearthly beautiful smile that sends goosebumps across my skin. Coming to a stand behind me, facing away from the crowd, he presses his steel chest into my back, once again reminding me of his size. Every cell in my body flares to life, when he slides his hand down my arm and threads his fingers in mine, the strength in them clasped around my more delicate bones. At the scratch of his mask against my neck, I tilt my head, allowing him full access. "What I wouldn't give to peel this dress off of you. Slowly."

"They're watching us, aren't they?"

"I approached you intentionally, Isa. I'd hate for anyone to make the mistake of thinking you're fair game."

"Including you."

"Especially me."

Desire simmers in my blood, when his lips press against the pulsing vein in my neck. "You're the most confusing person I've ever met."

"And you're the most irresistible." He kisses his way up my neck to my ear, where he nips my lobe, and I squeeze my fingers in his.

"I gave you the green light already. What more do you need?"

"That's just it. What I want, and what I need, are two edges of the same blade." With my head still tipped, he licks the shell of my ear. "I want you to tell me if any of these men proposition you tonight. Do you understand?"

"Why? What will it mean, if they do?"

"That's my concern, not yours."

"And if I welcome it?"

His fingers tighten around mine, and he exhales a sharp breath against my throat. "That will be my concern, as well."

I hate that I'm putty in this man's hands. That all it takes is a few poetic words and expert placement of his lips to leave me panting like an eager puppy.

"I meant to ask you. You could've had anyone play for you tonight. Why me?"

"Anyone else wouldn't have been half as enthralling to watch as you." With a tug, he leads me away from the cage, toward the piano.

The members of the orchestra set down their instruments, and the room falls quiet, as I take my seat on the bench.

Fingers to the keys, I exhale a shaky breath and close my eyes. The first notes of *Nocturne Op. 9 No. 2* echo through the room. Some of the partygoers have gathered around the piano. Others resume their conversations, but I keep on playing.

Through the crowd, I find Lucian standing in a circle of men, staring at me over the rim of his drink. The most handsome and

279

intimidating of all, even with the mask concealing half his face. He remains riveted, while the men lean in, obviously prattling on as he ignores them.

The intensity of his eyes is too much, and I have to look away, for fear of faltering in the song I've chosen to play. At another glance, I see he hasn't conceded so easily. His gaze remains unmoved. One of the men beside him pats his chest, breaking into laughter. It's painfully awkward to watch when Lucian sips his drink, not bothering to share in the man's hilarity.

The way he watches, like we're the only two in the room, makes me wonder what he'd do right now, if that were truly the case.

For the next hour, I run through the songs I know best, and when I reach the final note of the last, I glance around the room, noting Lucian has disappeared. Without much pause in between, I begin to play the song that he composed. The one I helped him capture in his notebook. Closing my eyes, I allow his notes to wind through my mind, while I imagine his roaming hands, and once I've finished, my audience claps, and I rise from the bench. Eyes scanning the crowd, I search for Lucian again, as the members of the orchestra return to their seats.

"I noticed you never once flipped through the music." The voice has me spinning around to a masked man with gray hair behind me, wearing a standard tuxedo, and he lifts his mask just enough that I recognize Mayor Boyd.

His comment brings a smile to my face. "A freakish talent."

He leans in, keeping his hands crossed in front of his body. "I think you mean extraordinary. One must never downplay the gifts God bestows upon us."

Flush with the discomfort of his compliments, I nod. "That's true." Once again, I search the crowd for the most handsome face, but find no one familiar, aside from the man beside me.

"You're looking for someone?"

Giulia's words hit me again, about staying near Lucian, but

I've met Mayor Boyd before, and the man hardly seemed danger-ous. My fingers fidget with the unease of chatting with the father of Lucian's dead wife, while just moments ago, I imagined his former son-in-law tearing away my dress. "I just ... no. No one in particular."

"Ah. If I were twenty years younger and had a stunning beauty like yourself on my arm, I surely wouldn't let you out of my sight for long."

Surely, he's forgotten that I'm only nineteen. If he's as old as I think he is, twenty years younger would still make him twice my age. And again, what an awkward conversation to be having with this man.

A change of topic is definitely in order, because if my cheeks get any redder, someone will think the man slapped me. "My apologies for not giving you a heads-up about Mrs. Blackthorne the last time you were here."

"I didn't realize Laura had declined so dramatically in the last few years. It's a shame to see her that way. She was always such a vibrant and bold woman."

"I've only worked with her for a short time, but I can imagine. She must've been quite a character."

"She was. She treated my Amelia so well." The first quiver of his lip knots my stomach, as his eyes shine with tears. "My sweet, sweet girl." He lifts the mask, tugging a handkerchief from the pocket of his tuxedo, and daubs his eyes. "I'm sorry. I don't think a father ever gets over losing a child."

"It's okay. I understand." I don't understand, at all, but it's all I can think to say to him.

"I know this might sound strange, but ... may I hug you?"

My whole body freezes at his request, and I am officially and utterly at a loss for words. "Uh. Well. Sure, I guess."

Without a moment's hesitation, he leans forward, wrapping his arms around me, as he pulls me in for a hug. Squeezed tight against him, my breasts smashed into his chest, he holds me there, and the broken sniffles in my ear only heighten the discomfort and alarm pulsing through me right now. It's then I realize I'm holding my arms away from him, uncertain what to do with them.

"I just miss her so, so much." He shifts his body against me, sliding my breasts across his chest, and I cringe at the sensation. "I couldn't even save her soul. I only pray the Lord spared her decision."

Shrugging to break his embrace, I feel him lower his hands to the middle of my back and tighten around me.

"I see you've met my pianist." Lucian's voice, laced with a small bit of antipathy, is a welcomed sound, and thankfully, Mayor Boyd releases me.

"She's very good. Very talented."

"She is. And if you'll excuse us, Patrick, I have a private matter to discuss with her."

"Of course." Taking my hand in his, Mayor Boyd bends to kiss my knuckles and smiles. "I look forward to continuing our conversation after you speak with Mr. Blackthorne."

I'd rather stare at the candles for the next three hours.

Sliding my hand out of Mayor Boyd's, Lucian leads me through the crowd to a door made of glass, which he opens onto the courtyard outside. The full moon shines down on the decaying foliage that climbs the outer walls of the atrium, and we come to a stop in the shadows. From here, we can still see the crowd inside, but remain concealed by the overhanging trees and the stone wall of the castle.

With a bit more force than I expect, my body spins around, and the cold wall presses into my back. Lucian steps toward me, diminishing the space between us.

"When did I give you permission to play that piece?" Malice burns through his fingertips where he squeezes my arms, and once again, he's irritated with me. When is he not?

"You didn't, I--"

"I didn't. That's right. And yet, you took it upon yourself to play it, anyway." He gives a slight shake, his lips peeling back with his anger. "Why?"

"It's a beautiful song. So haunting, I hear it every time I close my eyes. And I'm sorry I played without your permission. It was wrong of me. Please forgive me."

"What did he say to you?" he asks through clenched teeth, cluing me in to what I'd bet is the real source of anger pulsing through him.

"Mayor Boyd? Nothing, really. He just talked about his daughter."

"What about his daughter?"

"Just that he misses her. What's wrong?"

Hand to my throat, he lifts my chin, amber eyes drilling into mine. Licking his lips, he breathes hard through his teeth, the mask concealing his face enough that I can't get a sense of whether he's pissed at me, or Boyd. "He touched you. Why did he touch you?"

"He asked if he could hug me."

"And you said yes? You *allowed* him this comfort?"

"Yes. Though, I'm not going to lie, I regretted it immediately."

A tiny fissure cracks his veneer. Jealousy practically oozes out of him like a dangerous poison to anyone who dares touch it.

"And what about me? Would you regret it, if I kissed you right now?" His pride dangles before me like a flitting string, one I want to recklessly pull to see what it means to unravel this man.

"Are you asking my permission?"

"I don't ask for anything. When I want something, I take it."

The intensity staring back at me through the holes in his mask is nearly sex itself. Never has a man looked at me this way, with such possession.

"Then, what are you waiting for?"

Warm lips crush mine in a kiss that demands my surrender, as he keeps his hand propped at my throat. His other hand slides up the slit of my dress, his finger hooking the string of my panties and pulling them down my thighs. The fragile bands dig into my flesh as he nudges my legs apart with his knee.

Beneath his sensual touch and the longing in his eyes lies something filthy and depraved. Tension and hostility radiate from every pore in his body, and it suddenly occurs to me why. He can't control himself. If he could, he'd have left me at the mercy of Mayor Boyd.

A part of me wants to laugh at the victory, but the sad truth is, I'm just as weak as he is.

The moment his fingertips make contact with my bare skin, he groans into my mouth, while gathering up the slick arousal that belongs to him. "You always have to be fucking wet, don't you?" The air of violence in his voice stokes my excitement for some reason, I can't explain why.

The very thought that my arousal turns him on feels like a whole lot of power in my hands. "Maybe you should stop, if it makes you so angry."

"I can't stop. All I think about is this." He drives his finger up inside of me, and I arch into him on a moan. "Day and night, I think about your taste. Your scent. The softness of your skin against my tongue."

"You said you love the torture. Now you don't?"

"I'm beyond torture. I'm on the brink of madness," he says, in a voice that sounds like he's on the verge of cracking. Squeezing my throat tighter lifts my chin into the air, my mouth gaping for a breath, and he closes his lips over mine once again. In and out, his fingers pump into me, the wet sucking slide and our harsh mingling breaths the only sound between us. "I have to fuck you. I shouldn't. It's wrong. But I have to."

Releasing me, he lowers to his knees and throws off the mask. The second he lifts my dress at the slit, the cool summer air hits my bare sex, and at the tearing sound, I look down to see he's broken the string of my panties. The garment falls to the ground beside us, and he hikes my leg up, his movements frantic and rushed, as if he fears he'll stop himself any moment.

Soft lips clamp to my clit, and as his tongue drags over the sensitive bit of flesh, my belly clenches, and I reach down to grab a handful of his hair. "Oh, God!"

He laps up my juices, tonguing my flesh as though he can't bear to leave one drop behind. His scars tickle my skin, and I dig my nails into his scalp, crying out, while he eats like a ravenous beast who hasn't had a meal in days. The merciless tug of his lips draws my hips away from the wall, and I tip my head back, palm against the stones behind me, searching for something to squeeze.

"Lucian! Please." I don't know what I'm begging him for. More? Mercy? An end? All I know is my belly is tight, and my muscles are burning for this man and his delicious wrath.

"Hold your dress open." His voice is husky and demanding, and I do what he says, holding it open for him. Without breaking contact with my flesh, as he loosens his belt with a jerk of his arm, springing himself free. Tilting my head to the side, I watch as he strokes himself, the sight of his thick and obviously hungry cock winding a thrill inside of me.

I squirm against his mouth, the scratch of my dress against the stones only adding to the sounds of lust filling the air, as I let out a moan.

"Lucian? Lucian?" The distant sound of Laura's voice sends a rush of panic through me, and I push at the top of his head to break his hold of me.

"Wait. It's your mother."

At first, he doesn't stop, but with a bit more prodding, he backs away from me. I drop the fabric, watching him tuck his still fully-erect cock back into his pants. "What the hell is she doing out of bed?" Swiping his mask up from the ground, along with my discarded panties, he straightens to a stand, wiping off the small bits of grass from his slacks, and replaces the mask over his face. He tucks my panties into his pocket and takes my hand, leading me back in through the glass door.

The room is dead silent.

The music has stopped.

We make our way through the crowd toward the center of it, and I skid to a halt and slap a hand over my mouth.

Lucian turns his face away, shrugging out of his coat. "Jesus, mother."

"Lucian, there you are." Laura's face beams with a smile, as she stands in the center of the packed atrium without a single stitch of clothing on her body. Like she's oblivious to the gasps and stares of onlookers.

My heart hurts for her, as I absorb the humiliation she apparently doesn't yet feel.

Rand wraps a coat around her, and I slide my mask up, grab Lucian's coat, and lurch forward, using the second one to conceal the front of her body where it's still exposed.

"I'll take her back to her room." Shielding her as much as I can, I push through the crowd and guide Laura out through the atrium doors.

Twisting against me, Laura physically objects, turning in the direction of the party. "Where are we going? I need to speak to Lucian."

"Laura, where's Nell?"

"Who's Nell? Have you seen Amelia? I can't find her anywhere."

Halfway to the elevator, we run into Nell, whose eyes grow wide and panicked as she hustles toward us. "Where was she?"

"She walked right into the masquerade. Everyone ... everyone saw her." I flinch at the mental replay of it. "God, where were you, Nell?"

"I just stepped away a moment for a cigarette." Taking the lead in front of us, she holds onto Laura's arm and pushes the elevator button.

The doors open, and we take it up to the second floor, where Laura squirms to break our hold. "I need to speak to my son. Why won't you let me speak to my son?"

"Laura." Setting a hand against her cheek draws her eyes to mine, the rheumy sadness in them tugging at my chest. "I'll ask him to come up here to speak with you. But please, you need to get dressed and get into bed, okay?"

Her gaze flits to Nell, who, to her credit, doesn't say a damn thing, and Laura nods. "Okay, but I need to speak to him right away. It's urgent."

Helping her to her bedroom, Nell and I gather up fresh underwear and a nightgown. The pad on the bed where she lay earlier is soaked, which is what likely prompted her to remove her clothes. After helping her to the bathroom, Nell gives her a quick shower, while I clean up her soiled bed, replacing the old with new sheets. The dress rubbing against my bare skin has me feeling as exposed as Laura was as I move about, but I ignore it. When the two emerge from the bathroom, Laura is fully clothed again.

As I help her to bed and tuck the blanket around her, Laura smiles up at me. "She never pays attention anymore."

I glance back to Nell, uncertain whether Laura is aware of what happened this evening. I hope she isn't. I hope whatever has taken over her mind protects her from this. "Who?"

"Amelia. She always kept those pills out on the dresser, and I warned her Roark would get to them."

Another glance back at Nell, and both of us frown. "What happened?"

"Well, what do you think happened? She wasn't paying attention. You must always pay attention to your children. Always."

For a moment, I wonder if she's lucid right now, because she has never once acknowledged that her grandson was missing, or dead. What she's suggesting is that her daughter-in-law essentially murdered her grandson by leaving pills where he could reach them.

Warm, wrinkled hands grab hold of my arm, and she lifts her head off the pillow. "Promise me you won't leave the pills out, the way she did."

"I promise I won't."

"Good. You'll make a much better mother to my Lucian's children than she ever was."

I clear my throat, the embarrassment of her words heating my cheeks.

"I'm going to sleep now, if that's okay."

"Yes, of course." I exit the room with Nell in tow, my mind spinning with questions.

Nell closes the door behind us and blows out a breath. "Way too much excitement for one night."

The humiliation still coursing through me on Laura's behalf swells to anger. "Why would you do that? Why would you leave her alone like that?" Perhaps what I'm feeling is irrational, but I don't care. Tonight wasn't fair to Laura. Stepping away for a smoke isn't a good enough excuse for what this poor woman just went through.

Face screwing up into a frown, she gives me a onceover. "Don't you fucking judge me. Not when you had her son's face between your thighs." Her words hit my conscience like a punch to the gut.

"You saw us? You were watching us?" My momentary shock and embarrassment twists into disgust. "That's why you didn't hear her get out of bed. Why you didn't see her get undressed, or leave the room. You were too busy spying on us?"

"Kinda hard to miss when you guys were out in the open."

We weren't, though. She'd have had to look for us, in order to see where we were, hidden in the shadows. "Do you have any idea how humiliating that must've been for her? All those fucking people seeing her like that? And Lucian! My God, if he can even look those people in the eye after this--"

"Oh, poor Lucian. Let me tell you something about your little Romeo. He didn't want kids. He didn't want Roark. And I'm guessing he didn't want the baby Amelia was pregnant with when she killed herself. In fact, I'd bet that's *why* she killed herself."

"How the hell do you know she was pregnant?"

"One of her labs was accidentally entered in Laura's medical chart. At first, I thought it was Laura's, until I looked up the medical record attached to it. Amelia Blackthorne. HCG positive two weeks before she committed suicide."

"Laura said--"

"I don't give a shit what Laura said. The woman just walked into a crowded room naked. You think she knows what the hell is going on with her family? Aside from her *precious* Lucian ..."

"You're jealous."

"Jealous of what? You and the Devil of Bonesalt? You can have your murdering piece of shit. And if you don't believe me? Ask Giulia. Amelia never left those pills where Roark could reach them. Never. Roark was afraid to come into her room because of those fucking dolls."

Giulia told me the same thing the first night I stayed in that room. She said that Roark refused to come into the room, that he was terrified of the doll on the nightstand. Still, that doesn't implicate Lucian in any murder—Amelia, or Roark's. Assuming Roark is, in fact, dead.

"You're making assumptions about him without proof. You don't even know that Roark is dead, and you're willing to accuse Lucian?"

"You don't know anything about him. He's got his ugly face so far up your dress, you're blind to everything around you. I've seen men show up at the house. Sometimes? They don't leave. Did you know this castle is built on a big pile of bones?"

The unbidden memory of the man being escorted by Makaio

and Rand into the elevator flashes behind my eyes. The one I'm certain was Franco. The horrific look on his face when the elevator doors closed, as if he suddenly realized something. I didn't recall having seen him leave.

The first tendrils of doubt crawl over the back of my neck. "Why are you still here, then?"

"It doesn't matter. And whether you believe me, or not, I don't give a shit. But my advice? Pay closer attention."

CHAPTER 38

LUCIAN

Seven years ago ...

Hunched over paperwork strewn across my desk, I cup my face in my hands, mentally trying to block out the screams of my month-old son, Roark, two rooms down. The minutes of the last investors' meeting are my only prep for the report I'm supposed to present to my father later today, and I'm suddenly wishing I'd made the drive to Gloucester, for the peace and quiet of my office there.

The high-pitched squeal is more than I can take, and I slam my pen onto the desk and push up from my chair. Whatever the hell nanny my mother hired when he was first born must be deaf not to hear those goddamn screams.

"Anna!" I growl, stepping out into the hallway.

A minute later, she still hasn't appeared, or answered me.

"Anna!"

Still nothing but the incessant wailing from his nursery that, I have no doubt, was intentionally set up in the same hallway, just to piss me off.

I storm down the corridor to the door where the screaming is loudest, and slam through. "Anna!"

Instead of the nanny, I find Amelia sitting in a rocking chair, staring off with her head tipped to the side. She doesn't make any effort to calm the baby, doesn't bother to acknowledge me when I enter the room, either.

No sign of the nanny we've assuredly paid handsomely to keep this kid quiet. "Where's Anna?"

At first, I don't think my voice can reach her over the sound of Roark's crying, but Amelia lifts her eyes to mine. How much she's changed over the last few weeks. The bright young girl, once vibrant and witty, now wears the dark circles of depression and misery. Something I refuse to take credit for. "She didn't come in today. Had some … errand to run." Every word arrives as if she's out of breath and weak, hardly audible over those wretched screams.

"Are you going to quiet him, or let him scream all hours of the day and night? I have an important meeting I'm trying to prepare for."

Her gaze slides toward the cradle, where Roark still hasn't quieted. Tears fill her eyes as she shakes her head, her bottom lip quivering. "I can't."

My mother says it's post-partum depression, but I can't stand it, just the same. She does nothing for him. Won't even hold him. Why she didn't arrange to have a backup nanny is beyond me.

A screech echoes through the nursery, and Roark almost sounds in pain, his wail shaky and tormented.

Groaning with frustration, I cross the room to his cradle, and find him lying in a pile of blankets, wearing nothing but a diaper. His naked body is red from crying, his face scrunched with agony, as he trembles like he's been hit with a stun gun.

I've not held him once since his birth, mostly because I'm not experienced in holding babies and they tend to make me uncomfortable. But also because a part of me can't help but think this child was the scheming of both my mother and Amelia. A means of roping me into a relationship with a woman I didn't love.

Rubbing my hand over my head, I screw my eyes closed, the sound of his screams innervating some part of my brain that makes me want to throttle something. Breathing hard through my nose to calm the rage, I look down at his tiny hand, which shakes with his cries. Before I can stop myself, I reach out to touch it, drawing back my hand on finding him ice cold.

Jesus.

I pull the blanket up around him, covering his hand that remains propped beneath it, and with his shivering, the blanket covers his face. Seconds tick by as I stare down, his cries hysterical now, his small form squirming beneath the blanket. For the briefest moment, I wonder if it's better to spare this child from a life of parents who didn't want him. To let him suffocate now, rather than watch him suffer a lifetime of slow and painful asphyxiation.

Instead, I tuck the blanket under his chin, and exhale a breath as I slide my hands beneath his little body. I lift him from the cradle, and the hysterics heighten midair, until I pull him to my chest. As I awkwardly try to wrap him up, he slips a little from my grasp, and a gasp flies out of me before I catch him. *Fucking hell.* My heart slams against my chest at the near miss, and I curl him into the crook of my arm.

His cries die down to whimpers.

Whimpers die down to thumb sucking.

And then his eyes meet mine.

Blue, like Amelia's, and brimming with curiosity as he stares up at me, going to town on his tiny thumb. What hits me most of all, though, is the trust swirling in them. Does he even know who I am to him? Is that why he stopped crying?

I scan my gaze over the length of him, noticing his miniature feet sticking out of the blanket, and I cover them one-handedly.

When my gaze returns to his, his eyes are still riveted, like the kid can't get enough of staring at me.

"How dare you look me in the eye like that," I say, watching the bold little shit stop sucking his thumb for a second, as if he's trying to study my voice instead. "Do you know who I am?" Only pausing a second, I lift him a little higher. "I'm your father. And you're really fucking up my concentration with all that crying."

The awe sketched across his face as he continues to stare up at me leaves a strange feeling in my chest. I can't explain it. It isn't pain, or anger. Bitterness, or apathy.

Warm tingles crawl beneath my skin and congregate inside my chest. Everything around me seems to slow down, like I'm floating underwater, just me and him. There's the apprehension of not having taken in enough breath, but at the same time … contentment. Perhaps even slight euphoria.

My son.

The words echo inside my head while I watch his eyes grow heavy with sleep. A glance back at Amelia shows her sitting in her chair, staring off once more, as if oblivious to us.

When I turn my attention back on Roark, his eyes are closed, his small mouth gaping, chest rising and falling with sleep. The red tone fades to baby white skin, and I dip my head just enough to breathe in the scent of him.

I don't take my eyes off Roark's sleeping face as I exit the nursery and make my way back down to my office. Rounding the desk of scattered papers, I take my seat on the leather chair and lay Roark against my chest, where my shirt is partially unbuttoned. Kicking my feet up on the desk, I hold him against me, focusing on the breaths that flutter in and out of him.

My son. Each time the words chime in my head, a rush of tingles follows.

This small, trusting little bundle is mine. Truly mine.

Annoying as hell, but mine. Perhaps the only thing that will ever really belong to me, for as long as I live. The thought of such a thing stirs something inside of me. A sensation pulled from the depths of me, because it's surely one I've never felt before.

I think about him lying in that crib moments ago, screaming and cold, with his mother only a few feet away, and my lip peels back in disgust. Petting his back, I take in his tiny size against my chest. So small and fragile, and suddenly, I want to protect him.

My son.

For the first time, I understand my father's words all those years ago.

And I would kill for what's mine.

CHAPTER 39

LUCIAN

Present day ...

I lead the group of men through the long and winding tunnels of the catacombs. A cold chill skates over my skin as we pass the sarcophagus I had carved for Amelia, as well as the much smaller one for my son. Even now, years later, after the many times I sat down here alone with my thoughts, an ache still blooms inside my chest at the sight of my son's memorial.

The tunnels open up into a wide cavern, where tables line the perimeter of an enormous floor medallion made up of black, gray and brown pewabic tiles I had imported from Detroit. The center of the medallion carries the likeness of the moth with its skull on the thorax.

Patrick Boyd is led into the circle of tables, blindfolded as every member in the room once stood. Each of the men takes a seat, all of them still wearing their masks from the party.

Following the fiasco with my mother, I had all the women leave at once, along with anyone else not a member of our collective, and I'm looking forward to the end of this inquiry so I can seek out distraction for my humiliation in Isa.

Seeing Patrick's hands on her triggered a potent rage inside of me, an uncontrollable desire to break every one of his fingers. The sooner I get him out of my sight, the better.

Friedrich Voigt, whom I've come to have a completely different relationship with since my time spent at the institute, takes his seat at the head of the table.

I take my seat directly beside him.

Standing before the members, Friedrich clears his throat, a sound that echoes in the cavernous room. "Gentlemen, we are here today based on an inquiry into our collective. It's come to my attention that Patrick Boyd--"

"Former mayor," Patrick interrupts, and I mentally groan. If he's granted membership, he'll learn very quickly that Dr. Voigt isn't one who appreciates interruptions. Particularly the rude and unnecessary variety.

"Has come to us in search of knowledge and a deeper understanding of the human psyche," Friedrich goes on, ignoring Patrick's ignorance. "For decades, our group has studied behavioral epigenetics of sadism. And now I ask you, Patrick Boyd, what contributions do you feel you would make to our collective?"

Fingers entwined, Patrick swirls his thumbs around each other, a nervous habit, as he stands quiet, seeming to contemplate the question. He shifts on his feet and clears his throat. "Well, I'm not a doctor, or scientist on the subject, but I am a former teacher, and I have encountered a number of personalities throughout the course of my political career that make me question if there may be a link between politicians and this psychopathic behavior that you're studying."

"Sadism, specifically. And we already know there is a link between politics and psychopathy. Organizational psychopaths tend to be naturally drawn to leadership roles, which allow them to control a large number of people. While your curiosities are interesting, I'm afraid they're nothing new." The boredom in Friedrich's tone is telling, and I suspect he's already made up his mind about Patrick's inquiry.

A long pause follows, and Patrick lowers his head, perhaps feeling defeated. I already knew, from my conversation with him, that his motivations weren't aligned with our group.

"I actually have a twin. Identical. He's serving a life sentence in prison for a ... very brutal murder." His confession skates down my spine, and I look back at him, wishing I could rip off that blindfold to see his eyes, to know that he's bullshitting the group for the sole purpose of gaining entry. "We didn't grow up together. I was adopted by a good family. He, on the other hand, grew up in a very poor community. I don't talk about this because ... well, why would I? But I would like to understand. To know if whatever he endured was based on genetics that might affect me. Or if his environment contributed to his violence."

Friedrich sits forward, and the intrigue on his face sends a sinking feeling to the pit of my stomach. It seems Patrick isn't as stupid as I thought. Seems he's done his homework.

The entire foundation of this group is rooted in the study of twins, specifically identical, as their genetics represents the best model for study. Of course Friedrich would find this compelling. "Interesting." Tapping his fingers together, Friedrich scans the group. "We'll take a brief moment to discuss this as a group. I'll ask that you leave the room, Patrick."

One of the members escorts Patrick out of the cavern and down the hall. Once he's out of sight, Friedrich exhales a sharp breath. "Well, that was certainly a turn of events there."

There's no way I'm going to let the bomb Patrick dropped blow up in my face. "One worth investigating. He may be lying."

"Certainly. And we will need to determine that. However, if it's true, he may be the perfect specimen for our study." Friedrich sighs, leaning back in his chair. "If only your son were here today.

We'd have a third generation sampling to see if those genetic markers are present in him, as well."

"My son was not a *sampling*. He was a child." I have to be careful with the man. One wave of his hand, and I could instantly become an enemy to this group.

"I meant no disrespect, Lucian. As you know, I value and respect your place in this collective. Your great-grandfather was one of the progenitors of this study. Of this group! If you feel he's not right for what we're trying to achieve, know that your vote holds weight."

"I feel Patrick's interest is selfish. All around this table sit wealthy and very powerful individuals." I glance around at all of them, successful business owners and politicians, physicians and high-ranking military officials. All with one thing in common: they find pleasure in hurting others. It's practically a favor to Patrick, convincing this group to deny him.

And if he is denied, he'll be watched. If he so much as whispers one word about the collective, he'll vanish into thin air, never to be seen again, because that's how strongly they would protect their anonymity. Surveillance is already in place, and when Patrick leaves this party tonight, someone will be following him home.

"I fear this myself. We've managed to keep the motivations of this collective pure, but I must say, this new information threw me. However, we will need to look into the validity of it."

"We've not yet had a twin for the study." The older man beside me, perhaps in his late sixties, is the owner of a chain of home improvement stores, his face the logo for the company. His mask sits on the table in front of him, while he sits rubbing his jaw. "It is a curiosity, to me, anyway."

I want to ask him if it'd be worth the public finding out he's a sexual sadist who enjoys hogtying women and flogging them.

Another member at the opposite end of the room, a senator from Massachusetts, shakes his head, having removed his mask, as well. "Boyd is sloppy. The scandal involving the girl was an absolute mess. Not worth the risk, in my opinion." His thing is cutting subjects with razors. He once left over a hundred cuts on a man who sought out the collective.

"Years ago," the older man beside me volleys back. "I doubt anyone but stiff political competition would even remember."

The senator sneers and waves his hand in dismissal. "The man couldn't get elected to an ass wiping committee, let alone the senate."

Bored with their arguments, I turn my attention back to Friedrich. "My vote is no. And if you don't need anything more from me, I'd like to be excused."

"If that's your wish. Though, I would strongly advise you to make the effort of attending more of our meetings. Important matters are discussed that affect you."

"I'll have the next one added to my calendar." I push up from my chair and straighten my coat.

"Very good." Friedrich sighs, sitting back in his chair. "In the meantime, I'll request more information regarding Mr. Boyd."

E ased back in my office chair, I sip my liquor, staring across the room as the elevator dings and Isa steps out. I don't know why my pulse quickens at the sight of her, like any second she'll take off on a dead run and make me chase her.

As she edges closer, I don't take my eyes off her. Couldn't if I wanted to.

"You changed out of your dress." I drink in the beauty of her in a simple T-shirt stretched over supple breasts, and tight leggings that hug her toned calves. My mind rewinds back to earlier in the night, when I had my face buried between her thighs, while her moans echoed all around me.

"It was uncomfortable." Something is different about her, the way she doesn't volley some smartass remark and hasn't met my gaze once since walking into the room.

"What's wrong?"

Her brows flicker, and she winds her fingers in the hem of her shirt. "You had Rand fetch me."

"And?"

"And ... it just felt a little ... strange. After what happened in the courtyard tonight."

"You'd have preferred I come myself."

"Would've felt more personal. Less like a business transaction."

I polish off the rest of my drink, setting the glass down on the coaster, and rise up from my chair. Dragging a finger over the smooth mahogany wood, I round my desk and come to a stop only inches away from her. The twitch of her shoulder, the quick rise and fall of her chest, the steady diversion of her gaze--small cues I notice that tell me she's nervous around me all of a sudden.

Reaching out a hand, I brush my knuckles down her cheek and catch the subtle tilt of her head away from my touch. "Something else is troubling you."

"I'm just tired."

"Bullshit. You took my mother back to her room. What happened then?"

"Nothing."

I curl my fingers around her fragile jaw and guide her eyes to mine. "What happened?"

Her throat bobs with a swallow. "Nothing happened. We ran into Nell at the elevator, and both of us helped your mother to bed."

"And where exactly was Nell when my mother entered the masquerade without any clothes?"

"She took a smoke break."

"How convenient. And how is my mother now?"

Eyes hidden beneath the long dark lashes, she nibbles on her bottom lip that I want to take between my teeth while I hold her pinned to the floor. Something was exchanged between her and Nell, this much is obvious to me. Earlier in the night, she practically begged me to fuck her, and now, she can't even look at me. "Why didn't you ask me about her right away?"

"You think I'm cold, and that I don't give a shit."

"I'm just trying to understand, is all."

"Understand this." I tip my head to gain her attention, and when she meets my gaze with those puppy dog eyes, it takes an incredible amount of control not to act on my desires. "There are few that I trust as a general rule. But I knew she was in good hands with you."

A flicker of a smile dances across her face, but I'm not sure I've broken down whatever shield she managed to construct in the last couple of hours. Still grasping her jaw, I lean forward and take those lips, setting my other hand to the crown of her head as I tilt her chin up. The taste of mint toothpaste greets my tongue as I prod past her teeth.

I slide my hands down her back to her ass, and squeeze just enough to make her squeak against my lips. Traveling further down to her thighs, I lift her up, never breaking the kiss, while I wrap her legs around me and carry her around my desk. The chair catches me as I lower the two of us onto it. Reaching up her shirt, I run my hands over her belly, and up toward her breasts, while I devour the flavor that lingers on her lips.

Straddled over my thighs, she pushes against my chest, pulling her lips from mine, and breathes hard between us. Quiet for a moment, she shakes her head. "I'm sorry for this, but I have to know. I have to ask. What really happened to your son?"

As soon as the question tumbles out, my suspicions about Nell are confirmed. It isn't the first time the woman attempted to scare off one of the staff here with her little conspiracy theories. We let her off with a warning the last time, on the grounds that it's not easy hiring help with the Blackthorne reputation looming over this place. She's not the first to try and piece together what happened to my son, and won't be the last, it seems, as much as I hoped otherwise with Isa.

With a light nudge, I back her off my thighs, and she clambers to her feet, standing before me.

"You want to know if I killed my son."

"If I offended you, I didn't mean ... I'm just trying to--"

"I want to show you something." I lean forward and open the largest of three drawers on my desk. The moment I slide it out, the familiar pangs of agony punch at my chest. Held within, are pictures and drawings, a few crayons, and Roark's favorite toys. The last remnants of my son that I gathered and stored away, keeping them for myself. I've never shown anyone my collection. Never gave a shit what anyone thought about me.

Isa kneels down beside the drawer and reaches in for a picture that I can't bear to look at right now. He was two and a half years old, and my mother had snapped a picture of us, as I'd just tossed him into the air and caught him. Roark's face was bunched with laughter, his tiny hands plastered at my cheeks as I held him up for a kiss.

"I'll admit, I didn't start out the best father. I hate myself every day for that. But he's the only thing in this world that I learned how to love." As if I've torn open an old wound, my chest aches with the admission, and I frown to keep the familiar anger from rising to the surface. I don't owe her any of this, but without it, I'm still the monster. The Devil of Bonesalt who murdered his wife and son. At least now she knows, even the devil was capable of love once.

Eyes brimming with sadness, she sets the picture back into the drawer and shakes her head. "I'm sorry. Lucian, I'm so sorry."

Words that fail to breach my disappointment. All my life, I've battled rumor and fairy tales, if not of my father's infidelity, then my mother's flirtations. The accusations about my son and wife are something I have to live with for the rest of my life.

It's fucking exhausting.

"I know now what first drew me to you." The familiar jab of pain strikes my temples, and I screw my eyes shut, trying to ignore the agonizing distraction. "You were different. You didn't cower like I was some kind of murdering monster. You looked me in the eyes when you spoke to me, like you saw right past all this shit." I gesture to my face where the disgusting vestiges remain, and shake my head. "But you are just like them. Just like everyone else who feeds into the bullshit lies."

"I'm not, Lucian, I swear."

Another stab of pain is lightning behind my eyelids, and I breathe hard through my nose, mentally counting to ten, just like when I was a kid, waiting for the chasing thunder. "Get out."

"Please. I'm sorry. I didn't mean--"

"Get *out!*" The anger comes too fast, pounding against my skull, and I slam the heels of my hands against my temples. Breathing. Keep breathing.

One-one-thousand, two-one-thousand, three-one-thousand, four-one-thousand ...

Like needles piercing the bone, the jagged edges of pain skate over my brain, throbbing and pulsing against the back of my eyes, until the incessant pounding finally slows. The waves of agony settle to a placid calm once more, and I open my eyes to find Isa is no longer there.

Breathing hard through my nose, I let the misery fall away. When I stand up from the chair, vertigo sets in, and I stumble back, letting the soft leather catch my fall.

With a trembling hand, I run my fingers over my forehead and close my eyes on the dizzying blur of the room.

"She's pretty." The melodic sound of a thick French accent ripples down my spine, and I blink awake to find Solange knelt down between my splayed thighs. Her nails rake across my trousers, and she pushes up to her knees, resting her belly against my groin. "Does she excite you, young master?"

She comes to me sometimes, when I'm stressed. I know she's not real, even if she feels real. Sounds real. Smells real.

"Yes," I answer, watching her unlatch my trousers, the wily smile showing off her one crooked tooth.

"She makes you hard, I see." Massaging the ache between my thighs has me grinding my teeth, and when she gives a light squeeze, my thighs come up off the chair as I let out a growl of frustration. "Why do you think that is?"

"I don't know."

"She's young. Delicious. And there is nothing more exciting than the forbidden fruit." With her hand shoved down inside my trousers, she slides her palm up my shaft over the thin, silky fabric of my boxer briefs. "Pretend I'm her. Take me any way you want, Lucian."

I set my hand over hers to make it stop. "No."

"You know the rules," she breathes, her voice louder inside my head. "You can't have both of us."

"Then, leave."

A shocked expression meets my gaze, as if she's just been slapped. "You would send me away? Why?"

"Lucian?" At the quiet pitch of Isa's voice, I freeze, opening my eyes to find my own hand down inside my pants, Solange nowhere in sight. "I'm sorry." Fingers fidgeting where she keeps her hands crossed in front of her, Isa's standing in the middle of my office again. "I know you said to leave, but ... who were you talking to? A second ago?"

There's an uncertainty in her voice, one I know very well. It's come in other forms from various people--strange looks, avoidance, and in the worst cases, has resulted in more treatments and drugs.

"Why are you still here?" I slide my hand out of my pants and twist my chair to face her.

"I wanted to make sure you were okay." Gaze cast from mine, she clears her throat. "Who's Solange?"

Christ, I don't even remember having said her name, at all. "No one."

Still not bothering to look at me, she nods. "I see that. But you were talking to her anyway."

"And you wouldn't have seen anything, if you'd have left as I asked."

Warm gray eyes finally lift to mine, the stubborn glint behind them telling me she doesn't intend to let this go.

The question isn't *should I tell her*, because at this point, anything I tell her will sound the same. It doesn't matter who Solange is to me. What matters is that Isa will have yet another reason to stay away from me.

Yet, maybe it's better that way.

"What do you want, Isa? To know if I'm crazy? The Mad Son everyone claims I am? The answer is *yes*. But then, that was never really a secret, was it?"

Feet still glued to the same spot, she shakes her head. "I never believed the rumors. It was your mother who told me about the hallucinations of your friend. Jude?"

Leave it to my mother to perpetuate the very rumors she feared back then. I stare back at Isa, my throat suddenly dry and parched, and I reach for the decanter to pour myself another drink.

"She told me he died when you were very young," she adds, finally taking a step closer.

Gaze buried in the liquor, I lick my lips, the scent of the bourbon already puckering my tongue, while an image of Jude's face comes to mind. "It used to be the mere mention of him would incite flashbacks. That awful sound of his screams over the crashing of waves. The look of fear in his eyes when he reached out for me, as the waves swept him to sea. I'd end up blacking out. Don't even know how long." I finally take a sip from my glass, letting warm liquid slide down my throat. "If not for the pictures I have from when we were young, I'd wonder if he was ever even real."

"Why do you say that?"

A quiet chuckle escapes me as I swirl my drink. "I don't think you want down that rabbit hole, Isa. It's dark, and there is no bottom."

"Try me." The resolution in her eyes is remarkably attractive somehow. Almost fearless.

"All right. Solange was … an affliction of a different sort. Unlike Jude, she never actually existed. Yet, she taught me things that, to this day, are very real for me." I study her reaction for a moment, waiting for that familiar flicker of disbelief.

Instead, the intensity of her stare speaks of intrigue. Fucking intrigue.

"What kinds of things?"

Forget that I just told her I dreamed an imaginary woman who taught me things, she wants to know what.

"An appreciation for the line that separates life and death."

"The reason you seek out an adrenaline rush." It's not a question from her, but rather my unspoken confession.

"Yes. She taught me breath play and knives."

If I could crack open her skull right now, I'd probably hear the blare of a warning, telling her to run.

"You still see her? This Solange?"

"Only when my head is in a messed up place."

She looks away, still fidgeting. "I put you in that place. When I asked about your son."

I don't answer that. "This is why I warned you to stay away. Welcome to my crazy."

"Your mother said she tried to help you."

With a snort of laughter, I tip my glass for another sip of liquor, needing the buzz, all of a sudden. "Yes, she tried to help me. By putting me in a place that sought to *cure* my sexual *deviances.* The only thing they managed to cure was my desire to live."

Frowning, she shakes her head and crosses her arms. "I don't care. I don't care that you have hallucinations. I don't care that you like knives, and whatever else they considered to be crazy. None of that matters to me."

What the ever-loving hell is wrong with this girl?

"While I appreciate your sentiments, this is the universe telling you to walk away." I polish off the rest of my drink and set the glass on my desk. "Heed the warning."

She lurches toward me, but stops herself. "I don't give a damn what the universe, or anyone else, thinks. I make my own decisions."

Her tenacity is something else. If I wasn't so caught up in the humiliation of her having seen one of my little episodes, I'd take her against my desk right now. "Leave. You'll be grateful I spared you the heartache later."

"What heartache?"

"Of knowing I'm the kind of selfish bastard who will fuck you before I push you over a cliff." I don't want to do this, but this girl is as stubborn as they come. The truth is, I don't have the courage to watch her fall apart, when she realizes that Blackthornes aren't designed to whisper sweet words and fall in love. We annihilate, and revel in the aftermath of destruction. My mother is a fine example of that. My father could've left her, but the sadistic bastard got off on watching her slow death. The whole purpose of Schadenfreude is to prove that level of bastardry is genetic, and it's clear I've not been spared, so why would I subject Isa to that? A teenager who has her whole life ahead of her. A whole slew of broken hearts and true love.

"So, what happened in the courtyard earlier …"

"Was fun."

"Fun." The lack of humor in her voice is telling of the rage and confusion that must be clamoring inside of her.

I want nothing more than to sweep her off her feet like the white knight she's probably dreamed about since she was a little girl, but to what end? So she can be as miserable as my mother? As miserable as Amelia was? Like a bird trapped inside a box with no holes to breathe.

Gaze lowered, she shakes her head. "I don't get you, Lucian. I want to, but I don't."

"You're not the first, and I doubt you'll be the last."

"So you ... you want nothing to do with me."

That couldn't be farther from the truth, but I answer with more lies. "I want to do a number of things *to* you, but that's all, I'm afraid."

"And what if I was okay with that?"

This girl. This excruciatingly beautiful, exotic girl who has my dick ready to tear through the zipper right now.

"I'd think you were a very foolish girl."

Lips pressed together, she nods. "Well ... you're not the first, and I doubt you'll be the last." She finally backs herself toward the door. "For the record? Aside from the mishap with your mother, tonight was the best night of my life," she says, and she spins around toward the elevator.

Every muscle in my body is wound tight, listening to the evidence of her retreat. The ding of the elevator. The sniffles. The sliding of the doors. My opportunity to have her slipping out of my grasp.

The moment she's gone, I pour myself another drink, hand trembling with fury.

This is my curse. The legacy my father left behind, of mindless sex and misery.

I raise the glass for a sip, teeth grinding inside my skull, but slam it against the desktop so the liquid splashes out onto the wood.

Screwing my eyes shut, I succumb to the visual inside my

head. The look of ecstasy on Isa's face, her legs wrapped around my body, her moans echoing off the walls.

I need her out of my system, out of my head. Every waking thought is wrapped around this girl, strangling my opposition, begging me for one taste. One touch.

I want the forbidden. I want the one thing that irritates me more than anything. The one thing I shouldn't want.

Isa.

CHAPTER 40

ISADORA

A soft tickle down my leg rips me out of dreams, and I slide the blade from beneath my pillow, kicking my feet back. In the blackness of my room, the knife hits something, and I keep it propped there while scrambling for the lamp beside me. The chain brushes my fingertips, and I give a hard yank, the darkness blinking to light.

Lucian's hulking body looms over me, like a black squall ready to take me under, as he holds himself propped on outstretched arms.

My blade at his throat.

The seeds Nell planted inside my head earlier in the night failed to bloom once I saw the relics of his son, and I left his office feeling like every other asshole from Tempest Cove who believes the rumors about him. I fell asleep hating myself for failing to do the one thing that makes me different from the others in this town: think objectively. Still, murderer, or not, the man carries an edge of danger about him. An aura that triggers my instincts, warning me to be careful. So I keep the blade where it's at, while my brain unwinds from the confusion.

My attention falls to his bare chest and torso, momentarily distracted by the tight cords and deep ridges of hard-earned muscle. The scent coming off him is an intoxicating mix of spice and a more primitive, masculine aroma that waters my mouth. Something burns in those infernal eyes. Dark and wicked. For a moment, I wonder if I'm dreaming, until he shifts, and I feel my pants slide down my thighs.

"Wait." I squirm beneath him, never lowering my weapon, and grab hold of his hand, which makes him pause.

"You've got the knife, Isa. Use it." He lifts his chin, exposing more of his throat to the blade's unforgiving edge, but even so, he goes back to tugging my pants down my thighs.

Once they're off my legs, he tosses them to the floor, and I lie vulnerable beneath him. Metal clinks while he works the buckle of his belt one-handedly, his eyes never wavering from mine as he loosens his pants and springs his cock free. Thick pulsing veins feed the long and stiff erection captured in his fist, the sight of which tickles my stomach.

"What are you doing?" Still half asleep, I double-blink, trying to determine if this is the real Lucian, or the one I've dreamed of for the last month.

"I'm fucking you. With, or without, the blade at my throat." His voice, pitched low and deep, dances across my skin, leaving goosebumps in its wake. My panties slide down next, his eyes shimmering with reverence as he pauses a moment and pries my knees apart. "Or you'll be fucking me, it seems." The awe in his voice mimics the expression on his face as he licks his lips.

Without ceremony or apology, he pushes two fingers up inside of me, and I gasp at the intrusion. His fingers glisten on the withdrawal, and closing his eyes, he shoves them into his mouth. He shudders, shaking his head, and his hand balls into a tight fist. "Tell me to stop, Isa. For fucks sake, tell me to stop, and I will. I swear it."

Swallowing a gulp, I set the knife onto the nightstand and shake my head, my whole body trembling. "No."

For a moment, we stare back at each other in a battle of wills, until he finally groans, slips my panties off, and tosses them away. "I'm selling my fucking soul for this, so I hope it's as good as I imagined." Taking hold of his cock, he strokes himself while he seems to admire my body, biting his lip as the iniquity dances in his eyes. Darkly erotic, he reminds me of the bad twin in my dreams. The one who fucks me without apology. The one I secretly desire most, for reasons I can't begin to explain. "I'm no lover, and I'm not equipped to offer the emotional security a girl your age requires. To be clear, I'm here to fuck you. Hard. That's all."

His words send a shiver of anticipation down my spine, and my thighs twitch. "I'm not looking for a pep talk from you."

"Then, it's settled. I gave you a choice." The rough and ragged texture of his voice oozes desperation and tenuous restraint. Trembling muscles, and the unyielding spark in his eyes, make me wonder if I really have a choice, at all. If a powerful man like Lucian can be pushed to the brink of taking without asking.

It doesn't matter. I've dreamed of this. Of him. Coming to me in my sleep. I want the savage beast that I imagine lies beneath the thin mask of control he wears. The devil who whispers in my ear while I dream, spinning depraved promises. "I want you," I whisper, lying back against the pillow.

Lowering himself, he slants his mouth over mine, and I swallow his moan. He fists my shirt, yanking up the hem of it, exposing my bare breasts beneath, and the growl of appreciation vibrates over my skin when he dips his face to suckle me.

I cup the back of his head, squirming against the merciless tug at my nipple. A zap of pain comes with the scrape of his teeth, and I cry out, closing my fist around a handful of hair. "More, please." Drunk with lust, I mindlessly reach down between my thighs and take hold of his straining shaft.

Drawing his hips forward, he allows me to stroke him, while he holds himself propped on outstretched arms. He slowly rocks into my palm, his cock harder than before. So hard, I can't imagine him fitting it into me.

I stir my hips beneath him, rocking in the same tempo as his imagined thrusts, and the moment his eyes finally lock on mine, desperate and starving, I know I'm in trouble. I've finally pushed him over the edge.

"Please, Lucian."

"I could." The length of his cock slides across my soaked entrance that's aching to be filled. Teasing and taunting me. "But I want to watch you squirm beneath me like hooked bait. Desperate."

Biting my lip, I focus on the sensation of his skin against mine, rubbing across my sensitive slit every time he drives forward. The lust burning in my belly like hot coils ready to ignite.

"I want my name to echo inside your head like a blade across your skull, because that's what you are to me. The knife that cuts deeper and deeper." Every word that pours from his lips is like my own blade dragging across my arm, and I moan at the thought of such relief, that moment when the blood seeps through the burn.

"Please," I whine, my body tense and trembling, waiting for it. Rolling my head on the pillow is all I can do to fight the feverish passion burning through me. The craving I feel for him right now must be what every junkie on the planet suffers, just before that needle plunges into the vein. "I need it. I need you."

The tearing sound draws my attention to where he rips a condom free of its foil of between his teeth, and he slides it down his length before tossing the wrapper onto the nightstand. "You love this. You love what you do to me, don't you?" Sheathed cock in hand, he slings my legs over his shoulders and drives forward, my body tensing with his size, and I breathe hard through clenched teeth.

"Relax, Isa." He inches further, working his way deeper, stretching me with his girth. As he pushes to the hilt, filling me, his teeth come together in a hiss that ends on a curse.

Like an invisible string pulling my chest, I arch into him and cry out.

Capturing my screams in his mouth, he eats my cries of pain, devouring my breath, and thrusts deeper. A growl vibrates against my lips, and his cock slides in and out of me, creating a wet glide.

"Fuck, Isa," he says against my mouth. "Fuck!" His breaths are broken and fervent, teeth scraping across my jaw.

Solid muscles flex and tremble beneath my hands, where I hold tight to his shoulders, drawing him into me. On a single-minded mission toward climax, he ravages my body, taking what he wants from me. Fiery and restless, he fucks as if his entire existence rides on pleasure, as if it's a requirement for his survival, and I'm the food source.

All I can do is hang on and hope I survive the aftermath.

Skin slick with sweat, he reminds me of a starving animal cut loose from its confines, one determined to feed to the point of gluttony.

My stomach tightens at the sight of him, the smell of his skin, and the slapping sounds that echo in the room, as he works himself toward what he needs from me. I'm shaking with excitement and fear for what's to come. The uncertainty of what it means now that we've crossed this line.

In my experiences with sex, which have been nothing more than quickies in the backseat of a car, there's nothing beyond this. The guy does up his pants and drops me off at home. I wish I could say that I trust Lucian completely, and know he won't discard me afterward, but I can't trust what I've never known. As much as I want to come and give in to the pleasure alongside him, I don't want the moment to end, for fear of the black void. The humiliation and shame that inevitably follows.

I offer myself up like a sacrifice, letting him tear away my skin, down to my bones, where the vulnerable parts of me are buried so deep, I don't even recognize them anymore. Secret fantasies wrapped in delicate black ribbons, just wanting for a man like Lucian to pull the strings and unravel my tightly-woven facade.

We're just having a little fun.

The tiny compartments inside my mind open to the voices from my past, and eyes screwed shut, I shake my head, willing them away.

No, please. Not now. I won't let them ruin this moment.

You're dirty. Nothing but a dirty fucking slut.

A spasm of pain sends jagged lights behind my eyelids, the panic seeping in from the fringes. "No," I whisper.

A soft caress against my cheek draws my eyes open to Lucian. My dark knight. The shadow on my wall when I sleep. The tickle on my skin when I'm alone.

A man. Not the selfish and childish boys of my past, who take without permission, and touch without invitation.

He slows his thrusts, his eyes burning with concern. "Isa, what's wrong? Am I hurting you?"

It's only then I notice the tears slipping down my temples, and I shake my head.

"Why are you crying? This is what you wanted, isn't it?"

I reach up to touch his face, running my thumb over his scar. "Have you ever wished one moment could last forever?"

Tipping his head, he seems to study me, then leans forward for another kiss, this one less demanding, gentle. He slides my legs off his shoulders and lowers himself to his elbows so that our bodies are closer together, my breasts pressed against his chest. Forehead resting against mine, he rolls his hips, smooth and steady as a metronome, in a lazy and languid tempo. "I'll hold out as long as I can, but I can't lie, you've got me burning up right now."

I lift my head to kiss him and wrap my legs around his back. "No. I'm ready. Just promise me, afterward? You won't treat me like shit." More tears spring to my eyes, and I hate myself for ruining this. I hate that my past is filled with so much baggage I could start my own fucking luggage company. I hate that he now knows perhaps my worst weakness.

He kisses the tear streaking down my temple, and his eyes are locked on mine. "I told you, there's a difference between getting fucked by a boy and getting fucked properly." Hand stroking my hair, he wears an earnest expression. "You're mine. And I would never hurt what's mine."

Lips pressed to mine, he ups his pace again, winding my body back up.

You're mine. Perhaps it slipped from his lips unintentionally, because only moments ago, he told me all he came to do was fuck me. Hard.

You're mine.

Mine.

His.

"Yours," I whisper mindlessly, watching in awe as climax crests over his face like the sun rising on the edge of the ocean. The rush of blood beneath his skin, the blaze of violence in his eyes, with every thrust inside of me. He tips his head back, and the veins in his neck pulse with the tight clench of his jaw, while his hips hammer into me.

"Again," he says, raggedly.

"I'm yours." Panting through my nose, I grip the bedsheets at either side of me, scrambling for something to hang on to, as the pinnacle of ecstasy draws closer and the fragile strings grounding me begin to fray. My senses blur to nothing but Lucian. His eyes.

The scent of him filling my brain with a voracious craving. The delectable flavor of his skin on my tongue.

Quick, controlled movements have his cock pistoning in and out of me, his powerful thighs slamming into mine. He dips forward for another kiss, sealing our lips together as my body thirsts for oxygen. I turn my head to break the kiss, but he takes hold of my jaw, suffocating me with his mouth. I moan and shift against him, my body in a frenzy. A maelstrom of agony and promise.

He doesn't stop.

Body jerking for air and the need for release, I climb higher and higher. Tighter and tighter. I close my eyes to a flash of blinding light, and arch my back, finally breaking the kiss on a gasp of breath, and the warm rush explodes through my veins. Crying out, I arch higher, my body paralyzed with the pleasure pulsing through every muscle.

The bed squeaks as he bangs out the last few seconds, and his curse bounces off the walls around me. Jets of warm fluid leak down my thigh, and he directs more onto my belly, where he's ripped off the condom and began stroking himself. White ribbons spring from the head of his cock, collecting in a pool of hot fluids.

He takes my hand, smoothing my palm over his sticky release, and kisses me hard. "You feel that? Weeks of pent-up torment, all for you. Wear it like a fucking crown, because no other woman has made me come so much in my life."

His words are crude, but hot, and when he slides his hands beneath me, lifting me up from the bed, I'm so exhausted, bone-less and satisfied, that I can barely wrap my arms around him.

"Where are we going?" I ask, out of breath.

"I'm going to get you clean, and then I'm going to fuck you again." His comment tugs a weak chuckle from my chest, as I rest my head against his shoulder. "You find that amusing?"

"I find that amazing." The getting clean part, in particular. No one usually sticks around long enough to clean me, aside from tossing me a rag from some compartment in their car. Perhaps that's the difference, as he warned me, between fucking a boy and a man.

"Well, brace yourself. Because the only thing that gets me off more than knives is water."

CHAPTER 41

LUCIAN

Five years ago ...

"There's a meeting at the Institute this week. I'll ask you that you go in my place. It'll be good for you to get acquainted with some of the members of the Collective." My father leans back in his chair, his feet kicked up on the ottoman, as if the request is of no consequence to him.

Across from him, I sit forward and frown. "It's not a good week. Roark's been waking up with nightmares—"

"He has a mother. You have a job. And one of your duties in said job is to attend meetings on my behalf."

"This isn't a real meeting," I bite back, staring at him beneath lowered brows. "It's a waste of time. Precious time that I could be spending with my own son."

"A waste of time. A waste of time?" The tone in his voice is a warning, the rack of a gun pointed at my head. "You being afforded time to spend with your son is entirely made possible by the Collective who pulled your grandfather out of a shit life. If not for this group, you'd be at fucking sea for months out of the year, begging for shark scraps so you could feed your precious little family!"

"A debt that's been paid decades over in blood."

"A debt that will never be paid, you ungrateful shit!" Liquor spills over his glass onto his shirt with the jerky movements of his anger.

"I hate to disappoint you, Father, but I don't harbor your love for making my son miserable. I'm not a fucking sadist who gets off on watching the torture of another man."

At the sound of something shattering in a nearby room, followed by what must be Anna's shrieks, I snap my head toward the door. In an instant, I'm pushing out of my chair, and I stride out of the library and down the hallway, to find Anna and Roark in my father's hobby room.

Small bits of porcelain lay scattered at Roark's tiny feet, as he stands picking at his lip, watching Anna scramble to clean it up. From the coloring on each piece, it would appear to be one of my father's many beer steins that he's collected over the years.

Kneeling down beside Anna, I help her pick up the pieces before Roark can step on one.

"I'm sorry, Master Lucian. We were playing hide and seek, and ..." Petite, and perhaps only just twenty years old, Anna always seems nervous around my father. No doubt, she's probably ready to peel herself right out of her skin to avoid his wrath for this.

"It's all right."

"What's going on here?" My father knocks into my shoulder as he passes, and when he bends forward to pick up a much larger chunk of the stein, a look of shock registers on his face. "This was the last Thewalt ever made. Do you have any idea what you've done?" He lurches toward Anna, but turns toward my son, taking hold of his shoulder.

At Roark's first cry, I jump to my feet on a rush of pure adrenaline.

My father draws back his hand to strike him, but I catch his wrist, my teeth grinding in rage. A blinding fury explodes inside of me, and I shove hard against his chest, knocking him backward, over the coffee table, and he tumbles onto the floor.

Roark cries when I lift him into my arms, my whole body trembling with potent violence, and I breathe hard through my nose to catch my breath. "I ever see you raise a hand to my son again, mark my words, I will take pleasure in your suffering."

With one hand holding his arm, he sits forward and chuckles drily. "I see the trait's alive and well within you, after all."

CHAPTER 42

ISADORA

Present day ...

The warmth of the bathwater surrounds me like a cozy blanket, as I sit on Lucian's lap, my cheek pressed against his chest, listening to his heart. After another round of sex in the bathtub, he's already washed every inch of me, including my hair, leaving me relaxed and content to fall asleep right here.

A part of me hates this comfort I feel with him, after we both agreed this was nothing more than sex, but I couldn't have anticipated the emotions he's stirred inside of me, the safety and trust. I expected him to treat me like every other asshole who's taken a piece of me, and I hate myself for secretly wanting more from him, like some kind of betrayal.

Arms stretched across the edge of the tub, he breathes deep, and I lift my head just enough to peer up at him. The steam from the bath added to the soft glow of a candle casts a shine across his skin, emphasizing the muscles in his arms and chest.

He looks like a god. One roughened by life and wounded in battle.

Eyes on his, I bend forward and lick the dew from his skin, running my tongue over his nipple. Jerking forward, he bites his lip and growls, the expression on his face a warning. "You are a vision of temptation in the flesh, Isa. A man's greatest weakness." His eyes fall to my lips, and he leans forward to kiss me.

"And you should've been a poet, instead of a big, bad shipping mogul."

"I'd have been happier for it."

I feather my lips over his and kiss along his jaw to his throat. "What makes you unhappy?"

"At the moment? Knowing this bathwater is going to get cold soon, and we'll have to get out."

Smiling against his throat, I drag my teeth over his skin, and he shifts beneath me.

"If you keep doing that, we might not be going anywhere for a while, though. Cold, or not."

"We'll be prunes."

"A fitting match for my face, then."

One arm wrapped around his neck, I trace the scar along his lip with my finger. "I happen to like your face very much."

His palms glide up my thighs, coming to rest at my hips, while he leans into me for a kiss. "That'd make you the first."

"I find scars *very* attractive."

The sound of his chuckle echoes in the steamy room. "Is that so?"

"Yes. They tell the story of an interesting man."

Brows lowering, he turns his scarred half away from me.

"I'm sorry. I didn't mean to say something upsetting."

"There's nothing interesting about these scars. The only story they tell is regret and pain."

I look down between us, to where the skinny lines mar my forearm. "Mine, too."

He takes my wrist in hand and rubs his thumb over the scars. "Tell me."

I don't want to speak of it now and ruin the contentment, but his eyes implore me. Trusting and brimming with sadness, I recall the same look when he opened one of his own wounds, showing me the pictures of his little boy earlier in the evening.

What could be worse than the pain of losing a son?

Casting my gaze from his, I muster the strength to tear open these scars and let them bleed out for the first time in months. "It was January. My senior year. Everyone was counting down the days, and I was just ... trying to hold on. I had no idea what I was going to do once high school ended. And it's not like I loved the place, you know? Everybody hated me there, except Kelsey."

"She's your friend."

I nod, running my fingers over his fine chest hairs. "Like a sister." The smile on my face withers with my frown.

"What happened?" Lucian's voice is a distant sound to the music blaring inside my head, as my memories transport me back to that night.

"I went to a party with her. Wasn't my thing, but ... it was senior year, and she begged me to go. Some guy she wanted to see there. Brady was his name." I can smell the stale beer and the skunky, pungent odor of weed, from when we entered the house that night. The promise of bad things on the air and across my skin. "There was a boy there. One I'd seen around. Maybe nineteen. Everyone thought he was so hot. I used to hear the girls talk about him in the bathroom. Things they wished he'd do to them." Shaking my head, I sneer at the stupidity, the naiveté of those girls now. "Imagine my surprise when he sat down next to me. He talked to *me*. Out of all those girls. I felt so ... unique, for once. And he was nice. He talked about books, you know? Something I could relate to."

"And where was Kelsey when you talked to this boy?"

"She walked off to find the guy she wanted to see there."

Closing my eyes adds vivid colors to the scene--the red lights around the room, the music blaring from the speaker, red cups of alcohol scattered over the floor. Red. "It was so loud. Everyone was drunk. Seemed like, just minutes later, she was stumbling after the guy out to the pool house."

"Brady?"

I stare off, lost to the memory. The blur of the scene I've spent months pushing away with therapy and dark shadows. *We're just having a little fun.*

"She stumbled after Brady?" The sound of Lucian's voice draws me back to the present, and I nod.

"Yeah. Sorry. The *beloved* son of Tempest Cove," I go on.

A flash of his naked torso flickers in my head, over the distant echo of laughter.

"She got drunk."

Screams pierce my ears, and I screw my eyes shut, breathing hard through my nose as the sketchy memories arrive like half-drawn pictures with the edges erased.

"He tore her clothes off. And she was so intoxicated she couldn't even fight it."

The sharp tip of a blade scrapes over the stark white paper, connecting the lines of the image in pale gray scratches. I can't bring myself to look at the mental image forming inside my head--the naked body of a girl lying on the floor. As if I'm looking down at her, scored onto the page in rough strokes.

"There were more of them. His teammates. Maybe four, or five, I can't remember. They laughed, as he raped her. All of them watching, begging for a turn."

A blackness stirs in the pit of my guts as the rest of the story seeps out of its locked compartment, the images clearer as more lines converge on the image, dark scratches filling with cold black ink, bringing details to life. Her half-drawn lids. The dirty carpet beneath her. Bruising marks where he held her too tight.

"Where were you when this happened?" Lucian's voice fades

beneath the remembered sounds of grunting and slapping skin, curses and crying.

"I was hiding. Hiding from all of them. I couldn't breathe. But then I screamed. I screamed so loud, but no one could hear me." I don't even realize I'm clawing at Lucian's chest, until my eyes focus in on the scratches streaked across his skin.

"What happened to the girl?"

What happened to the girl? His voice echoes inside my head.

"She screamed louder. Our screams were finally heard by a neighbor, who shined a flashlight. They all got spooked and ran off."

"And the girl. Did she get away?"

"She did." Like a movie reel, the memory continues to spin inside my head.

Wrapping my arm around Kelsey, both of us stumbling out of the pool house. The cold bite of winter air against my face, as the two of us made our way back to the car.

The urge to break down tugs at the back of my eyes, and I push off Lucian's chest, concentrating on each breath, as my therapist told me to do whenever the anxiety struck me. Closing my eyes, I focus on every count, inhaling and exhaling, in and out, until the thrum in my veins slows, and when I feel Lucian's arm tighten around my back, I open my eyes again.

"That must've been very traumatic to watch. I shouldn't have been so rough with you tonight." His comment lures me out of the dark thoughts, pushing them back inside their boxes.

"There's a difference between roughness and rape. Someone completely betraying your trust. Making you feel small and weak. Worthless."

"What I wouldn't give to have been in that room that night." The shadows behind his stare send a curling shiver down my spine as I imagine what unseen thoughts have captured his focus. "They would've regretted laying a hand on that girl."

In spite of the distress humming through my veins, I try to

picture that. The Devil of Bonesalt teaching those adolescent boys a lesson in karma. What a different outcome it might've been, and perhaps I wouldn't have been plagued with so many nightmares after. "You're the first time I feel safe."

"And you're the first time I've felt anything in a long time." He kisses my forehead, squeezing my nape. With each passing second, the memories seal tighter, and my muscles tremble less.

"Tell me about the music. How did you come by such a gift?" His change of topic is a welcomed distraction from the few lingering sensations still humming inside of me.

I exhale a shaky breath, mentally willing my head to let go of the phantom images still clouding my head. "No idea. My dad, maybe? Except, I don't know anything about him. He died when I was young. Definitely wasn't my mother, though."

"What do you intend to do with it?"

Shrugging, I shake my head. "I haven't thought about it." Leaning forward, I press my lips to his and feel his hands slide down to my hips. "Enough about me. I want to know about you. How did you get your scars?"

"I'll tell you sometime, but not tonight." Thumb tracing the edge of my jaw, he seems to be lost in thought again. "It's a long and unpleasant story. And you need sleep."

CHAPTER 43

LUCIAN

Four years ago ...

I park the Ducati on the arc of the drive at the manor and kill the engine. It's not often I get to ride it these days, but the first day of spring brought warm weather, and the long ride to the office sounded a whole lot better, with the wind zipping past me at speeds that'd make my mother's eyeballs spin.

My father stands in his office window, watching me, as I dismount the bike. Almost thirty years old, and I'm still hawked like a teenager.

As I jog up the staircase, Rand meets me at the door, and I toss him my helmet.

"Nice job negotiating that contract, Master," he says in passing.

No doubt, my father told him of the deal I struck with one of his vendors this afternoon, securing millions for over the next couple of years. More security for Blackthorne Enterprises.

"Thanks. Roark in his room?"

"I believe that's where I last saw him."

I make my way to the second floor and hang a left down the hallway, along which Roark's nursery has officially been turned into a Formula One pit stop. Only three and a half, and the kid's already taking after me. I enter to find him sitting on the floor with his toy cars, and I lean against the doorframe watching him for a second.

Zooming his car over a carpet track, he talks to himself. "Yay, I'm da winnah! I winned dah wace. Oh, wanna wace again? Yes!"

I chuckle watching him, and when he turns around to face me, those blue eyes light up.

"Daddy!" He drops the cars and dashes across the room, and I kneel to catch him. Crashing into me, he nearly knocks me on my ass. "Do you see my new caw, Daddy?" He points to one of his discarded toys on the carpet. "Uncle Wand gabed it to me."

"Uncle Wand, huh? Where did Uncle Rand get a toy car?"

"Him buyed it at dah store."

With a smile, I run my hand over his blond hair. Another trait he earned from Amelia. "How was your day, buddy?"

"Good. Did you worked?"

"I did. Nailed a big deal, too." I hold my hand up, and he leaps to high five.

"Wanna pway wace wif me?"

"Let me get showered and finish up some paperwork real quick, and I'll go a couple laps with you."

"Yay!" He jumps up and down and throws himself at me.

Arms wrapped around him, I pull him in for a hug and kiss his cheek.

A figure sweeps by us as Amelia makes her way into his bedroom. "Okay, Roark, bath time."

The two of us don't speak much, with me being gone most of the day, but she doesn't sleep as much as she did for a while there. Lately, she's been up and dressed before ten, as I understand, and has even started taking Roark and Sampson for walks in the garden. We'll never be what she imagined, but at least we won't be what I imagined, either. Hands stuffed in her pocket, hair pulled back in a loose bun, she wears jeans and a flowy top that isn't what she would've worn ten years ago. She looks older. Still pretty, but aged with stress.

"How'd it go today?" My mother must've filled her in, as I certainly didn't tell her what was on my agenda.

Even so, I answer, "Fine. You?"

"Fine."

An awkward silence follows, as it always does. Usually, she tries to fill in the gap with benign conversation about the weather, or my office. Most of the time, I think she's looking for me to slip and tell her I'm fucking someone at work. Tonight, I don't give her the chance.

"I've got some paperwork to finish." Directing my attention back toward Roark, I point at him, backing myself toward the door. "I'll see you in a few, buddy. Get in a couple warmup laps, okay?"

"Okay, Daddy."

"Lucian," she calls after me, bringing my escape to a halt. "I was thinking … if you're up for it tomorrow. Maybe we could have dinner? Together? Nothing special. Just … catching up."

On four years of ignoring each other? Two of those years I spent resenting her. The three of us have never eaten as a family. I either grab something on the way home from the office, or eat alone later, after everyone's already gone to bed.

"I'll think about it."

"Fair enough. I'm going to go to bed after Roark's bath. Can you make sure he gets to sleep?"

"Yeah. Where's Anna?"

"I gave her the night off. Just trying to get …" Gaze cast downward, she shakes her head. "Never mind."

"Trying to get what?"

331

"Back to being a mother." It's strange to hear those words from her, considering she spent the first year of Roark's life avoiding the role. "I don't want my son to be raised by someone else."

Tight lipped, I nod in approval, though I haven't been around Amelia much these days to know what kind of responsibility that might be on her.

"Anyway, let me know about tomorrow."

"I will. 'Night."

"Your father is incredibly proud of you." My mother stands in the doorway, arms crossed, while I sit hunched over the small bit of paperwork I'm hustling to finish so I can hang out with Roark, as promised.

"I'm sure he is. All the more reason to toss this shit aside."

Sneering, she enters the room and saunters over to the liquor that's set out on a tray. Glass clinks as she stands with her back to me, pouring a drink, and when she turns around, she's carrying two, one of which she places down on the desk.

Plopping into the chair in front of me, she raises her glass. "Cheers to your successful negotiation."

I raise my glass and nod. "Thanks."

Seconds pass quietly, before her lips widen with a smile. "Amelia seems to be feeling better these days."

"Seems to be."

"If the two of you would like some time to get away, I'm happy to watch Roar--"

"No. That won't be necessary."

"Lucian, she's trying. You have to give her that."

"I appreciate her efforts, but I'm not here to play pretend. I didn't choose this." The only thing that solidified my decision to play, at all, was the paternity test results that came back positive that I was the father. For the sake of my own son, I gave the family shit a chance.

"And you think she did?"

"Why are you here, Mother? To lay another guilt trip on me?"

Lips pursed, the way they do when she's trying to cap a smartass remark meant for my father, she sets the glass on the desk. "Consider having dinner with her tomorrow. The two of you *are* still married, after all. It's important to build what you can before the real hate sets in."

"Like you and my father? Why bother to stay together? You could be doing your own thing right now. Following your heart's desire, instead of playing into his little games of power."

"Because divorce is messy. And expensive. Besides that, the heart is a dangerous organ that isn't meant to be free. Why else would God have built a cage for it?"

If there was any question as to where my lack of faith in love and relationships originated, I'm staring at half the reason right now. "No promises. But I'll think about dinner. Now, if you'll excuse me, I need to finish this so I can hang with my son."

"Of course." My mother gathers up the half-sipped glasses of liquor and exits the office.

I glance at the clock on my desk, and at my watch that reads twenty-to eight. "Ten more minutes."

A cold, hard surface presses against my cheek, my jaw aching, and I open my eyes to white sheets of paper. Pain pulses inside my skull. Eyes screwed shut on the agony, I sit up and rub the sleep from them.

The clock reads almost eleven.

Shit.

I fell asleep. I don't even remember doing so.

Shit.

Having grown up with a man who never played with me as a child, and never kept his promises, I make it a point to do both with Roark.

On my feet, the room spins for a second, and I shield my eyes behind my palm until it slows to a stop again. *What the hell is wrong with me?*

Stumbling out of the office, I stagger down the hallway toward Roark's bedroom, the portraits of ancestors on the wall going in and out of focus. I must be utterly exhausted.

When I enter the dark bedroom, I find Roark's sleeping form on the floor, surrounded by his toys. It isn't unusual for him to fall asleep while playing. It's why Amelia asked that I check on him. Without anyone physically putting him to bed, he'll stay up all hours of the night until he crashes.

I try to shake off the dizziness and cross the room, where I kneel down next to him. Something sits off to the side, and I frown once I realize what it is. A pill bottle. Small blue pills lay scattered on the floor. I lift the bottle, turning it over to find Amelia's name printed on the label, and below it, Lorazepam.

Ativan.

Panic tightens its fist around my chest, and I turn Roark over, immediately taking note of the white pallor of his skin, the blue of his lips.

"Roark!" I shake his small body to wake him, every muscle in my body quaking with the urge to throw up. "Roark!"

His eyelashes flutter, his lids opening to show dilated pupils that can't seem to focus on me. "I'seep, Daddy," he says weakly.

"No, no. Don't sleep." Stroking his hair, I try to keep him awake. "Don't sleep, buddy, okay?" I lift him into my arms, pressing him against my chest. "You can't sleep yet."

"I wan dede bew." His teddy bear.

I don't have time to look for it. I don't even know if I have time to reach my phone. "Help me! Somebody, help me!" My shouts echo down the hallway, bouncing off the walls. Racing back toward my office with Roark in my arms, I find my phone on my desk and one-handedly dial *9-1-1*.

"I'seep, Daddy."

"No, no. Stay awake just a bit more, Roark."

"Nine-one-one, what's your emergency?" At the sound of another person on the other end of the line, all the urgency pours out of me.

"My … my son! He … he got into my … he took Ativan."

"Calm down, sir, is he with you now?"

"Yes!" I tuck the phone against my ear to grip the back of Roark's head, and gently lay him down onto the desktop.

His eyes are closed again, and if possible, his face a ghostlier shade of white.

"No, no, no! Roark, wake up!"

"Master Blackthorne, is everything all right?" At the sound of Rand's voice, I hold out my phone.

"Talk to her for me! It's emergency. Roark got into Amelia's pills!" The moment he takes the phone from my hand, I turn back to my son. "Hey, buddy. You need to wake up." I give a light shake and gently pat his cheek. "Roark, wake up."

"Ambulance is on its way, Master." Rand's voice is a distant sound to the rush of blood pounding inside my ears.

"He won't wake up. I can't fucking get him to wake up!" I lean down, pressing my ear to his chest, listening for a heartbeat.

Nothing.

"Roark?" When I shift toward his mouth, I don't feel the warmth of his breath on my skin. "He's not breathing."

"The operator says you need to perform CPR on him, Sir."

"I don't fucking know CPR!"

"Allow me, Master." Setting a hand on my arm, Rand urges me aside, placing himself between me and my son, and within seconds, he's going to work on his chest, while talking to the woman on the phone. Rounding the desk, I watch through a shield of tears as the only thing in this world that ever mattered, that ever gave me purpose, lies slipping out of my grasp.

Amelia enters the room, darting toward Roark, and at the sight of her, I imagine wrapping my hands around her throat. Squeezing until her face turns as ghostly white as Roark's.

"What happened? What's going on?"

A muscle in my jaw tics, as she stands beside Rand, stroking the boy's hair.

"What did you do?" I grit past clenched teeth. "What the fuck did you do?"

The rage in my voice must reach her loud and clear, because she slowly lifts her gaze, eyes wide and cautious as if a monster stands before her.

"I didn't do anything," she says in that disgusting meek voice that, in this moment, makes me want to tear her vocal chords right out of her throat. "I swear I didn't do anything, Lucian."

"Your pills were in his room. Scattered on the floor around him."

Her body jerks with a sob that she caps behind her palms, and tears spring to her eyes. She shakes her head. "I didn't leave them in his room. I don't know how he got to them."

"He got to them because you're fucking careless. Care. *Less.*"

"Master, please." The desperation in Rand's voice bleeds through his words as he resumes his compressions.

There's no movement from Roark. No sign that his efforts are working.

Rand lifts the phone for the operator. "It's not working. He's not breathing, at all."

"Keep with compressions until paramedics arrive," I hear the operator say through the phone.

"Oh, God, Roark!" Amelia lowers her head to the table, her hand clutched to his face, and her sobs are nothing but an irritating distraction from the pain that waits to swallow me up. The agony that I can't bear to face, for fear I'll do something stupid.

Minutes tick until two men in uniform enter the room, followed by my mother.

"Lucian? Lucian!" Her voice is frantic, and when her gaze slides toward Roark, she collapses beside the couch across the room, holding her chest. "Oh, no. Oh, not my sweet boy. Not my sweet, baby boy!"

More minutes pass while they hook him up to machines and tubes and a contraption that pumps air into him. One of the men finally speaks into a radio comm, and all I pick up from that conversation is *asystole* and *no pulse*. He ends the conversation with, "I'll notify dispatch. Thank you."

"What's going on? What's happening? Are you taking him to the hospital?" The desperation and despair in Amelia's voice is enough to curl my lip, and I fear what I'd do, if not for all these people standing around us.

"I'm sorry, ma'am. There's nothing more we can do. An officer is on his way. They'll gather information for the coroner."

"Coroner? As in … he's … no. No." She falls into one of the chairs behind her, wailing into her palms.

"He was talking. An hour ago. He told me he felt sleepy." I can't see through the blur of tears. "He asked for …" At the memory of his last request, I stride through the small crowd and out of the room, down the hall, to Roark's bedroom. Scanning the toys lying about, I find his Dede tossed onto the bed. Snatching it up, I race back down the hall to find Amelia sobbing beside Roark, stroking his hair.

My father stands off to the side as emotionless as I'd expect.

I make my way around the desk, away from Amelia and the paramedics, and lower to my knees. Taking his small, cold hand in mine, I wrap his teddy bear in his limp arms.

"Roark, you have to wake up." For a moment, it's as if there's no one else in the room except me and my son. I press my face to his soft baby cheek and inhale the scent of him. The lavender soap of his bath from earlier. "I should've left the paperwork. If I'd known ..." The pain in my chest is unbearable, like an animal eating me from the inside out. The air turns thick and suffocating, and suddenly I can't breathe. I can't fucking breathe. I slide him off the desk, clutching him against me as I fall to the floor. The agony rips through my chest as I rock him, just as I did the first time I held him in my arms. When he stopped crying. When he looked at me with trust and wonder in his eyes. And he stopped crying.

A broken sound of rage and suffering echoes through the room, and I realize it's coming from me, as I clutch my son for the last time.

Voices reach the void inside my head.

I don't even know how long I've stared at the spot on the desk where Roark's body lay before he was taken away. An officer outside the office talks with my father, finally drawing my focus away, and in the thick of conversation, he makes eye contact with me and offers a sympathetic nod. When I lower my gaze, I notice the signet ring he's wearing, and the conversation sharpens to clarity.

"We'll make sure not a word of this breaches these walls," he says, shaking my father's hand. "Not a single word."

I push to my feet, my body moving on its own, and I exit past the officer, who pats me on the back. Down the hall, then staircase, until I finally reach the foyer.

"Master?" Rand asks from behind. "Where are you going?"

I don't answer him. I swipe the keys from the console where I left them earlier, and make my way toward the door.

"Master, you shouldn't go anywhere right now." The warning

in Rand's voice fails to breach the haze of determination, as I head toward the door. "Lucian!"

Once outside, I hustle down the staircase, toward my bike still parked on the drive. I need something, I don't even know what. Speed. Air. Adrenaline. Something that will take away this intense pain. The massive hollow in my chest that's doubled in size over the last hour. The emptiness and numbness that waits to devour me the moment I let down my guard.

"Boss!" Makaio calls, as he and Rand plod down the stairs after me.

I start up the bike, rev the throttle, and take off down the drive. Cool air whips past me, stealing my breath, as I pass through the gates of this hell. Flickering images of Roark slip through my mind, and I feed the bike more gas. Trees zip through my periphery, the buzz of the bike the only sound over the distant memory of Roark's sleepy voice. Before I know it, the trees give way to the seaside, the winding road ahead calling to me.

More speed.

I think of the moments earlier, when I stood in the doorway, watching him play. What if I hadn't bothered with the paperwork? What if I'd dropped it all and played with him right then?

More speed.

The visual of picking up the bottle and finding Amelia's name on the label sends bullets of rage through my veins, and I clench my teeth together.

More speed.

I curse God for giving me something so meaningful, so crucial, only to swipe it right out of my hands.

Lights ahead approach fast, and somehow, they're coming right at me. That's when I catch sight of the line I've crossed on the road, and I swerve to avoid the crash. My hand slips from the throttle, flying into the air. The pavement crashes into my shoulder and tears into my face, as I drag across the concrete. Fire streaks up one half of my body, while the rest of me goes numb, and red gathers in my periphery, the world stands tilted on its side. A white hot pain rips across my skin. I see lights. Shadows looming over me.

Standing in front of them is Roark, clutching his teddy.

"Hi, Daddy."

CHAPTER 44

LUCIAN

Present day ...

"Roark!" I snap out of the nightmare, momentarily disoriented as I search the room for familiarity.

My son. Gone. Dead.

Bile rises in my throat, my head spinning out of sleep, while my surroundings come into view.

The dark chandelier, white curtains, dark Victorian décor, all tell me I'm in Amelia's room.

Amelia.

Turning to my side, though, I find black raven hair fanned out against the stark white pillows, her equally black lashes fluttering in dreams. Not Amelia. *Isa.*

Isa.

Shaken to my core, I drag her body into mine, where her small frame perfectly melds into my much larger form. With my face pressed into her nape, I screw my eyes shut, mentally pushing away the lingering images of my nightmare. My son. Pale and cold and dead.

Her scent penetrates the chaos inside my head, the warm and inviting aroma that's a mix between sweet vanilla cream and her own personal fragrance. I drag my lips over her soft skin, kissing her shoulder, while my breaths calm, my pulse slows. Wrapping her tighter against me, I feel her body tick with life, her heartbeat and steady exhale like a metronome that lures me back to the present. I've had nightmares before, and woken up to cold sweats, sleepwalking, sometimes swinging out at nothing but shadows. Tonight, I'm grateful for Isa's presence. The way she soothes the restlessness that claws inside of me. The wretched demons of my past spoiling for their usual nightly torment.

With her back to my chest, she shifts and moans, and I kiss behind her ear to settle her. For years, I've shunned the idea of sharing a bed with a woman. But Isa is delicate. A fragile bird in the palm of my hand, whose vicious bites are the result of cruelty and neglect. She needs direction and guidance, security and protection. Things I could give her, if not for my trepidations.

I've been careful to avoid repeating the mistakes of my past, of tangling myself in another web of commitments and responsibilities, but this girl is different somehow. I can feel my defenses crumbling when I'm around her, and as much as that might frustrate the hell out of me, I don't hate it, either.

Thoughts of her story from earlier come to mind, the way my body reacted to her distress, tense and shaking with anger. There's more to what happened that night, something she's leaving out, but I didn't push it. I wanted to punish those who put the panic and fear in her eyes, while she spoke through detached words, trying to convince me that she left that party unscathed. I know better than that. A girl doesn't sleep with a blade under her pillow and cut up her arms in the name of a friend. I don't care how close they were. Those boys hurt her, too, and in turn, I wanted to hurt them—still do.

I would find joy in their misery, pleasure in their suffering, while gifting them with a slow and agonizing penance.

Perhaps I am a sadist, after all.

I would've destroyed every last one of them for her.

My raven beauty.

My Isa *bella*.

CHAPTER 45

ISADORA

The intoxicating scent of cologne rouses me from dreams. A rich woodsy, masculine flavor dances through my senses, and I stretch against the solid body pressed against me. His strong palm slides over my belly at the same time as a deep, growly sound rumbles in his chest, and I turn to face him. Eyes still closed, he seems to fight waking, but the small bit of early morning light coming in through the curtain is hard to ignore in the otherwise dark room.

The steady cadence of his breathing expands and contracts his back, where resting muscles protrude beneath his skin. Broad shoulders taper down to narrow hips and tight buttocks, his magnificent body shamelessly on display. Everything about Lucian, from this angle, oozes unearthly perfection.

Full irresistible lips beg to be kissed, and I lean in, feeling the light tickle against my mouth as I brush mine over his. His hand slides lower, lips quirking to a half smile, and he turns to his side, dragging my leg over his hip.

Pressed against his naked form, I feel the enormous shape of his erection prodding my belly. When I shift against him, he finally lifts his eyelids, exposing those beautiful golden irises. The scarred half of his face lies buried in the pillows, and from my angle, all I see is the flawless half. The side of him that he doesn't turn away when I stare at him, like I am now.

I reach up to trace his perfectly trimmed hairline, down to his chiseled jawline. "Has anyone ever told you that you're very handsome when you're not being a jerk?"

He snorts a laugh, turning his face into the pillow, away from my touch. "There she is," he mumbles. "The smartass."

"It's true. It's like the clouds break open to the heavens and ..." I make a choir sound that scratches my throat, knocking out a barky cough.

Face still buried, he shakes his head. "Should've stayed in my own bed." His voice is muffled by the plush fabric. "At least I'd get another hour of sleep."

"There's plenty of time to sleep when you die."

"Which will be long before you."

"I heard sex keeps you young. *Virile.*"

Turning to face me again, he raises a brow, the sight of him ruffling the butterflies in my stomach. "And if she happens to be over a decade younger than me?"

"You're practically a god."

His grip tightens like a band around me. "Then, I've no reason to leave this bed. And neither do you."

"I actually have to pee, so ..." As I twist away from him, an arm reaches out, dragging me backward. Long, deft fingers dig into my sides, and I howl with laughter, the urgency to pee squeezing my bladder. "Lucian! Please! I'm going to pee my pants!"

"You're not wearing pants."

"I swear to God I'll wet the bed!"

"After last night, it's due for a change of sheets."

"Lucian! Stop! Right now!" I giggle, squirming and twisting in his unbreakable grasp. "I'm begging you. Please!"

"Yes, I like to hear you beg. It warms my bastard soul."

Reaching back, I take hold of his swollen balls and squeeze, giggling when he groans and the tickling stops.

"That was a dirty move."

"Sensitive this morning?"

"As a matter of fact they are. Take your piss and get back here, before I decide to take my chances on a golden shower."

Wearing a smile, I slide on his discarded shirt from the night before, not bothering to button the front, and scamper across the room toward the bathroom. Lifting the fabric to my nose, I breathe in the scent of his cologne as I relieve myself quickly, followed by a cursory brush of my teeth and hair. When I return, Lucian is propped on his elbow, a vision of divine masculinity, his muscles all bunched up while he stares down at something in his hands.

As I approach, I notice the picture. The one I found beneath the nightstand.

"I'd forgotten about this day." The somber tone in his voice echoes the expression on his face that I recall from the picture.

Crawling into the bed beside him, I slide in close, trying not to disturb whatever thoughts have his eyes so fixed and contemplative.

"It was one of Amelia's good days. A rarity."

"You look so unhappy? Why?"

"I never liked pretending, and when she was happy, the lies just became more obvious."

"What lies?"

"That we were in love."

"You didn't love her?"

"Never."

"Have you ever loved a woman?"

He seems to hesitate for a moment, but shakes his head. "It's the only brand of pain I refuse to inflict on myself."

"Why is that?"

He sets the picture down and lifts my arm, tracing my scar

with his finger. "When you cut yourself with a blade, there's an open wound, and blood and pain, but the pain comes to an end and the wound seals to a scar. So you cut yourself again and again, because you forget how much it hurt the first time. The heart is a different animal. A caged, lonely scavenger that feeds on its own wounds. Its scars never heal, because you can't mend the very thing it needs to survive. So the wound continues to fester, until what's left of the organ is eventually consumed by its own self-mutilation."

I hate that his words penetrate deep, and that I know so intimately their meaning. The world would call his sentiments depressing and morose, but it's the most honest definition of love I've ever heard.

I run my thumb over the scars along his arm, the tips of my finger traveling over the jagged, irregular edges of wounds that didn't seal properly. "You've hurt yourself, too."

"I'm not the devil they make me out to be. The heartless, *callous* monster. You can't do this shit to yourself without feeling something. That's the problem. I feel everything. I feel it very deeply."

Monsters and devils don't keep drawers full of their son's old pictures and toys. They don't intervene when violent drug dealers make terrifying threats. And they certainly don't kiss like the world might burn down at any moment.

"You're no monster," I whisper, climbing over his body, urging him onto his back. Legs straddling him, I feel the warmth of his hands trail over my thighs to the curves of my hips and higher. My breasts, heavy and pulling at my shoulders, jut forward with his wandering fingertips, nipples hardening beneath the pads of his thumbs.

His tongue sweeps over his lips, his eyes seeming to devour every inch of my body, as he pushes aside the edges of my borrowed shirt. "How can you be so fucking perfect? It's maddening to look at you."

"Why?"

"So many things I want to do to you. I never know where to begin." He gives a tiny tug at my nipples, and I arch toward him, which seems to please him, from the way he bites his lip and grinds me against his erection. "You should be grateful that I don't have a pair of cuffs at my disposal."

"I've personally found your hands to be just as effective."

His lips stretch to a wily smile, and before I can react, he knocks me to the mattress, flipping me onto my stomach with ease. In two rapid movements, I'm beneath him, lying on my stomach with my face smashed into the pillow. Big palms grip my wrists at either side of my head, pinning me to the bed. His cock glides between the cheeks of my ass, and the heat of his breath falls against the back of my neck. "If my hands weren't occupied, though, they could hold your thighs apart while I eat your pussy for breakfast."

"You assume I'll try to get away from that?"

"Maybe not." He licks the shell of my ear, the tip of his cock prodding my entrance. "But it's better when you *can't*."

From the nightstand, he tears another condom from the strip, two of which we've already used.

Turning to the side, I watch him rip open the package with his teeth.

"Do you always use condoms?" I ask, the self-conscious side of me rearing its ugly head. Back home, guys wore condoms with me because they assumed I whored myself out.

"Yes. It's nothing personal." After sliding the barrier down his shaft, he grips the base of his stiff erection and moves up my body. "I've no intentions of becoming a father again."

"Ever?"

"Ever."

It doesn't hurt my feelings, as I don't intend to become my mother, either--pregnant before I have my shit together. As he holds himself behind me, waiting and teasing, as usual, I raise my hips up and stir my ass against his groin to taunt him.

A firm hand grips the back of my neck, squeezing hard enough to make me still. I try to lift my head, to see if I've pissed him off somehow, but he holds me down, like a lion affirming dominance over his female. He's a man who likes to be in control of his body, and perhaps my teasing caught him off guard.

"You love to taunt me. Yet, you tremble in my grasp."

"I can't tell if you're angry."

"I am angry." Sliding my hands up to either side of the pillow, he holds me captive as he drives forward, filling the ache between my thighs. In slow and easy thrusts, he pumps in and out of me, jerking my body with each rough invasion. "I hate that fucking you has become my favorite thing in the world."

"Then, stop, if it troubles you so much."

"I can't stop. Once I'm inside of you, and I can feel that tight little hole gripping my dick." He bends my arms, and holds my wrists behind my back like that of a criminal about to be cuffed. His arm slides beneath my stomach, propping me up onto my knees, and with one hand holding my wrists captive, he grips the back of my neck again with the other. "It's impossible to stop," he grits in my ear, hips slapping against my ass as he pounds into me with fervor. "This is what you do to me. My head. My body. It's madness. And I'm going to fuck you until I no longer feel this violence inside of me."

I don't know where, or when, I developed a desire for rough sex, but everything about this sends a wicked thrill through my body. The idea that I've stirred this lack of control, made him want me to the point of savagery, it almost feels like too much power in my hands. Like I'm holding the reins of an untamable beast.

Like I'm the one in control.

It's strange, the way he makes me feel this way, as comparatively small and inexperienced as I am.

I turn my head into the pillow, breathing hard against the cotton, and my thoughts take me back to the night before, when his lips sealed off the oxygen as I climaxed. How exquisite it felt, the tug for air, the tightening of muscles, my body in a frenzy for release.

Pace escalating, he grunts while he ruts against me, the force of his body knocking what little breath remains out of my lungs.

I focus on his stiff length slipping in and out of me, the way my breasts jitter beneath me on each forward thrust.

Oh, God.

My head urges me to turn and steal a breath, but I can't. I want the burn in my chest, the cramping in my womb, and the tremble of my muscles, as it culminates inside of me.

"Keep your head in the pillow." Lucian's voice is ragged and strained, his fingers digging into my wrists, keeping me hostage as he drives into me.

My body jostles like a ragdoll beneath him, helpless to his relentless assault, and I curl my fingers in his grasp, desperate for air, desperate for release, desperate for the pleasure he's stirred inside of me.

So close.

Chest pulsing for one sip of breath, I bite the sheets, listening to the perpetual sound of slapping skin echo through the room over his grunts and growls.

Long, labored moans escape my lips, captured into the pillowcase. The damp cotton fails to offer more than a small bit of air, not enough to fill my lungs.

My muscles tighten. Toes curl. Arms tremble in his grasp. I'm so close.

"Come for me, Isa."

The deep timbre of Lucian's voice sends me flying over the edge, into the stratosphere where the light flashes in my eyes. I scream into the pillow, while pleasure rips through my body, the dizzying poison exploding through my veins.

I turn my head to suck in a breath, drinking in the cool air that rushes into my chest. His palm slides beneath my throat, my wrists still bound in his other hand, and he squeezes as he lies across my back and runs his teeth over my jawline. Thrusts slowing, the groan in his throat is long and tortured, and he releases my neck to push off of me. As cool air hits my back, Lucian's curses bounce off the walls.

As he jerks out the last of his orgasm, I lie weak and exhausted, reeling from my newfound thrill.

"You enjoy the lack of breath." He rests his head against my shoulders and kisses my damp skin.

I nod, still panting from the exertion that has every muscle feeling like jelly. "I think I just figured out my new favorite thing, too."

"You and I are going to get along very well, my little raven." Teeth nipping my skin, he tightens his grip around me, drawing my arms in and caging me beneath him. "As tragic as that may be."

CHAPTER 46

LUCIAN

Four years ago ...

Voices echo around me. Sterile scents invade my senses. I can't tell if I'm awake or asleep. The incessant beeping in my ear grows louder, until I open my eyes to see white walls and a half-closed white curtain, enveloping me in with two men in white coats.

Am I dead?

A flash of blinding light hits the back of my head, making my eyes instinctively screw shut, and I feel the flames burning my skin.

I jerk awake, but when I try to sit up, my body doesn't move.

"Relax, Lucian. Your heart sounds as if it might gallop away any minute." The voice is foreign to me, in this place that feels like a dream.

"Where am I? What is this?" The words arrive stiff and clipped through an ache in my jaw that pulses in my ear.

"I'm Dr. Thames, and this is Dr. Mayer," he says, gesturing to the shorter, stocky man beside him. "He's an expert in the field of reconstructive surgery."

"Wh-what are you talking about?"

"You've been in a coma for about a week. In that time, we've done some minor patches to your face and jawline, but wanted to wait until you were stable before taking you to the OR."

"Patches? For what?" A fog swirls inside my head, dancing around the dull throb that beats through my sinuses.

"You were in an accident and sustained some fairly serious injuries, particularly to your jawline, shoulder, arm and thigh. Your shoulder took the brunt of the impact, but you have a number of broken bones in your face, collarbone and ribs. There was quite a bit of head trauma, as well. The coma was induced to reduce some of the swelling on your brain. We placed a drain that, I'm pleased to report, we were able to remove yesterday afternoon, along with weaning you off the vent. You've remained stable since."

My mind replays the last thing I remember. The lights. The fire. Roark holding his teddy bear. "My son. Where's my son?"

"Your mother tells me there was an accident at home? That was the nature of you hopping on a bike with no helmet."

"Accident?" I say the word aloud, and the movie reel inside my head rewinds further. *Roark sleeping. The pill bottle. No pulse.* My chest expands as the panic blooms behind my ribs, until I can't breathe.

Something beeps inside the room.

"Hey, hey. Calm down, Lucian."

A hand touches my shoulder, and I want to throw it off me, but can't. Nothing moves. I can't feel anything but the agony tearing through me. "He's dead."

"I'm sorry to hear that. As difficult as it may be, the best thing you can do right now, Mr. Blackthorne, is focus on your recovery."

Tears distort his form, as I stare up at this man I don't even know. One who thinks he knows what's best for me. "What's the point?"

～

Two weeks have passed since the accident. Two weeks of rehab. Caring too little. Thinking too much. Drowning in the misery and guilt of having failed my son. It's there every time I look into the mirror. The mangled remains of my face, so riddled with scars and metal plates that I don't even feel human anymore. My punishment for being a shitty father. For putting myself first, when it should've been Roark.

His body was eventually returned to us and buried in a small sarcophagus down in the catacombs. It's a place I can't bring myself to visit. Not for a while.

"It was an accident. That's all. An oversight," my father says, sitting in his chair across from me, Amelia, and Mayor Boyd. "No one is really at fault here."

At my father's words, I lift my gaze from the condensation trickling down the glass of water that I've been staring at for the last twenty minutes. "He got his hands on her fucking pills. How is she not at fault?"

"I have told you repeatedly, Lucian." Amelia's voice has grown weaker, more fragile than before. "I would never--"

"But you did." My jaw remains stiff, with more titanium in my face than a Russian submarine. "And now he's dead."

"And you'll just keep punishing and punishing me and punishing me," she whispers.

"All right, all right." My father waves his hands in the air, the tone of his voice laced with irritation. "Enough of this bickering like children. We have a much bigger issue to contend with, which is what to tell the media. They've been all over us since Lucian's little circus sideshow."

"Sideshow? Look at me. Can you even look at me?" I tip my

head to catch his gaze, a zap of electricity striking my skull as I grind my teeth. "This is what you wanted of me, remember? To be a father. A fucking monster, like you."

"Careful, boy. Now's not the time. The point of this meeting is to discuss next steps. If word gets out that Amelia's pills were the cause of his death, she'll be strung up like a Salem witch by this town. It'll be bad for her, for Mayor Boyd, and for us. Everyone who had contact with Roark that night, down to the goddamn dispatcher who took the call, has been informed to remain quiet."

In other words, threatened to be buried six feet under. The beauty of money and power.

"You think you can keep this from getting out? Someone is going to talk. They're going to slip." In spite of the pain, I steal the opportunity to chuckle. "I hope they do."

"And we'll address it when the time comes. For now, we're going to inform the media that Roark has gone missing."

"I'm not lying to the media about what happened to my son."

"You don't have to. I'll be speaking on behalf of his *distraught and grieving* parents. There will be a reward for anyone who has information about him. All you have to do is keep your mouth shut and play along. Sheriff Townsend has agreed to do the same."

Of course he has. He's one of my father's little cult buddies, and will, without question, take the secret to his grave. They all will, because that's the Blackthorne curse. That's what's earned us the reputation of crossing paths with a black cat. That's why no one will dare dispute a word of this, and Roark's death will forever remain a mystery.

I turn my gaze away from my father, from Amelia, and Mayor Boyd. "This is wrong."

"Welcome to the world of power, my boy."

CHAPTER 47

ISADORA

Present day ...

Freshly showered, Lucian exits the bathroom, wearing only a towel wrapped around his lower half, the perfect V disappearing into the crisp white fabric. He leans in to kiss me, where I lay on the bed, having left the shower ahead of him. This is the moment I've dreaded. When we part ways and the awkwardness settles between us. I almost wish he'd been a dick afterward and ditched me last night, because at least then I'd be familiar with this. I'd know what to expect between us.

"You're welcome to stay here today, if you'd like," he says, tucking a strand of hair behind my ear. "No sense packing up, just to turn around and come back."

The idea of staying seems even more awkward, especially when I haven't figured out if this was just a onetime thing between us. A weekend of sex, and we'll be back to boss and employee come tomorrow, when the work week starts over. "I can't. I have to run a quick errand in town, and I told my aunt I'd have lunch at The Shoal."

"I see." The disappointment in his voice almost sounds as if he'd prefer that I stay. "I guess I'll see you when you get back, then."

"You could come with me." I flinch as the words tumble out of my mouth before I can stop them.

Again.

Especially when the expression on his face is what I'd expect if I'd just eaten a bowl full of maggots in front of him.

"Have you seen the crosses along the road? They call me the devil, in case you've forgotten. The mere sight of me will have them all believing the apocalypse has arrived."

The thought of such a thing brings a smile to my face. What I wouldn't give ... "I don't blame you. They treat me like shit, too." With a sigh, I sit up on the bed, holding the crumpled sheet to my breast, and glance around the room. "If I lived here, I probably wouldn't want to leave, either."

"They treat you like shit, too. Why?"

Shrugging, I pull my knees up to my chest. "Because of my mom, mostly. I guess I inherited her reputation."

"Isn't that always the case." It's not a question, and there's a kindred spark behind his eyes as he studies me.

"It was really bad, my first couple years of high school. The other kids and their parents, teachers, they all treated me like I was some kind of plague." Memories of my first day filter in, when I sat eating lunch under the staircase, just looking for a place to breathe. "It gets easier after a while. Almost like their hate becomes part of your skin." I run my finger over the tiny ridges of scars along my forearm. "Surface. As long as it stays on the surface, it can't touch who you are inside."

"On second thought, I would like to accompany you today."

A zap of surprise washes over me with his sudden change of heart. "Really?"

"Really. I'll drive."

~

E xpecting to see Lucian dress casual is like expecting a star to be less brilliant. No matter what he's wearing, he always looks like a million bucks.

As he takes my hand, leading me down a hallway I haven't yet ventured into, wearing a short-sleeve, black button-down and dark jeans, I have to remind myself not to stare at his ass the whole time. It's uncanny to me, the way the man can fill a pair of denim with the same ruthless sex appeal as when he's dressed in one of his sharp suits.

A delicious orange sandalwood scent trails after him, watering my mouth, as I follow behind.

The hallway ends at a door, which Lucian opens before flipping a switch on the wall beside him. Lights flicker on, illuminating what reminds me of an airplane hangar, as enormous as the room is, with high ceilings and massive shelves storing two wrapped boats. On the open floor of the place are rows of vehicles, maybe two dozen. Luxury, compact, sport. Various colors and sizes, makes and models.

"Oh, my God," is all I can muster, as I scan the room.

"I like cars." He takes the lead once again, toward a sleek, black contraption that looks like something Batman would drive. Specks of light from above dot the polished black exterior like stars across the night sky--fitting for Lucian.

"Do you, um … have a costume hidden somewhere? Like, only pull it out when the signal goes up? What even is this car?"

"A Bugatti Chiron. One of the fastest, most powerful cars in the world." He opens my door on the black leather duet of seats and shiny chrome interior.

The only two-seater I've ever been in belonged to Griff, one of the local fishermen who gave me a ride home from the library, when Aunt Midge got tied up at The Shoal one night. He'd removed his entire backseat to fit all his gear, because he couldn't afford a truck.

I'm almost afraid to sit down in this thing, but I slide into the seat. Like sitting in a cockpit, the leather practically hugs me, and it smells as if it's never been driven in its life.

Lucian falls into the seat beside me, his eyes immediately darting to my exposed thighs. The only reason I opted for the airy dress, one of a few that Amy left at the Manor, is that it's supposed to get up to eighty-seven degrees today, and I can't bring myself to risk sweaty thighs and pit-stains on my first official outing with the guy. The dress is cool and lightweight, and I'm only going to The Shoal. It's not like any of the regulars there will even notice, and if they do, Aunt Midge will surely bop them upside the head.

His gaze lingers for a moment, the two of us sitting in silence, until he shakes his head. "Sticking toothpicks in my eyeballs would be less tortuous than trying to keep my hands off you in that dress," he says, firing up the vehicle, the sound of its powerful engine echoing in the garage.

I turn away to hide my smile, pressing my knees together at the warmth he's stoked between my thighs.

A wall ahead lifts, revealing an inclined road, and when he drives forward, my head hits the seat behind me, and I remember that I forgot to strap my seatbelt. Once I'm clicked in, I settle into the cool leather seat, as he drives toward the gate.

"You look and smell incredible," he says, not looking at me at all, as if refusing to do so.

"As do you." Outside my window the massive stretch of lawn, with its broken fountains and unkempt hedges, takes me back to my first day here, when everything felt dead and abandoned. I've since found it doesn't matter that it's midday, the manor always carries a dark and gloomy aura. And yet, it's strange, how in the thick of all this decay, I've never felt more alive.

"There's a gift for you in the glovebox."

Frowning, I glance toward it and back. "For me? Why?"

He jerks his head that way. "Have a look."

I open the compartment to the small, but telling, blue box tucked inside. I may have grown up in a small fishing community, but even I know a Tiffany box when I see one. "Lucian ... what did you ..."

"Open it."

I flip the box open to a gorgeous bracelet inside. Two thin chains, that I have to believe are white gold, link to either side of a large, princess-cut diamond. It's breathtaking, and probably cost more than everything I own combined. "Oh, my God."

"Put it on."

Sucking my bottom lip, I shake my head. "I'm afraid."

"It's yours."

"What if I break it?"

"Then, I'll whoop your ass until you bleed."

I snap my gaze toward him, frowning, until his stoic face breaks into a chuckle.

"I'm certain the company that *makes* these things are quite capable of *fixing* them when they break."

"Yes, but you said we were strictly sex. Buying me gifts doesn't sound like filler. It screams plot to me."

"I'm not following. What's filler?"

"It's like ... in romance novels, when the main couple do things together that doesn't really move the plot forward. Just kind of fattens the book."

"It's a bracelet, Isa, not a ring. Please. Put it on."

Fingers trembling, I one-handedly latch the bracelet onto my wrist. A month ago, it would've looked out of place on me, ridiculous even, but paired with my dress, it almost seems fitting, aside from the tattoo just below it. The most beautiful and delicate thing I've ever been given. "You didn't have to do this."

"You like it, then?"

I spin the diamond to the top of my wrist, wishing he hadn't done this. It's too much. Too much for what we agreed on, and it'll only be harder when it all comes to an end. In spite of those thoughts, I nod. "I never want to take it off."

"Good. Then, don't." There's a serious edge to his voice, as if removing it would be an insult to him.

It takes twenty minutes to reach downtown, and as we approach the main street, I set my hand on his arm, feeling his muscle twitch beneath my palm. "Wait. Can we make a quick stop?"

"Sure."

I direct him toward a strip of shops, where he parks the car in one of the many open spots there. Through the window, I stare up at the sign that reads *Vellichor*.

"How did I know we'd end up at a bookstore at some point?" His comment brings a smile to my face.

We climb out of the vehicle, and as we reach the door, I turn to look back at him, only just now realizing, in the brightness of day, how much he sticks out from the surroundings. Like a dark storm cloud on a sunny day. Sinister, and as foreboding as his reputation.

A man you don't cross, with his equally menacing black car.

Lucian couldn't fit in this town if he tried. He'd be the rogue puzzle piece that doesn't want to line up in its empty spot. A thought that has me smiling when he follows after me inside.

The scent of old books invades my senses when I push through the door and set the bell chiming. Like wrapping myself in a cozy blanket with a hot cup of coffee.

"Rhea, you here?" I call out to the woman I visited about three times a week during high school.

Unable to afford the number of books that I plowed through, I often lived at the library, or here. Probably about half my adolescence was spent here. Rhea let me read whatever books I wanted, in exchange for helping her straighten up around the shop. Not that much ever needed to be done. Most of her business came from out of state, when collectors would call looking for a rare and hard to find book.

"That you, Izzy?" Graying hair pulled back in a ponytail gives some insight into her age, as she slides on her spectacles. In spite of her age, though, the woman is sharp with her wit.

"Yeah, I brought a friend today."

"I see that. A mighty fine-looking friend." When she says this, she doesn't mean it sarcastically. One of the reasons I'm glad I brought Lucian here first. Rhea is predictable, real, and as kind as it gets. I'd like to think it's her worldly understanding that comes from a lifetime of reading, but some people are just good people with good hearts. "Where you been, kiddo?"

"Around. How's business?"

"Ah, you know. Online, I'm killing it. Here? Not so much. Brick and mortar ain't what it used to be. Folks have entire libraries on their devices nowadays." Rolling her eyes, she shakes her head, the large, gold hoop earrings swinging at either side of her face. "Don't get me wrong, I got one of those Kindly things." She means Kindle, and the error has me biting back a laugh. "Call me old-fashioned, but I just prefer flipping pages."

"Same." It's sad to me that so few are interested in physical books these days. My favorite thing in the world used to be the sound of the book's spine cracking open on a new adventure inside. "Anything new?"

She offers a wink and smiles. "Got a few shipments in toward the back you might like."

Taking Lucian's hand in mine, I don't lead him to the back right away. Instead, I peruse the shelves that hold books I've read over and over. From classics to contemporary. At the end of the row, I stop before a glass-encased leather-bound, and stare down longingly at the book.

"Bram Stokers Limited Edition *Dracula*. I've drooled over this thing for years. Thought for sure someone would've swiped this one up. It's practically a steal at two-hundred dollars."

"Then, why haven't you bought it?"

I don't tell him that most of the people on this island don't have two-hundred to drop on a book. That, and I don't want him to buy yet another gift, not after the bracelet. That wasn't the purpose of bringing him here. I just couldn't bring myself to pass this place without stopping in to see an old friend.

"Nowhere to store it at Aunt Midge's. It'd be ruined if I brought it home. It's better here. Rhea takes good care of it. Was my favorite book growing up, though. Have you ever read it?"

"Does it have pictures?"

"Never mind. I forget you think literature is ridiculous."

"There are darknesses in life and there are lights. You are one of the lights." A quote from the book. He turns his eyes to mine, and I swear there's a flickering flame in them. *"The light of all lights."* He leans into me. "For the record, I read quite a bit."

"Impressive."

We spend the next few minutes rummaging through books, before Lucian grabs an old copy of *Kidnapped* by Robert Louis Stevenson, along with a few others he decides Laura might like to read, mysteries mostly.

At the cash register, Rhea greets him with her signature bright-eyed smile that had the power to light up my days, back when I wandered in sad, or upset. "My first flesh and blood customer in ages! I thank you for your patronage, sir."

"Of course." As he slips his wallet from his back pocket, he nods toward me. "Why don't you head out to the car, get it cooled down, while I finish checking out." The object he hands me doesn't look like a key, at all, but a folded up pocket knife, or something, with a leather strip down the center that reads *Chiron*. On the back is a lock and unlock button, but no key. "There's a button on the dash to start it up. Just don't go taking off anywhere."

"No promises," I say, backing toward the door. "Take care, Rhea."

Brow quirked, she smiles. "You too, Miss Izzy."

Once outside of the bookshop, I shield my eyes against the blinding sunlight that beats down on my shoulders as I make my way to the car. Hot leather stings my bare skin when I fall into the seat, and my hips thrust me away from it as I awkwardly press the start button for the engine. Tugging my dress down pulls at its neckline, exposing more cleavage, but I refuse to burn my legs again. I roll down the window as the still-warm air blasts from the vents.

Once again, I find myself staring down at the bracelet on my arm, and I smile.

"Oh, look, the asylum must've had a field trip for psychopaths." The sound of the familiar female voice outside the window skates down my spine, and I can't bring myself to look up and face Brady's mother.

Weeks after the incident at the party, she went out of her way to smear mine and Kelsey's name through the mud, making us out to be two reckless delinquents, hooked on all variety of drugs. Because her husband is chair and commissioner of the entire island, something she likes to make clear to everyone, she's taken it upon herself to bully anyone she deems a threat.

For whatever reason, it seems I'm still her target.

On reflex, I open my mouth to say something, but cap it. I'm not getting in trouble for this woman. I refuse.

I finally lift my gaze just enough to see her and another woman sitting around a small table, just outside the ice cream shop next door to Rhea's.

The woman across from her, who I'm guessing is her best friend Joan, turns her head to look back at me, pausing to lick the double-scoop dripping down her thumb. "Is that who I think it is?"

Casting my gaze from theirs, I contemplate whether, or not, to roll the window up. What the hell is taking Lucian so long?

"Who else would dress like a whore to visit a bookshop?" The derision in her voice sounds more like jealousy, perhaps brought on by the fancy car, than that of a mother looking out for her son.

I'm anxious to pull the front of the dress up to hide the cleavage she can likely spot from where she's sitting, and I want more than anything to look up and say something. *Say something*, my head urges, but neither my limbs, nor brain, will act at my command, the silent warning of the last time I spoke up paralyzing my vocal chords.

"Her aunt works at the bar, right? Chatty one who reeks like smoke all the time?" Joan's voice is louder than before, as if she wants me to hear her.

"Yeah. That's her. Brutish one everyone calls *Butch*."

The car door swings open, and I snap my focus toward Lucian, who slides the package down alongside my legs onto the floor.

Their chasing cackles don't seem to have snagged his attention yet. Meanwhile, my fingers twitch with the prodding of my head to climb out of this car and stand up to this wretched bitch who made my life hell for all those months. But I can't. Partly because of the dress I'm wearing that, in truth, makes me feel out of my element. A fake and a phony. The other part is because my mouth has gotten me in trouble before.

Ignore them, I can hear Aunt Midge telling me, as she always did. Which is weird, because she never ignored them herself. In fact, she got into a yelling match with Brady's mom a few months back, when the woman accused me of being in a satanic cult. Probably based on how I was dressed at the time.

But for whatever reason, Aunt Midge insisted that I ignore them.

I suddenly wish we were back at Blackthorne, in the dark

gloom where I felt shielded from all of this. It's no wonder Lucian's family never really venture out much. Why would they subject themselves to an entire island of ignorance and judgment?

"How much you think he's paying her?" Joan snorts, and both women giggle at her remark. "Enough to fund another tattoo?"

Finger on the ignition button, he stills, his expression hardening, and he sits forward in his seat like he's starting to catch on. He stares through the windshield. I wait for him to start the damn car and get out of here before I do something stupid, but instead, he opens the driver door.

I grab him by the arm and, gaze lowered, shake my head. "Trust me, retaliation doesn't work with them. It only adds fuel." It's true. The last time I volleyed insults back at her, I found myself sitting across from a police officer over some harassment accusation she made up. "Let's just go."

"They're talking about you?" he asks, his hand still on the door handle.

"Maybe. Maybe not, though."

"Only whores tattoo themselves! Whore!" Brady's mother calls out to us, the target of her insult unmistakable as she stares right at me.

Lip caught between my teeth, I bite back the urge to scream, and screw my eyes shut to the visual of her choking on that goddamn ice cream cone.

"Fuel meet fire." Lucian climbs out, and every muscle in my body pulls tight as I watch him round the vehicle toward the women.

With the window still rolled down, I can hear snippets of their whispers, as Lucian approaches.

"Sorry to interrupt your ice cream, but my lady friend over there seems to think your comments are directed at her." There's an eerie calm to Lucian's voice as he stands towering over them, while both women squint to look up at him. "If that's the case, I'll ask that you apologize to her for being so rude."

"Do you even know who you're talking to, asshole?" Joan asks, lifting her hand to shield her eyes from the glaring sun that must be directly in her face, maybe why she doesn't seem to recognize him and those infamous scars.

"Any chance you might know who *you're* talking to?"

Hand covering my mouth, I swallow back a laugh, watching these clueless women rile the Devil of Bonesalt.

Brady's mom scoffs and takes another lick of her ice cream. "Tell me, so I can report your ass for harassment."

"Lucian Blackthorne." He bends forward, holding out a hand toward her. "Pleased to make your acquaintance."

Both women gasp in unison.

Brady's mom slowly lowers the ice cream from her mouth, the top scoop plopping onto her lap with her trembling. She glances toward Joan, who hasn't moved in nearly a minute now, as if he's already turned her to stone. Neither woman returns his shake.

"Perhaps the gossip hasn't truly done me justice," he says, and slips his hand back into his pocket. "Feel free to report my *ass*, if you'd like. I'll give my lawyer a heads-up. And in the meantime, I strongly suggest you watch your words when you speak, or refer, to Isadora Quinn."

Not a word is spoken between the two women, and I'm beginning to wonder if he cast some kind of dark spell over them, because I've never seen Brady's mom so silent after a confrontation.

As Lucian makes his way back toward the car, I exhale a shaky breath, trying to figure out whether to laugh, or cry, at the fact that he just verbally Hulk-smashed the bane of my existence.

The moment he falls into the seat beside me, a burst of laughter escapes me, and I double over, my muscles still trembling with the adrenaline rush. Catching a glimpse of Brady's mom cleaning up the mess from her lap, I laugh harder. "You are so on her shit-list now."

"Whoever did her hair this morning should be, as well," he says, throwing the car in reverse. "Where to next? The Shoal?"

"Yes. What took you so long in there? Thought I was going to have to send in a rescue squad."

He shrugs, looking calm and collected, the way he leans back in his seat with one hand on the wheel. "Caught up in conversation. Who were those women back there?"

"Tempest Cove clowns."

"I'm serious."

Huffing, I stare out the window at the sidewalks bustling with tourists. Strangers who know nothing about me. Have no idea about my reputation. "Brady's mom and her friend, Joan."

"Why do they have a problem with you?"

Pangs of remorse still needle my gut for not having stood up for myself. If not for my desperation to get out of this town, I'd have chanced another harassment claim, just to shut her up myself. "This whole town has a problem with me."

"I can see why." At his remark, I snap my attention back to him, scowling and mouth gaping for something to say. "Young. Beautiful. Intelligent. I'd be pissed, too, if I looked as unoriginal as the two of them."

Chuckling, I shake my head. "I never know whether to slap you, or kiss you, Lucian. It's the most confusing feeling in the world."

Eyes on the road, he sets his hand on my thigh in a possessive way. "Nobody fucks with you when you're with me. Ever."

The Devil of Bonesalt. The Mad Son. The monster of Tempest Cove.

Not even.

About a mile and a half up the street, he pulls into the parking lot of The Shoal, where I notice Aunt Midge's old junker parked off in one of the designated employee spots toward the back of the lot. A nervous thrum of anxiety pulses beneath my skin as we exit the car. Rhea was relatively harmless. It's hard to say with Aunt Midge. She knows Lucian played a part in helping with the drug dealer, but whether that's enough to change her perception of him is up in the air.

The tired boards of the deck creak below our feet, as we walk the pier to the front entrance, the salty sea air and sound of seagulls taking me back to life before Blackthorne Manor. After passing through the invisible curtain of grease at the entrance, we step inside, the scent of seafood smacking me in the face. Irish pub music drones on in the background, where the regulars--Mac, Joe, Doherty and Paul sit in their usual seats around the bar. Conversation withers like a frosted vine, the moment they turn their heads toward us. Behind the bar, Aunt Midge eyes me up and down, and frowning, she tosses a towel onto the counter behind her before shuffling toward us. "What's this?"

"We're here for lunch, like I promised."

"We?" She tips her head, and the moment she crosses her arms, looking past me toward Lucian behind me, I know she doesn't approve. "Can I talk to you for a sec?"

"Sure."

Warm palms grip my shoulders, and perhaps Aunt Midge notices the way my skin reacts to Lucian's more intimate touch because her frown deepens. "I'll grab a table." He strides toward one of the many open spots at the back of the bar, and I watch the other men eyeing him as he passes.

Once out of earshot, Aunt Midge tips her head to get my attention. "What do you think you're doing?" Her gaze dips to my dress and back. "Wearing dresses now?"

"I told you. We're having lunch. The dress was the only thing I had to wear in ninety-degree heat. Here." I slip the check Rand issued me this morning for another week of work. "To help with the mortgage. Already signed it."

"I'll deposit it for you, but I'm not taking the money." She folds the check, slipping it into her apron.

"C'mon, Aunt Midge. Don't be difficult."

"That's another discussion. Right now, I want to know why you brought *him* here."

"Why not?"

"Sounds too much like a date." Again, her eyes trail down to my dress and back. "Looks like a date, too."

"What if it is? I'm nineteen. An adult."

"And he's nearly twice your age, child!" She's the master at whisper-yelling, but I don't think she went unheard this time, as I look around the room to see all the men, Lucian included, staring back at us. "Look, I know he helped out with that Franco. But you don't need to be getting involved with him, okay? It's bad news."

"You guys get a load of that? The Devil of Bonesalt himself." Mac, one of the older fishermen sits at the end of the bar, hiking his thumb toward Lucian. "Since when do we allow monsters in our fine establishments?"

Two of the men chuckle, and only one of them shakes his head, but smiles as he's doing it.

"Since the day you walked in, smelling like you crawled out of a watery grave," Aunt Midge answers over her shoulder, as I lurch toward him. Always quick with the quips, which I imagine comes from working with these assholes all day.

Lucian waits in the corner, quiet, not bothering to respond to the man, at all.

"You don't know anything about him." My response is directed toward Mac, but my eyes are on Aunt Midge.

"Neither do you."

"What do you suppose a man has to tell himself when he's staring at that every day in the mirror?" Mac chimes in again, no doubt drunk.

"The same--"

Aunt Midge cuts me off, setting a hand on my shoulder, and shakes her head. "Enough, Mac. You can keep those comments to yaself."

Still, Lucian doesn't say a word, and I can't tell if the idiot's ignorant comments are starting to get to him, or not.

"I should've known better than to bring him *here*." Teeth gritting, I shoot a glare toward Mac that he doesn't bother to notice, too caught up in staring back at Lucian.

"It's not my fault he's garnered the reputation." Aunt Midge glances back toward the bar. "These guys are assholes. What'd you think? They were going to welcome him with open arms?"

"Okay, well, if I can't have my opinions, maybe a suggestion." Mac is one slap away from my wrath. "I propose the ugliest bastard in the room buy a round of drinks for everyone."

If fire could shoot from my eyeballs, the old man would be engulfed in flames right now.

"I could certainly afford that tonight," Lucian finally says, sitting forward in his chair. "But I suppose that'd leave you broke every other night."

There's a moment of deafening quiet, before the other men at the bar belt out laughter, and Aunt Midge shakes her head again, chuckling as she heads back toward the bar. "All right, now that deserves a round."

Mac shakes his head, burying the next smartass retort in his beer glass.

Still fuming, though, I make my way toward the table, knocking the old man in the shoulder along the way, and take my seat across from Lucian. "Here, I thought I had to protect you."

"You underestimate my bastardly charm."

"Indeed."

Aunt Midge sets a mug of beer in front of Lucian. "What can I get the two of you to eat?" She nudges my shoulder. "Already know what you want."

"I'll have whatever she's having."

"Two bowls of cat piss. Comin' up."

Frowning, Lucian leans back in his chair. "What?"

"I think she's trying? It's hard to tell with her sometimes." I chuckle, staring back at him.

Tipping back a sip of beer, Lucian grimaces when his throat bobs with a swallow, and he sets the glass down. "Speaking of cat piss."

"Yeah, everyone here calls it Nasty Light. I probably should've warned you."

It takes twenty minutes for our meal to arrive: two Cokes with two sloppy lobster rolls, and when I bite down into mine, I realize how long it's been since I've had the non-gourmet variety of food. Closing my eyes, I savor the taste of familiarity, the flavors of Aunt Midge's cooking, and let out a quiet, "Mmmm." When I open them, Lucian is watching me, his jaw slowing working the food as he chews.

"You eat like you're making love to it."

"I missed Aunt Midge's cooking. And I like food."

"I like a number of things that I don't indulge in as passion-ately as you with that lobster roll."

"That's a shame. You should always approach the things you enjoy with passion."

Setting the lobster roll down, imperfectly perfect lips smile again, and I know he has another punchy comeback ready to go. Instead, he studies me in silence for a moment. "I have to admit, you're not what I expected."

"What were you expecting?"

"Not you."

"Good? Bad?"

"Good, unfortunately."

"Why is that unfortunate?"

"Because this is supposed to be filler, but you're making me curious about the plot."

Lowering my gaze, I bite back the smile itching to break free. "What are you curious about?"

"How a girl like you isn't fighting off every swinging dick in this town."

I lean in, keeping my voice low so Aunt Midge, or anyone else, can't hear me. "Maybe I like yours best of all, Mr. Blackthorne."

His eye twitches with a smirk. "Careful. That's how innocent girls get dragged off into the woods by the devil. Isn't that how the story around here goes?"

Snorting a laugh, I nod. "Something like that. And is that a threat, or a promise?" Gaze locked on his, I lean forward and capture the straw with my lips, taking a sip of my Coke.

"Both."

"Well, then, I better lock my door tonight," I say, just above a whisper.

"I insist that you don't." Beneath the table, his knee brushes mine, and the way he stares down at me, licking his lips, before he bites into his sandwich, sends a ripple of excitement down my spine.

We finish our lobster rolls, and as I suck down the last of my soda, Lucian stands up from the table, dropping two hundred-dollar bills for a twenty dollar meal.

Aunt Midge scurries over, frowning down at the cash atop the bill. "I'll see what I have for change in the till."

He waves his hand in dismissal, sliding his hand in mine as I push up from my chair. "A round of drinks. Courtesy of the ugliest bastard in the bar."

Mac makes a growling noise in his throat, lifting his beer in the air.

"Next time keep your mouth shut," Aunt Midge says over her shoulder, stuffing her hands into the pockets of her apron. "Was nice meeting ya, Mr. Blackthorne."

"You, as well."

"And, you." Her eyes dip toward mine and Lucian's clasped hands, and when they fall on me again, they're winged up with worry. "Behave, all right?"

I sneak a glance toward Lucian and smile as I nod. "Always."

Once again, we're back in Lucian's car, and as he fires up the engine, his eyes cruise over me and down to my legs. "Any other errands this afternoon?" he asks, sliding his sunglasses over his eyes.

"Nope."

"Good. One more second in this town, and I might burst into flames."

"I always thought the devil was one to *cast* flames, not succumb to them." I slide the seatbelt across my body, where it slips between my breasts, and I click it in place.

He seems to take notice, staring for a moment, before he throws the car in drive. "So did I. Until you decided to wear that dress."

CHAPTER 48

LUCIAN

The speedometer hovers around a-hundred-twenty on the ride back to the Manor. The trees that whip past the window are nothing but a black blur beneath the moon that sits high overhead.

Beside me, Isa curls her fingers into mine, squeezing and releasing, as the anxiety undoubtedly escalates with every mile the car swallows up like a reckless game of Pac-Man. Only the quiet hum of the motor can be heard beneath her nervous whimpers.

"Okay, this is ... really fast." If not for the belt strapping her in, she looks like she's ready to crawl out of her skin.

"You're nervous." The needle edges past one-thirty. One thirty-five.

"We ... we're ... almost going a-hundred-fifty miles-an-hour."

I slide her hand onto my lap over the rock-hard erection that's been pressing against my zipper for the last hour. The pressure through the fabric is enough to send a zap of ecstasy shooting up my spine, and on reflex, I hit the gas harder.

She slices her gaze toward me, eyes wide on my groin, where her hand grips my shaft. "Jesus. You're like stone right now."

Adrenaline courses through me, the speed and her delicate hands drawing me closer to the edge. But that's not the only reason.

Being with her today, seeing her in this element, how she's learned to survive with all the shit life has thrown at her, has only made her more irresistible to me. I want to steal her away from these vultures who'd pick at her bones until there's nothing left of her. The same ones who've picked at me. Ones who've ravaged and discarded her. I want to shield her from their petty scorn and judgment.

I've been careful to avoid repeating my mistakes, but Isa is the kind of girl to make me pile them up like a fucking stack of pancakes with syrup on top. She makes me reckless and possessive.

With a squeeze of her hand, the car accelerates. Faster and faster. I tighten my fist around hers, grinding my teeth to keep from combusting, but it's not enough. I need more.

I press the brake and jerk the wheel toward the shoulder of the road, squealing to a stop that sends her hands flying out to keep from bashing into the dashboard.

"What are you doing?"

"C'mon." I flick my fingers for her to climb onto my lap. That dress has been messing with my head all night, and I can't take it anymore. I want her. One taste.

There isn't much room in the car, but she slides over the console and wedges one knee beside me, the other propped up on the driver's door panel. Grabbing either side of her face, I pull her in for a kiss, rougher than I intend.

Doesn't matter how many times we do this, her lips always taste like candy. A sticky, strawberry lollipop that I could lick for hours and never tire of the flavor.

My phone buzzes against the console beside me, but I ignore it, instead focusing on the softness of her skin as I eat the soft moans that leak from her lips.

The phone buzzes again.

Isa breaks from the kiss and looks down at it. "It's Rand."

"Fuck Rand," I say, pulling her to my face again.

"What if it's your mother?" she asks against my mouth, and at the mere mention of the woman, everything inside of me deflates. With a groan, I swipe up the phone. "Yeah." The irritation in my voice is both unmistakable and intentional.

"Forgive me, Master, but I just received a call from Dr. Voigt. He's been trying to reach you in your office."

"I'm not in my office." As Isa slides back toward the console, I squeeze her thigh to keep her from moving off my lap.

"I realize that, Sir. Um, I didn't know you'd planned to be out this afternoon."

The aggravation is killing my libido by the second. "What is the nature of his call?"

"He asked that you make a trip up to the Institute this week. He apparently has some important matters to discuss with you."

Important matters. I can't think of a single thing he'd need to discuss that would warrant a trip to Vermont.

"Can you give me any hints?"

"I'm afraid he didn't divulge any to me."

Throwing my head back against the seat, I pinch the bridge of my nose to settle the urge to throttle something, as Isa climbs back over to her seat.

Like I have time for this shit.

Not going to Vermont means that Friedrich starts nosing around in my affairs again, though.

"Fine. I'll fly out first thing tomorrow. Get it over with early in the week."

"Very good. I'll let him know. Again, my apologies for interrupting you, Sir. He seemed quite adamant that you make this trip."

"I'm sure. Thanks." I click out of the call and toss the phone onto the console, my mood officially soured. "Should've ignored it."

"I'm sorry. I just thought--"

"It's not your fault." I lean to the side and seize her lips for another kiss, wanting nothing more than to pick up where we left off, but the frustration of having to play along with Friedrich to keep those bastards out of my hair is the equivalent of grinding my dick against a cheese grater.

Just not in the mood, all of a sudden.

Leaning back into my seat, I start up the engine and throw the car in drive.

The sooner I get home, the sooner I can take an ice cold shower.

CHAPTER 49

ISADORA

Mondays have always been the dreaded first day of the week, but today is significantly less dreadful, in spite of the noises that kept me up again last night. At first, I thought it was Lucian, sneaking into my room, but when I flicked on the light, there was nothing there.

There's something inside these walls, though. I can't say what it is, as I'm always half asleep when I wake from it, but I feel it watching me.

I've never believed in ghosts, or the many myths that plague this island, but I'm beginning to wonder if I should.

I take the elevator up to Laura's room, spinning the gorgeous bracelet over my wrist. No one has ever given me something so beautiful in my life, and I want to tuck it away so it doesn't get lost, or broken, but I made a promise to Lucian that I wouldn't take it off.

If Laura asks, I'll just have to work up an excuse, like I found it in a McDonald's bathroom, and when I tried to return it, the owner told me to keep it. I chuckle to myself at the ridiculous story that, even in her mental state, she wouldn't buy.

After Lucian and I returned from running errands yesterday, he decided he needed to get some work accomplished, and I haven't seen him since.

He claims this is nothing but sex between us, and I'm okay with that, since he made it clear from the start. Except, all weekend long, he referred to me as his.

You belong to me. You're mine. Mine.

I've been with guys only looking for sex, and not a single one told me I belonged to them after. In fact, they were quite content to keep their distance, and so was I, if I'm being honest. It's not that I set out to fulfill my mother's destiny for me through meaningless sex, it's just that boys tend to be nicer when they think they're getting laid.

I guess I just liked believing in their bullshit sometimes.

Lucian is an enigma to me, though. A big black question mark at the end of a long sentence. Could've been a heat of the moment thing with him. Guys sometimes say weird things during sex, but then I'm still left wondering why he bothered to run errands with me. Why spend the day with someone you've no intentions of pursuing?

A part of me wants to ask Giulia if he's ever claimed *she* belonged to him when they fucked. Maybe that's his kink: collecting girls like his mother collects dolls.

Another part tells me to leave it alone.

When I reach Laura's sitting room, Nell already has the older woman dressed for the day and in her wheelchair, ready to go. Odd, considering it's still about five minutes before Laura usually wakes on her own.

I cross the room toward them, where Nell huffs, seeming to struggle with pinning a broach to Laura's blouse. "Here. Let me." When she steps aside, I take the broach in hand and offer Laura a smile, as I slide the pin through the silky fabric. "What's going on?"

"Rand asked that we come down to the office. He wants to speak with us. All of us, apparently."

Rand? Surely, if it was something I've done wrong, Lucian would've given me a heads-up over the weekend.

"Did he say what it was about?" I study Nell's expression for any flicker of emotion, any hint of what to expect from this meeting.

Her face is as impassive as her voice. "No. Just that he wants us down there in five minutes." She unlocks Laura's wheelchair, while I shuffle ahead of them, back toward the elevator.

I press the down button, and when the doors open to show Lucian against the rear wall in a crisp black suit, glancing up from the phone in his hand, my breath hitches.

He quirks a brow, as I step inside and press the button to hold the door open for Nell and Laura.

"Lucian!" Laura's face lights up at her son, pride beaming in her eyes. "My, you look dashing today. Doesn't my son look absolutely dashing, ladies?"

"He does." Pursing my lips to hide a smile, I back myself alongside him to make room.

Nell doesn't say a word as she pushes Laura onto the elevator, her eyes directed away from Lucian, and she turns her back to us.

The elevator doors close, and I feel a warm hand snake beneath my shirt, across my back. I stiffen at his touch, and turn my head just enough to catch the smile tugging at his lips, while he keeps his gaze ahead.

"Lucian, will you be joining us for breakfast, darling?" Laura asks, leaning over the side of her chair, seemingly oblivious to Lucian fondling me behind her.

"I'm sorry, Mother, but I have a very important meeting this morning. Perhaps another time."

"Pity. I miss talking to you. Oh! And hearing you play piano. Amelia plays very well, don't you, dear?"

Eyes closing, Lucian shakes his head. "It's Isadora, Mother. Not Amelia. Amelia is dead, remember?" It's strange hearing him respond so frankly, when I've tiptoed around the subject.

"Oh." She slumps back into her wheelchair, raising a trembling finger to her lips, as if in contemplation. "How could I have forgotten that?" She shakes her head and leans over the chair once again. "Anyway," she says, waving her hand in the air. "You should come listen to her play sometime."

Another handsome smile greets me, when I slide my gaze toward his again. "I'll have to do that."

Nell's head kicks to the side, not enough to see the two of us, but clearly interested in the exchange, perhaps picking up on the slight amusement in his voice. The doors open up to the first floor, and she pushes Laura out of the elevator, and into the hallway.

As I follow after them, a grip of my wrist stops me in my tracks.

"I'd like to speak with Ms. Quinn for a moment. Go on ahead, and she'll catch up."

Still not bothering to look, Nell gives a nod, and Laura tips her chin in what I'd surmise as suspicion as the two head off in the direction of Rand's office.

Once out of sight, Lucian spins me around and, as the doors close, pushes me back against the elevator wall. His lips crush mine in a fervent kiss, while his hand travels the length of my thigh. "I should've snuck into your bed last night."

"I thought, for sure, I'd get to pull a knife on you again. What gives?"

"The very thought of that makes me regret sleeping alone."

"So, why did you stay away?"

"Because there's a saying ... *absence makes the dick grow harder*, or something."

Snorting a laugh, I shake my head. "Ah, I think you're

mistaken. I believe the phrase you're looking for is, *makes the heart grow fonder.*"

Taking my hand in his, he guides my palm to the massive bulge in his slacks. "I'm not mistaken, at all."

Swallowing hard, I run my hand over what must be one painful erection tenting his slacks. "Oh." Another moment of touching, and he releases my hand. "Well, I wish you would've, because I heard noises in my room."

"What kind of noises?"

It somehow feels silly saying it aloud to him, like I'm admitting I believe in ghosts. "Just shifting of the walls, I guess. It's nothing."

"This place can be haunting at times." His palm slides down my belly, only the tip of his finger breaching the waistband of my khakis. "However, if you feel something touching you while you sleep, just keep your eyes closed and roll with it."

The thought of that makes me chuckle. "I'll try."

"I have a meeting out of state this afternoon, and will return this evening. Expect me."

"Out of state?"

"Yes. Vermont. I trust you'll wear something appropriate."

"I don't have anything sexy, if that's what you mean."

"Ah, then, we'll have to rectify that." Warm lips press into mine again, his tongue dipping past my teeth. "In the meantime, wear something expendable."

"Expendable? As in, I don't care if something happens to it?"

"Exactly."

"Can I ask what for?"

"You can ask, but I'm not going to tell you." He bends forward and seizes my mouth in yet another kiss. "I'll see you tonight."

As he pulls away, I reach for his arm. "Hey, do you have any idea why Rand called us down?"

Glancing toward his reflection in the elevator wall, he straightens his tie and jacket. "Yes. I'm firing Nell." The playful tone from seconds ago dulls with indifference, as if her firing doesn't matter to him, one way, or the other.

"Wait. What?"

"I can't have someone in this house who constantly accuses me of murdering my wife and son. Call it a conflict of interest."

"But what I told you … I didn't want her to know."

"She won't know."

"Well, it's, like, *obvious.*"

Gaze shifting back to me, he plants his palm against the wall as he leans in. "And if her accusations were directed at you, what would you do?"

"Confront her."

"Which is the purpose of this meeting. The outcome depends on her response. Either way, it's out of my hands." He straightens again, rolling his shoulders back. "Rand does the hiring and firing for me."

"And if it were me?"

"What about you?"

I cast my attention from his impervious stare that suddenly has me feeling childish and insignificant. "Never mind. It was a stupid question."

"You're trying to navigate what this is. If I'd treat you like an employee, or the girl I'm fucking."

"Like I said, it was dumb."

"In my experience, the two have always been one and the same. But with you …" His jaw tics, eyes on my lips. "I'd find it very difficult to let you go. My confrontation with you would be on a much more personal level."

Another cryptic response that doesn't fit the *sex only* rules I've come to know with other guys. "Then, I trust you won't stand me up tonight."

"It would take an act of God to keep me away." Another small kiss, before he pushes the button to open the elevator door and exits toward the front entrance, while I make my way toward the office.

When I enter the room, Laura is parked in her wheelchair beside Nell, who sits with her hands fidgeting in her lap. Offering a stilted smile, Rand gestures toward the empty chair beside Nell, and my stomach flips over on itself as I plop down beside her. Now that I know the purpose of this meeting, all I want to do is disappear.

Clearing his throat, Rand entwines his fingers and stares over the top of his spectacles. "It's come to my attention that there has been some discussion regarding Master Blackthorne's involvement in the disappearance of his son."

The moment the words are out in the air, I can feel Nell's stare burning into the side of my face.

"As you were made aware, when you first took the position here, the master values his privacy above all else. Gossip, of any kind, is frowned upon." As he prattles on, my mind is spinning with questions, like *why the hell was I asked to sit through this?* and *why was Laura hustled out of bed so early this morning to sit through this as well?*

"If this is about me, I haven't said shit." Nell crosses her arms, sinking down into her chair.

I shoot her a glare. If she thinks she's going to pin this on me, she's wrong. Lucian knows the truth.

"And what about you, Miss Quinn?" Rand turns his gaze on me this time.

"What happened with his son was before my time here. From what I have come to know of Lu--um, Mister Blackthorne, I've no reason to believe he's harmed anyone."

"Of course you wouldn't," Nell bites back, the anger radiating off of her. "Not when your lips are practically sewn together."

Cheeks heating with embarrassment, I avoid looking at Rand, and Laura, in particular. "What I do is none of your business."

"If you don't want anyone in your business, perhaps you

should be a bit more discreet." If I didn't happen to know she's terrified of Lucian, I'd think the bite in Nell's tone screamed of jealousy.

"It's funny you should mention that, Miss Anders." Rand presses the button on a remote that's set out in front of him on the desk, and the wall behind him slides open for a flat-screen television. When he clicks another button on the remote, the screen lights up to show Laura's sitting room. At the sound of Laura's screaming in the background, the older woman perks up from where she's sat quietly in her wheelchair the whole time. In the scene onscreen, it seems she's having one of her nightmares, though it's out of the camera's view to know for sure. A figure staggers into the room, and when he turns around and falls on the couch, I recognize Lucian, with his tie undone, his shirt unbuttoned, holding a glass of liquor.

At first, I think it's the night I went to check on Laura that first week, but I notice Lucian's tie is burgundy in this clip, not black like before.

"In an effort to be thorough, I've done some digging around, and I found this." He fast-forwards the video, and from the corner of my eye, I catch Nell shifting in her seat.

In time lapse, another figure enters the room onscreen, and Rand plays the video at normal speed once again.

Lucian appears to be passed out, where he lies back on the couch, his hand covering his face. The second figure is Nell, who stands over him with her head tipped, as if curiously watching him. When she kneels down between his thighs, the hairs on the back of my neck stand up. I can't bring myself to look at her, as I sit paralyzed, watching her make a move on him in his sleep.

Nell shifts again and clears her throat. "We get it. I fucked up, okay?" The nervous edge in her voice is as uncanny as her behavior in the video. Like watching two completely different personalities.

"Ah, well, I think it's important to establish a motive in these cases," Rand says, his attention seemingly fixed on the screen.

As she unzips his pants and springs his cock free on camera, I feel compelled to look away. It's like watching something forbidden take place. Something I shouldn't be privy to, but I can't stop watching because I need to know how far she goes. The moment she takes Lucian in hand, he startles awake.

"What are you doing?" The slur in his voice confirms that he's drunk. "Stop."

"Shhhh," she says, swatting his hand away when he reaches for her arm. "Just relax."

"Get the fuck off of me!" He shoves her hard enough to send her tumbling backward onto her ass, and fumbles to zip up his pants. Pushing up from the couch, he stands over her, swaying a bit. "You ever touch me again, I'll make sure you never work another job on this island," he says, before striding off, out of the camera's view.

Rand pauses the video, and when he turns around, there's a smirk twisting his lips. "It seems rejection is a rather touchy thing for you, Ms. Anders."

"He came onto me first, before that video."

"No, I don't think that's true. Master Blackthorne has remained ever professional in his interactions with you. It is you who have behaved inappropriately."

"Is that what he told you?"

"He's not told me anything regarding this incident. I had to find it myself. And on the grounds that you have failed to uphold your end of the contract, I'm afraid we'll be letting you go."

"What? Letting me go? You can't … I need this job."

Suddenly, she's concerned about her job? I want to tell her she should've thought of that before she decided to smear the boss's name, but I guess some people are clueless.

"I'm sorry, but it is a conflict of interest to allow you to stay."

"What's that supposed to mean? Conflict of interest? How?"

"I understand you've been reporting back to a private investigator, who's been busy trying to build a case against the Blackthornes and Doctor Powell."

The look on Rand's face reminds me of those cop shows, when the detective finally calls bullshit and all hell breaks loose. Who knew that people still hired private investigators? I always thought that was a low-budget TV thing.

"You've certainly contributed to that with your lies and gossip," Rand continues.

"I've been documenting care, as I am directed to do. If he's gained unauthorized access to my progress notes, that has nothing to do with me."

Tipping his head, Rand narrows his eyes on her and opens the drawer beside him. He pulls out a photograph that's slightly grainy, like it's been blown up to a larger size, and pushes it in front of her. In it, she's sitting across from a man I don't recognize, smiling in a way I'd consider flirtatious even if I'd never met the woman. "You've spent quite a bit of time with Mr. Goodman, it seems."

Shoulders slouching, she frowns while staring down at the picture in silence.

"Get out of here, Miss Anders. And if I find you snooping around the manor again, I'll have you arrested on the spot for trespassing."

She doesn't bother to look at me as she pushes up from the chair. It's when she passes that she grabs my arm, and I startle at her touch, thinking she's going strike out at me. Instead she gives a squeeze, and her brows wing up to something that appears to be more sympathetic than angry. "Watch yourself, Isa. Don't trust anyone."

"Out. Now." Once she's left, he turns to me. "I apologize for making you sit through that, Miss Quinn, but I thought you should be aware, in the event you've shared any private conversations with her."

My mind rewinds to conversations I've had with her, where I could've easily said something personal. Something that would've had me, or Aunt Midge, under scrutiny. Namely, the issue with the drug dealer.

He huffs, the frown on his face deepening. "I wasn't aware of this until recently. Tell me, have you noticed any unusual behaviors in your time working alongside her?"

"Just … she asked me to cover once, so she could sort something out. I assumed it was with her son."

"I see. And what was the nature of you covering for her?"

A quick glance toward Laura shows her staring back at me. "Just keeping an eye on Mrs. Blackthorne for a few hours."

"We try to keep a nurse on hand at all times. On the weekends, when Nell leaves, Shauna takes over. Therefore, it's important that you communicate these things to me."

"My apologies. It won't happen again." I lower my gaze from his, fingers fidgeting. "I'm assuming Lucian told you what I told him."

"He did. And while I find her actions to be quite serious, we came to the conclusion that she would be let go immediately."

"It just doesn't seem like …"

"What?"

"She said she's been working so hard to get her son back." I don't bother to tell him that she struggled through rehab to get clean prior to becoming a nurse. "It seems strange that she'd let anything get in the way of that."

"Some people have a very self-destructive approach to their wellbeing."

"Well, I, for one, never trusted her." Laura sits with her hands folded in her lap and shakes her head. "The things she would say and do. Wretched girl."

"What kinds of things would she say?" Rand asks, turning his chair to face her.

"She said that Isa had stolen from me." Laura scoffs and

glances away, frowning, and I lower my gaze to keep from having to look at her.

I could tell her it's true right now, and clear Nell's name of at least one accusation, but when I lift my gaze to Rand, he's shaking his head, the expression on his face a warning.

So I don't bother. Nell is gone now. I suppose clearing her name is pointless.

CHAPTER 50

LUCIAN

The Institute is the one place on the east coast I wish I could set fire to and watch burn. Doing so would certainly spare the country of half its psychopaths. A chill settles across my nape as I walk the halls that, just a few years back, bore witness to my suffering and torment. Now, the place merely serves as somewhere for the Collective to meet, but I don't think I'll ever fully erase the harrowing images of my time spent here.

The idea was to prod me into an aggressive state, so they wouldn't have to explain away a false-negative result in my DNA. By rejecting my sadistic tendencies, I essentially discredit the entire organization, since my lineage represents the most well-studied of any member. There are so many samples of my DNA, sperm, and stem cells stocked here, they could probably begin generating my clones. Unless they already have, and that's the nature of this otherwise useless meeting.

I reach the door to Friedrich's office. After a couple knocks, it swings open, and the man himself stands there, wearing a smile that could house a small village.

"Lucian, wonderful to see you! Thank you for making the trip up." He ushers me inside the office, patting my shoulder as I pass. Prick wouldn't dare lay a hand on me the way he did when I was sixteen, with as much as I've filled out over the years. Not to mention the funding he'd risk losing, if he did.

My unpredictable nature likely puts him on edge, too.

Good.

Nowadays, it's only a careful placement of his hand on my shoulder. Cautious responses.

Gesturing toward one of the chairs in front of his desk, he makes his way to the other side and falls into his own.

"I'm assuming you have something important to discuss, as you've requested face-to-face, rather than a Skype meeting." I lean back in the chair, wishing I had a drink to numb me from the science bullshit he'll undoubtedly spew in the next ten minutes.

"You know I don't trust meetings held over the computer."

Of course I do. And I was swept over with a metal detector at the front entrance, to ensure that I didn't have a recording device on me, including my phone. Since it's not my first rodeo, I left that in the car with the driver I hired.

"The purpose of this is to let you know that I did look into Mr. Boyd's family history," he started. "And it does seem he has an incarcerated twin. But the interesting piece in all of this is *who* he murdered."

"And who might that be?"

"Their biological father. Who also had a criminal record for assault and the murder of their mother, when both boys were quite young."

"That sounds like one messed up family tree."

"Indeed. Which makes Patrick a very curious specimen. I'd love to pick his brain about what he remembers of his childhood."

I'm sure he would. Literally, with an ice pick. "I take it my vote no longer holds any weight."

Hands in the air, he smiles and shakes his head. "Now, I didn't say that. We don't have baseline studies on him, so much of the data will be inconclusive, anyway. It's more curiosity on my part. Was Amelia his only offspring?"

I shrug, already beyond my limits of boredom. "As far as I know."

"We'll verify that, of course. For now, I'm going to observe before making a decision about him."

"And this is what you requested an in-person meeting for?"

"Of course not." He rises up from his chair and shoves his hands into the pockets of his lab coat. "Come with me. I'd like to show you what your generous funding has provided."

With a quiet huff, I follow him out of the office and down the hallway, toward the elevators I took to get up here. Once inside, he pushes the button to the bottom floor of the institute. A place where all the magic of this shit-show goes down.

The research department.

The doors slide open to a too-bright hallway, where fluorescent lights leave me squinting.

He leads me down the white hallways, with white doors and white tiled floors, that smell of potent disinfectant. "Have you considered more extensive surgery on your scars?" he asks over his shoulder.

Prick. "No." I gave up on trying to remove all traces of my accident. If nothing else, it serves as a reminder that I am not, and never was, as invincible as I liked to think.

"Shame. I know a surgeon, if you change your mind."

"Thanks. I'll let you know when I give a shit." The irritation of having made this trip has seriously soured my mood.

The smile he flashes me is fake and oozing contempt. Our benevolence toward one another is separated by a thin layer of bullshit.

A loud throaty scream brings me slamming to a halt in front of a door whose small, square window shows a dimly-lit room on the other side. I catch sight of a figure crouched in the corner, shaking and scratching at the walls. A girl, given the long, disheveled hair that sticks up around her head and over her shoulders.

Curiosity pulls me closer, until I'm standing at the door, staring straight in. From what I can see of her profile, the girl's lips are moving, but all I can make out is quiet mumbling through the door. I knock, and she pauses her scratching of the walls, where long streaks of red, which must be blood, indicate she's rubbed her fingertips raw. When she finally turns to look at me, I frown back at the familiar face.

"Melody Lachlan." Friedrich moves into my periphery as he stands beside me. "Daughter of--"

"Daniel," I interrupt, studying the girl, as she resumes her scratching. "I know her."

A flash of memory dances through my head, of a warm summer day at her parents' estate. Her father owned a chain of luxury hotels, and had invited my family to a charity event at their home. I was only eleven at the time, which would've made her around seven. While our parents mingled, she took Jude and I out to the garden, where an elaborate cage housed a bright and colorful bird. The moment Melody stuck her finger inside, the bird flew to the fleshy perch, and I watched as Melody nuzzled and kissed her pet. She was the most gentle creature I'd ever met, always kind and vibrant. Smiling. Unlike most girls born into wealth, she was grounded and genuine.

"What happened to her?" I can't peel my eyes away from the dirt streaked up her arms and across her face, mixed with what I guess is blood.

"Her father asked that we run some tests on her, seeing as we didn't have much of a family history gathered on him."

From what I understand, the man was a self-made millionaire, who my father often jabbed as nouveau-riche.

"In doing so," Friedrich continues, "we stumbled upon a

trigger that led us to believe she may have been assaulted, or abused, at some point."

Melody slams her palms against her ears, screaming as she rocks in the corner. It's possible her father could've hurt her.

"What will you do with her?" I ask.

Friedrich sighs, and tips his head, still peering through the window. "Well, she's certainly not fit for release at this point. We'll continue to run tests."

My own experience tells me they've no intentions of curing her mental state. "What is the nature of these tests?"

Friedrich's cheek twitches as if he might smile. "In order to study a subject's propensity for violence, you must prod them a little." He points toward the corner opposite where Melody sits, and I follow the path of his finger to a pile of birds scattered on the floor, their heads detached from the bodies. At the sight of white droppings across the cement, I lift my gaze to the birds perched on the ceiling rafters above. About a half-dozen colorful birds, like the one in the cage all those years ago.

"She's begun biting their heads off, like a feral cat. It's remarkable to watch."

"What have you done to her?"

"Nothing that wasn't in her all along. Think of the repercussions, if she'd have snapped outside of these walls. She might've killed someone. We merely gave her violent tendencies an outlet." He clears his throat and turns to face me. "Come. I've more to show you."

We keep on down the corridor, and come to a stop in front of a door, through which he ushers me inside a room that opens up to a glass dome, around which a number of chairs are set out. In the chairs, sit a number of men with wires attached to helmet-looking contraptions on their heads. Below them, on the lower level, a man is laid out on a table, held down by restraints. Another in a lab coat wears thick gloves, as he lifts a branding stick with a red-hot slab of metal on its end. The man on the table whimpers and squirms in his binds, screaming against the bit caught between his teeth. At the first crackle of burning flesh, something flashes in my periphery, and I turn to see monitors that seem to be capturing waves. Brain waves, I'm guessing.

"We're trying to measure empathic neural response by using EEG recordings."

"Empathic? As in, trying to see if these people give a shit that you just branded a man with hot metal?"

"Precisely."

"Couldn't you have just played a video of someone getting branded? Why this?"

"Could you not practically taste that burning flesh on your tongue just now? I would venture to say your gamma waves were off the charts watching it."

Shoving my hands into the pockets of my slacks is all I can do to keep from throttling the motherfucker. This is what my father has been pumping money into all these years? This is what the bastard insisted I *keep* pumping money into, when he finally died? To make sure these assholes continue to produce bullshit studies.

And they're one of the bigger reasons I'd never attempt to pursue Isa. If they thought, for one second, that I was serious with her, she'd be stalked and monitored, her whole history dissected in secret. My mother didn't know a damn thing about Schadenfreude, but they knew everything about her, down to her menstrual cycle.

"In this case, the subject is a known child predator," Friedrich prattles on.

"We're offering payment to child predators now?"

"No. We offered payment to the prison that incarcerated him." He drifts across the room toward the monitors, studying the various waves onscreen. "There is no criminal more despised than the child predator. It's interesting that this particular segment of our species garners the justification of violent retribution. Even the most empathetic human being can muster the *apathy* to watch these individuals suffer." Still wearing a smile, he glances back at me. "We like to use them as a control group. And if it helps your conscience to know, they never leave the Institute." As he makes his way back toward me, I catch the other lab coat heating up the metal rod for round number two. "This is what your funding has provided. Each room focuses on a particular sadistic behavior. The next room over is sexual sadism. Would you like to see?"

"No. I wouldn't. I fail to see how this is considered science, at all."

"These individuals are homozygous for a particular genotype--"

I raise a hand and shake my head. "I don't need a dissertation. I'll be honest with you, Friedrich. I don't give two fucks what you hope to learn from all of this. I'll keep providing the funding, because my father willed it and, to your advantage, put someone other than me as an executor on it. But I want no part of this shit-show anymore."

Rand would be puking his guts onto the clean white floors right now, if I'd brought him with me.

Glad I didn't.

"Who, um … who do you think you're talking to Lucian?" It's uncanny the way this guy's smile never falters, even when it's clear I've slapped him in the face with insult. "Do you think you're talking to one of your father's employees? This *shit-show*, as you called it, can bury you without anyone noticing you're gone."

"Then, why haven't you yet?" With a smirk, I tip my head. "Oh. That's right. Because the funding only lasts so long as there is an heir. Meaning, it dies when I die. You have some very powerful connections, no doubt, but face it, no one was as committed as my father." Slipping my hands in my pockets, I take another step toward him, invading his personal space. "Don't ever threaten me again."

Clearing his throat, he steps back. "Very well. Quarterly meetings. That's all I ask. And the occasional medical update. You don't have to participate in the experimental studies."

"I'll think about it." I pat him on the shoulder, catching his flinch, and exit the room.

There was a time this place weaved nightmares like a spider's web, always present on the edge of my brain, waiting to wrap me up in its terrifying fibers.

Now, it can't touch me.

When I finally reach my car, I find two texts from Rand on my phone. At first, I think he's going to respectfully rail into me for what he'd surely consider another disastrous meeting, but his second text instructs me to check my email. When I open it, I find the remaining report that I requested of him last week. The more extensive research into Isa's past.

One of the documents is a police report describing the attack at the party, mostly true to what she narrated, but there's something new.

Something I had my suspicions about.

Something she's managed to keep hidden away.

I can't help the smile tugging at my lips as I flip through the other attached documents: therapists notes from her weekly sessions.

My raven beauty is far more dangerous than I imagined.

Darkness settles over the manor as I make my way up the staircase, the anticipation burning through me, even after a three hour flight. The box tucked beneath my arm is a gift, and one I spent far too much time choosing, just before I left Vermont.

The door to Isa's room is closed, and when I click it open, the lights are off inside. Cracking it open just enough to slip through, I find her sleeping form stretched out on the bed, the sight of her stirring a sinister craving for soft moans, nails, and teeth. Coming to a stand alongside her bed, I set the box aside and lean down to kiss along the smooth curve of her neck.

A twitch of movement, and she startles awake, flipping onto her back. Silvery bands of moonlight shimmer across her face, drawing my attention to full pouty lips I want to bite.

I'm convinced she's my punishment from God. My curse.

A forbidden touch.

A stolen kiss.

My temptation in the flesh.

As I lean in to kiss her, soft, warm lips greet mine, pulling me into fantasies of keeping her all to myself. My own little doll, just like the clusterfuck collection my mother keeps. Everything inside of me begs to resist, knows too well not to get swept up in the illusion of this, but the enticement is too strong. She's fast become a weakness, a preoccupation I can't seem to shake, and a dangerous gamble for a man with as many enemies as my father has amassed in the Blackthorne name over the years.

I push off her, grabbing the box I left at the foot of the bed, and her eyes widen at the sight of it.

"Another gift? Lucian ..."

"Open it."

With a small bit of hesitation, she tears at the thick, red ribbon and lifts the lid of the box to reveal sheer, white lingerie within. I watch her surprise dissolve into a demure sort of smile, and she lifts the skimpy lace panties and matching bralette.

"You want me to put this on now?"

"No. Not yet. I want you to come with me." I reach down for her, and help her to her feet, drinking in the sight of her in nothing more than a thin white T-shirt and a pair of shorts.

"You said expendable. Should I throw on some pants?"

"That won't be necessary."

"Shoes?"

"Shoes, if you want. It's a walk across the yard to the water."

"Water?" Glancing back toward the few sandals and the pair of mucks lined against the wall, she shakes her head. "I'll be fine."

Taking her hand in mine, I lead her out of the room, down the hallway. A heavy stillness hangs on the air, as everyone seems to be asleep.

Except for Sampson, of course. He greets the two of us in the foyer, his tail wagging, as Isa pauses to pet him.

"He's taken a liking to you, I see."

Kneeling down to the floor, she lifts her chin, allowing him to lick her jawline. "And I've decided he's not the mean and scary monster I first met."

"Funny what happens when you take the time to get to know someone. I've decided the same thing about you."

With that signature chuckle of hers, she rises to her feet. "Where are you taking me?"

"I figured, since you so graciously showed me your favorite place yesterday, I'll show you mine." Giving a light tug of her arm, I lead her out the front entrance and down the familiar path toward the knoll. The moon is full and high in the sky, illuminating the well-worn path across the yard. I twist to see Isa looking around, her expression guarded, as if she's waiting for something to swoop down at her. The manor is always somewhat eerie, but at night, it almost seems as if the shadows come alive.

Once at the threshold of trees, I halt and tap my shoulder. "C'mon. On my back."

"What?"

"The branches will tear up your feet. Hop on."

Taking hold of my shoulders, she does, and I wrap smooth, toned legs around my body as I grip the bottoms of her thighs and trudge through the brush.

The small copse of trees opens up to the path downward,

along the perimeter of the cave. A cool breeze mingles with the warm summer air, creating a slight chill. The incessant crash of the waves takes me back to years ago, when I sat in this cave for hours at a time. I set her down onto the soft sand and remove my coat to wrap around her, which she accepts appreciatively.

The tide has begun to rise, but not yet to the point of filling the cave. I toss away my shoes and dress socks, and roll up my slacks.

"We're going into the water?" she asks.

Before she has a chance to protest, I hoist her up over my shoulder, smiling as she giggles, while I slosh through the water to the cave's entrance. A few feet inside, the sand is still dry, and I set her down in front of a boulder. Kneeling before her, I reach into the pocket of her borrowed coat to retrieve a small flashlight that I flick on and hand off to her, as well as a pack of matches. In a slow turn, her gaze trails over the surroundings, and when it lands on me, her eyes seem to sparkle with wonder.

"I used to come here as a kid. Was the only place I could sneak away from my parents."

"Really? You live in a freakin' castle. With separate wings."

"You'd be surprised at the lack of privacy. Someone always watching." Two pieces of driftwood and dried seaweed scattered about the cave bed make for the perfect kindling, which I quickly gather. Situated far enough from the water, I dig a shallow pit in the sand and pile the desiccated tinder in the dip of it. With a strike of the match, I set the kindling aflame and the small flickers blaze with an orange glow that casts shadows on the walls.

Having fully scoped out the cave, her gaze falls on mine, and she flicks off the flashlight. "What were they watching you for?"

"When I was very young, my best friend drowned. Right here in this cave."

Brows dipping to a frown, she glances around again, as if I've hidden his remains somewhere inside. "So … how is this your favorite place?"

"The hallucinations started here. For hours, I'd sit and talk to him. Conversations I'd never have the opportunity to have with him again. It felt as if he never left. Which brought me some peace."

"So, they were watching for these hallucinations?"

"They were always watching." I think back to the many times I felt someone's eyes on me. The cleaning staff. The kitchen staff. All advised to pay attention. "Hallucinations, or not."

"That must've been hell when you got older."

"It was. Until I learned to stop hiding. Once everything was out in the open, they stopped watching." My thoughts take me back to the day my father insisted that we lie to the media about Roark's death. The way it felt, as if he threw me back into a sealed box again. "Unfortunately, you can't always be an open book. Some secrets aren't meant to be exposed."

"Like what?"

"You asked how Roark died. The media painted a story that he went missing from the castle. They made the assumption that he might've ended up here, and water washed him away." I stare off beyond her, the memories of that night playing on the fringes of my thoughts, and I will myself not to delve too deep into them. "Amelia was always very careful about her medications. I know this. But one night, she wasn't, for whatever reason. He found them." Frowning, I lower my gaze to my hands, where I rub my thumb over my palm, as I recall the weight of my son in my arms. The curve of his head in my palm. "It was an accident."

"I'm sorry, Lucian. I'm sorry I ever doubted you."

"You'd be a fool to ignore the rumors entirely. The lies never added up quite right, but they were there to protect Amelia." At the mention of her name, screams echo inside my head. "She just couldn't live with what happened, I guess. Anyway, I've never told anyone the truth about that night until now."

"I swear I won't speak a word of it."

"I know you won't. It's why I told you." I reach out to run my fingers down the edge of her cheek, and grip her chin, studying the soft gray of her eyes. "There's a certain freedom in confession. I feel somehow liberated with you."

Taking the hem of her T-shirt in hand, I pull her into me for a kiss, and rub my palm over her toned belly, goosebumps bobbling against my skin that aren't only from the cold. The band of her panties greets my fingers as I run my hand lower. "Lie down on the sand," I whisper in her ear, palming the cheeks of her ass.

Without hesitation, she lowers before me and lies back on the sand, pulling her knees together as my jacket slips from her shoulders. The waves have already begun to reach for her, and it won't be long before they find her.

I sink to my knees and pry hers apart, while she stares down her body at me.

Running my palms down her thighs, I dig my fingers into her flesh and squeeze, anxious to have them wrapped around my shoulders. At the first nudge of the rising waves, she looks up toward where the sea plays with her hair.

"Should we move back?" she asks, flicking her gaze between me and the waves.

Shaking my head, I unbutton my shirt, eyes locked on her as I peel it off my shoulders and toss it to the side. I hook the string of her panties and slide them down her thighs, over her knees, and chuck them somewhere behind me. "Put your hands on your knees."

Once her palms kiss her knees, I slide her ankles wide and she gasps, looking down at me.

"Don't move your hands, understand? You keep them there, no matter what. Do you understand me?"

She nods, curling her fingers over her knees, the digging of her nails and rapid contractions of her chest telling me she's nervous.

Dragging my gaze from hers, I stare down her thighs to where the pink shell of her pussy begs to be eaten.

The first, heavy wave rolls in, splashing up over her shoulders to wet the thin T-shirt that turns almost translucent over her delectable, braless tits beneath. Round globes peek through the sodden fabric, and I lean forward to suck the salt across her nipple, taking the hardened flesh between my teeth.

She squirms and writhes beneath me, her fingers running over the top of my head.

Breaking the rules.

I nip her flesh, inciting a squeal, and set her hand back atop her knee. "Hands where I placed them."

Taking the fabric of her shirt in a tight grip, I tear it down the center, jostling her pretty tits, before I let each half fall against her chest. Eyes wide, she lifts her head, staring down at her tattered shirt.

She looks like a mess I want to lick clean.

The sight of her exposed skin tempts my fingers, and I run them over her breasts, giving one a light slap before I take her now fully exposed nipple into my mouth again.

Another wave splashes over top of her, and her muscles jerk against my lips, while I work my way down her body, trailing kisses across her wet stomach, until I reach the apex of her thighs. Once my tongue reaches her sensitive skin, the sweet flavor hits the back of my throat, and my eyeballs damn near roll back in my head.

Like sucking the juices from an overripe peach.

Arms wrapped around her thighs, I draw her closer and lower to my stomach, while the sound of her soft moans echo in the cave.

Another wave, and she jerks in my grasp.

"Lucian." The breathless tone of her voice, laced with a small bit of panic, spirals down my spine. "The waves ..." A push to the top of my head fails to break my tonguing of her pussy, and I reach up to place her hand back on her knee. Again. "The water ... it's rising." Another moan bounces off the cave walls, as she seems to fight to stay focused.

"I'll stop when you come."

Panting, she squirms on the sand, thighs trembling in my palms. "I can't ... I'll drown before then."

"Then, I suggest you quit talking and relax."

One long suck of her clit, and her whimper dissolves into a moan, her back arching up off the sand. Another wave crashes around us, and her thighs flex, but I hold her down and flick my tongue along the silky walls of her narrow seam. Her fingers curl over a handful of my hair, only this time I don't bother to place her hand back on her knees, because she opens herself wider to me. "Good girl."

Another wave follows the first, this one splashing against my face, and when I lift my head from her slippery flesh, I notice the water level is at her ears. I dive in again, and she cries out, nails digging into my scalp.

More licking.

More sucking.

The waves come faster than before, the tide rising with every ticking second.

Her moans begin to heighten, and another wave crashes over top of us, the salt in my mouth while I eat her underwater. A cough sputters from her throat, and she sucks in a gasp, before another wave rolls over top of her.

I slide two fingers up into her velvety depths, while the wave retreats, and she arches again, her outcry cut short by yet another wave.

The water begins to linger, the tide rising higher and higher with each passing second. Pushing to my knees, I pump my finger in and out of her, watching as another wave comes over top of her.

She tries to sit up, but I slam my mouth against hers, kissing her as I ease her back into the sand.

"Come for me, Isa," I say against her lips, before another wave mutes out the world. This one doesn't retreat, and the burn of her nails digging into my skin, muscles stiff and trembling, is her body finally edging toward climax.

I can feel it culminating inside of her, as she squirms less and trembles more, as if saving her oxygen for the big finale.

She jolts up on a gasp and tips her head back, exhaling the most tortured moan I've ever heard. A cross between pleasure and agony while she seizes and twitches. Tiny contractions pulse around my fingers still lodged inside of her. Deep heaving breaths saw in and out of her, while the waves knock her body around. When her eyes find mine, there's something new swirling in their depths.

Something darker.

Sexier.

I want to taste it on her lips like an addict watching someone get high for the first time.

With a handful of her hair in my fist, I yank her head back and seize her mouth, eating the drunken euphoria of her climax.

She climbs onto my lap, wrapping her arms around my neck, as she kisses me with the ferocity of a wild animal. "What happened to me?"

"*La petite mort.*"

"What does that mean?" The satisfied purr of her voice only stokes my need for release, like hot coals on the verge of igniting.

"Death," I say, shoving a hand down into the pocket of my pants, from where I fish out a condom. I nudge her up off my lap just enough to undo my pants and spring my cock free. Tearing the condom from its packet, I slide it down my shaft and line my tip to her entrance. Back against the wet sand, I scoot the two of us away from the rising tide, closer to the warmth of the crack-ling fire, and she impales herself down my length. Palms to her hips, I lower her onto my eager dick, and the sound of her moan coils around my senses like a poisonous vapor. Won't take much after watching her climax, and holding her steady, I stare up at her flawless face, while hammering my hips into her tight little body.

This girl has corrupted every fiber of my being, and no one will ever be good enough after her. No one will ever compare to the flesh and blood fantasy before me. She's mine.

The breath of new life. The steady pulse in my veins. The long-awaited beat of a heart that's been dead too long.

My kindred flame.

Every muscle in my body is a wire ready to snap, as this girl works me to climax. I want to come so fucking bad, but I wait. I wait for her, because in the last two days, I've learned one thing about Isa Quinn: there is nothing more beautiful in the world than watching her shatter. A sight I could eat for breakfast every day.

The waves climb higher, splashing around us in white, salty spray.

Her moans escalate, penetrating down to my bones, and I let out a groan, my stomach tight with excitement, as her juices wet my cock on every withdrawal. She pants through her nose, the first flicker of climax breaking across her face.

Brows winged up, she digs her nails into my chest, clenching her jaw.

"Come on, baby." I guide her hips along the length of my cock, driving deep each time she comes down on me.

She cries out, back stiff, muscles trembling, and the sound of her long, tortured moan is music to my ears.

I draw my dick out of her, and she scrambles off of me, as I tear away the condom and stroke myself to finish. White ribbons of cum spring from my tip, captured by her mouth.

"Ah, fuck." I stare down my body, watching her lap every drop, as bullets of pleasure shoot through my muscles, bathing them in a warm, tingly aftermath. Panting hard to catch my breath, I feel her tongue dance over my stomach, lapping up the fallen drops of my release.

When she lifts her head, I want to frame her face that wears the shine of my cum glistening across her mouth.

Ravishing.

The day I learned to climax while holding my breath, I thought I'd touched heaven, while traipsing the line between life and death.

It turns out, heaven is a nineteen-year-old girl who sleeps with a pocket knife under her pillow.

And I'm the selfish bastard who intends to keep her all to myself.

CHAPTER 51

ISADORA

Another week seems to fly by, and somehow it's Friday again. Each day is spent stealing glances of Lucian, shy smiles, secret touches, and hiding away from the other staff to make out in the shadows. We're like children, sneaking around the manor, as if they don't already know what's going on.

Every night, Lucian comes to me and takes me for hours, in positions I've never imagined, before he carries me to the bathroom to clean me up. Most mornings, he's gone before I wake.

I've not yet seen his bed, which I suspect is his way of ensuring that I remember what this is between us, and I do. But I want more, and I hate that about all of this. I hate that his touch lingers for far longer than I care to admit, and that the sound of his voice consistently leaves my panties a soaked mess, as if I've somehow been primed and trained to respond to it that way. The dreams of him, in his absence, have grown more vivid, darker than before, and I've begun to fear them less. Just as the sounds and shadows in my room at night no longer startle me awake.

My cravings have also intensified.

This morning, during my shower, I let the water from the spigot run over my face, as I touched myself, aroused by the lack of breath. The memory of Lucian's riveted expression in the cave that night, sparkling with some kindred understanding, swirled inside my head while the evidence of my climax ran down my leg.

I haven't decided yet, whether I'll go home for the weekend, or spend it at the manor, as Lucian insisted. Aside from the brief visit to the bar, I haven't seen much of Aunt Midge. But maybe I need a couple days away from him. To distance myself from this growing obsession that's sure to destroy what we've established between us.

I don't know what's happened to me in the last week, but since that night in the cave, my preoccupations with the master of this manor have brought me to a heightened need that scares me a little. As if he's the only one who could possibly understand my sudden fascination with this newfound thrill.

Outside, a black object flutters by my window, breaking my thoughts. It hobbles and flits about the sill on the other side, but the black wings are unmistakable. A raven, or crow. When it finally settles, it tips its head, and I stare down at the bird with the missing eyeball. Perhaps the one I saw the first day, while riding with Aunt Midge. The strange bird caws and flaps its wings again, and in seconds, it takes flight, smacking into the glass.

My muscles flinch, and I step back, frowning. The bird hits the window again. And again. As if it's trying to come inside, not aware of the barrier there. Its squawks grow louder, and its determination to come through has me backing farther into the room, until the door on the opposite side hits my spine. The obnoxious cawing continues, and I slip out of my bedroom, deciding to head to Laura's room early today. A tremor hums beneath my skin as I glance back to my room, to be sure it didn't break through, before shuffling down the hallway to the first floor.

When I enter Laura's room, Dr. Powell is packing up his bag, stuffing a stethoscope inside. Laura smiles as she sits watching him. The new nurse, who I've not yet met, bustles about the bed, and pauses to toss the blue pad into the trash.

"Ah, look who's here, Laura. Your babysitter has arrived!"

"Companion. And she isn't *terrible*. I suppose." She seems to have her wits about her more today. Perhaps the doctor's presence has this effect? Or maybe the new nurse is a welcomed change.

"I've altered her dosing a bit, so she should be less ..." Dr. Powell circles his finger next to his ear, his words confirming my observations of her. "Cuckoo."

"Stop it." Laura slaps his arm and gives a lighthearted chuckle. "I'm not losing my mind just yet."

"You were for a bit, there." I tuck the blanket around her legs, and smooth down a flyaway hair.

"Well, I certainly haven't forgotten in that time what a nuisance *you* are."

"She's warming up to you nicely, I see." Brows lowered, the doctor jerks his head. "May I have a word with you? It'll only be a moment."

"A word? Alone? Is it about me?" Running her fingers over her necklace, Laura smiles up at Dr. Powell.

Bending slightly forward, he takes Laura's hand and leaves a kiss to her knuckles. "Of course not, darling. I'm sure it'll come as a surprise to know not every topic is about you. I'm off to my next appointment, so you stay out of trouble."

"You don't know me very well, then."

A sly grin crinkles his face, but once outside the room, it sobers to something more serious, as he closes the door behind him. "I, um ... thought, rather than have you find out through Laura, I should tell you that Nell was found dead very early this morning."

The air deflates inside my chest as I stare back at him, confusion and shock waging war inside my head. "Dead?"

"Yes. It seems she overdosed."

"Overdosed? That … that doesn't sound right."

"She's been skimming pills off Laura for quite some time. I never said anything because, well … I didn't exactly have proof. Just scripts running out faster than they should've. But as far as I know, it was heroin. The housekeeper at the motel found her."

I know heroin abusers. Nell certainly gave off the addict vibe, but there's no way she was actively abusing it all this time. This has to be a relapse.

I lift my gaze back to his. "Motel? What was she doing at a motel?"

"One of those pay-by-week things."

Unless I got bits of the story wrong, I was certain Nell had her own place. "What about her son?"

"Son? I wasn't aware she had a son."

Maybe she didn't talk about him much, or didn't divulge anything personal like that. "Was it in town? On the island?"

"The motel? Yes, it's, ah …" He taps his finger to his chin, contemplative for a moment. "Crow's Nest Motel."

I know that one. About a mile and a half from where Aunt Midge works. They not only rent by the week, but by the hour, as I understand. "I can't believe she'd throw everything away."

And yet, I absolutely can, because that's how junkies work. There is nothing more valuable than the drug. Not even a child. I know that from firsthand experience, which is how I got dumped on my aunt's doorstep.

"Well, she was always a little shady. Used to hang out at some skeevy bar. She liked picking up the locals to take back to the motel and shoot up."

"The Shoal?"

"Pretty sure that's the one."

Sure, there are some interesting characters that end up at The Shoal, but I've grown up with a lot of those guys. Worked summers with some of them. They're not the most upstanding citizens on the island, but I can't imagine any of the regulars taking a young girl back to a motel to shoot up drugs. I've seen much skeevier places than that bar.

Then again, maybe I don't know any of them any more than I thought I knew Nell.

"Anyway, I need to go, or I'll be late. I just wanted to let you know."

"I appreciate it. Thanks."

I head back into Laura's bedroom, where she sits with one eyebrow quirked, and I shake my head. "Just giving me some info on your new meds."

"So, it *was* about me. That man is such a liar," she says with a smile.

I want to ask her if that's true, and to what extent would he lie. "It's beautiful outside. I was thinking maybe we could sit in the garden and read."

"What garden? You mean the cemetery of vines and shrubbery in the yard?"

"Yes. Unless you're up for a game of basketball, or something."

Her face scrunches to a frown. "Reading, it is."

I wheel her down to the first level, and out into the ruins, as I call them. The sun is bright today, but the news of Nell somehow dulls its warmth. Taking a seat on a stone bench half covered in bird crap, I flip the book open to where we last left off, the picture of young Lucian and his friend acting as the bookmark.

"I think I'd prefer to hear your story, instead, today."

Peeling my attention from the new chapter, I frown. "Mine?"

"Yes. Have you always lived on the island?"

I don't know why I hesitate to answer her at first. "No. My mother and I moved around a lot when I was little. Every month, it felt like."

"Was she in the military? Or business? Engineers move around quite a bit, don't they?"

Engineer. The only thing my mother managed to engineer was a shit life for both of us. "She was neither of those."

"Well, what did she do to keep moving you around so much?"

"Drugs. She was a junkie, and … we ran quite a bit."

The sidelong glance she shoots back at me is overflowing with judgement, but I don't care. Hiding my past has become an exhausting exercise as of late. "That doesn't sound like a healthy environment for a young girl."

"Not at all."

"And your father?"

"He died before I had the chance to meet him."

"So, how did you manage to avoid following your mother footsteps in life?"

"My Aunt Midge raised me from the time I was ten."

"It took *ten years* for your mother to decide she couldn't manage? Or did something precipitate the decision."

In the pause that follows her question, a flickering image flashes through my head.

A child holding a glowing heart. Darkness all around. But the child's face practically glows. It's sad eyes. Gentle hands. A red heart. Deep breaths. Red. Everywhere, it's red.

I blink out of the thoughts, the book in my lap coming back into focus.

"Well?" The expectant tone in Laura's voice carries an air of annoyance. "Why ten years?"

"I don't know. I guess she just gave up."

"That's not how mothers operate, darling. My guess is, you'll never know. Women do what they have to do, sometimes. Even at the risk of unimaginable pain."

There's a very lucid texture to her voice, and I have to look away from her eyes, which seem to be searching me for something, though I can't say what.

"Is that why you and Lucian don't communicate much?" It's a

tricky question with Laura, given the way she obviously feels about her son.

Instead, she sneers at my question, staring off toward the yard. "He resents me. He felt I forced him into marriage." Rolling her shoulders back, she lowers her gaze toward her hands resting in her lap. "As if I had a choice."

"You loved Amelia, though. Didn't you?"

"Love is a strong word, child. Best saved for your own children."

"You don't believe in romantic love, then?"

"If I did, I suppose my husband might still be alive, assuming the heart grows stronger when you love." She rubs her hands together and tips her head. "Has my son fucked you yet?"

My God, her blunt questions will never cease to keep me on edge. Even now, there's a thrum of anxiety beating through me.

While my mind scrambles for something to say, short of lying right to her face, she waves her hand in the air. "Never mind that. I'm sure he will eventually. A young thing like you is far too much temptation for the appetite of a Blackthorne man. His father was the same way. The younger ones always seemed to draw his attention most. Disturbing really. Had Lucian been a daughter, instead of a son ..." She seems to stare off for a moment, her eyes glassing over with each passing second, brows creeping toward a frown. "I'm tired. I'd like to go lie down now."

CHAPTER 52

LUCIAN

Four years ago ...

A rush of cold air casts a chill across my skin and drags me out of the void. At the sound of wind, I push up onto my good elbow and double blink the sleep away. Across my dark bedroom, the door to the balcony stands open, fluttering the sheer white curtain beneath the drawn drapes.

The hell?

I roll to my side and clamber out of bed, the frigid ambient air becoming painfully apparent outside of the covers. The cast on my right side was finally removed, but the ache of pins and plates seems more intense in these cooler temperatures. As if the cold has an affinity for the metal through my layers of skin and flesh.

Hobbling toward the door, I notice the flickering movement on the balcony, and find Amelia standing there in nothing but a silk, pink nightgown, her blonde hair dancing in the breeze.

"What are you doing?" Sleep still clings to my voice as I approach her from behind, and I rub my eyes, to be sure this isn't some strange nightmare. It wouldn't be the first, but they've settled some in recent weeks.

"Do you remember that night in the atrium ... when we kissed?" she asks, not bothering to turn around.

Rubbing the back of my neck, I blink hard to focus. "Yes."

"It was the best kiss I've ever had. For weeks, I dreamed about it. About you. I was certain that I was going to be the girl who won Lucian Blackthorne's cold, unattainable heart."

Though the anger that I feel toward Amelia still courses through me, it's lessened with time, as I've watched her slip into depression alongside me. I know now that it was a mistake on her part, leaving those pills out. A simple, human error. But I can't bring myself to forgive her, and whatever this is she's doing, it only solidifies my feelings, as I can't bring myself to care about a childish kiss, either.

The death of my son has turned me into a broken husk of a man. If ever I was capable of such frivolities as love, that time has long since passed.

"When I got pregnant with Roark, I had a choice. Keep the baby, the son of the man that I knew I was destined to marry. Or destroy it and, along with that, all ties to you." Her hands reach out, gripping the railing of the balcony, and she stares downward, the sight of which sets my teeth on edge.

"Why don't we talk in here?"

"This is what excites you, isn't it? Staring death in the face?"

"Amelia. C'mon. Talk inside."

She turns around, and with the red, puffiness of her eyes, I can see she's been crying. "I loved Roark. I know you don't believe that, but I did. Every morning, I woke up and thought, *Today is the day I'm going to be the mother he deserves.*" The crack of her voice sets off another round of tears that she quickly wipes from her cheeks. "And every day I failed him. I failed him because I was distraught over how to understand and please my husband."

417

Of course, she'd blame that on me, but I don't risk igniting her mood, seeing as I don't know what the hell she came to do out on my balcony yet. "I'm sorry. I'm sorry that I didn't give you a chance. Come inside." I hold out my hand to her, flicking my fingers. "We'll talk about this in here. In my room."

"I think I get it now, though," she says, continuing to ignore my request. "That freedom of knowing that, in the next breath, you could easily cease to exist. Do you think Roark felt that?"

Heart pounding in my throat, I step toward her, and that's when she hikes her leg over the railing, literally straddling the line between life and death.

"Amelia, don't do this. You don't have to do this. Let's talk. We can start over." I don't even know what I'm saying to her, or if I even believe such a thing is possible, but the urgency to get her back on this side of the balcony seems to have taken over my vocal chords. I take another step, and she shifts, the abrupt movement forcing me back to keep her from doing something stupid.

"There's no starting over. The night Roark died? I saw pure hatred in your eyes. If you ever felt anything for me, it died alongside him. And I don't blame you." Her gaze lowers from mine, as she seems to catch her breath. "But I kept loving you in spite of it. There's never been a time when I stopped loving you, Lucian." She slips, tumbling over the edge of the railing, and panic explodes through my muscles, jerking me forward on instinct as I reach out and grab her arm. It's not until I capture her hand that I realize my mistake. Pain bullets up my wrist and into my shoulder, while the full weight of her dangles from my once-broken arm.

"Ah, fuck!" I grit out through the agony tearing up my muscles. "Somebody, help me!"

Tears shine in her eyes, as she stares up at me, captured only by her delicate wrist. "You can let me go now."

"No." Bracing my foot against the edge of the railing, I reach out with my good arm. "Take my other hand. Please, Amelia. I can pull you up with this hand."

"I want you to let me go. I want to be with Roark. I promise I'll be a good mother to him this time. You won't have to worry."

My arm trembles as I lean further over the railing and attempt to reach for her with my stronger arm. I can't even lift her enough to capture her wrist. "Please, take my hand. I'm begging you."

With intense focus, I try to flex my shoulder, to pull her up so I can grab her, but an agonizing sensation tears through my muscles, as if it's separating from my body.

She manages to wriggle loose.

A sound of excruciating pain rips through my chest, echoing in the night.

In seconds, she hits the pavement, and a red pool crawls over the cement creating a halo of blood around her head that's visible in the triggered floodlights.

Balling my trembling hands into tight fists, I rest them against my temples and slide down the edge of the wall. The world slices me open once again, and I bleed out the misery trapped inside of me.

CHAPTER 53

ISADORA

Present day ...

I have to know. It's a nagging, needling thought inside my head that won't go away. Did Nell really overdose? Was she a regular at my aunt's bar? Was she lying the whole time? What the hell was the warning before she left all about? And why was she working with a private investigator?

So many questions slamming around inside my head.

If I come right out and tell Aunt Midge about what happened, it'll just be more gossip about the Blackthornes. She'll warn me to stay away from this place, and tell me I'm asking for trouble with Lucian.

But what if Nell didn't overdose? What if something happened to her? Maybe Aunt Midge saw her at the bar. Maybe she saw her leave with someone.

I can at least put my mind at ease a little by asking.

I'm sure, by now, the whole town knows a woman was found dead in a motel room. That kind of thing just doesn't happen frequently enough in Tempest Cove to get swept under the rug entirely. And if there's one person I know who's gotten the skinny on it, particularly as it's only a little over a mile up the road, it's Aunt Midge.

I shove a couple outfits into my bag for the weekend, my mind made up about taking a couple days away from this place, but pause at a knock at the door.

Shit. Lucian.

He seemed insistent earlier that I stay, and I've been trying to formulate a non-suspicious excuse for him for the last hour.

"Isa?" Giulia's voice bleeds through the door, and I exhale a relieved breath.

"Come in."

The door clicks as she enters the room, her face etched with worry. "You heard the news of Nell?"

Nodding, I sit down on the bed, resting my hands in my lap. "I can't believe it."

"I can't believe it, either." The skepticism in her voice proves the point. "I've known Nell for a couple years now. There's no way she would've thrown everything away. I watched her work so hard through school."

Unfortunately, I happen to know how easily an addict will throw everything away to feed their craving. Even at the expense of losing what they love most. I wish that was the most troubling part about this, because at least I'd be able to dismiss that. It'd make sense to me. The problem is, if Nell was just another junkie out to ruin what she worked hard for, why would she go out of her way to work with a private investigator, and to warn me away from the Blackthornes? Addicts don't give a shit about anything but their next fix.

"She was fired last week. Maybe that triggered a craving."

"Maybe." After glancing back at the door, she shuffles across the room and sits beside me on the bed. "Can I tell you something? You have to promise me you won't say a word."

"Yeah. Sure."

The way she glances around the room makes her look almost paranoid, but then again, maybe rightly so after the nights I've spent here. "I told her things," she whispers. "Things I shouldn't have talked about. She asked me about that secret group and the men involved. What if they found out?" Wringing the apron of her dress, she lowers her head and exhales a sharp breath. "What if they come for me next?"

"Why would they come for you?"

"You don't know who these men are, Isa. What they'll do to remain anonymous. To protect their identity. What they do. And they know everything about me. And Jackie." Face screwed up in panic, she clutches her stomach and leans forward as if she might throw up. "Oh, God, what if they go after my daughter?"

Go after her daughter? "Lucian is part of this group, as well?"

"Yes. But it's different with Lucian. He doesn't entirely share their philosophies."

"On what?"

Releasing a sharp exhale, she looks up at me. "They pay money to torture others."

Tendrils of ice crawl up my spine. "What do you mean? Like … *hurt* people?" All this time, I was under the impression they were some high-rolling escort service.

"People come to them with problems. Say me, for example. I needed a way out. So some, they physically hurt for money. Others might be used in other ways." She casts her gaze from mine, as if she can't look at me. "For money. The common thread is pain. These men get off on doling it out and watching it."

What she's saying makes no sense. A group that pays to torture people? It's the kind of thing that only happens in the dark recesses of the internet. Not here. Not in a small fishing community like Tempest Cove.

"People *come* to them to be hurt? *You* went to them for this? And worse yet, you suggested *I* go to them for this?"

"Remember how desperate you were? Imagine thousands of dollars paid to you. Money you don't have to pay back. All your debts and problems? Gone."

"Desperate, or not, I was trying to *avoid* being tortured and killed."

"Because you didn't know the terms, or the limits." She turns toward me, her eyes imploring. "But imagine if that drug dealer had outlined exactly what he would do to you, and afterward, your debts were clear. You never had to see him again."

Maybe. Maybe I was desperate in the moment. Who knows? I was certainly willing, at the time, to proposition the Devil of Bonesalt.

"Lucian does this? He pays to hurt people?"

"I don't think he participates. I think he's just one who provides the funding."

"Why? What could he possibly get in return for that?"

"I don't know, okay? I shouldn't even be telling you."

"How did you even learn about this group?"

"I heard through someone else about them. On the streets, they're like ... gods." There's a sparkle in her eyes when she says it, as if she believes it herself. "To be chosen is a lifesaver, for some."

"They tortured you?"

"My circumstances were such that ... they weren't interested. I was a single mother with a child. For what I was willing to do, they weren't willing to take both of us in. I'll admit, it was stupid. But we were starving, and you don't realize the depths you'll sink to when you have a hungry child. Had Rand not approached me, I'd be walking the streets of Boston looking for Johns. I'm not proud of that, but I'll do anything for my little girl. *Anything.*"

"So you made a deal with Lucian ..." I was aware from the start that he was fucking her, but to hear the reasons behind it somehow doesn't sit well with me.

"Yes. But that was before you came along. He hasn't touched me since."

"And has he ever physically hurt you?"

"Never." The unyielding tone of her voice dissolves when she adds, "He has asked me for things, though."

"What kinds of things?"

"To cut him."

"Cut *him*? As in, he's the one who bleeds?"

"Yes. I hated it. Every minute. It's sick and disgusting. But I did it, whatever he asked of me. For Jackie."

I knew Lucian had a penchant for knives, and admitted that a blade to his throat got him off. The scars on his skin, separate from the injuries, confirm that he has hurt himself, too. It's just strange to hear that he'd request that from her. "Why would you tell any of this to Nell? Why would you risk it?"

"They know where Jackie goes to school. A police officer has apparently visited her, called her down to the office to ask questions about Lucian and me."

"About the group? I'm not following." Frowning, I shake my head, trying to make sense of what she's saying. "What makes you think they know where she goes to school?"

"The ring. Jackie said he was wearing a ring with a moth. The same one Lucian wears. The same one they all wear. He's one of them."

"So, why didn't you have her removed? Why didn't you pick her up, the moment you heard about this?"

"Because I'm certain, if I run, they'll find me." She raises a trembling hand to her face and wipes at a tear that streaks down her cheek. "If something happens to me, I need someone to know. To protect my daughter. That's why I told Nell."

"And you don't trust Lucian to protect her."

"I want to. But how can you trust the man who funds these people?"

Funds them. My mind scrambles to wrap itself around what

she's telling me. Lucian funds a secret group who pay to torture people. *Pay* to torture. No matter how many times I repeat it in my head, it still comes out wrong. "Who are these people?"

"You met some of them at the masquerade. They're powerful and wealthy. And they have connections to other powerful and wealthy people."

"How could you not know this would happen? That they would be watching you after? That they'd question your relationship with Lucian?"

"How long did you think about it before you mentioned the group to Lucian? A minute? Ten? Do you think you teased out every consequence? No. You were desperate. That's what you do when you're desperate. So don't you sit and judge me."

"I'm not. Listen, I'm going to look into what happened to Nell. I'm gonna talk to my aunt. There's a chance she might know something."

She gathers my hands in hers and squeezes, her eyes pleading. "Please don't tell Lucian that I told you all of this. I can't risk that he'll throw Jackie and me back on the streets. Especially now."

"I promise. I won't say a word to him about this."

Makaio slows the car to a stop along the curb in front of The Shoal. "You sure you don't want me to drop you off at the house?"

"No, I'd like to hang out with Aunt Midge for a bit." I gather up my bag and set my hand to the car door, instead of waiting for him to open it for me.

"How long?"

I pause at the question. "Excuse me?"

Hiking his elbow over the back of the front seat, he cranes his neck toward me. "How long do you plan to hang out with her?"

"Is there a reason you're asking me this?"

"I need to know how long I'm waiting here."

"Um. I planned to stay the weekend. That's why I brought a duffel."

"The boss told me to drive you back."

"Well, can you let him know I decided to stay?"

"No." The expression written across his face is as unyielding as his response, and a creeping sensation of discomfort climbs my spine.

"No? Why?"

"Because you're to return to the manor. That's what I was instructed to do. Bring you back."

"Um. I'm … off the clock."

"I'm not. So, I'll wait here for you."

"I have a choice of where I want to go on the weekends, and I chose to come home," I volley back, the frustration blooming hot beneath my skin.

"Well, seems the boss wasn't made aware of that. So, here I am. Waiting for you."

"Well, you'll be waiting a long time, I can tell you that."

"How long?"

"Three hours. Maybe four, if I decide to eat here."

"Okay, cool." He lowers his arm, turning back around in his seat. "I'll just be waiting here in the parking lot, then."

"Fine. And I'll be sure to have words with Lucian about this."

"Whatever you two spat about is none of my business. I'm just over here doing my job." The dismissal in voice gnaws at me, and I can't get out of this car until I know he's going to let it go and not wait for me in the parking lot, like some psychotic bodyguard I never hired.

"This is crazy, Makaio. Seriously, just go. I'm fine. I'm with Aunt Midge."

"Your timer already started." He taps his wrist that's absent of a watch. "You're wasting minutes talking to me."

Frustrated, I storm across the parking lot, throwing back the door of the bar to find Aunt Midge leaning on the counter, chatting with Mac and Doherty.

"Ahh, look what the wind blew in, fellas!" she says, straightening as I approach.

"Can I talk to you for a second?"

"Am I in trouble? Judging by the scowl on your face, I'd say so."

"No. I'm just ..." *Pissed.* "Can we talk?"

"Yeah, sure." She directs her attention toward the two older men across from her. "You guys let me know if anyone else strolls in." With a jerk of her head, she leads me into the office behind the bar and closes the door. "Everything all right?" The air of humor in her voice from moments ago switches to concern.

"Yeah. I just had a question. Last night ... did you notice a young girl at the bar, at all? Maybe slightly older than me? Think she comes in pretty regularly."

"You're talking about the Anders girl?"

"You know her?"

"Not personally," she says, shrugging a shoulder. "She comes in sometimes, to meet with a guy. Older guy."

"Did you see her last night?"

"Yeah, she was here. With him."

"What did he look like?"

Puffing her cheeks, she blows out a breath. "Gray hair, kinda heavier build. Glasses."

The private investigator, I'd bet.

"She ever drink? Or leave to party somewhere else with any of the guys?"

"Ah, well, what they do when they exit through those doors ain't none of my business." Finger waving in the air, she shakes her head. "But I ain't never seen her drink. She typically orders a Coke. You know her?"

"She was a nurse for Mrs. Blackthorne."

"No shit?" The sudden intrigue in her eyes makes me wish I

hadn't said a word. No doubt that bit of information will spread through the island like a bad case of herpes. "Whatever she pumped in her veins was apparently some hard-hitting stuff. Doesn't seem like a good candidate for a nurse."

"Yeah, I guess not. None of the guys ever mentioned hanging out with her at the Crow's Nest?"

"Nah. Only guy I ever watched her leave with was that older guy. You sure everything is okay?"

I nod, rolling my shoulders back. "Just kind of a shock."

"Was to us, too. Don't get a dead body like that very often. Not the young ones, anyway." Staring off in silence, she blinks out of her thoughts. "So, you stayin' this weekend? Thought I'd cook up a pot of chili tomorrow."

"Yes. I just have to … deal with something first."

"Nothing serious?"

Just an enormous Hawaiian bodyguard who refuses to leave.

I shake my head, pulling my duffel bag higher up onto my shoulder. "Hey, you think I can use Jack's computer for a bit?" I'm curious to know if Nell ended up in the news, and if they happened to mention anything about her son. The owner of The Shoal often let me use his computer for school, when I couldn't get to the library, for whatever reason.

"Knock yourself out. You want anything?"

"Maybe just some cheese fries and a Sprite?" It was a go-to favorite of mine when I was in high school, and the smile that lights up Aunt Midge's face tells me she appreciates the nostalgic request.

"On it."

The wooden chair creaks when I sit down at the dinosaur computer that's still equipped with a disk- and CD-drive. Ages seem to pass before the internet browser finally pops up onto the screen, and when I click the search bar, it's a ten second pause before I can type in the first inquiry.

Anelle Anders Crow's Nest Death.

The only relevant result that pops up is a brief article in the Gazette that mentions she died of a drug overdose, and that police are investigating. Nothing more. No mention of her son, or how long she's been a resident on the island. Nothing but a small bulletin on her death.

There's also no other trace of her. No Facebook. No Instagram. No social media, at all, which isn't exactly strange to me, seeing as I don't keep up with that myself. Mostly, I'm just struck by how little there is on her death.

Just another junkie.

It's sad to me, that someone can live and work hard, and the most anyone can say about her is that she died of an overdose.

Aunt Midge enters the office, the concern on her face creasing her forehead as she sets the food down on the desk. "Hey, there's a man out there. The one I was telling you about, who came in with that girl. Says he's an investigator. Wants to ask you some questions about her, I guess. If you don't want to talk to him, I'll throw him out. Must've known you two worked together, or something?"

"I'll talk to him." I push up from the chair and follow Aunt Midge into the bar, taking note of only a handful of regulars scattered about, though it'll soon be packed with tourists.

Standing off from them is a heavyset man with gray hair and glasses, exactly as Aunt Midge described, who waves with what seems like a friendly smile. As I approach, he holds out a hand toward me, which I shake with some reluctance. "Al Goodman. You're Isadora?"

"Izzy is fine."

"Nell told me a lot about you. Can I have just a quick minute of your time?"

"Sure."

We find a booth toward the back, and I scan the room to make sure Makaio hasn't wandered in. The last thing I need is to have him report back to Lucian that I met with the same investigator Nell was fired for chatting with.

Aunt Midge shuffles over with my fries and Sprite, setting them down on the table. "Can I get you anything?" she asks the stranger.

"Just a Coke." As soon as she walks off, he leans in. "I'm assuming you've heard about your co-worker, Nell?"

"It's a small town. I'd venture to say most know about it by now."

"I'm just going to get straight to the point." His eyes scan the room, before he leans in closer. "In spite of what you've been told, Nell didn't die specifically from a heroin overdose."

Branches of ice climb my spine as I stare back at him, searching his eyes for a lie. "She told me she abused drugs in the past."

"She did, yes. Which made this awfully convenient. But she did not overdose on *heroin*. My sources are sketchy, at best, but that much was confirmed. On the streets, it's called gray death because it looks like concrete. It's heroin, fentanyl, and an elephant tranquilizer. Dangerous and deadly. Therefore, I have reason to believe she was murdered."

"By?" My heart gallops inside my chest, and I wonder if he'll come out and tell me it was Lucian.

"If I knew, I wouldn't be sitting here with you now."

"You think *I* know who killed her?"

"I think if anyone has insight into who might've wanted to kill her, it's you."

"I hardly knew her. We worked together for a few weeks, is all."

"And I know the nature of your working together, for the most part. What I don't know is what led to her being fired."

I don't even know if this guy is the real deal. He could be a reporter. "She was skimming pills and spreading rumors. Look, I'll admit, I only have a vague understanding of what you do from old eighties shows, but don't you have access to police reports and stuff? I don't think the Blackthornes decided to show up at her motel room and pump her full of drugs."

"She didn't rent that room. It was under a different name. One I can't seem to track down, because it doesn't seem to be associated with an actual body. And in this case, the police haven't been playing nice with me."

"Can you just … tell me what you're thinking, then? Because I really hate puzzles."

"Are you familiar with Schadenfreude?" Once again, his eyes make a sweep of our surroundings, and he's practically stretched across the table, leaning into me.

"No. What is that? German, or something?"

"It's a German word, yes. In essence, it means finding pleasure in another's suffering. It's also the name of a secret group I've been investigating for a while now. Would you know of any group that might pay for the pleasure of watching someone suffer?"

Again, I find myself contemplating how much I want to tell this guy, and thoughts of Giulia and her daughter pop into my head. "I might've heard of it. But I wouldn't know anything about it."

"Assuming you did hear about it, how would you have learned of it?"

As paranoid as Giulia was, I'm not going to throw her into this guy's lap. "Who hasn't heard of it?"

"A number of people, that's who. They happen to be very good at keeping themselves hidden below the radar. I'm only privy to their name through a contact who was found dead in a New York hotel room, a month ago. I'm here to investigate the activities of this group."

"Who hired you?"

"I can't divulge names, but it's the family of a girl who ended up dead."

"Local?"

"Again, I'll not go into detail, except to say, I believe she may have somehow gotten tangled up in this group."

"What do you want from me?"

"Tell me what you know about Lucian Blackthorne."

At the mention of his name, I instinctively look away, for fear he'll see the obsession written all over my face. "I don't know anything about him. He's not a very transparent man."

"I know that you and he have become quite close." *Jesus*. Did Nell tell this guy everything? "I did a bit of digging into your background, as well."

Trying to keep a poker face, while my whole body is screaming from the inside, is impossible.

"I know there was an incident a few months ago at a party. I know you spent some time in a therapist's chair."

"I don't see what that has to do with your investigation."

"I know you live with your aunt, because your mother is a drug addict who gave up parental rights when you were ten years old."

Pushing the plate of food away, I slide along the booth to leave, and at a grip on my arm, a flare of panic explodes through my muscles. All I have to do is scream, and damn near everyone in this bar would be on this guy.

He reaches into a bag that's on the seat beside him and pulls out an envelope. "I have a feeling you'll be quite interested in knowing what's inside."

Gaze on the envelope, I suddenly wish I had X-ray vision, because no way this guy is about to hand over whatever he seems to think would be important to me without some condition. "What is it?"

"Tell me what you know about Lucian."

"You're asking me for information, when I don't even know that what's in that envelope is worth it."

"It's worth it. And I'll assure you, this offer doesn't come without risk to me. I've more to lose than you in this exchange." Which means my curiosity just ratcheted up a notch, just not enough, until he says, "It contains information about your father."

Shit.

No. No way he's privy to that.

All my life, I've yearned to know the answer to that question. I've inquired and dug around to no avail.

But what if it's true?

My gaze falls to the envelope again. What if my father's identity is right there? Practically at my fingertips.

Rubbing my hand across my brow, I close my eyes and shake my head. I'm not telling this guy jack about Lucian and risking someone watching me, like Giulia. But for information about my dad, I'll tell him what I know for certain. "He didn't kill Nell. He was with me the night before she was found dead."

"Come now, you know he doesn't have to carry out the murder himself. A man like Lucian Blackthorne can't afford the blood on his hands, with the kind of past he has. Perhaps the only thing the man can't afford."

"You're suggesting he had her killed?"

"She was meeting regularly with me. They knew it. The question is, why wouldn't he have had her killed sooner?"

"And now I risk the same fate."

"Give me what I'm looking for, and you'll never hear from me again. I swear it."

"What are you looking for?"

"Have you seen, or met, any of the members of Schadenfreude?"

According to Giulia, the men who were present at the masquerade were members, though I didn't see any of their faces behind the masks. Except for Mayor Boyd.

"Only one. But I don't even know if he's a member. He might be innocent."

"Who?"

"Mayor Boyd."

Lips curved upward, he snorts. "Amelia's father. The scandalous Mayor Boyd who had an affair with a seventeen year old girl. Trust me when I say he's not innocent. He's the only one you've seen around the manor?"

"Yes."

"And do you know in what capacity Lucian serves this group? Have you ever seen one of his slaves, or noticed any unusual activity? Anyone coming to the manor who, perhaps, didn't leave?"

"Slaves?"

"Yes. This group is known for sexual slavery and sadism."

"I ... know he's helped Giulia. A maid who works for them."

"I'm aware of Giulia. Any others?"

"No." I don't bother to tell him about Franco, because that would open the box to more digging, and I don't need a drug dealer seeking me out for having ratted him out.

"I'm afraid I need one more piece of information before I hand this off to you."

"What's that?"

"Would your aunt happen to have a yearbook handy? From, say, your mother's sophomore year?"

"Yeah. I guess. My grandparents had some old stuff stored away. Why? They have copies of yearbooks at the library."

"I know. That particular year is missing."

With a huff, I glance around the bar one more time. "Sure, I can look in the storage stuff in the attic."

"Would you like me to drive you there?"

Makaio would probably go ballistic, if he saw the two of us leaving the bar and getting into his car.

"No, it's not that far. I'll run home, and I can be back here before dark."

"Are you sure? I don't mind offering a ride."

If Nell's fate was sealed by having been caught hanging

434

around a private investigator, I sure as hell don't want to be caught hanging around said investigator.

"No, I won't be long. Can I ask what you're looking for?"

"Any pictures your mother is in."

I frown at that, my suspicions slowly creeping back in. "What does she have to do with your investigation?"

"She doesn't have anything to do with Schadenfreude, so far as I know. But she does have something to do with what's in this envelope," he says, holding it up again like a dangling carrot to a starving rabbit.

"Okay. I'll be back." I slide out of the booth and am greeted by the look of confusion on Aunt Midge's face, as I pass the bar toward the back entrance, so Makaio won't see me leave. "Gotta grab something from home real quick."

"Like home-home? Or castle home?"

"Home-home."

"Why you going out the back door?"

"Cutting through the alley."

"You're *walking* home?"

"Yeah. It'll just take a few minutes."

"Hey, Mac, any chance you can give Isa a ride to the house and back?"

Before he can answer, I shake my head. "He's been drinking. Look, I don't get out much these days. It'll be nice to walk. Haven't jogged in almost two months. I need the fresh, sea air. Kinda stuffy in a castle, you know?"

Arms crossed, she sighs. "Be back before dark, okay? That girl may have just overdosed, but that crap makes me paranoid as all get out."

She has no idea. "I promise."

∾

435

I t takes a half hour to walk from uptown to my neighborhood. The early morning strolls along the boardwalk, with the warm salty air, is something I've missed since taking the job at Blackthorne. Dead body aside, Tempest is a relatively safe island, overall. Murders happen, but rarely, and when they do, it's all over the place, which results in more eyes watching.

Probably should've told Aunt Midge what I'm doing, seeing as I hate lying to the woman, but she's like an endless vacuum of worry. Besides, I need the time to process everything. Between Giulia and Mr. Goodman, my head is spinning like a hurricane. Snippets of conversation stand out like a word cloud, but none of it makes sense to me.

You don't trust Lucian?

He has asked me for things. To cut him.

Tell me what you know about Lucian Blackthorne. A man like Lucian Blackthorne can't afford the blood on his hands with the kind of past he has.

I want to believe that these are all as much rumor as everything else on this island, and that I shouldn't trust any of it any more than I trusted the idea that he kept a refrigerator of human blood, but my head is swimming in lies and facts that flit past like quick minnows in the shallow. I can't grasp anything, and the throbbing ache in my temples is a migraine about ready to wreak havoc on my skull.

Crossing the neighbor's front yard, I finally arrive home, and jog up the stairs to the front door. *Locked.*

She finally started locking up? Only took the death threat of a drug dealer.

I fish for the key I stuffed in my pocket earlier, and push inside to find the house still and dark. As much as I try to shake it off, there will always be a small part of me that feels uneasy without a knife in my pocket.

When I came to live with Aunt Midge, she insisted that I leave the knife at home, because a fifth grader carrying around a pock-etknife at school is a no-no. We compromised, and I began sleeping with it under my pillow. Aunt Midge didn't particularly like the idea, but that's the thing about growing up as a kid from the streets--people treated me a little differently. I got to eat lunch in the library, while my classmates played at recess. I got out of gym in middle school because I didn't want to change in front of the other girls, and of course, my counselor assumed something had happened to me to make me that way, so he excused me from the elective. In high school, nobody gave me a hard time, when I skipped the occasional class to sleep in, or read at the park, because I had decent grades, and at least I wasn't plotting to shoot up the place.

I've always been, and felt, different thanks to my mother, who gifted me with ten years of constantly having to defend myself against whatever predicament she got us into. It doesn't go away, either. The instincts. The edginess. I feel it even now, padding through the empty house toward the attic. Like something might jump out at me any second.

Tugging the hook on the attic door, I yank it down and slide out the ladder. I can't remember the last time I ventured up here. Years ago, it was a place where I hid away with books to read, undisturbed.

The small, cramped space smells like damp wood and moth-balls, and my muscles twitch at the possibility that I might stumble upon a small critter up here.

I tug the chain, and a naked bulb casts a dull light over the room. Most of the stuff in here belongs to my grandparents. Old dresses and costume jewelry, tucked away in wooden crates and bins. I head toward the back, where Aunt Midge's old trophies for softball are set out on a shelf above a stack of cardboard boxes. I pull the first one down and rifle through pictures, and posters of bands from the eighties sporting ratted-out hair and endless spandex.

One particular picture catches my attention, and I lift it from the stack. My mom and Aunt Midge. My mom must've been fifteen, or so, seeing as she wasn't pregnant. That I can tell anyway.

While living on the streets, she didn't keep any pictures from home, so I never really got to see what she looked like as a teenager, aside from the couple of school pictures hung on the walls downstairs.

Long, red hair hangs loose around her shoulders in lazy curls, and her bright eyes are framed by thick, dark lashes that look like she's wearing mascara. She had an exotic beauty, and paired with her slim, developed figure, it makes sense to me that she'd draw the stares of hardened fishermen on this island. Like bagging their own mermaid.

Tossing it back into the box, I continue my search, and after about ten minutes, I find the yearbook buried at the bottom.

Any pictures your mother is in.

I flip to the index and search for her name, finding three pages where she's listed. The first is her yearbook picture, in which she smiles between long, red, side-swept bangs. So young and vibrant back then. The second is a picture of her in choir, and in it, she wears a long, purple gown, with a black stole to match the school colors. The third is a National Honor Society picture.

I had no idea my mother did well in school. She never talked about it much, and neither did Aunt Midge. I stare down at her, where she stands amongst a small group on risers, and I scan the other faces, coming to a stop on one very familiar.

Holy shit.

Mayor Boyd stands at the opposite side of my mother, that too-white smile stretched across his face. The darkness of his hair puts him somewhere around forty, I'm guessing, which would make him the only adult in the photo. A mentor, I bet.

I flip back to the index to look up his name, and find him on a few pages, as well. A staff picture whose caption is 'Government', the National Honor Society picture, and a third: track, which he apparently coached. Below the picture is a list of names, and one catches my eye. *Not pictured: Jennifer Quinn.*

The woman in these pictures is nothing like the one I've come to know. It's like looking at her doppelganger, or something. As I tuck the book under my arm, I catch the dimming light through the porthole window, telling me it'll be dark soon.

I climb back down the ladder, fold it up, and push the door closed. When I spin around, a figure is waiting in the living room, and I let out a shriek.

My mother sits on the couch, flicking her cigarette into the ashtray on the coffee table. "Hey."

"Hey."

"Midge ... she doesn't know I'm here."

"How'd you get in?"

"She gave me a key." She reaches into her pocket and pulls out what looks like a wad of cash, which she holds out to me. "I just wanted to drop this off."

I don't accept it, but keep my feet planted where I'm at.

She drops the cash on the table. "Just thought it might help out."

"Now, you're suddenly interested in helping out?"

She bites her lip and scratches her head with her cigarette-toting hand. "How you been? Heard you, uh ... got a job working at Blackthornes."

Instead of answering, I let her keep on with her one-sided conversation. I have no interest in telling her anything.

"Midge says you been spending a lot of time with Lucian Blackthorne." A smile creeps across her lips as she raises her cigarette. "Like mother, like daughter, eh?"

"I'm nothing like you."

"You're more like me than you know," she says around a mouthful of smoke that she blows off to the side. Her gaze falls to the bracelet on my wrist, and I'd be willing to bet she's calculating how much coke she'd score for what it's worth. "That's a whole lot of power for a girl so young. Be careful with a man like that."

As if she has any room to advise me on men. "So, what is this? Redemption? You think a little cash is going to make up for dumping me on her doorstep?"

"I'm ... just trying to make things right. Get my shit together."

"Why bother? You're halfway to the grave. Why turn around now?"

"I want ... I want my family back. I want you back, Izzy."

"Don't hand me that bullshit. I know exactly why you're here. You found out I was with Lucian Blackthorne and you decided it might be an opportunity for you."

"No. No, that's not true. In fact, I think you should stay away from that whole fucked-up family."

"I'm sure. Except it was Lucian who got you out of trouble the last time."

She stares back at me confused, as if it's the first time she's hearing this. "What's that in your hands?"

"Nothing."

"My yearbook? What for?"

"You want to do me a favor, *Mother*? I'll give you one chance. One opportunity. You want to make things right and be a family again? Tell me who my father is."

Turning her face away from mine, she flicks the ash into the ashtray again, and when she brings the cigarette to her lips, I catch the tremble in her hands. "I can't do that."

"Why? Because you fucked so many men you have no idea who he is?"

"Because he's a piece of shit who never deserved to be in your life."

"Ah, perfect. You two made the perfect match, then."

She snorts a laugh and bites her lip, the way she does when

her pride has been wounded. "You're right. Maybe I should've stayed with him." Jaw shifting, she sniffs and drags her arm across her nose. "I couldn't, though. I refused to stay on this shit-hole island with him."

"You're selfish. You've always been selfish. And this crap about having a family again? It's just that: a steaming pile of dog shit."

"You don't understand, Izzy. I didn't …. I'm … not telling you because of me. That's not what I meant to do."

"Do you hear yourself? How ridiculous you sound? The drugs have warped your head so much. Whatever you were in this …" I hold the yearbook up in the air. "Isn't who you are now."

"You're right. You're absolutely right. That girl is gone. Long gone."

"I'm out of here. Lock the door when you leave. And do Aunt Midge and I a favor--lose the fucking key. I don't need *you*, Mother. The little girl who did is gone now, too. Long gone."

My blood pulses with white hot fury, as I slam through the front door and cut across the neighbor's lawn. The walk back is riddled with confusion and anger, and I don't immediately notice the sleek, black Bentley parked at the corner, about a block ahead of me, until its lights flick on.

"Shit!" I slam to a halt and bang a right through the adjacent park, running across the massive stretch of lawn, until I have to stop and catch my breath. Bending forward, I force deep inhales and long exhales, trying to settle my nerves.

The darkness settles over me, and in the silence, I clamp my eyes to the mishmash of information pounding at my skull. I want to cry, but I won't.

Get it together, Isa.

Another minute, and I push upright to hustle back before Makaio can catch up to me, when a shadow steps into my path.

"Well, well. Look what we have here." The sound of Aedon Ross's voice scrapes at the back of my neck.

I turn around to go the other way, but bump into Brady

441

standing behind me. Fear and panic churn in my stomach, muscles tingling with the shock that crawls beneath my skin. "You're … you're not supposed to come near me." Based on a court order, we're not to talk, or go anywhere near each other, which has been easy up until now, with the two away at college.

At the sound of Aedon's chuckle from behind, I spin around, desperate to keep my eyes on both of them. On instinct, my hand swipes over my pocket, where my knife should be, but I left it back at the manor.

"No, no, sweetheart," Aedon says, edging closer. "It's *you* who are supposed to stay away from *him*. But we won't tell, if you don't."

I lunge to the left of Aedon, darting around him, but he captures my arm. I swing out with my free arm on reflex, failing to connect with my intended target. A scream rips through my chest, but is tamped down by his hand covering my mouth. My body is dragged backward, my heels digging into the grass, as they haul me toward the building behind us.

The park restrooms.

The potent smell of sewage fills my nose, when we slam through the door. Urinals stand off to the side, the concrete of the bathroom floor tearing at the soles of my shoes. Aedon holds me captive, one arm banded across my chest, while the other seals off the air to my mouth. Brady approaches me, the dark smile on his face brimming with malice and long-awaited revenge.

My whole body is quaking as I squirm in Aedon's grasp, to no avail.

From his back pocket, Brady tugs a pocket knife, much like my own, and twists it around in front of me.

Salty tears mingle with the snot that gathers in my nose, as Brady holds my legs, preventing me from kicking out at him. I reach behind to grab hold of Aedon's groin, and the dirty cement floor of the bathroom crashes into my spine as the two lay me out. Pain shoots up the back of my skull into my sinuses, and spots float before my eyes. Another scream escapes me in the melee, echoing off the walls before being quickly capped by Aedon's palm. He tucks my arms beneath his bent legs, and traps my head between his thighs, flexing hard against my ears. Brady gathers my legs beneath him, and I'm stretched out on the floor, imprisoned by both of them. Brady leans forward, still holding the blade, and buries his nose between my thighs.

"You smell like dick, Isa. You always smelled like dick." He raises the blade again, and I scream into Aedon's palm, squirming and writhing on the filthy bathroom floor. "I'm going to repay the favor for what you did to me. I'm going to make sure you never enjoy a good fuck again. I hear it's a common practice in some countries, removing the clitoris."

My head aches with the scream that fails to breach Aedon's palm. Dizziness settles over me. The surrounding blackness closing in.

The sound of a slamming door yanks me out of that abysmal descent, and Brady turns away from me.

"What the fuck?" I hear Aedon say over me.

"'The fuck you want, asshole, get out!"

I stare down my body to where a massive, shadowy figure takes up the width of the doorway.

Makaio.

In the next breath, Brady's body is hefted up off the floor and thrown backward, crashing through the door of the nearby stall.

Aedon releases me, and I feel him scrambling about my head.

I steal the moment to kick myself back against the wall, watching as Makaio makes easy play out of these boys, throwing them around as if they're nothing more than ragdolls. Hands against my ears, I try to block out the sounds of their screams.

The sounds of my nightmares.

My body is lifted up off the floor, the world feeling light as

I'm spun around, and Makaio carries me out of the bathroom as if I weigh nothing.

I finally wrap my arms around his neck, while he strides across the park, my whole body cold with terror as I stare off at the restroom over his shoulder.

When the weight of it all finally hits me, a sob tears through my chest.

Finally, we reach The Shoal parking lot, and he settles me into the soft, plush leather of the Bentley and closes the door. As he rounds the car, I steal a glance at the bar. All I want right now is Aunt Midge's arms wrapped around me, but I can't bring myself to go back inside and tell her what happened just now. For months, she tried to pull me out that blackness, and I can feel it rising up from my gut like dead bodies in a murky lagoon of bad memories. I left the yearbook back at the park, but that's the least of my worries right now, as my body shivers, desperate for warmth.

Makaio falls into the driver's seat, and for a moment, he sits quietly, not bothering to look back. "Are you okay?"

I sniff, blinking to hold back the tears. "I don't know."

"If I tell him what happened tonight, he'll want them properly punished."

Properly punished. What does that even mean, with the information I've been given about Lucian in the last few hours? What would he do, if given the opportunity?

I have nothing to say in response, because the truth is, if Lucian was standing here now and asking me if I wanted Makaio to go back and punish the hell out of them, I'd probably tell him yes. "How did you find me?"

"The bracelet."

Frowning, I stare down at the adornment on my wrist. "You tracked me?"

"For exactly what happened tonight. He wants to keep you

safe." The engine roars to life and lurches forward, and Makaio turns out of the parking lot.

"Can you please just take me back to my aunt's house? Please, Makaio."

"No. You're safer with Lucian now."

CHAPTER 54

LUCIAN

The investigating officer sits across from my desk, his partner in the chair beside him. From the looks of it, the rookie was trying out the big boy wheels, by asking all the questions, while his mentor sat quietly beside him. Observing me, no doubt.

Too bad for them, I hold fucking degrees in bullshitting. It's wound up in my DNA alongside my eye color, dark hair, and penchant for rough sex. These guys will be lucky to walk away with one straight answer by the time this inquiry is over.

"I understand she worked a couple years for you, as a nurse to your mother."

Rookie boy's attempt to sound official is thwarted by the uncertain glance toward the seasoned cop beside him, the sight of which, tugs at my lips for a smile. I'll give the kid some credit-- he's trying to be thorough, just doing his job, but if they think they're pinning another murder on me, after the bullshit I've gone through with my dead wife and son, they're nuts. I'm not going to be this town's designated scapegoat every time a body floats to the surface.

"She worked for an agency that we hired."

"Okay. And, um …" Face buried in his notes, the kid doesn't seem to have a single thought of his own about this investigation. He's spent most of the time staring at whatever he wrote down before knocking on my door. "She was fired the week before. What was the nature of that?"

"My mother's pills have gone missing."

"So, you fired her because she was stealing pills?"

"I fired her because she wasn't the right fit. Happens, sometimes. Some people just aren't cut out for certain jobs."

His partner rubs his hand across his face as if to hide the smirk I catch, and I eye the signet ring on the older man's finger. With his cockeyed, misbuttoned shirt, and hair that looks like he trims it himself, the guy seems the type to harbor little patience for anything, especially some wannabe badass on training wheels.

"We did find a prescription bottle for Laura Blackthorne."

"And is that why you decided to interrupt my evening?"

The kid looks to his partner, then back to me, frowning. "We're just following up."

"Was there evidence of foul play?"

"No, we … dusted for prints. Didn't find any outside of the maid and Miss Anders, of course. The lab is checking out what she injected in the syringe. But the room was rented under a James Smith. Does that name ring a bell?"

"Yeah. It's probably the most common name in this country. You got a credit card? Camera footage?"

"No. It appears the room was paid in cash for the week. And the Crow's Nest doesn't have any outdoor cameras, from what we understand. Just one in the office to make sure their employees aren't stealing anything."

"Then, my guess? She wanted a place to get high without anyone finding her."

"Funny, that was my guess, as well," the older officer says, leaning forward. "I think that's all the questions we have for you,

Mr. Blackthorne. Thanks for your time." Pushing to his feet, he reaches out a hand, which I shake from across the desk.

"Of course. Anything I can do to help the investigation, I'm happy to assist."

"One more question." Once again, the rookie buries his face in his notes, his eyeballs shifting back and forth as they scan the page. "She worked for you a couple years. Why would you suddenly decide she wasn't the right fit out of the blue?"

"I try not to delve too deeply into the personal affairs of those I employ, but I will say, there's been a gradual decline in her performance. We recently had an incident where she left without informing anyone, which put my mother at risk. I also found her to be increasingly impatient with my mother."

"Do you mind if I … chat with your mother for a minute?"

"I do. My mother won't be any assistance to you. Her mental faculties aren't what they used to be."

"Still, it might be--"

"We're not *chatting* with Mrs. Blackthorne. We've got more pressing issues than a drug addict who decided to hole herself up for the weekend and overdose on heroin."

"Of course. Thank you for your time, Mr. Blackthorne."

The officers exit my office, along with Rand, who didn't bother to say a word from the time he showed them in up until now. I pour myself a drink, carrying the glass back to my desk, and pulling out my phone, I check my texts.

The last one I received was Makaio, telling me Isa had apparently left the bar to walk back home. Why? No idea. On the way back, though, it appeared she caught on and ran from him, through the park. And that's when Makaio got in touch with me.

I dial his number, which answers on the second ring. "Yeah, Boss, I found her."

"And?"

"She's okay. Shaken up a bit. Some little pricks in the park were messing with her."

"I trust you intervened."

"That I did."

"Everyone still has a pulse?" I pitch back the entire glass of liquor, trying to erase the mind-numbing exercise of having entertained an infant cop for the last hour.

"Yes."

"Good. I don't need another investigation thrown in my lap."

"Rest assured, I only smacked them around a bit."

"Enough to serve as a warning, I hope."

"I don't think they'll mess with her again. And if they do, I'll be sure to make it clearer."

The comment makes me smile as I fill another glass of bourbon. "I want her brought directly to my office when you arrive."

"Sure thing, Boss."

As I hang up the phone, the elevator dings, and Rand strides toward me.

"Is there something you want to tell me?" I ask, falling back into my chair and kicking my feet up on the desk.

"I can assure you, I carried out your orders to the T. I let the woman know we were aware of the private investigator, and I let her go. That was the last I saw, or heard, from her."

"I don't like surprises. Having two police officers show up at my door is definitely a shitty surprise."

Arms crossed in front of him, Rand lowers his gaze. "My apologies, Sir."

"Did you have any awareness of her addiction?"

"Based on the information of our contacts, I was aware she had a history of drug abuse, but her tests have since been clean."

"Guess it was a bad night, then. Relapse, maybe."

The warm buzz of alcohol begins to dull my frustration from before, and I switch my mind to something else, no less concerning, but more worthy of my attention. "I appreciate the information on Isa. It appears she had a run-in this evening while in town."

"She's okay, I hope."

"Yes. According to Makaio, she's a little shaken. If I find out it has anything to do with the bastards who attacked her before, I'll have their dicks severed and sent in a gift-wrapped box to their parents."

The nervous shift of his feet tells me Rand believes every word of my threat. "Is that wise, Master? Given the attention Ms. Anders has brought our way?"

"I don't give a fuck whether it's wise, or not."

The elevator dings again, and this time, it opens up to Makaio and Isa, who looks a bit disheveled and pale.

"That will be all, gentlemen, please excuse us."

Both Rand and Makaio quickly exit the office, disappearing behind the closing elevator door, while Isa stands in the center of the room, her gaze downward.

In the silence between us, I scan over her, making sure not a single bruise mars her skin, the sight of which will trip my slowly budding temper. "Exciting night, as I understand."

The way her eyes shift, glassed over with tears, makes me wonder if Makaio left out something important.

"What happened?"

Instead of answering, she shakes her head, and the quiver of her lip raises the hairs on my neck. One thing I've learned about Isa in the last few weeks: she doesn't cry easily.

"They hurt you." I can hardly say the words past the clenching of my teeth, my body wound up to throw a fist through something, depending on her answer.

When she shakes her head, I exhale the rage on a shaky breath, mentally willing my muscles to ease up.

"Makaio arrived before anything happened," she finally says. "Your gift. It's a tracking device."

"It is."

"Why?"

"The answer is fairly obvious, I think."

"Why do you feel the need to keep track of me?"

Time for another drink.

I lean forward and pour the decanter into the awaiting glass. "Why do we put GPS on our phones. Our pets? Anything we don't want to get lost?"

The indignant expression on her face is a sure bet she doesn't like that answer. "Is that what I am? An object? A pet you don't want to run away?"

"I didn't embed it in you, Isa. It's a fucking bracelet."

"That you insisted I never take off."

If this night gets any worse, I might be inclined to buy a lottery ticket. Pushing up from the chair, I round the desk toward her. "You're angry. Shaken. You need to rest."

The second I reach out for her, she recoils, throwing her arm back like my fingertips are hot metal. "Don't you fucking touch me."

I lurch toward her, but she scampers back. Catching her arm, I yank her into me, holding her against me, as she squirms and pushes at my chest in a slightly humorous, yet failed, attempt to get away.

"Why did you run off?"

Another shove to my chest fails to break my grasp. "Why did you instruct Makaio to bring me back here? Are the weekends no longer my free time?"

"Not when one of my former employees was found dead in a motel room."

She stills at that, her eyes blazing with accusation as she stares up at me. "Did you kill her? Nell?" There isn't even a hint of apology this time, unlike when she asked about my son, which tells me she's really pissed off at me about the bracelet.

"No. I didn't. It seems the rumors are true this time. She overdosed."

"And what about Franco? Did you kill him?"

I study her eyes, searching for explanation into why she

suddenly has all these questions for me. What happened when she left the manor? Why did she run off? "No."

"No? You're lying to me, then?"

Tricky, this one. "No. I didn't kill him. Technically. Makaio did." Since the fight seems to be out of her at the moment, I loosen my grip, but don't yet release her. "He threatened to kill your mother and your aunt. Was I supposed to stand by and do nothing?"

"You could've given me the money. Struck a deal with me." She shoves at me again, this time with her teeth clenched and bared like a cornered little wolverine. "Instead, you're a murderer!"

"Now you're a saint? You didn't seem troubled to know he was out of your life when the threat was still alive in your head."

"I would never have asked you to kill on my behalf."

"Well, too fucking bad. Because that's what I do when someone threatens what's mine." Squeezing both of her arms, I give her a shake that's rougher than I intend, but hell if this girl hasn't wound me up all night with her antics. "I didn't ask for this, Isa. I kept my distance. I warned you to stay away from me. But you didn't. And now? You're going to find out just how protective I am over the things that belong to me."

"Belong to you? I never belonged to you. We made that clear in the beginning, remember?"

"No. I made it clear that I couldn't pursue a relationship with you. That doesn't mean I won't kill a bastard for laying his hands on you."

She flinches and twists her arms, trying to wriggle out of my grasp. "I don't need your protection!"

And I don't need to remind her of what happened tonight, proving she does. Not because I don't think she can take care of herself, but because she doesn't have a clue what she's up against, if Friedrich and the others find out about her.

Still frowning, she stops trying to break free. "I don't know who the hell is lying and who is telling the truth anymore."

"So, why don't you start paying attention to the facts."

Again, her eyes are like laser beams ready to split me down the center. "That you keep women as sex slaves? That everyone who works for you is terrified of you? That you have the power to silence what threatens you without repercussions? Which facts should I pay attention to, Lucian?"

I back her toward the couch, and with a small shove, she falls over the arm of the chair onto the cushions, where I cage her beneath me. I'm about a second away from muzzling this girl with my lips. "Nell overdosed on drugs. What more do you want me to say? What is it that you want?"

Lips peeled back, she looks like she would tear right through me if she could. "I want out of here. Nothing to do with this place. Nothing to do with *murderers*. Or *slavers*. Or you!"

My patience finally explodes. I grip tight to her jaw, breathing hard through my nose to keep the rising fury in check. "I'm not a murderer. And no woman has been kept here against her will." Eyes falling to her lips, I want more than anything to kiss her right now, but I'm certain she'd steal the opportunity to bite my fucking lip right off my face.

"Prove it. Let me go."

"You want to go? You want to leave?" The very thought of her leaving is like a punch to my chest. A hard, *steal-your-fucking-breath* punch that has my head spinning out of control, my muscles wound up in tight balls of rage.

"Yes."

Grinding my teeth, I stare back at her, urging myself to stay away from those lips. I release her face, and it takes every ounce of strength in my body to step away from her. "Fine. Makaio will drop you off first thing in the morning."

CHAPTER 55

ISADORA

The buzz of my cellphone rips me out of dreams, and I sit up in bed. Morning light shimmers through the curtains, while I wipe the sleep from my eyes and lift my phone to see a call from Aunt Midge. I texted her last night, letting her know I decided to stay the night at Kelsey's. I hate having to lie to her, but the truth will only make her worry.

"Hello?"

"Isa … you need to come home." Even through the phone, her voice carries the weight of grief and sends a shiver of goose-bumps across my skin.

"What is it? What's happened?"

"Your mother … she was found dead this morning. You need to come home."

Makaio closes the passenger door of the Bentley, and as he rounds the vehicle, I catch Lucian standing in the window of his office, staring down at me. Hands stuffed in the pockets of his slacks, he carries the same stern body language as when I first arrived, and I know he's angry with me. I didn't bother to say goodbye, or tell him about my mother.

There's no point.

My return to Aunt Midge is merely to be there for my aunt.

The news of my mother didn't exactly come as a surprise to me, seeing as I've waited nearly a decade for that call to come in. A person doesn't get to live that perilously without fate kicking in at some point. A part of me feels hollow and cold, empty inside, but not from the same sadness that will surely crush Aunt Midge over the coming days. Mine is a yearning. A craving to find some small piece of me that still gives a shit about something.

My disconnect with Lucian the night before was like snipping the only other thing that mattered to me, aside from my aunt. Now, I feel like I'm drifting. A flitting scrap caught up by the wind.

As the car pulls away, my heart withers inside my chest. For a fleeting moment, I was certain what I had with Lucian was real. That, for the first time in my life, I felt something genuine.

There is safety in Lucian, insofar as I'm willing to take a leap over the edge of a treacherous cliff to reach it. I should've known better than to get involved with a man like him—a deity of wrath and flames, when I'm nothing but a mortal, playing with fire.

I didn't grow up with the kind of power he wields, the kind that can eliminate threats and competition without consequence. The kind that can hunt down a dangerous drug dealer and bury him right under my nose. I was naive to think that he'd struck a deal with Franco, or paid him off. How foolish to imagine two predators could come to some mutual understanding that way.

Sharks don't compromise, they hunt to kill, and Lucian is one of the more cunning in this sea of corruption.

By the time we reach Aunt Midge's house, Makaio hasn't spoken a single word to me. I find myself torn between wanting to thank him for coming after me, when Aedon and Brady had me pinned down in the nasty park bathroom, and fearing him. Like Lucian, he's apparently quite capable of eliminating whatever gets in his way. And I certainly don't want to be the source of his wrath today.

I unclasp the bracelet and set it down on the console table beside me. When Makaio opens the door, I step out onto the sidewalk, and he reaches for the duffle bag in my hand. This time, I set a hand on his shoulder to stop him. "I've got it."

He eases back a step and rests his hand on the door, instead.

"Makaio ..." Words are hard for me. Words of thanks and appreciation are impossible. "If you hadn't shown up last night, I know that would've been a very bad situation. I had nightmares about what could've happened."

"I was told to protect you. The boss told me to keep you safe."

I shake my head, the few lingering pieces of confusion still kicking around in there, searching for answers. "Why? He couldn't have known they would attack."

"He isn't worried about them. Those shitheads are small potatoes."

"Then, who is he worried about?"

Casting his gaze from mine, the giant rolls his shoulders back. "Look, I've known Lucian a long time. Years. I've never seen him act this way toward another woman. Ever."

"What way?"

"He's crazy about you, Isa. Lost his mind, crazy. You should know, he won't just let you go that easily. He'll give you space for a while. But this isn't over for him."

"He'll change his mind when he understands that it's over for me. I can't be with a man who murders people like it's any other day. I don't care if they're bad people. It doesn't give him the right to take someone's life."

"We try to be civilized, us human beings, but ultimately, we're animals. All of us. And in the kingdom of animals, only the strongest survive."

I lower my gaze and shake my head. "His world isn't my world. Goodbye, Makaio."

"You take care of yourself."

I step past him and head toward the front door of the house. Hand to the doorknob, I watch him leave, and once he turns the corner, I open the door and find Aunt Midge sitting at the kitchen table, smoking a cigarette.

The whole house smells like tobacco and coffee, and my muscles tense with the thought that I'm going to have to slog through her sadness over my mother. I don't feel what she feels, and I don't want to.

I slide into the chair beside her. Her eyes are red and puffy, swollen from hours of crying, which has given rise to black circles. Unkempt hair sticks out around her face, the evidence of her having run her hands through it all morning. She looks like hell.

"I, um. Have to go ID the body later." She flicks her cigarette against the edge of the ashtray and takes another drag of it. "I guess a morning jogger found her on the beach beneath the pier. They think she might've gotten high and drowned."

With a sigh, I push away from the table and walk to the cupboard for a glass. From the fridge, I nab the carton of milk and pour some out, and keeping my back to Aunt Midge, I suck it down.

"That's it? That's all she gets from you?" The tension in her voice isn't really directed at me, I know this. She's angry and sad, and I'm going to be her emotional punching bag, the same way I was when Uncle Hal left her when I was fourteen.

"Are you really that surprised?"

Jaw cocked with a retort, she shakes her head. "You really are something, kid."

Setting the glass down, I grip the edge of the counter to keep from throwing *something* across the room. "I'm sorry, I'm supposed to *what*? Be sad that she destroyed our lives, then continued to destroy hers until the very end?"

More tears slip down her cheeks, her lips pressed to a hard line as she smashes her cigarette out into the ashtray. "He didn't want you. I know I'll probably go to hell for sayin' it, but it's the truth."

"What are you talking about?"

"Your dad." Wiping her tears away, she sniffs and clasps her hands together. "The rotten bastard didn't want you. She did, though. Whether you believe it, or not, she wanted you." Her eyes seem to go out of focus, as she stares off as if she's slipped into a scene in the past, and when her brows lower, I know it's a place she doesn't want to be, but I stay silent. Because I need to know. I've waited too long to hear this.

"If you would've asked her back then, she would've said she was in love with him. Maybe she was. They say there's a bit of mystery in all of that, and I believe it. She got pregnant with you. I remember the day she and I sat in the bathroom. I'd gone out and bought the test, because if my parents found out, they would've tossed her to the sharks, the next time my pop went out to sea." She laughs through the tears and shakes her head. "Not really, but she was scared, anyway. When the two lines showed up, I told her it could be wrong. I offered to take her to the clinic in town, have it confirmed before she said anything, because I knew lives were going to be ruined by this. Ruined." Exhaling a breath, she pauses for a moment, rubbing her hands together, before she reaches for her pack of cigarettes again. "Once it was confirmed, she decided to tell him. By then, I think she could've gone either way with the pregnancy. Kept it. Got rid of it. She didn't really have a plan." The way she recites, it's hard to believe she's talking about me, as detached as it sounds. "But she knew she wanted to talk to him. And when she did, he became furious. He called her a whore, and told her it could've been anyone's baby. And then he threatened her. He said, if she didn't destroy it, then he'd just have to do it himself." More tears gather in her eyes, as she taps the cigarette against the table, and at the sight of her, tears gather in my eyes, too. "Doesn't take a detective to read between the lines. But your mom … your mom was fire and brass balls, and she refused to destroy you. She was scared, though. Scared for you, and scared for herself, so she left the island. And she quickly found out how hard it is to be a single mother. By God, she tried, though. For a long time, she busted her ass to make a life for the two of you. But life never cut her a break, no matter how much she worked."

I trail my gaze over the walls to keep from having to look at her. To keep from showing the tears in my eyes. "Why didn't you tell me?"

"She didn't want me to. She thought it was better this way. Better for you, anyway. She, on the other hand? Didn't fare so well." Her voice cracks at the end, and it begins to make sense to me why Aunt Midge has always been so adamant, so uncompromising, when it comes to my mother.

"Who is he?"

Hand still trembling, she sets the cigarette to her lips, cheeks caving with a long drag, and she shakes her head. "I made a promise, Isa. She made me swear never to tell you."

"Please. I have to know."

Still shaking her head, she lowers her gaze from mine.

"You've kept every promise to her, Aunt Midge. Every single one. What does it matter now? She's dead!"

"It matters now, more than ever."

"Please. I'm begging you."

Silence hangs on the air between us, my impatience growing stronger with each ticking second.

"Why would she bring me back here? Don't you think that's a little stupid of her?"

"She didn't have a choice. Believe me, she wouldn't have."

"So, why did she, if it's so dangerous?"

Brows pinching together, she looks up at me as if she can't believe I'd ask such a thing. "You honestly don't remember anything?"

"About what?"

Breathing a sigh, she shakes her head. "You're asking me to open too many cans at once, Isa."

"And you're still holding all the worms. Give me something. Anything. I've spent my whole life believing my mother was a piece-of-shit junkie, and you're trying to tell me she's not. I need to know what made her come back here. What made her risk bringing me back to the man who wanted to destroy me."

"Does *Uncle George* ring a bell?"

No sooner do the words pass her lips than they unlock thoughts inside my head, images, like a skeleton key.

A child holding a glowing heart. Darkness all around. The child's face practically glowing. It's sad eyes. Gentle hands. A red heart. Deep breaths. Red. Everywhere.

My mind falls into a trance, pulling me into the memory. "I called him Uncle George. He was ... Aunt Tessa's husband."

"She wasn't really your aunt. She watched you when your ma had to work, or when she went out. An older woman who lived in the neighborhood. Your mom trusted her."

"I woke up in the middle of the night. Somebody was whispering in my ear. I saw a picture of a child on the wall ... holding a glowing heart." The memories arrive faster, more vivid, and I shake my head. "No, not a child. It's a man. Jesus, maybe?"

"Yes, Jesus's Sacred Heart. Your mother told me she was very religious. Keep going."

"He told me ... to relax. That my mom wasn't coming to pick me up. That it was just me and Uncle George hanging out." A coldness fills my chest, the crystal branches of fear crawling out from somewhere deep inside my gut. "He put his hand ... on my stomach. And down my pants." I screw my eyes shut, as if doing so can block out the memory that continues to play behind my lids. "I screamed, and he told me that if anyone heard me, he'd have to hurt them. I remember the pain. So much pain that I blacked out from it." I exhale a shaky breath, and open my eyes to find Aunt Midge staring back at me with more tears in her eyes. "When I woke up, there was blood everywhere. So much blood. And my mom, she was there, and she picked me up into her arms." Voice cracking, I break into tears. "She said, '*It's going to be okay, baby*', and I looked over, and he had blood on his throat and all over his hands."

"She got into her car, and she drove for miles, until she arrived here on this island. When she brought you to me, you still had his blood all over you. Uncle Hal and I took you in, and I washed it off and wrapped you in a blanket, just holding you while your mom broke down." She sniffs and wipes the freshly fallen tears away, while mine sit trapped in a jiggling shield across my eyes. "She told me she had to leave you with me. And she made me promise to protect you. To never tell you who your father really is."

She reaches out a hand, setting it on my arm, and as she grabs something from her purse that's hanging off the edge of the chair and slides it in front of me, the tears finally break. All of my school pictures lay in a pile atop a large picture of my mom and me when I was small, maybe five years old. She's smiling and pointing at the camera, her face healthy and lit up, framed by those fiery red locks.

"I gathered these this morning. From where she was camped under the viaduct. I'm no mother, so I'm certainly no expert on what makes a good, or bad mom. But one thing I know for sure is, she loved you. As much as a drug addict can love, she loved you."

I finally break down and feel Aunt Midge's arms wrap around me, drawing me into a hug. "I said horrible things to her. And now she'll never know how sorry I am."

"She knows, baby. She knows."

CHAPTER 56

LUCIAN

I swirl my drink in the glass, staring at the empty bed on camera. Teeth grinding in my skull, I recall her last words before she left. *Let me go.* They echo the night Amelia dangled from my arm, trying to pry my fingers loose.

I chuck the glass across the room, and it shatters against the wall. "Fuck!"

What the hell was I thinking, getting involved with this girl? I knew the consequences of falling for an unbridled thing like Isa. A young, sassy, package of poke-my-eyeballs-out-with-a-chopstick kind of girl. Like trying to contain a hurricane inside of a test tube. She's whipping winds and half-torn rooftops, treacherous waves and dangerous undertows, and I can't fucking get enough of her, for some reason. I don't know if I'm a weatherman at heart, or a bona fide masochist who loves the torment.

The elevator dings, and Rand steps out, staring down at the broken pieces of glass as he skirts around them on his way to my desk. He lays the bracelet I gave Isa across the desktop, and my hand balls into a fist at the sight of it.

"I've gotten word that another dead body was found this

morning," he says, taking a step back and crossing his hands in front of him. "Another drug overdose, it seems."

"And why do I care?"

"It was the body of Jenny Quinn. Isa's mother."

Easing back into my chair, I stroke my jaw in thought. "She never said anything when she left."

"No, I suppose she wouldn't."

"Any connection to Nell? Any similarities?"

"Just that a needle was found lodged into her arm. Heroin is suspected with her, as well. Though, as I understand, Isa's mother has been an addict for quite some time. I suppose there wouldn't be anything unusual about that."

"Any word on Isa? How she's doing?"

"Nothing, I'm afraid."

I push to my feet and tuck my cellphone into my pocket.

"Master … perhaps a couple days might be in order. To let her mourn, and all that."

I've made a point of ignoring Rand's advice over the last couple of years, since my father's passing, finding his council mostly useless, but perhaps he's right on this one. Maybe she needs time. "I'd like to attend the funeral. As soon as it's known, make me aware of the date and time."

"Absolutely."

"And, Rand, what are your thoughts about this? Coincidence?"

"It's hard to say. I don't see any reason someone would go after Isa."

"Unless that someone knew what she meant to me."

"True, but the only one who might have motive is Stefano Scarpinato, and he seemed relatively appeased by your offer, when we met."

It so happens, Rand isn't privy to the meeting I had with Friedrich. I haven't dismissed the possibility that the cocksucker is testing me, and if that's the case, he'll have more than a lack of funding to make his asshole pucker.

"Makaio tells me her attackers in the park were the two who gave her trouble a few months back at that party. I want to keep an eye on her."

"I'll dispatch Makaio at once."

"No. She snuck away that night to *avoid* Makaio. I don't need her running off, the moment she catches sight of him. And let's face it, Makaio blends in like a clown at a funeral."

"Should I look into hiring someone?"

Twiddling my thumbs, I chew the inside of my lip in thought. "Yes. I think it's time we have a chat with our private investigator friend."

"Mr. Goodman? I'm not sure that's a good idea, Master."

"Neither was killing Franco, but I did it, anyway."

CHAPTER 57

ISADORA

I hate funerals. If I was a grief eater, I could feast all day on the sadness and misery that comes with being forced to stare at a casket. Why do we do this to ourselves? Why do we prolong the anguish by shoving our faces in it for a full day?

Is it supposed to make it easier? Do we reach a point where we're so sick of staring back at a lifeless body that we accept death?

My mother lies in a casket, surrounded in white silk and flowers. Four-dozen roses sit in pots on the floor around her, which I'm guessing came from Lucian, though the attached card was signed *A Friend*. Her long red hair has been curled, the tracks on her arms covered in thick makeup. That's the other thing about funerals: they lie. If they were about truth, my mother would lying in a cardboard box, her hair half-cocked in a greasy ponytail, with a bunch of used needles around her.

Aunt Midge opted for an emerald dress that makes her look like the doll encased in Laura's collection.

Something that isn't real.

Her complexion, glowing and perfect, as if the drugs never even touched her blood. The pictures Aunt Midge gathered lie about her body, and I focus on the one of her and me, as the pastor rattles off some scripture I couldn't begin to understand.

I opted not to give a eulogy, and instead wrote a letter for my mother, to be burned with her ashes. Speaking in crowds was never my thing to begin with, but being asked to share thoughts and feelings about a mother I spent most of my life despising isn't something I care to eulogize, at all.

Only a handful of people show up, mostly the guys from the bar where Aunt Midge works, who came out to support her. Taking my hand in hers, Aunt Midge sobs into a tissue, as we watch the others pay their final respects. The woman must be an endless reservoir of tears. At some point, it has to dry out, and perhaps that's where I'm at. It must look strange that I'm the only one at the funeral whose eyes are dry as a bone.

I need air.

Desperately.

This place is suffocating.

Smothering me.

Aunt Midge gives a squeeze of my hand, sending another round of panic shooting into my chest. An oncoming anxiety attack, I bet. I suffered them frequently after the attack of Aedon and Brady, and the tightness in my chest, the spinning of the room, serve as warning signs of another episode.

Mac stumbles over to the two of us, undoubtedly drunk, and plants a kiss on the top of my forehead. As he wraps Aunt Midge in a whiskey-scented hug, I set my palm on hers.

"I'm going to get some fresh air."

"Okay, sweetheart," she says, her voice muffled by Mac's embrace.

How she can stand it right now, I don't know. I'll probably hyperventilate if someone tries to hug me, which is a good reason to walk away. This is when the hugs begin. When the sorry's and memories and regrets pour out of everyone like a river of sorrows.

Breathing hard through my nose, I exit the showing room, down the hallway, through the foyer, and out the front door of the funeral home. Gripping the staircase handrail, I suck in deep breaths in an effort to calm my pounding heart.

Breathe, Isa. Just breathe.

Opening my eyes on a long exhale, I find a familiar face standing before me.

"Hey there, Isa." Mayor Boyd stands with one foot propped on the staircase, his hand resting on his thigh. "How are you?"

"I'm good. What are you doing here?"

"I just, uh … I saw in the paper that Jenny passed. She was a student of mine. Back when I taught high school." As he talks, my mind replays the pictures of him I found in my mom's yearbook. "Haven't seen her in … decades."

"She moved around a lot."

"Yeah. I heard that."

An awkward pause hangs between us, and I hike my thumb over my shoulder. "You want to … go inside? The service is over. Everyone's just doing the final respects thing."

"No, no. I don't want to intrude. I am curious, though. How do you …. How did you know her?"

"She was my mother."

"Your mother?" There's an edge of surprise in his tone, and he clears his throat, adjusting his glasses. "That's interesting. I don't suppose she had anything good to say about her favorite government teacher." The laugh that follows is goofy and awkward, and somehow inappropriate for the mood.

"Um. We didn't get along very well when she was alive."

"Ah, that's too bad." He rolls his shoulders back and clears his throat again. "Say, I don't suppose we could--"

"Hello, Isa." The voice that interrupts is a deep rich sound that tickles my ear, and I lift my gaze past Boyd, to where Lucian stands behind him. Decked out in a perfectly tailored, crisp, black suit, he's almost hard to look at, and my body instinctively responds, in spite of the bad terms we left on. Tucked in the pocket of his suit is a black rose that's actually fitting for Lucian. Even at a funeral, though, he doesn't belong in this town.

Boyd cranes his neck, and in doing so, stumbles back a step, chuckling as he catches himself. "Well, speak of the devil ..."

I frown at that, not recalling any mention of Lucian in our conversation.

With one hand shoved in the pocket of his slacks, Lucian steps toward me, his other hand running across a day's worth of stubble that draws my eyes toward the scar at his jaw. My heart literally aches at the sight of him.

"I'll just ... let the two of you have a moment of privacy." Boyd steps down onto the sidewalk, twitchy and rolling his shoulders back, like he's uncomfortable around the looming darkness that stands behind him. "Isa, we'll catch up later."

Ignoring him, I keep my eyes on Lucian, as he ascends the staircase. "What are you doing here?"

"I heard about your mother. I wanted to make sure you're okay."

Crossing my arms, I peel my gaze away from him, noticing his car at the curb. The same car we almost had sex in, when I swore Lucian Blackthorne was the most incredible human being I'd ever met in my life. "I'm fine. I take it the roses were from you?"

"Yes. You look good."

"It's only been a week since I saw you last."

"And I've thought about you every minute of every day since. It's fucking maddening, the way you've infected my brain."

I don't bother to tell him that every night I've awakened in cold sweats, calling out his name. I've imagined his hands on me, his lips on mine, the lack of breath, the pounding of my heart, all the chaos that explodes around me when I think of him.

"Yeah, well. Too bad I don't have a clue who the hell you really are." I spin around to leave, but at the tight grip of my arm, twist to face him. "Let me go."

"You're the only person in the world who really knows me." He gives a sharp tug that yanks me forward, and I fall into him. "Everything I've shown you is what I am."

"I want to believe that. Believe me. I want to think I'm the only girl who cracked the Devil of Bonesalt. But I don't think you're that stupid, Lucian. I don't think you're that careless, to let some local girl into your world."

He doesn't respond to that, and instead traces a finger down my temple, his touch almost unbearable, as much as I've missed it. "I want you to come back. Come back to me."

He cups my face and plants a kiss to my forehead, and I swear it takes every ounce of strength not to wrap my arms around him and get lost in his embrace. I want to, so badly. These last few days, I've felt lost, drifting. I've yearned for someone to pull my strings and ground me, to hold me down and keep me from losing myself.

"Whatever you need, just ask and it's done," he says.

"I need time." I've spent the last few days convincing myself that Lucian killed Franco simply to protect me, without any other motive. That he isn't the devil who tortures people for pleasure. "And answers."

"Fair enough. I'll give you time. But this thing between us? It's happening, Isa."

"We'll see." I glance back toward the funeral home, where I can see movement through the window of the viewing room. "I better get back."

"I'll be in touch." Taking hold of my chin, he presses his lips to mine, and my head prods me to hang on tight and not let go. Instead, I break the kiss and step away, and if I thought my head was spinning before, I've gone full-on tilt-a-whirl.

He descends the staircase, the ease of his stroll like a man who can show up to a funeral without a care in the world, and leave as if he's stolen the last sip of air.

I want to follow after him with blinders to what I've become privy to--the lies and truth that clash inside my head.

I turn around and head back inside the funeral home.

The ashes of my mother fill the urn that sits on my lap, while Aunt Midge drives us back to the house.

"She would've hated every second of that, your mother. Not one for attention." Tears still weigh heavy in her voice, like she might break again.

"I never liked the attention, either."

"You'd be surprised how much the two of you had in common."

"Like what?"

"Piano, for one."

I frown at that, staring down at the brass urn. "My mother played?"

"She sang and played and danced, and was smart and athletic. She was everything I wasn't, and I spent years battling the jealousy."

"Is that why you kept letting her in? Why you couldn't turn her away?"

Staring toward the windshield, she shakes her head. "When you love someone, it's hard to *unlove* them. They make mistakes, they do things you hate, things you don't agree with, things that drive you absolutely mad, but when it comes down to it? You still love them. You can't help it. I suppose that's why I never really grasped the concept of Hell and the devil. The idea that God, or Jesus could turn his back on the ones he loves so much, just doesn't make sense to me. Even if you murdered someone, Isa. I might be deeply disappointed, but to stop loving you? That'd be impossible."

Her words somehow penetrate deeper than ever before, and I can't help but think of Lucian.

"Aunt Midge, if I did something terrible, but I did it to protect you, could you forgive that?"

"Did you do something terrible?"

"No. It's just a hypothetical."

"Of course I'd forgive you. That's what I mean. There is nothing stronger than love."

I wonder, if she knew that I was talking about Lucian, would she answer differently. "How do you know if you love someone?"

She glances down at the urn in my lap and back to the road. "When you try to imagine a world without that person, and can't, then you know it's love."

For a week, I've tried to forget about Lucian, and I can't. I've tried to ignore the images of his face. The sound of his voice. The smell of his skin.

I can't, and it physically aches to think that I may never see him again, in spite of what he says.

We arrive back at the house, where a strange car sits parked at the curb. I peer through the driver's side window at Mr. Goodman, who waves back at me.

"What the hell is this?" Aunt Midge says beside me. "How'd he find out where I live?"

"He's an investigator. It's what he does."

"Or did you tell him."

"I didn't." Once the car rolls to a stop in the driveway, I climb out and hand the urn off to Aunt Midge. "I'll just be a minute."

"This guy gives you trouble? Scream."

"I will." I wait for her to hobble inside the house before making my way toward the car. "If you're looking for the yearbook, I lost it."

"I understand. No need to trouble yourself. I just felt that, with the information you were so willing to give, I owe you this." He holds the envelope out toward me. "For what it's worth."

471

Staring down at the package, I hesitate a moment, before snatching it out of his hands, anxious that he might change his mind.

"I heard about your mother, and I'm sorry for your loss."

"Thank you. What is it you were looking for in the yearbook?"

"Proof."

"Of what?"

"That your mother could've possibly come in contact with the devil himself."

Frowning, I stare back at him with an even stronger need to know what's inside.

I open the envelope and slide out the document contained within. Unfolding it reveals the intake form, which looks like it was written in my mother's handwriting. Eyes scanning down the page, I find the field I've searched for my whole life. The one that reveals who my father really is. The one she intentionally left blank on my birth certificate.

Sickness churns in my stomach as I stare at the name scrawled across the page there.

Patrick Boyd.

CHAPTER 58

LUCIAN

I've come to the understanding that everything in life comes down to a rule of threes.

For me, the rules have always been simple:

Never give into temptation

Never show your cards

Don't fall in love

With Isa, I broke all three. At least, I'm fairly certain I did. I've never actually felt this kind of love before, but I figure wanting to kill anything and everything that comes within close proximity of her must count for something.

And seeing Boyd approach her at the funeral home somehow whisked up an inexplicable rage inside me. As irrational as it may sound, I could've easily snapped my former father-in-law's neck like a dandelion, for being so close to her.

I stroll up to the park bench, flicking away my half-smoked cigarette, and take a seat opposite the man at the other end. Staring out over the sea, I drink in a moment of peace before the shit-storm of questions begins.

"Thank you for reaching out to me, Mr. Blackthorne."

"I didn't. My associate reached out to you."

"Yes, Mr. Rand?" He clears his throat, shifting on the seat as if he's got a bad case of hemorrhoids. The guy reminds me of a cross between a true gumshoe and the lonely IT worker who masturbates to tentacle porn, decked out in his short sleeve plaid shirt and gray chinos.

"I'm a private investigator--"

"I already know who you are, and what you're looking for."

"And you agreed to this meeting?"

I keep my gaze ahead, not bothering to give him the satisfaction of staring at my scars. "I have my reasons for doing so."

"Fine. I won't waste your time with formalities. I want to know who the members of Schadenfreude are."

"No you don't."

"Excuse me?"

"Knowing puts you at grave risk. Consider it a favor that I keep you in the dark. By telling you, I'll essentially place a big-ass bullseye on your back, and all that hard work you've put into this case? Gone." Lips pressed to a hard line, I shake my head. "I'm not naming members."

"Okay. Then, what is your role?"

"My role is obscure. I'm neither subscribed to their philosophies, nor bound by their laws. I'm a floating entity, tied only to them through a long lineage of loyal membership and shitty genetics."

"You're saying you don't agree with them, but you follow them, anyway."

"If that blows your skirt up, then I guess that's what I'm saying."

The sound of him huffing is laughable, like a toddler who's been denied candy. Even if he has a clue what the group was about, there's a skyscraper of an iceberg beneath the surface that'll take him decades to chip away. "You agreed to this meeting for an exchange of information, and so far you've given me nothing."

"Perhaps because that's exactly what you're searching for. Air. A void. The pause of an inhale. The space between one sentence and the next. Even if I gave you all the information you're looking for, you'd never find them. They've spent years perfecting the art of hiding what they are."

"Okay ..." He shakes his head with a mirthless chuckle. "What's the point of this, then?"

"I'm glad you finally asked. The real puzzle in all of this is what happens to Isa."

"Isa? What about her? What does she have to do with Schadenfreude?"

"Or better, what *doesn't* she have to do with it?" A quick glimpse at him, and I cast my gaze back toward the endless sea. "The future of this collective lies with me. When I'm gone, they have no funding. No research. No validity to their bullshit."

"Yet, you don't subscribe to their methods, at all."

"Have you been paying attention, Mr. Goodman?" A sailboat sits on the edge of the horizon, nothing but a dot on the line. A point of convergence. Reference. Direction in a vast sea. The more I stare at it, the more it seems to encapsulate my thoughts. "Beyond Isa Quinn is a black void for me. A point on the horizon that I can't see past. If you want answers, I suggest you pay close attention to her."

A beat of silence follows, before he clears his throat. "Are you asking me to follow her?"

"I *insist* you follow her."

"To what end? You haven't given me anything valuable."

"I have. By admitting what's most valuable to me. But if that's not enough, I'm willing to double whatever you're currently being paid to be a pain in my ass."

He snorts and rubs his forehead, as if a headache is blooming there. "Fine. You consider her valuable. Then, I'll keep a close watch on her."

"Good. And should you need to contact me, here is where you can reach me directly." I slide a business card across the bench, which he accepts by sliding it toward him.

"Thank you, Mr. Blackthorne. I'll be in touch."

CHAPTER 59

ISADORA

The small Tupperware container filled with my mother's ashes sits in the sand beside me, as I tip back a bottle of Boone's Farm I stole from Aunt Midge's stash.

I've taken just a small bit of the ashes to scatter into the ocean, the one place I know my mom would love to be. The spot is a small cove where Aunt Midge brought me to swim, when I first arrived in Tempest. Away from all the tourists and meddling eyes, a small piece of heaven that belonged only to us.

"Do you remember the night, when I was eight years old, you and I ran down to the ocean? We plopped in the sand, and you let me try strawberry Boone's for the first time. You told me it was your favorite, because it reminded you of hot summer nights and sunsets in Tempest Cove. And afterward, we stripped down to our underwear and jumped into the waves for a night swim." Staring into the bottle of pink alcohol, I smile. "I think that was my favorite moment with you." The setting sun casts vibrant colors over the surface, as I tip back a sip of the drink and slam the bottle into the sand beside me.

I swipe up the container of ashes and dig open the lid, careful not to spill any of the contents prematurely. With my blue jeans rolled up to my calves, I wade into the water, letting the waves crash against my ankles. Arm outstretched away from me, I sprinkle the ashes into the shallow waters around me, and watch as they gather on the surface, the bigger fragments sinking to the sand.

In seconds, a school of tiny minnows gathers around me, nibbling up the small ashes of my mother's remains.

The fucking fish are eating her.

Within minutes, I'm surrounded by small fish feeding off the tiny bits still floating around, and laughter cracks through my chest. I bend forward, laughing so hard, I'm afraid I might piss myself. For five straight minutes, the hysterical laughter pounds through me, and I let it take me under.

Mom would've laughed, too, I'm certain of it. If there's one thing we did share, it was humor for the macabre. Dark humor, for which she was bold enough to laugh when others might keep quiet. Perhaps that's one thing I loved about her.

In seconds, the dust of her remains is consumed, and the school disperses back out into the deeper waters.

Sighing, I stare out over the ocean, thinking how incredible it would be to end up in the tiny bellies of fish. To forever be part of the sea.

About three quarters of the bottle remains, and I toss what's left in one of the nearby trashcans, then gather up my shoes from the sand. For the last hour, I've sat here, contemplating what to do next, now that I hold all the missing pieces to the puzzle.

Back when my mother was pregnant with me, Boyd was apparently working toward his first run as mayor. He had a wife, a daughter, an entire life built around the facade of a well-respected man. An affair with one of his students who ended up pregnant would've blown all of that to bits. It would've annihilated his opportunities in politics, and possibly his marriage at the time.

But what about now?

With his wife having left him, his career destroyed by some scandal Aunt Midge told me about, and his daughter dead, would he still feel the same hatred toward me? Would I still be unwelcomed?

Would I even bother with a man who once threatened my mother to destroy me?

I walk along the path toward the house, the warm sea air leaving a saline mist across my face. At the sound of an engine, I turn to see a vehicle slowing alongside me. Inside, Patrick Boyd stares back at me, his smile bright and friendly, as usual.

I wonder if he knows who I am. If he recognizes himself in me.

"Need a lift?" he asks through the rolled-down window.

"No, I'm just heading back to Aunt Midge's. Thanks, though."

The car comes to a stop, which brings me to a stop, and I turn to see him climb out of the vehicle.

"Isa, we need to talk." The tone of his voice has changed and carries an edge of confession. It's vastly different from the man I've met on a few occasions. One clearly versed in polish and veneer. "I know … who you are. What we are. And I just want to say, I was such a stupid, selfish bastard back then." Coming around the car, he folds his arms over his chest and leans against the hood. "I was scared, and your mom … she was so young. But so incredibly beautiful and smart and funny." Smiling, he stares off like he's lost in the thought. "But we were wrong together. Still, I shouldn't have scared her away. I feel like everything that happened was my fault. And I want to make things right with you."

There's a part of me, a niggling sensation that tells me to run away, but it gets tamped down by the authenticity of his voice. It's unnerving how genuine this sounds to me.

I'm a girl from the streets, though. And I always go with my gut.

"How did you know I was here?"

"Your aunt told me where to find you."

Bullshit. Aunt Midge wouldn't have told an FBI agent where to find me, let alone this guy. "Look, I really need to get back. Aunt Midge is waiting for me. She's got lunch planned."

"I'd love to give you a ride and talk more on the way."

"I appreciate it, but I need some time to process everything." I don't even realize I'm backing away from him at first, until the guardrail hits my leg.

Lips pressed together, he nods. "Of course you do." He reaches behind his back, and something flips inside my head. A warning.

Run.

I twist on the ball of my foot, and dart forward.

A *pop* sounds behind me, and pain explodes in my ankle, white hot streaks of it climbing my leg. A throaty scream rips from my chest as I collapse to the ground, and I pull my knees up to find blood seeping out of a dark red hole, where a small bit of white peeks out. Every muscle in my body is shaking on a rush of adrenaline, while I watch the blood trickle down my skin to be wicked away by the sand. Nausea gurgles in my stomach, my hands cold and clammy, and I swallow it back the bile that rises to my throat. "Oh, God, oh, God, oh, God."

At the sound of approaching footsteps, I crawl toward the opposite direction, kicking away from him with my one good foot. "Somebody, help me!" Fingernails digging into the sand, I pull myself along, my body burning with urgency.

"I'm sorry, I didn't want to do that. But I had no choice. You're as stubborn as your mother." He reaches down into my pants pocket, sliding out my cellphone, and pitches it toward the ocean.

Arms snake beneath mine, and when he tries to lift me up, I

scratch at his skin and scream again. "Please, somebody, help me!"

There's nobody here. Nothing but cliffs, and the soft rustle of trees over the distant crashing of waves.

This is where I'm going to die. Fish food, just like my mother.

"Freeze, or I swear to God, I'll pull the trigger." Relief bursts inside of me at the sound of familiarity and I turn to see Mr. Goodman pointing his gun at Boyd. "N-now get down on your knees, and p-p-put your hands behind your back. Where I can see them."

Eyes brimming with malice, Boyd keeps his gaze on mine, as he releases me and lowers to his knees.

I kick away from him over as much distance as I can, and whimper when the pain of the bullet flares to life inside my ankle.

"Pressure, Isa. Put p-p-pressure on it." Mr. Goodman takes his eyes off Boyd for a split second to glance down at my ankle, and that's when Boyd twists like a snake, tossing a dust cloud of sand into the air. "Ah, shit!" Eyes clamped shut, Mr. Goodman stumbles backward. "Run, Isa!"

Dread ruptures inside of me again, and I roll onto my belly, pushing to my feet.

A piercing scream echoes behind me that's quickly cut short, followed by a thud.

Don't look back, my head tells me, as I hobble over the guardrail, down the sandy incline. The agony throbs in my ankle, air burns in my chest. There's nowhere to hide. Only the endless sand and dunes for miles, but I keep on, trudging over the soft surface that kicks up into my wound. A crashing sound from behind has me skidding to a halt, and I turn to see Boyd's car barreling toward me through the sand.

Oh, my fucking God!

Screams tear through me, echoing in my ear, and I limp forward, desperate to ignore the agonizing pain with every step. My feet tangle beneath me, and the earth crashes into my face.

The car comes to a stop, and I scramble to get back to my feet. Once upright, my foot flies out from beneath me and my shoulder smacks into the sand. The gritty surface scrapes across my skin as my body is dragged backwards, and I kick out, the pain shooting through my ankle the moment it makes contact.

"Ah, fuck!" I cry out, and Boyd gathers up both of my legs, pulling me by my calves. I grapple for something to hang on to, but only soft sand slips around my fingers. Grabbing a handful of it, I toss it at him, employing the same method he used on Mr. Goodman, but he turns, dragging me behind him.

Once alongside his car, he releases my legs.

Pushing to my elbows, I sit up from the ground to flip over, and a flash out of the corner of my eye is the only warning before a knock to my jaw rattles my teeth. Another hit kicks my head to the side, and I lie disoriented, staring at my reflection in the chrome hubcap beside me.

Jaw throbbing, I blink hard to focus.

"I'll give you this, you young bitches don't go down easy. Last one didn't, either."

He killed Nell. It wasn't Lucian, or Schadenfreude. It was my father.

The world shrinks to a pinprick and swallows me whole.

CHAPTER 60

LUCIAN

My phone buzzes, and I glance down, frowning to see Friedrich's phone number flashing across the screen. It's rare that he calls my phone for anything, so I'm guessing this is important. I answer it on the third ring.

"Lucian, I just got off the phone with our contact, who has been in touch with Mr. Boyd. It seems you were wrong about his offspring. There is one illegitimate child who might prove to be of some interest to our study."

Doesn't surprise me. Boyd had a number of affairs during the course of his marriage. Probably got a prostitute knocked up. "And what does this mean now?" I ask.

"It means he might be worth considering, given his background. She appears to be young but has a bit of a history herself. Her mother was a student of his, who apparently passed away just recently."

A student of Boyd's. Local girl, then. "Who is it, if you don't mind my asking?"

"Her name is Isadora Quinn. I'd like to bring her to the Institute. Run some tests on her. At the very least, prove his paternity."

Motherfuck, fuck. Muscles burning with tension, I curl my hand to a tight fist at the thought at the thought of Friedrich getting his hands on Isa. They'll lock her up and study her like a guinea pig, like they did me, or worse, like Melody Lachlan, rocking in the corner with a pile of dead birds on the floor. "Do you have her now?"

"No. Not at the moment. He mentioned that he'll get back to us after he's had the opportunity to talk to the girl. In the meantime, I've dispatched someone to Tempest Cove to retrieve her once we hear back."

"And you've not heard back from him yet?"

"No. Not yet. I suspect he's meeting with her, as we speak."

Meeting with her. In contact with her. I'll kill the prick myself. "And you don't happen to know where?"

"No. Unfortunately, I don't."

Rubbing a hand down my face, I inwardly groan. "Thank you for the update, Friedrich. I look forward to hearing from you."

"Of course."

I hang up the phone and dial Rand's phone number, not even giving him the opportunity to greet me when he answers. "I need Mr. Goodman's contact number. Now."

"Yes, of course. Would you like me to get in touch with him?"

"No! I need the number now!"

As he rattles it off, I jot it down onto a sheet of paper from my desk, and as soon as I have it, I click out of the call.

I dial the number.

It rings and rings.

No answer.

I dial it again.

It rings and rings.

"Fuck!" Adrenaline courses through me, and I shoot out of my chair, scrolling through the apps on my phone. I click on the tracker app linked to Isa's bracelet that I handed off to the investigator at the end of our meeting. The blinking dot skates along State Rd. like the asshole is in transit.

At the ding of the elevator, I lift my attention to Rand, who shuffles across the room, into my office. "You sounded distressed, Master. Is everything okay?"

"No, it's not fucking okay." From my desk drawer, I lift the gun stored there and pop the magazine to find it packed with bullets. Stuffing the weapon into my pants, I swipe up my phone from the desk, watching his eyes widen. "Friedrich called. They've taken an interest in Isa."

"Whatever for?"

"She's apparently my sister-in-law. Go fucking figure." I round the desk and stride toward the elevator. "How did our contact miss that little detail?"

"Her birth certificate didn't list a father," he says after me, when I pass. "Master, I'll have Makaio fetch the car."

"He's welcome to follow me, but I need something faster."

CHAPTER 61

ISADORA

An earthy scent pervades my senses, until I can practically taste it on my tongue, as I blink out of the black void. A hard thump rattles me awake, and I open my eyes to the surrounding darkness of trees, beyond the halo that shines down from a floodlight overhead, the grit of dirt pressing into my cheek.

Confusion hangs like a thick cloud inside my head that's throbbing with an intense ache. I squint my eyes against the pain and attempt to raise my hand, which doesn't move. Stretched behind my back, both arms are bound together by a band of rope, or something, that bites into my wrists. Moving my legs proves equally impossible, and I stare down myself to find white nylon cord tied around my ankles.

Panic settles over me, my muscles cold and stiff.

Another thump reaches my ear from behind, and I twist over top of my bound arms to find Boyd slamming a shovel into the ground, the mound of dirt beside him telling of a hole he's dug.

A scream cracks through my chest, and I squirm and tug at my arms to get loose. "Somebody! Somebody, help me!"

In the pause, Boyd raises the dirt-filled shovel on a grunt and tosses it onto the mound. "Scream as much as you want. No one can hear you out here."

Another scream tears out of me, louder than before. And another. I scream for what feels like minutes, until my voice is hoarse and a cough sputters in my throat.

"Told you. No one can hear you."

Still caught up in a spell, I turn into the ground, gasping for a breath. "Why ... are you ... doing this?"

He jabs the shovel into the earth and, with his shirtsleeves rolled up, wipes his arm across his forehead. "Tell me, Isa. Do you know anything about politics?" he asks, striding toward the trunk of his car. Popping it open, he peers inside for a moment, and swings his gaze toward me, as if he expects me to answer.

Instead, I remain silent.

"It's the most intense game I've ever played in my life. A dirty match between you and the public. Every move dictates whether you ultimately win, or lose, and there is no room for error, because let's face it, people are fucking unforgiving pricks." He reaches into the trunk and hauls the private investigator up onto the edge of it. The sight of his lifeless, glassy eyes staring back at me, while half his body hangs out of the trunk, sends a wave of nausea to my stomach. Boyd rolls his body over the side, and it topples to the dirt below. "When your mother told me about you all those years ago, I was on a winning streak. Perhaps the best years of my life. If I'm being honest." Hooking his arms beneath the investigator, he drags him toward the awaiting hole he's dug.

Behind my back, I curl my fingers over the rope, my fingertips in search of the knot to loosen.

Dropping him alongside the shallow grave, Boyd remains bent, hands on his thighs, as if to catch his breath. "Finding out she was pregnant was like someone knocking me out of the game. This town would never forgive the beloved teacher and coach and future mayor who fucked his student and knocked her up."

"Maybe you should've thought of that before you put your dirty hands on her."

Chuckling, he kneels down and shoves at the investigator, pushing him into the hole. "I've always had a thing for young pussy. Tight, pink, sometimes bare. It's always been my kryptonite. The one vice I couldn't give up, if I tried." He nabs the shovel from beside him, while a cramp settles in my fingers as I scrape my nails over the too-tight knot of my binds. "I remember the first time I cornered her in the locker room. It was after practice. She always waited to change until after the other girls left." Lifting the dirt from the mound beside him, he drops it onto the private investigator's body. "Being more developed, she was always ... self-conscious. With good ... reason." His voice is broken by the toil, as he buries his victim. "Her tits ... looked like implants ... so perfect."

"You're sick. And fucking disgusting!"

Pausing, he straightens and smiles back at me. "Am I? Seems your beau likes young pussy, as well. He's not much younger than I was, in fact."

He also wasn't my teacher and coach, and I'm not sixteen years old, but I don't bother to argue with this crazy asshole.

"Not that I blame him ..." Shovel piled high with dirt, he grunts as he dumps the last bit into the hole. "If you weren't my daughter, I'd be all over that tight little ass of yours, too."

The thought of that sends bile up my throat, and I have to press my lips together to keep from throwing up.

Eyes on the grave, I breathe hard through my nose to calm the hysteria itching to break free. "What do you plan to do with me?"

He tosses the shovel towards the woods and rubs his hands together. "You're my ticket to power. Ironic, isn't it? The daughter who nearly ruined my career is the only one who can save it now."

"How?"

"When you're knocked out of the political arena, and the

fickle crowd shuns you, the only thing that can put you back in the game is money and power. At the moment? I have neither." Setting his hands on his hips, he inhales and exhales deeply, glancing around. "This used to be my domain. My kingdom. And now it isn't. But with the right connections, and power in my corner, I can own this whole fucking state. And Lucian Black-thorne, for that matter."

"What does this have to do with me?"

"I happen to know someone who will be very interested in meeting you."

My heart hammers inside my chest when he stares back at me wearing that evil politician's smile he's perfected. "Who?"

"Doesn't matter. You wouldn't know him. But he's perhaps the only man your little boyfriend wouldn't dare cross." As he strides toward me, I kick myself back in a laughable attempt to get away from him. He kneels to the ground beside me, and when he reaches out to touch my hair, I crane my neck away, my whole body trembling with rage and fear. "I understand a number of these men enjoy young pussy as much as I do. Once they're finished poking and prodding you, I'm certain they'll have a number of unorthodox tests to run." Hand stroking my head, he grips a handful of hair in his fist and gives a hard yank, sending hot streaks of pain across my scalp. "They'll test your tolerance for pain like you're a fucking guinea pig in a blender."

"He'll find you." My voice chokes on the tears that I won't give him the satisfaction of seeing. "Lucian will kill you."

"Lucian bows to The Collective. If I prove to be of interest to them, then my life becomes far more valuable than yours."

According to Giulia, Lucian never subscribed to the ideologies of Schadenfreude, but he funds them, just the same. What if Boyd is right?

What if Lucian's loyalties are stronger than his feelings for me?

CHAPTER 62

LUCIAN

The engine roars down the highway as I feed it more gas. The dot on the tracker app appears to have stopped in some remote part of the island. A wooded area with cabins that the locals like to rent out on occasion.

So much for trusting the private investigator.

I should've known his interests would be selfish. I asked him to contact me if anything seemed sketchy, but the gumshoe in him must've looked at it as an opportunity to take out one of the bad guys singlehandedly.

A few miles behind me, Makaio follows in the Bentley, struggling to keep up. My adrenaline is through the roof, and if I happen to get my hands around Boyd's throat, I might just snap it by accident.

An ache throbs inside my skull, casting a flash of white light behind my eyes, and I shake it off, rubbing my temple with the heel of my hand.

Not now.

It'd make sense that I'd get hit with a migraine, though, because God has a morbid sense of humor, and what better time to have my vision go blurry than when I'm cruising at one-hundred-fifty miles per hour?

Through the haze and white fog, I concentrate on the solid yellow line that separates me from oncoming traffic.

Another zap of electricity strikes my skull.

One one-thousand, two one-thousand, three one-thousand, four one-thousand.

The throbbing ache settles deep inside my head, and I work my jaw in a desperate attempt to make it go away.

I set my thoughts on Isa. Her smile. The sound of her voice. Soft skin beneath my fingertips.

Relax.

The blur begins to sharpen at the edges, while the pain dissolves. The air thins in my lungs, and I exhale as clarity seeps back into the fringes.

The dusky orange sky gives way to the dark cover of trees, and I check my phone one more time to see the dot hasn't moved. About a mile up the road, from the looks of it. I slow the vehicle and catch sight of the *Whitman Woodlands* sign off to the side. Turning into the narrow drive, I kill the lights. Gravel pops beneath my tires as I roll down the obscure path. Before reaching the cabins, I turn the Bugatti off the road and throw it in park.

A half-mile up the drive, a row of cabins sit in darkness, with one lone vehicle parked out in front. I stalk through the woods toward them, careful to stay in the shadows. Sweeping a hand over the gun tucked inside my jeans, I trudge through the brush, pausing when I feel the slight vibration of my phone against my hip. Tugging it out of my pocket, I glance down at the dot blinking on the screen and halt my approach. Using the dim light from the screen, I angle the phone downward and scan the ground. A mound of dirt ahead catches my eye, and as I get closer, I notice what appears to be fingertips sticking up from a fresh grave.

The private investigator, I'm guessing.

Tucking my phone back into my jeans, I keep on toward the cabin, careful to avoid the floodlight's halo, and once I reach the south wall, I flatten myself against it and listen for voices inside.

Nothing.

Keeping low to avoid being seen, I peer through a window and spot Isa strapped to the bed, all four limbs tied to each of the four posts. My attention is drawn to the white gauze wrapped around her ankle, dotted in what looks like blood. Silver tape covers her mouth, and she squirms and writhes on the bed in a disastrous attempt to get loose.

Tugging the gun from my pants, I rack the chamber and let it lead the way, as I creep around the house and up the staircase to the front window. Scanning the rest of the interior shows no sign of Boyd. Only sparse furniture and an open kitchen. Carefully turning the knob on what appears to be the only door, I push it open, cringing at the chasing creak of its rusted hinges.

Isa stills on the bed, only her legs in view from around the corner, as I make my way toward the back room.

"Don't move." The familiar voice arrives from behind, and I halt my steps, keeping my gun held out in front of me. "Pass me the gun. Behind your back."

"You hand her over to them, you'll never see her again."

"Pass me. Your fucking. Gun." Boyd has always carried an edge of fake benevolence in his tone, and the hostility that bleeds through is strange, coming from him. "I've got a bullet with your name on it, Lucian. All I have to do is pull the trigger."

From the other room, Isa's muffled screams tell me she can hear our exchange.

The cold rush of adrenaline pulses through me as the seconds tick off before this motherfucker'll lose his patience. "You killed Nell, didn't you?"

"That meddling bitch just couldn't keep her hands out of it."

"You were afraid she'd find out the truth about Amelia. And Roark. And Isa."

"She was out to destroy everything. She told that fucking investigator *everything*." The words hiss through his teeth.

"How do you know what she told him?"

"Who do you think hired the bastard?"

Boyd is the last person I suspected. In fact, I'd have pegged Friedrich before this asshole. "Why?"

"There were things I needed to know. Things you weren't telling me. And then I learned of Isa. The daughter I never knew."

"So, why would you hand her over to them?" I kick my head to the side, catching a shadow of him in my periphery, a few steps back, along with the gun pointed directly at me.

"If I thought cutting her up into tiny pieces and giftwrapping her organs would get me into Schadenfreude, I'd do it in a heartbeat."

And I'd do the same to him, if I got wind he was behind it. Only I wouldn't bother to giftwrap the shit. "You're a heartless prick, Patrick. A sick and disturbed man."

"Says the Devil of Bonesalt."

"Did you kill Isa's mother?"

"Jenny? What do you think? That I would stand by and let some junkie whore slink back into my life like a nightmare?"

I thought I had problems with women. This guy is the Godfather of bad decisions. "You kill me, and they'll come after you. You know that, right?"

"I don't have to kill you. You're going to hand me that gun right now."

"Now, why would I do a stupid thing like that?"

"Because I know the truth about your girl. Why she came back to Tempest Cove. What really happened the night of that party."

"You're not telling me anything I don't already know. Good one, though." What really happened was served to me in an envelope from Rand, dug up from one of our many contacts.

"Pass me the gun."

"Fuck off, Patrick."

"You really are the *Mad Son*. Pass me the fucking gun!"

"No."

"You like to straddle the line between life and death? Huh? Let's see how long you hang there with a bullet in your skull."

At the sound of a gunshot and shattering glass from behind, I drop to the floor. I don't know who fired, just that it didn't come from my gun, and the tortured pitch of Patrick's outcry is a sure bet that a bullet hit him, somehow, instead of me. I twist around to see a massive figure standing on the other side of the broken window next to the front door.

Makaio, I'll bet.

A hard thump vibrates over the wooden floor planks, and I glance back to see Patrick holding his knee to his chest, scooting back against the wall across the room from me. When his eyes meet mine, he scrambles for his fallen gun, and I fire a shot, just missing his arm, which he recoils back.

"Motherfucker!" he grits out, reaching for it again.

Not a second later, I twist back around, and a shot rings out, its bullet flying over me, hitting the wall ahead on a puff of drywall dust.

The chasing sound of Isa's screams through the tape skate down my spine, and my first thought, my only thought, is that she's been hit by the bullet. Urgency ignites in my veins. Another gunshot echoes in the room. A fourth. Isa's screams heighten. I keep low on another shot, and don't even allow myself to do a sweep, or look back at Patrick, before I army crawl into the next room to get to her.

Another bullet whizzes past, and a cold hot pain streaks across my shoulder. "Fuck!" I grit my teeth and ignore it, until I'm through the door, separated from Boyd by the bedroom wall.

Isa's screams, still muffled by the tape across her mouth, draw my attention to where she struggles against her binds on the bed.

I climb over her, covering her body with mine, feeling her

jerk and twitch with another gunshot. Patrick screams again, as if he's been hit a second time.

Finally, the melee settles to quiet.

At the sound of heavy footfalls across the floor, I point my gun toward the bedroom door, muscles sagging when Makaio steps into the room carrying two guns.

"Boss? You okay?"

"Peachy." Pushing off Isa, I tear the tape away from her mouth and give her body a onceover, looking for any sign of injury, or stray bullets. The only blood I see is the small bit that dripped from my shoulder onto her cheek, and the oozing wound at her ankle. The streak of red at my shoulder, without an actual hole, tells me the bullet only grazed me.

"Lucian," she says out of breath, before breaking into tears. "I'm sorry. I'm so sorry."

"Shhh." I stroke a hand over her hair and kiss her. "You're going to be okay. Relax, Isa."

After checking my own body for sign of injury, I loosen her binds, and the sound of groaning from the other room makes me pause.

"You didn't kill him?" I ask Makaio.

"You said you didn't want any more investigations on your hands, so I shot him once in each leg. If you want, I can finish him off, though." He lurches toward the man who sounds like he just got his ass handed to him.

"No." Sliding my hands beneath Isa's body, I lift her into my arms. "He's her father. He deserves better than that."

Makaio opens the front door of the cabin, and I halt at the approach of distant headlights. Ducking behind the adjacent wall, I dodge the bright beam crawling up the driveway and nod to Makaio, who slams the door shut.

"You're fucked." Boyd's weak voice is broken by the hard pants of breath while he sits bleeding out of his bullet wounds. "I called ... them. To collect her here."

495

Teeth grinding in my skull, I lower Isa to the floor, my mind spinning with what to do.

"Want me to take care of them?" Makaio slides his gun from its holster and I shake my head.

"No. You'll set off an investigation that I don't need."

Obnoxious laughter bounces off the walls, steeling my muscles, and I snap my gaze to Boyd, who's undoubtedly trying to drum up as much noise as he can. Swinging my attention back to Makaio, I give a quick jerk of my head toward the noisy prick, and the hard *thunk* of a punch silences the man.

Crouching low to peer out through the window, I see the men haven't yet exited the car. "There's a window in the back room. Get the two of them out of here."

I don't yet have a plan in mind, all I know is, I'll be the one leaving with Isa.

No matter what.

The tight clutch of my arm draws my focus to where Isa grips me. "I'm staying with you."

"If they find you, you might as well be dead for what they'll do to you. Go with Makaio." Finger hooked beneath her chin, I press my lips to hers. "Now."

With Boyd's limp body hoisted over his shoulder, Makaio takes Isa's hand, guiding her toward the back room.

After giving them a moment to break away, I swing back the front door to find three Blacksuits standing alongside the sleek black vehicle parked beside Boyd's. Two of the men, I recognize as Dominic and Louis. Haven't seen the elders since they visited my office two months ago. The other man I've seen a couple times, but never formally met. A tall, beefy guy who could probably rival Makaio in size.

"Gentlemen," I say, stepping out onto the porch. "Good to see you again."

"What are you doing here, Lucian?" Dominic asks, around a

thick cigar that sticks out from between his lips, as he grips the porch's handrail at the foot of the stairs.

I close the door behind me to shut out any scuffling sounds as Isa and Makaio make their escape through the back window. Not that the old man would hear much with his hearing aid, anyway. "Friedrich contacted me. Asked me to look into a call he received from Boyd."

"Funny … he asked us to look into that very thing. Seems a bit redundant."

Poker face in place, I nod. "Perhaps he thought I'd catch him first."

"Catch him?" The dubious tone in Dominic's voice plays on my nerves.

I could pull my gun and take my chances on killing all of them where they stand, but that would leave far too many questions for Friedrich to inquire about. "Seems he took off with the girl."

"Now why would he do that when he was the one who contacted us?" The voice of the stranger has me lifting my gaze to where he stands next to Louis, arms crossed.

It seems he doesn't yet know who I am in this Collective to speak with that level of contempt in his voice. "He has a long-standing history of molesting young girls. Perhaps he found her too tempting."

"If you don't mind, we'd just like to have a look for ourselves." Dominic glances back toward the beefy guy and jerks his head.

As he passes me on the way inside, the asshole knocks me in the shoulder and my muscles burn with the urge to clock the bastard in the skull.

Louis stands off from Dominic, quiet as always, staring back at me, while my head spins with a few different scenarios on how this will all play out.

The beefy asshole shooting me in the back.

All three of them dragging me into the car.

Makaio jumping out from the shadows, killing them all, and me having to explain the shit to Friedrich.

Awkward silence hangs on the air between the three of us, while the stranger tromps through the cabin. When he appears again, his eyes are brimming with accusation. "There's blood everywhere in there."

"Yes. There is. It appears Boyd had a bit of a confrontation with an investigator who was after him. I suspect he might be the reason the two fled." I nod my head toward the shallow grave just outside of the floodlight. "You'll find what's left of him over there."

With jerky movements, the two older men twist around, and Louis hobbles over to the spot I pointed out, before he turns back to Dominic and nods.

"That's all fine and dandy, but why do you have blood on your shoulder then?" If I don't end up killing the bastard behind me tonight, it'll be a miracle. "Come to think of it, why's his car still here if he fled so quickly?"

I don't bother to turn and face the asshole, and instead keep my eyes on Dominic. "Everyone on this island would recognize his car. Surely they'd take notice of a young girl after his many indiscretions, as well. Might've taken the investigator's instead."

"No." He moves closer into my personal space and my fingers twitch with the compulsion to draw my gun and take my chances. "I think you're lying. I think you know exactly where the girl is. Boyd, too."

"Can't say I give a fuck what you think." Still keeping my back to him, I flex my fingers around the gun's grip tucked inside my waistband. "And I'll kindly ask that you back off before I teach you a lesson in boundaries."

"I'd like to see you try—"

"Enough!" Tugging his cigar from his lips, Dominic glances over his shoulder toward Louis, and gives a silent nod that could mean any number of things, but I'm guessing it signals my death.

The moment I catch sight of Louis pulling his gun from its holster, I take hold of my own weapon, and feel the tight grip of my shoulders. In one sweeping move, I pivot just enough to aim the gun at the ribcage of the man beside me.

Before I can pull the trigger, the quiet pop of gunfire stops me short. The vacant, bewildered look on the beefy guy's face seems a muted reaction for the hole in his skull that marks the bullet's path. The grip of my shoulder falls away, followed by a hard thud, as he crumples to the ground beside me.

I blow out a breath and nod, my muscles releasing their tight grip of my chest, and I shift my attention back to the two remaining Blacksuits. "Well, that was an interesting turn of events."

"To be frank, I don't give a good goddamn why you were here or where the girl is. As far as I'm concerned, we never saw either of you." Dominic's eye squints as he shoves the cigar back between his lips and puffs it. "Isn't that right, Louis?"

"Never liked that bastard." The foreign sound of Louis's grumbled voice only intensifies the pulses of shock still beating through me. "Boyd either, for that matter."

The two older Blacksuits make their way back toward the car, and with one hand on the passenger door, Dominic twists to face me again. "I'll send a cleaner to take care of the mess. Make sure you get that shoulder looked at, Lucian. Wounds fester when you ignore them."

CHAPTER 63

ISADORA

I open my eyes to the dimly lit room, staring up at the ceiling where a bright ornate painting of Greek gods in battle casts a glow overhead. Lifting my head from the pillow, I frown at the unfamiliar surroundings, and scan the room until I find a shadowy figure sitting off in the corner, staring at me. Double-blinking, I struggle to focus through the fog of exhaustion clouding my head.

"Where am I?"

"My bedroom." The unmistakable sound of Lucian's voice hits like a tuning fork, and the relief I feel brings tears to my eyes. "Dr. Powell removed the bullet from your ankle. He gave you something for the pain. You've been out for a whole day."

Resistance keeps my arms from moving when I try to sit up, and I crane my neck to find black leather cuffs attached to my wrists.

A gasp of panic escapes me, and I wriggle against them.

"You kept trying to pull out your I.V. My bed was the only one equipped with restraints."

I don't know why the thought of that pisses me off, but I sneer at him. "For your *slaves?*"

"For you. I had them installed for you, that weekend I asked you to stay."

"To keep me imprisoned?"

"The thought crossed my mind." There isn't a trace of humor in his voice when he answers. He sits forward, resting his elbows on his thighs. "Aside from your ankle, how are you feeling?"

The question makes me snort a laugh. How am I feeling? To know my father is a murdering bastard who killed my mother? One who probably had every intention of killing me, as well. "It's a lot to process."

"It is. You could've died. One stray bullet. That's all it'd have taken."

My thoughts quickly sober with the serious tone of his voice, and the gravity of the situation presses down on me again. "How did you find me?"

"The bracelet. I gave it to the investigator."

"I should've never taken it off." A dull ache throbs in both my ankle and my head, and I turn to the side, where a glass of water sits on the nightstand. "Is that for me?"

"Yes. There's a pill there, if you need it. It'll knock you out, though."

"Any chance you can un-cuff me? My fingers are starting to tingle."

He stares back at me, as if hesitating, and his comments from before, of keeping me imprisoned, slink back into my thoughts. After idling a minute more, he pushes up from the chair and crosses the room, coming to a stop beside the bed, and traces his finger down my temple. "I thought I was going to lose you. That's a level of insanity I don't ever want to experience again."

Another moment of staring, and he unbuckles the restraints at my wrists.

I rub my irritated skin for a moment, running my finger over the ligature left there, before I reach for the glass on the night-stand, tipping back the cool fluids that coat the dryness of my throat and practically sizzle when I swallow. "He's my father," I say into the glass. "Is he dead?"

"No. I insisted that he remain alive. But I promise he won't hurt you again."

Two weeks ago, I would've insisted on knowing why. How. I would've inquired about the group that pays to torture others. But having been at the mercy of a psychopath, I've come to the understanding that there are some questions that don't need answers.

"I was so scared." Setting the glass in my lap, I take notice of the bandage at my forearm where the IV must've been placed. "The moment he pulled up beside me in his car, I knew something was wrong."

"Of course you did."

"What?"

"Most predators harbor natural instincts like that. It's how we survive."

"*We*? What are you talking about?"

"Tell me something, Isa ..." Lucian stalks around the perimeter of the bed, dragging his finger across the blanket, and comes to a stop opposite me. Perhaps it's the light of the moon that makes his eyes flicker like a burning flame, as he stares back at me, fingers curled around the footboard. "The night those boys attacked you at the party. What happened next?"

A tickle at the back of my neck is a warning, though of what, I'm not sure. "Why are you asking me about this?"

"Because I want to hear it from your lips."

I told him what happened weeks ago. Surely, he hasn't forgotten already. "I ... I gathered up my friend and drove her back to her house."

"And then?"

"We called the police."

His frown breaks to a partial smile that's plagued by disbelief. One that tells me he knows more than what I told him. "You skipped too far ahead. Go back a little. What happened immediately after you drove Kelsey back to her house?"

Panic blossoms inside my chest as I stare back at him, the memories of that night crawling out of their airtight boxes, the tiny compartments I've constructed inside my head. "Why?"

"Tell me."

"I ... don't ..." *Remember.* But I do. In the long pause that follows, the images in my head seem to project on the wall behind him, playing like a movie reel. "I went back to the party. Alone. And I found Aedon, Brady, and all their friends back out in the pool house. Drinking and smoking. I nearly choked on the cloud of marijuana clinging to the air."

"Why did you go back?" His voice is distant, reminding me of days spent sitting in the therapist's chair while he probed my thoughts for answers. Reasons that would compel me to do what I did.

"I was angry. I wanted to confront them."

"Wrong. What did you do when you found them in the pool house?"

What did you do?

What did you do?

The words of Aunt Midge echo inside my head.

"I told Brady that ... that I wanted him. Only him. So he sent the others out."

"And?"

An urgency in my head begs me not to answer his question, but I do, anyway, my mouth commanded by an unseen force. "I took my shirt off, to show him I was serious. And he removed his pants."

Lucian tips his head and strokes his jaw. "Did you want to fuck him?"

"No." My thoughts are still tied in the dream--or nightmare, rather--spinning inside my head. "The sight of him disgusted me."

"So, what happened?"

"I knelt down in front of him, like I was going to put my mouth on him. He closed his eyes. And I pulled the knife from my back pocket. I stabbed him. Over and over, I stabbed his groin." I screw my eyes shut to block out the memory, but it's all there inside my head. The screams. The fury. "All I saw was blood."

"It wasn't Kelsey that Brady tried to rape that night. It was you."

Eyes still clamped, I shake my head, but the truth in his words are too strong for the months of denial that has served as a shield. Because if--if--I'd so much as dipped a toe into those dangerous waters, there's no telling what damage I would've done to myself in the aftermath. I wanted Brady more than anything my senior year, and when he finally showed interest, all my good sense went out the fucking window. I became a statistic. Another after-school special, warning girls of the dangers of drinking alcohol at a party. Only, instead of Brady looking like the villain, my retaliation made him the saint in all of this, and I became the psycho.

"It was Kelsey's testimony that kept you from being locked up, wasn't it?"

"Yes." I finally open my eyes, exhaling a shaky breath. "She witnessed everything, except the stabbing."

"Tell me about Uncle George. Do you remember how his throat ended up sliced open?"

Lowering my gaze, I shake my head. "I blacked out."

"He lived. Miraculously, given the depth of the cut. But his wife found the knife in your hands."

Tears wobble before my eyes, distorting the dark gray sheets. *Hold still.* I can hear his raspy voice in my ear, smell the beer on his breath, as he yanked down my underwear. The grunting and groaning that churned a sickness in my stomach, while he tried to breach my barrier, too small for his size. The burn. The pain. The sight of his pocket knife sitting on the nightstand next to the wooden horse he carved for me. A knife he always carried around and used to clean his nails. "He tried to hurt me."

"All of them tried to hurt you. And if you'd had a knife in your hands the other day, when Boyd pulled up beside you?"

"I would've cut him with it."

Lucian rounds the bed, and sits beside me. "Your whole life, you've been ridiculed and treated like a monster." He strokes his hand down my cheek, and at the gentle nudge to my chin, I lift my gaze to his. "And all you've done is protect yourself."

"I didn't want to hurt anyone."

"But we do what we have to."

"I tried to forget it. I desperately tried to forget all of it, but … it's always there, Lucian. It's always there. Playing over and over inside my head."

"And it always will be. Trust me, I know."

"Did you kill Amelia?"

Turning away from me, he sighs, and his eyes seem contemplative for a moment. "I did. Over the course of our marriage, I killed her a little bit every day that I didn't show love for her. I couldn't lie to her, though. Not even in the end."

"Are you capable of feeling love, at all?" It's a question I'm not supposed to ask, because we established what this is before it began. To hear him say no would only stab my heart at this point, so perhaps it's masochistic of me to inquire, at all.

"When I figured out that Boyd had taken you, and saw you tied to that bed. Helpless. Scared. Only one thought stirred in my head. That anyone who touched you would die a long, slow, and painful death at my hands. I didn't care who, or what, it was." Palm caressing my throat, he strokes his thumb over my jawline and chin in a way that demonstrates his possession. "I'd have given up my soul to the devil himself for you. If that isn't fucking love, then I don't know what is."

"My aunt says love is when you try to imagine a world without someone in it, and *can't.*"

"I've only felt that one other time. When my son died in my arms. I wanted to follow right after him, wherever it was that he went, because I couldn't face him no longer being in this world. I've only felt that one other time, since then."

"When?" I dare to ask him.

"The day you told me you wanted out. Out of this place. Out of my life."

"I was scared of you, then. I'm not anymore."

Hand still clasped to my neck, he lowers himself and captures my lips in a kiss. God, I missed the feel of this, the scent of him, the taste of him on my tongue and in my head, wrapped around every nerve ending in my body. "I want you to stay with me," he says against my mouth. "You'll never want for anything, Isa. And I promise you, no one will ever hurt you again."

"And what happens when you get bored of me? When the thrill of the forbidden is gone?"

"Impossible. You can't get bored of the very thing you need to stay alive." Lips devour mine in another kiss, and he squeezes his palm, just enough to steal my breath.

Hand against his chest, I break the kiss. "I want you to let Giulia go. Honor the contract by allowing her daughter to stay in school, but let her go."

"Done." His voice is as resolute as the expression on his face.

"And I want you to leave Schadenfreude."

"If I could, I'd do it today. But leaving puts both of us at risk. It so happens I'm privy to things that ensure I'll never be able to just walk away."

I let my hand fall from his chest and turn away from him. "So, you're still willing to make deals to fuck other women?"

"No. I'm no longer participating in the rituals. Only the occasional meetings."

"And what happens when they decide that isn't good enough?"

"Then, we follow our instincts, you and I." He strokes a hand down my hair and tips my chin up. "No one will hurt you again. Not even me. I won't allow it. Are you hungry?" he asks, placing a gentle kiss to my forehead.

"Starving."

"I'll get you something to eat. Stay put."

"Here? In your bedroom?"

"Would you prefer to hobble your way back down to your room?"

"Not particularly. I just ... never mind."

"Good. Then, stay put."

Upon his exit, the door clicks, and I turn over on the bed, breathing in the scent of him clinging to the pillows. The warmth and safety of my surroundings, or perhaps the lingering effects of the drugs, lulls me in and out of sleep.

"Isa, wake up."

At the sound of a woman's voice, I turn over to find a shadow on the wall moving like a lithe figure. It rushes toward me, and as I kick back against the headboard, Laura's face comes into view in the light from the window. Her long, silvery hair drapes delicately over her shoulders, and the red rims of her eyes only accentuate the deep black pools of dilated pupils that swallow the blue.

No cane.

No wheelchair.

No stagger in her movements.

"What is this?" I glance around the room, but find Lucian hasn't yet returned. "Am I dreaming?"

Wrinkled lips curve into a smile. "I didn't find you in your bed, dear. Figured you'd be here."

"My bed? Did you .... Do you need something?"

"No." Her eyes soften, and she tips her head. "I just like to watch you sleep. For weeks, I've watched you now. Twitching with nightmares. Gripping the knife under your pillow. Whispering my son's name."

The room falls to a brittle silence, and it feels as if the temperature has dropped about ten degrees. A chill tickles the back of my neck again, crawling down my spine. "Why aren't you …"

"Limping around?" She scratches at her own face, eyes lost for a moment, before she directs her gaze toward my ankle. "Oh, dear. You hurt yourself."

"Yes. Mayor Boyd. He shot me."

She gasps and rests her hand against my ankle from the end of the bed, setting my teeth on edge. The way she seems to study it has me drawing my knees up, sending her stare in my direction once more.

Trying not to be obvious, I slide my gaze toward the door again, catching the light beneath, and watch, waiting, for Lucian's shadow to appear there. "There's nothing wrong with you?"

"I suppose it depends on who you ask." Head tipped back, she inhales a deep breath. "How curious that it doesn't seem to reek of sex in here. With you lying sprawled out on his bed like this, surely he couldn't resist." Absent of the usual hobble in her gait, she practically glides closer me, her proximity sending a tremble through my muscles. "Such a telling aroma. Thick and heady. I remember the scent of sex very well. When you're married to the biggest man-whore on the island, you become something of a *hound* dog. He fucked just about anything in a skirt. Would've fucked you, eventually."

I shake my head, and she slaps her palm over my face, steeling my muscles.

"He would've fucked you. Yes, he would've. Whether you wanted him to, or not. He fucked Amelia mere hours after Lucian. How do you think she ended up pregnant?"

Oh, my God. My back stiffens as shock spirals down my spine. "Roark was Griffin's son?"

She lowers her hand. "I didn't think so at first. The paternity test came back positive for Lucian. Initially, we were just making sure it wasn't her own father's child, since Boyd always had a thing for very young girls. Most of the genetics between father and son are quite similar, though, I later learned. It's when I requested further testing that I learned the truth about Roark. That child went from beautiful grandson, to stepson, overnight."

The way the sparkle in her eyes dims to something darker sends a feeling of dread to my stomach. "Did you kill him? Did you give him those pills?"

The disturbing smile on her face doesn't disappear with the question. "She was pregnant again, you know. Considering Lucian wouldn't so much as touch the poor girl, who do you think the father might've been?"

"Did you kill him?" I ask again, desperate to know.

"She stopped taking her pills. Didn't want to affect the baby growing in her belly." Eyes spacy and unfocused, it's as if she's reliving the memory. "There is nothing more cunning and deter-mined as a scorned woman."

"Answer the question."

"I couldn't bear the humiliation. And poor Lucian. Believing Roark was his only son. It was too much. I snuck into Roark's room that night, because Lord knows, that child feared every-thing. Wouldn't come anywhere near the doll on Amelia's night-stand." The feathery touch of her fingers running up and down my arm sends goosebumps across my skin. "I fed him the pills. I watched him choke. His face went pale as freshly fallen snow. When Lucian entered the room, I hid in the boy's closet. And ten minutes later, my humiliation was no more."

The sound of shattering dishes snaps my attention to the doorway, where Lucian stands, his hands balled into fists at his sides. "What have you done?"

"What I had to. You don't think I know what your father pumped his money into? What he was so *desperate* to hide from me?"

"You killed my son."

"Your brother. He wasn't yours, Lucian."

"He was my fucking son! The only thing I ever loved."

"He would've destroyed your life. *She* was destroying your life, and he was the reason you almost died that night."

Brows lowered, he steps deeper into the room. "I've tried to forgive you all these years. For forcing me into marriage. Forcing me into that bullshit institute." Lips peeled back, he snarls and stalks closer. "What have you done?"

"Your father put you in that Institute. Not me. He put too much faith in that doctor. They both swore you'd forget that woman after a while."

Woman? Amelia?

It seems to dawn on him, and he lifts his gaze to Laura, eyes darkening with betrayal. "Solange?"

The woman whose name Lucian spoke when he seemed to be having a hallucination a while back. When I asked about her, he told me she wasn't real. She was a different *affliction*, he said.

"The sound of her name still makes me want to wretch." Laura grimaces, as if she might just do that. "I knew from the very beginning she was trouble. The way she paraded around you and your father."

"She was real." Uncertainty bleeds through his voice, as if he doesn't trust the answer.

"Of course she was real. It's a wonder to me that you ever fell for all that brainwashing."

Eyes narrowed, he stares back at her, his mind seemingly lost to unseen images. "You ... never acknowledged her."

"Why would I acknowledge the woman? She was nothing to me."

Brows pinched tighter, he lowers his gaze, as if more images are coming to mind. "The staff ... they always gave me strange looks."

Laura scoffs and rolls her eyes. "Of course. The two of you looked ridiculous together. It was obvious to everyone that she was obsessed with you, Lucian. The way she'd pet you and fawn all over you. She couldn't keep her hands off you."

He rubs his hand over his head, back and forth, as if he might rub the hair right off. "She'd disappear for days at a time. Days."

Rolling her shoulders back, Laura clears her throat. "I became privy to a cage your father kept in his chambers. Locked away in some secret little room. He'd lock himself up with her for days at a time, fucking her like his little pet, when he wasn't torturing her. I'm surprised you couldn't hear her screams through the walls."

A strange numbness settles over me, and I can't even begin to imagine what has settled over Lucian with this revelation. To think it even possible that he could've been brainwashed for so many years, into believing that woman didn't exist. And for what purpose?

"You … you tried to convince me she wasn't real." Clutching his skull, Lucian paces at the end of the bed, while I sit trying to piece together the how's and why's of such a thing. "Do you have any fucking clue what they did to me there? Their methods of making me forget!" His bellow bounces off the walls, and I flinch at the flourishing anger in his voice. Judging by the cold disgust creeping across his face, it must've been torture. "All the drugs they pumped into me!"

"All your father's brilliant idea. *He* figured since you suffered years of hallucinations with Jude, what was one more?" She sighs and mindlessly toys with a loose string on my shirt, making me lean away from her, eyeing the opposite side of the bed for escape. "Not like I'd ever let you run off with that dirty child molester, anyway."

Breath stutters in my throat at that, and I look back to him. "Lucian?" He'd only ever mentioned that she'd taught him things, never that he was molested.

He offers only a quick glance toward me, not bothering to dispute her choice of words. "She was twenty-five. Half the age of my father when he fucked her. And at least I consented. At least she didn't threaten me, if I refused." His expression hardens again as he stares back at Laura. "You killed her, didn't you?"

"How humiliating do you think it was, to know both my husband *and* son were fucking that filthy little harlot? Of course I killed her. And if I hadn't stopped your father, he'd be fucking *her*, too!" She points a trembling finger at me. "He wanted a grandson to offer up so badly, he was willing to make one himself."

"What do you mean, *stopped him*?" he says past clenched teeth. Bunched shoulders and the tension in his jaw are clues that he's one second from snapping.

Laura's dark chuckle is unfitting for the moment, leaving me to wonder if she'll snap, as well. "The heart attack? Your father's heart was as healthy as an ox, before I spiked his drink. Tell me life didn't get better when he died. Tell me you didn't feel free the moment Roark was no longer your responsibility."

Subtle, to avoid snagging her attention, I scoot myself toward the other end of the bed.

"You made me believe I was crazy." Lucian steps around the bed, his movements slow and careful, approaching as if she's an animal that might try to escape him. "You let them pump me full of drugs and left me there."

"A mother does what she has to. Tell me you weren't better off without her in your life." As I set my sights for escape, the cold, steel tip of a sharp blade presses against my throat. "Or this one, for that matter."

I breathe hard through my nose to calm the racing of my pulse.

The murderous expression on his face is one I've never seen before. Not even when Boyd was shooting at us. "Put the blade down. Now."

"I see it in your eyes, Lucian. The same look when you were fawning all over that French whore. Obsession. You're obsessed, and we know what happens when you become obsessed with something."

"I swear to God, I will kill you myself, if you so much as nick her skin."

"Dr. Voigt said obsessions aren't good for you. He told me it's important to eliminate the sources of your obsessions. She is the source."

"Mother, I'm warning you." Lucian rounds the end of the bed, and with the burn of the blade's edge peeling through a thin layer of skin at my throat, I don't so much as swallow.

This woman is crazy, and one wrong move might leave me bleeding out.

"Did you ever stop to wonder if she's even real?" She pets the top of my head, blade steady for a quick slice. "You know, there's only one way to find out."

Breath held, I smack her arm away, and the knife falls with a clang to the floor. I roll to the side, as she bends down to snatch it up, and at the sharp yank of my hair, a jagged light dances behind my eyelids.

Lucian lurches toward her, and she releases me. "I'll see to it that you spend the rest of your life in a cage," he growls.

Dodging her flailing, knife-toting hand, he backs her onto the bed, and I scramble for the other side to avoid the scuffle.

"I'd sooner die than be locked away like an animal!" Laura screams from behind.

A sputtering cough follows.

I hear the sound of a body falling to the floor.

When I turn back, Lucian appears almost paralyzed, where he stands with his palms up, shock blanching his face.

With blood on his skin.

CHAPTER 64

LUCIAN

A blinding light reflects off the hallways on my way toward the room at the end. The low droning sound of classical music plays over the speaker as, adjusting my cuffs, I come to a stop before the door. I open it to find my mother strapped to a bed, her hands and legs bound by restraints. She turns her head to the side, her expression softening at the sight of me.

"Lucian! Oh, I'm so glad you're here, dear. I'm ready to go home now."

I don't say a word as I stare down at her. The wound at her throat, where she dragged the blade, has healed to a grisly scar. Dark rims around her eyes tell of little sleep, and the straggle of her unkempt hair makes her look like she belongs in a straitjacket.

At the approach of someone from behind, I turn to see Friedrich enter the room, wearing his white coat, hands tucked in the pockets. He stands beside me and sets a hand to my shoulder. "Don't worry, we'll take good care of her."

My mother's eyes harden to fear, her brows pinched tight. "No. No, please. I want to go home."

With a light squeeze, Friedrich exits the room, leaving me alone with my mother once again.

"You tried to kill yourself." The flat tone of my voice is as devoid of emotion as my heart when I stare back at her. "Why is that?"

Gaze shifting from mine, she seems to think about it for a moment. "The way you looked at me. I've never seen such a thing in my life. Not even from your father, as cruel as he could be." When her eyes meet mine again, they flicker with fear. "Like death would've been better than what you intended to do to me right then."

"And is it, mother?"

Mouth open, she trails her gaze over the mostly empty white room, and her lip trembles. "Is this death? Purgatory?"

"You tell me."

Tears well in her eyes, and she breaks into a sob. "I'm sorry. For what I did to you. You have to forgive me. You have to. I'm your mother."

The tears, the weakness in her voice, the frailty of her appearance, like she might snap any moment, they have no effect on me. Not when all I can see is my son's sleeping face, lips blue with the death she gifted him. The truth is, had she not slit her own throat, I could've very well done it myself. "I'll never forgive you for what you stole from me."

"I'm better now, though. I'm not angry anymore. Lucian, please take me home."

"This is your home now." There isn't an ounce of empathy left in me for this woman. That she could so easily snuff an innocent life without a hint of remorse proves it doesn't take unsightly facial scars to make a monster. "Don't worry. Dr. Voigt said he'll take good care of you."

Eyes wide, she pants, tugging at her binds. "What did you tell them? What did you tell them about me, Lucian?"

"What do you think I told them, mother? That you're a child killer."

I sit across the desk from Friedrich, watching him jot notes into my medical chart.

Adjusting his spectacles, he looks up, holding the pen poised. "For years, we've watched you very closely. You neither show interest, nor choose to participate in any sessions. You've shown no history of abuse, as far as we know, and the maid you hired to fulfill your sexual needs reported no deviances, or unusual requests."

"Perhaps the gene for sadism only extends over a certain number of generations."

"Or perhaps you haven't been pushed far enough. Be careful what you choose to mock."

"My apologies." I'm only playing along for Isa's sake, nothing more.

He lifts his glasses and reads from the file in front of him. "It seems you requested the murder of Franco Scarpinato, but you didn't directly carry out this session. Instead, you solicited your bodyguard to torture him on your behalf."

"I wanted only the best to carry out his punishment."

My apathy must finally be getting to him, because he eases back in his chair and huffs, eyes appraising, as always. "You fear becoming your father."

"I'm sure I'm not alone in that thought."

"Of course not. But your fears are concerning, as it relates to our study. If you won't be honest, you could end up being a danger to yourself and others. We exist to provide an environment for you to carry out those sadistic tendencies. Unburdened by society, or morality."

Just send me to hell already. If I was back at the office, I'd be on my second drink by now. This guy isn't going to give up for as long as I have to be a part of this shit-show. That's how it works with these scientists. They'll beat a dead horse until it's nothing but a mangled piece of flesh, if it means proving their theories. "I'll confess that I have urges sometimes."

Sitting forward in his chair, he sets the file aside and entwines his fingers. The intrigue on his face is what I'd expect of a priest getting offered a free hand job by a nun. "What kind of urges? Sexual, like your father? Or non-sexual?"

"Non-sexual."

"And how do you deal with these urges?"

"Sometimes, I'll cut myself. But mostly, I just … try to think of something else."

"Would you be open to participating in a session? Nothing too involved. We have an older gentleman who comes in every so often. We think he might be developing an affinity toward some of the abuses. In exchange, his rent gets paid every month."

I probably just signed over my human rights for a guinea pig with this confession. "How light?"

"A few cuts. Nothing too deep."

Cutting myself has always been for the high, much like holding my breath under water, but Friedrich has always sought to turn it into something malicious and perverse. I don't get off on watching other people bleed. The innocent ones, anyway. "I'll consider that."

"Excellent. Then, we'll continue to observe. For now." Sliding my file open again, he jots a few notes, underlining one that leaves me inwardly groaning: *observation*. "I have to give you credit. Considering all you've been through, and the history of sadism in your family, you demonstrate tremendous restraint." Crossing his arms, he shakes his head. "How?"

"It can be a struggle at times, but I keep myself occupied."

"Any sexual thoughts that might be considered more violent?"

My thoughts slip back into the night before, when I was

buried deep inside Isa, the only violence in me from thinking what I'd do if anyone laid a finger on her, and going so far as to imagine severing said finger. "Not at all."

He snaps the folder closed and places my chart on the desktop. "It's a shame things didn't pan out with Mr. Boyd. That he would offer his daughter for study, then just take off with the girl without any word. Doesn't make sense. Never called. Never contacted us again. It's been months now."

"Shame. Perhaps he changed his mind about the program."

"Perhaps. Obviously, his interests were never aligned with our own."

"I guess not. Maybe we'll hear from him again one day."

The elevator door opens up onto the dark hallway of the catacombs, lit only by the few floodlights that line the hallway. Drink in hand, I stroll toward the room on the right and set my key in the lock to open the door. I whistle the notes of the song I wrote a while back, the one Isa plays for me on the occasions she tries to seduce me, and I flip on the lights.

Whimpers bounce off the walls as I make my way toward the cage that's against the far wall, within which Boyd sits hunched over himself, naked and bruised from torture. Parts of his skin show patches of burns, and when he tips his head back, the stitching over his empty eye socket looks red and swollen.

"You're picking at it again."

"S-s-sorry." His body trembles at my approach, and when I crouch down beside the cage, I tilt my head to the side and find bugs crawling over his last meal.

"Not hungry?"

Gaze lowered, he looks away and shakes his head.

"That's too bad." With a sigh, I rise to my feet and nab one of the long metal poles that's hanging on the wall beside other tools.

When I grab the mag torch from the counter, and light it to warm the end of the rod, his whimpers intensify, and he moves toward the opposite side of the cage. "A while back, when we first began these little sessions, you called me a sadistic bastard. Remember that?" In the blazing flame, I twist the end of the rod, until it begins to glow orange.

"I'm sorry. I'm …. I didn't mean to."

"No, no. It made me think. In fact, I've been thinking of what you said ever since. Tell me, Patrick. Do you know the difference between a sadist and a psychopath?"

He shakes his head, his bare feet scraping against the cement as he kicks himself farther back.

"I didn't, either, at first. But in recent weeks, I think I've finally come to understand. The difference is very simple: empathy." I set the torch on the countertop and dial off the flame. With the end glowing hot, I make my way back toward the cage and crouch down beside it. "I didn't think I had it in me to personally kill another man. My father made it sound so easy, and I was certain, my whole life, the bastard was a psychopath. But that's the thing. It's not about empathizing with the victim. In this case, it's empathizing with *your* victim, Patrick. All I have to do is imagine Isa tied to that filthy fucking bed. Your hands on her. Your breath in her face. Suddenly, I have all sorts of fucking feelings. Deep-seated feelings. Anger. Rage."

The tremble of his body rattles the cage against the stone wall.

"So, here's the deal. I'm going to give you a choice this time. We can keep this up for as long as you like, or I can plunge this rod right through your throat and watch you sputter for breath for the last time." I click the end of the rod against the cage, smiling when he twitches. "Your choice, Patrick."

It takes a few minutes before he finally looks up at me, and when he does, the decision written all over his face makes my heart swell.

EPILOGUE

ISADORA

Four months later ...

Blindfolds are the most frustrating thing when at the mercy of Lucian Blackthorne. I never know what I'm in for.

Who am I kidding? I never know what I'm in for, even *without* the blindfold.

The leather seat, warmed by the heater, is a welcomed comfort, with the temps having taken a dramatic nosedive in recent weeks. What I'd guess is the Bugatti's engine hums along at speeds I couldn't begin to calculate. Which is probably a good thing, with Lucian behind the wheel.

My stomach twists from the force of acceleration pressing down on my body. "Why the blindfold, though? I'd at least like to see death before it hits me." I squeeze the edge of the seat, desperate to hold onto something.

The sound of his chuckle is one I'll never tire from. Dark and wicked, it seems to have a direct link to the muscles in my thighs and prompts me to cross them all the time. "I promise it'll be worth it."

"Death?"

He chuckles again, twitching my thigh. "The blindfold."

"If you say so."

Ten minutes later, I can hardly stand it anymore. My temples itch with the silky fabric tied tight enough to keep me from peeking.

Thankfully, the vehicle rolls to a stop. His hand slides out of mine. The car door slams. In seconds, a blast of autumn air hits my side, and at the warm grip on my arm, I climb out of my seat. A gentle tug prompts me to step cautiously, one hand out in front, while the other remains imprisoned in his grasp.

We come to a stop, and something is curled into my palm. Cold and metallic, with teeth along the edge. I'm guessing it's, "A key?"

The blindfold slips away, and I focus past the floating objects, my vision coming into sharp focus on the sign overhead.

Vellichor.

I glance down to the key again, and to Lucian standing beside me. "What is this?"

"Yours."

A cold, tingly sensation slithers beneath my skin. Confusion renders me momentarily dizzy, and I stumble back a step to be caught by his arm. I open my mouth, my throat tight, trapping words inside my chest.

Shock, I'm guessing. Icy, numbing, *can't-spit-out-a-single-word* shock.

"I finalized the paperwork with Rhea the other day." His words add to the confusion, spinning in my head like an alphabet hurricane.

"Rhea?"

"The day I accompanied you on errands. You went out to the

521

car. I told her if she was interested in selling at any point, I'd like first refusal."

"So, you ... you ... bought this? For me?" I swallow hard at the first sting of tears. Trembles settle in, and I exhale a shaky breath. Any minute now, I'm going to wake up. This will all have been a dream. Lucian. Laura. Blackthorne Manor. All of it.

Don't wake up. Please don't wake up!

"If you're not interested in running it, we can hire management staff. Whatever you nee--"

Before I can stop myself, I leap into the air, wrapping my arms around his neck, and he catches me. Tears swell in my eyes, which I fight to hold back, because why the hell am I crying when I'm happy?

He sets me down on the pavement and seizes my lips in a kiss. "This place brought you comfort, when everyone shunned you. I'd have paid twice as much. For you."

The blur in my eyes sharpens to his face as the tears slip down my cheeks. "I can't believe you did this. Thank you."

He thumbs the moisture away and tips his head, staring at me as if he's searching for any sign of doubt. "I take it that's a yes? You're interested?"

With a chuckle, I nod. "Definitely." I rise up on my tiptoes and kiss him again.

"So, then, are you going to stand out here in the cold, kissing me all day, or are you going to open the door to your bookshop?"

My bookshop. Mine. Excitement swells in my chest at the thought of that.

"Rhea agreed to help you out, show you the ropes, though she mentioned, you had a pretty good handle on things having spent so much time here. I have someone who can help you with the financials. If you'd like, we can hire a cleaning crew and contractor to fix the place up a little."

"That doesn't leave much for me to do."

"You've got books to read. Lots of them, because a good sales*woman* should know her product inside and out, after all."

A giggle escapes me. A freaking giggle. I never giggle, but this man has me so giddy, I can't help it. "Lucian, did you buy me a bookstore just so I'd have a place to read books? You know I'd do that just about anywhere, right?"

"I've spied on a few of your baths, yes. But in this case, no. I bought it as an option for you. And to piss off the Township." His finger hooks my chin, and he lifts my gaze to his. "There are no obligations with this, Isa. You can walk away any time."

"Even if I wanted to, which I don't, you've probably had a tracking chip installed while I was asleep."

"Did you feel it, or something?" His stern face breaks into a smile when he kisses me again. "Go. The suspense is killing me."

I could pass for a clown with the permanent smile on my face, as I turn around and make my way to the front door. The skeleton shaped key slips into the lock, and the bell chimes as I push through the door.

A warm familiarity embraces me when I step inside, breathing in the scent of old books. My shop. My very own bookstore. It doesn't even feel real.

As I pass the shelves of old books, I run my fingers over their spines, and pause mid-row to find the glass encased copy of *Dracula*.

"I paid a little extra for that one. It's not for sale. It's yours to keep."

"Why did you do this for me?" I turn to face him, blinking hard to ward off the oncoming tears.

Hands tucked casually in his pockets, he looks around the place and shrugs. "I want you to be happy."

I'm glutting with happiness right now, and I can't help but feel like, any minute, the carpet will be pulled out from under me. In my world, happiness is fleeting, the high at the end of a long stretch of lows. In my world, when you hit a streak of good luck, you duck, because right around the corner is the next swing of bad.

This feels unbalanced, for the lows I've suffered in my life.

"What about you? Are you happy?" I ask.

"More than I've ever been, which I guess proves that we're not as fatalistic as we'd like to believe."

"How so?"

"When you feel dead inside, you inevitably reach for things that make you feel alive. Pain. Adrenaline. Drugs. That's how vices are born. That's how you became my obsession. You are what makes me feel alive. Like a breath of air after drowning."

Setting my hand to his cheek, I run the pad of my finger across the grisly scars there, ones I hardly notice nowadays. "I think I'm in love with you, Lucian Blackthorne. And you don't have to say it back to me." I can't be certain, because I've never loved a man in my life, and likewise, no man has ever spoken those words to me in return.

"Everything I've ever loved, truly loved, has been ripped away from me." Brows stern, he tucks a strand of hair behind my ear. "And that scares the shit out of me, where you're concerned." Even the times when he's hard and aloof, I've felt his care for me. I know something's there, just like the shadows on the walls back at the manor. I don't have to see it, or hear it, to feel it everywhere. He doesn't have to say it.

I push up onto my tiptoes to kiss him. Glancing around the shop, I sigh. "I'm a business woman now. You know what that means?"

"You'll be wearing skirts more often than not?"

"It means you'll get to see my ruthless side."

"They're books, Isa. Not million dollar mergers."

"You don't know book hoarders like I do. They take their assets very seriously."

Leaning to the side, I look past him to check the Closed sign on the door, and back away, removing my long winter trench coat.

Golden eyes watching my every move, he keeps his distance.

I drop the coat to the floor and step back, deeper into the rows of books, away from the front windows of the store.

He steps toward me, tipping his head in curiosity. "What's this?"

"Is it only boats you christen? Or bookstores, too? I'm not sure."

Sliding his black trench over his shoulders, he tosses the garment onto the floor beside mine. "I'm fairly certain you christen both, but you're not old enough for a bottle of champagne."

"That's too bad." I continue to back myself toward the wall of books behind me, until I'm well out of sight of anyone passing by the shop. "I hear it's bad luck if you don't. Sort of like crossing paths with a Blackthorne."

A crooked smile kicks up the corner of his lips as he steps toward me, until caging me against the books. "Then, I guess you're screwed."

"I guess I am."

Slipping his fingers beneath the hem of my sweater, he yanks it over my head, his eyes alight with fascination as he runs his hands over the lace bra, one he bought for me, no less. Tongue sweeping over his lips, he yanks the fabric down, popping a nipple free, and devours the hard tip of my flesh. He hikes my leg up over his hip, testing the seam of my A-line skirt, and his eyes roll back the moment his fingers make contact with damp panties. "Fuck me. You do this on purpose."

"If it disappoints you, I'm happy to wear grannies with panty liners from here on out."

"No grannies. And no liners. I like your panties wet." Burying his face in my neck, his mouth hunts my throat, licking and biting and kissing. Frantic and impatient, he leaves a hot, wet trail of kisses across my neck, over my collarbone and back up again, while his fingers dig into my thigh. I've never known a man to make my breath stutter and muscles tremble with his kiss, the way Lucian's does. It's like a full body reaction.

He hoists me up and sets me down on the smooth wooden surface of a nearby reading table, the same table where I once sat while losing myself in racy bodice rippers, dreaming of one day knowing that kind of passion. The hard edge presses against my palm, and I arch into him.

"You seem feisty today," I breathe, just before his teeth press against my throat, pushing a moan past my lips.

"I've never fucked you in a bookstore." The clink of his belt is the only warning before he springs himself free, and with my leg hiked, he pushes my panties aside and prods himself at my entrance.

"And that turns you on?"

"Everything about you turns me on." Flames in his gaze ignite, when he drives his hips forward, and I melt against him. His palm hits my throat, and he squeezes while his greedy lips devour the air between us. The intensity of his kiss is stronger than before, as if something is different between us, all of a sudden. He's not just kissing me. He's claiming me. Owning me. And every drive of his hips proves the point, as I willfully surrender to him.

Between the grip of my throat and his mouth on mine, I can't breathe. My chest tugs for air, while my muscles tighten and quiver, edging me closer to release.

Every slam of his hips is rough and determined, and the growls against my lips only punctuate the frenzy of his movements. With each powerful stroke, his muscles tense and flex as he takes me like an animal. Raw masculinity radiates from every pore on this man's body, and when he ups the pace, I realize just how small and fragile I am beneath him.

How easily he could break me, if he wanted.

The air wanes inside my lungs, my head growing dizzy with his relentless drive toward climax. As if sensing my urge to pass out, he releases me, and his eyes are pools of liquid flames searing me from the inside out.

Coated in a sheen of sweat, I tip my head back to a long and agonized moan that tears from my chest. Mouth to my breast, he sucks and licks the sensitive swell of flesh, before his palm swallows it in a tight squeeze.

"You feel so fucking good, Isa." Voice ragged, he grips my lower back, keeping one hand locked on my throat, and continues his relentless assault. Strong hands latch to my thighs, and he draws me closer, as if he isn't deep enough.

Yet, I feel him so deeply inside of me. Everywhere. On my skin. Behind my shuttered lids. Across my lips.

Lucian.

My moans drone on, shaking my ribcage, as a flash of light hits the back of my eyes, and in one last punishing thrust, his curses bounce off the walls around me. Tingles bullet beneath my skin, warming my blood, as he shudders against me. Our bodies pressed close, we breathe. Slower. Slower. Slower still. Until every muscle is soft and useless, our heartbeats pounding in tandem.

"From here on out, I want you in my bed. Beside me." The harsh rasp of his voice reflects his rough handling of moments before. He squeezes a handful of my hair and kisses my neck.

"That sounds an awful lot like plot to me," I say, equally out of breath.

"And?"

"Are you sure? I mean, sleeping in your bed ... that's quite a bit of commitment for you."

"I've done a number of crazy things since I met you. What's one more?"

I try to push him off in play, but his solid body doesn't move, and instead, he presses himself closer.

With my hair still caught in his fist, he tips my head back, guiding my eyes to his. In spite of his comment a second ago, his expression is humorless. "I'm not going to lie, Isa. My reasons are entirely selfish. I won't have anyone else touching you."

"What made you change your mind?"

"You." Expression weighted with vexation, he traces a thumb from my temple to my lips. "Being with me comes with some risk, though. I promise to shield you from it, as much as I can, but it'll always be there."

His words bring to mind something my mother used to tell me when I was a little girl, perhaps the only small bit of advice she ever gave me. "Love and danger make for one hell of a good life. Something my mom used to say."

"She wasn't wrong."

"She wasn't. So, I'll take my chances and stay with you."

"Good answer." Hands tightening around my back, he lifts me up into his arms for another kiss. "As fucked as I'll be for saying this, I do love you, Isa."

My heart flutters in my chest, eyes stinging with tears, and I wrap my arms around his neck. "You are so fucked."

It was my mother who first told me that there was no such thing as fairy tales with happy endings. That's because she spent her whole life waiting for the white knight to come and rescue her from the life she so desperately tried to escape.

I went in search of the villain, instead, and found him alone and in pain, living in a castle of bones. A darker version of my mother's knight, whose armor had dents and cracks, and his hands sullied with blood. A broken man who tasted of salt and depravity, and who took me selfishly, without apology. He's the curse my mother warned me about. The Devil of Bonesalt, the Mad Son, with whom I've fallen irrevocably in love.

This town may cast us off as a sick perversion, a tragedy in the making, but I don't care. Together, we are madness. And there is music in madness, and madness in love.

It doesn't matter what the world thinks of us.

Because we're the composers, the conductors of our own fate, and we write the notes to a beautiful, dark melody that no one else can hear.

∼

I hope you enjoyed Lucian and Isa's story.

Keep scrolling to download your FREE copy of the *La Petite Mort* Bonus Scene!

Please consider leaving a review. Long or short, your review is always appreciated, and along with telling a friend about the book, it is the most wonderful gift you can give an author 🤍

Thank you for reading.

THE GOTHIC COLLECTION

LOOKING FOR ATMOSPHERIC BOOKS LIKE MASTER OF SALT & BONES WITH A TOUCH OF EERIE AND TWISTED?

"I'm saying it now. This is hands down my favorite book of 2021. I'm going as far as placing it in my top 10 of all time. It was magical and so emotional my heart aches. I kept laughing because this book just felt epic. I disappeared within the pages and lived this story." *-Coffee and the Bibliophile Blog*

"A spine chillingly, majestically dark, engrossing read. Utter brilliance." *-Zoe, Goodreads Reader*

OTHER BOOKS BY KERI LAKE

THE NIGHTSHADE DUOLOGY
NIGHTSHADE

INFERNIUM

STANDALONES
RIPPLE EFFECT

THE ISLE OF SIN & SHADOWS

VIGILANTES SERIES
RICOCHET

BACKFIRE

INTREPID

BALLISTIC

JUNIPER UNRAVELING SERIES
JUNIPER UNRAVELING

CALICO DESCENDING

KINGS OF CARRION

GOD OF MONSTERS

THE SANDMAN DUET
NOCTURNES & NIGHTMARES

REQUIEM & REVERIE

Sign up to Keri's newsletter for a chance to win ARCs of upcoming
releases!

ACKNOWLEDGMENTS

This book would not have been possible without the love and support from these wonderful people:

My husband and children, who continue to put up with me (in other words, have not yet had me committed) in spite of the fact that I spend a number of hours out of the day hanging with my imaginary friends. I love you. And my friends said they do, too.

To my family who supports me without judgement and always has my back.

My long-time editor and friend, Julie Belfield, who unfortunately, has never had the pleasure of reading one of my stories without wanting to scratch her eyeballs out. In fact, she's probably cringing at all the misplaced commas in this, paragraph. Thank you for braving the very first draft, no matter how disastrous. Your support and investment in every book has meant more to me than you will ever know.

Books need a catchy cover and this one blew me away! Many thanks to Hang Le for, once again, rendering me speechless with her insane talent.

Massive thanks to Morten Munthe for his stunning photography and the beautiful, dark and haunting image that perfectly captured the mood and tone of this story.

As I mentioned, my manuscripts tend to be a cataclysm of thoughts thrown onto the page in an effort to get them out of my head as quickly as possible. Therefore, I have to thank my very fearless betas for braving the early drafts. Lana, Terri, Diane and

Kelly, thank you for diving in, without hesitation, to make this a better book.

If I look like I have my shit together, it's because I have an awesome assistant (fairy godmother) who keeps me on track. Thank you, Diane, for all that you do.

My Vigilante Vixens, who make me smile and give me a small corner of the internet where I can let go and be myself. Love and hugs to all of you!

To the bloggers who have taken a chance on my books and share the love with others, I see you and I thank you.

And finally, to my readers, without whom, none of this would be possible. As long as you keep reading, I'll keep writing. Your support means everything to me.

ABOUT THE AUTHOR

Keri Lake is a dark romance writer who specializes in demon wrangling, vengeance dealing and wicked twists. Her stories are gritty, with antiheroes that walk the line of good and bad, and feisty heroines who bring them to their knees. When not penning books, she enjoys spending time with her husband, daughters, and their rebellious Labrador (who doesn't retrieve a damn thing). She runs on strong coffee and alternative music, loves a good red wine, and has a slight addiction to dark chocolate.

Keep up with Keri Lake's new releases, exclusive extras and more by signing up to her VIP Email List:
VIP EMAIL SIGN UP

Join her reading group for giveaways and fun chats:
VIGILANTE VIXENS

She loves hearing from readers ...
www.KeriLake.com